A SPECTACLE OF CORRUPTION

A
SPECTACLE
of
CORRUPTION

A Novel

David Liss

RANDOM HOUSE
NEW YORK

Copyright © 2004 by David Liss

All rights reserved under International and Pan-American Copyright Conventions.
Published in the United States by Random House, an imprint of The Random House
Publishing Group, a division of Random House, Inc., New York, and simultaneously
in Canada by Random House of Canada Limited, Toronto.

RANDOM HOUSE and colophon are registered trademarks of Random House, Inc.

Library of Congress Cataloging-in-Publication Data

Liss, David
A spectacle of corruption / by David Liss
p.   cm.
ISBN 0-375-50855-4
1. London (England)—History—18th century—Fiction. 2. Private investigators—
England—London—Fiction. 3. Jews—England—London—Fiction. 4. Boxers (Sports)—
Fiction. 5. Judicial error—Fiction. 6. Elections—Fiction. I. Title.
PS3562.I78I4S64 2004   813'.6—dc21   2003054806

Printed in the United States of America on acid-free paper

Random House website address: www.atrandom.com

246897531

FIRST EDITION

Book design by Carole Lowenstein

HISTORICAL NOTE

In the course of writing this novel, I've taken considerable pains to try to convey clearly the relevant terms and concerns of early eighteenth-century British politics, but I've provided the following information for readers who may want a quick review or some historical context.

Time Line of Significant Events
Leading Up to the 1722 General Election

1642–49   England's civil wars are fought between the Royalists in support of Charles I and the Parliamentarians, who rebelled against the king's Catholic leanings and sought to instill a government based on radical Protestant ideals.

1649   King Charles I is executed.

1649–60   During the Interregnum, Oliver Cromwell and later his son, Richard, lead the nation, along with Parliament.

1660   The Restoration of the Monarchy, the army supports the return of Charles's son, Charles II. The new king is a declared Protestant but is suspected of having Catholic leanings.

1685   Upon Charles II's death, his openly Catholic brother, James II, becomes king. James has two Protestant daughters from a previous marriage but is now married to Mary of Modena, a Catholic.

1688   Mary of Modena gives birth to a son, also named James. Parliament, fearing the beginnings of a new Catholic dynasty, invites William of Orange, husband of Mary, the king's elder daughter, to take the crown jointly with his wife. James II flees, and Parliament declares that he has abdicated.

1702   Anne, James II's younger daughter, becomes queen.

1714   In accordance with Parliament's Act of Settlement, on the death of Anne the crown passes to the Elector of Hanover, Anne's distant German cousin, who becomes George I.

1715   The first significant Jacobite uprising, headed by James Stuart, son of James II and now known as the Pretender.

1720   The South Sea Bubble collapses, causing the first stock market crash in England. As a result of corporate greed and Parliamentary complicity, the country falls into a deep economic depression. Jacobite sympathy grows.

1722   The first general election since George became king takes place and is widely viewed as a referendum on his kingship.

Key Political Terms

Tories   The Tories were one of the two key political parties. They were associated with old money, the landed wealth, a strong Church, and a strong monarchy. They vigorously opposed changes to the law that would aid non–Church of England Protestants, and especially Catholics and Jews. Following the accession of George I, the Tories were effectively barred from power.

Whigs   The second important political party, the Whigs, were associated with new landless wealth, the stock market, nonconformist Protestantism, divesting power from the Church, and Parliamentary power over royal power.

Jacobites   Those who believed that the crown should be restored to the deposed James II—and, later, his heirs—were called Jacobites (from *Jacobus,* Latin for James). Jacobites often masqueraded as Tories, and Tories were often suspected of having Jacobite sympathies. Scotland and Ireland were strong centers of Jacobite support.

Pretenders   The deposed James II—and, later, his heirs—were known as Pretenders. The Pretender in this novel is James Stuart, the would-be James III, son of James II. He was also known as the Chevalier.

Franchise   Who was permitted to vote in eighteenth-century Britain and who was not can seem a very complicated issues to modern readers. Election districts were composed of two units: boroughs and counties. To vote in one of the counties, a person needed an annual income from property equaling forty shillings or more a year (an amount that had seemed like significant wealth when the law had been written, three hundred years before the events of this novel). Condition for election varied from borough to borough. Some had wide franchises, some were composed of a small body of men who met in private and voted among themselves. In rural communities, farmers were generally expected to vote as directed by their landlords.

A SPECTACLE OF CORRUPTION

CHAPTER 1

SINCE THE PUBLICATION of the first volume of my memoirs, I have found myself the subject of more notoriety than I had ever known or might have anticipated. I cannot register a complaint or a lament, for any man who chooses to place himself in public sight has no reason to regret such attentions. Rather, he must be grateful if the public chooses to cast its fickle gaze in his direction, a truth to which the countless volumes languishing in the scribbler's perdition of obscurity can testify.

I will be frank and say that I have been gratified by the warmth with which readers responded to the accounts of my early years, yet I have been surprised too—surprised by people who read a few lines of my thoughts and consider themselves near friends, free to speak their minds to me. And while I shall not find fault with someone who has read my words so closely that he wishes to makes observations on them, I confess I have been confounded by the number of people who believe they may comment with impunity on any aspect of my life without a moment's regard to custom or propriety.

Some months after publishing my little volume I sat at a supper gathering, speaking of a particularly noxious criminal I intended to bring to justice. A young spark, on whom I had never before set eyes, turned to me and said that this fellow had better be careful, lest he meet the same end as *Walter Yate*. Here he simpered, as though he and I shared a secret.

My amazement was such that I did not say a word. I had not thought about Walter Yate in some time, and I had no idea that his name had retained any currency after so many years. But I was to discover that, while I had not contemplated this poor fellow, others had. Not a fortnight later another man, also a stranger, commented on a difficulty I faced by saying I should manage that affair in the same fashion that I had managed my business with *Walter Yate.* He said the name with a sly nod and a wink, as though, because he had uttered this shibboleth, he and I were now jolly co-conspirators.

It does not offend me that these men chose to reference incidents from my past. It does, however, perplex me that they should feel at liberty to speak of something they do not understand. I cannot fully express my bewilderment that such people, believing what they do about this incident, should mention it to me at all, let alone with more than a dash of good cheer. Does one go to a raree show and make light with the tigers regarding their fangs?

I have therefore decided that I must pen another volume of memoirs, if for no other reason than to disabuse the world of its ideas concerning this chapter of my history. I wish no more to hear the name Walter Yate spoken in naughty and secretive tones. This man, to the best of my knowledge, did nothing to deserve becoming the subject of a private titter. Therefore, I shall say now, truthfully and definitively, that I did not act violently upon Mr. Yate—let alone with the most definitive violence—something which, I have discovered, the world generally believes. Further, if I may disabuse the public of another misconception, I did not escape the most terrible of punishments for his murder by calling upon the influence of friends in the government. Neither of those tales is true. I had never known of these rumors because no one had ever spoken them to me before. But now, having published a few words of my life, I am every man's friend. Let me then do the friendly service of revealing the facts about the incident, if for no other reason than that it might be spoken of no more.

Walter Yate died, beaten in the head with an iron bar, only six days before the meeting of the King's Bench, so I had mercifully

little time after my arrest to reflect on my condition while awaiting trial. I will be honest: I might have put that time to better use,
but not once did I believe, truly believe, that I would be convicted
for a crime I had not committed—the murder of a man of whom
I had scarcely heard before his death. I ought to have believed it,
but I did not.

So great was my confidence that I often found myself hardly
even listening to the words spoken at my own trial. Instead, I
looked out at the mob packed into the open-air courtroom. It
rained a fine mist that day, and there was a considerable chill in the
February air, but the crowds came anyway, crammed onto the
rough and splintering benches, hunched against the wet, to watch
the proceedings, which had attracted some attention in the newspapers. The spectators sat eating their oranges and apples and little mutton pastries, smoking their pipes and taking snuff. They
pissed in pots in the corners and threw their oyster shells at the
feet of the jury. They murmured and cheered and shook their
heads as though it were all an enormous puppet show staged for
their amusement.

I suppose I might have been pleased to be the subject of such a
broad public curiosity, but I found no gratification in notoriety.
Not when *she* was not there, the woman I most wanted to look
upon in my time of sorrows. If I were to be convicted, I thought
(only in the most romantical way, since I no more anticipated a
conviction than that I should be elected Lord Mayor), I should
only want her to come and cry at my feet, tell me of her regrets. I
wanted her teary kisses on my face. I wanted her hands, raw and
coarse with wringing, to take mine as she begged my forgiveness
and pleaded to hear my vows of love repeated a hundred times.
These were, I knew, mere fantasies of an overwrought imagination. She would not come to my trial, and she would not come to
visit me before my fanciful execution. She could not.

My cousin's widow, Miriam, whom I had sought to marry, had
wedded herself six months before to a man named Griffin Melbury, who at the moment of my trial busied himself with preparations for standing as the Tory candidate in the election soon to

commence in Westminster. Now a convert to the Church of England and the wife of a man who hoped to rise as a prominent opposition politician, Miriam Melbury could ill afford to attend the trial of a Jewish ruffian-for-hire, one to whom she was no longer attached by the bonds of kinship. Kneeling at my feet or covering my face with tear-wet kisses was hardly the sort of behavior to which she was inclined under any circumstances. It would surely not happen now that she had given herself to another man.

Thus, in my hour of crisis, I dwelled less on the possibility of impending doom than I did on Miriam. I blamed her, as though she could be held accountable for this absurd trial—after all, had she married me, I might have abandoned thieftaking and would not have brought myself into the circumstances that had led to this disaster. I blamed myself for not pursuing her more vigorously—though three marriage proposals ought to meet any man's definition of *vigor.*

So, while the lawyer for the Crown attempted to convince the jury to convict me, I thought of Miriam. And, because even as I dwell with longing and melancholy I remain a man, I also thought about the woman with yellow hair.

It must be seen as no surprise that my mind wandered to other women. In the half year since Miriam had married, I had distracted myself—not with the intent of forgetting, you must understand, but with the aim of making my sense of loss more exquisite—largely by indulging in vices, and those vices consisted principally of women and drink. I regretted that I was not of a gambling disposition, for most men I knew found that vice to be as distracting as the two I favored, if not more so. But in the past, having paid the high price of money lost at game, I could not quite grasp the entertainment in viewing a pair of greedy hands collecting a pile of silver that had once been my own.

Drink and women: Those were vices on which I could depend. Neither needed to be of particularly fine quality; I was of no temper to be overly choosy. Yet, here was a woman, sitting at the edge of one of the benches, who absorbed my attention as nearly as anything could in those dark times. She had pale yellow hair and eyes the color of the sun itself. She was not beautiful, but she was pretty and had a kind of pert demeanor, with her pointy nose and sharp chin. Though no great lady, she dressed like a woman of the middling ranks, neatly, but without flair or much of a nod to fashion. Rather, she let nature do what her tailor could not, and exposed to the world in a deeply cut bodice the expanse of a dazzling bosom. There was, in short, nothing that would have kept me from finding her a delight in an alehouse or tavern, but no particular reason why she should command my attention while I sat on trial for my life.

Except that she did not once take her eyes from me. Not for a moment.

Others looked at me, of course—my uncle and aunt with pity and perhaps with admonition, my friends with fear, my enemies with glee, strangers with unpitying curiosity—but this woman fixed on me a desperate, hungry gaze. When our eyes locked, she neither smiled nor frowned but only met my look as though we had shared a lifetime together and no word need be spoken between us. Anyone observing would have thought us married or sweethearts, but I had never to my recollection—none the best during those six months of hearty drinking—seen her before. The enigma of her gaze monopolized my thoughts far more than the enigma of how I came to stand trial for the death of a dockworker I'd never heard of two days before my arrest.

The rain had begun to fall harder and turn frozen when the prosecuting lawyer, an old fellow named Lionel Antsy, called Jonathan Wild to the stand. In that year, 1722, this notorious criminal was still widely believed to be the only true bulwark against the marauding armies of thieves and brigands that plagued the metropolis. He and I had long been rivals in our thieftaking efforts, for our methods were none too similar. I believed that if I helped honest folk to recover their lost goods, I should receive a handsome reward for my labors. Granted, my work was not always quite so principled. I was willing to track down elusive debtors, to use the skills I'd gained in the pugilist's ring to teach lessons to rascals (provided they deserved such treatment in my eyes), to intimidate and frighten and scare men who required such usage. I would not, however, inflict harm on those I believed undeserving of rough treatment, and I'd even been known to let a debtor or two escape my capture—always with an apologetic lie to my employer—if I heard a credible tale of a starving wife or sick children.

Wild, however, was a ruthless rogue. He would send forth his thieves to steal goods and then sell the same items back to their owners, all the while pretending to be the lone voice of London's victims. These methods, I admit, were far more profitable than mine. Hardly a cutpurse in London lined his pockets without Wild taking his share. No murderer could hide his bloodstained hands from Wild's scrutiny, even if the great thieftaker had ordered the murder himself. He owned smuggling ships that visited every port in the kingdom and had agents in every nation in Europe. The stockjobbers of 'Change Alley hardly dared to buy and sell without his nod. He was, in short, a remarkably dangerous man, and he bore me no love.

In our incompatible efforts, we had clashed more than once, though our clashes tended toward the cool rather than the hot. We circled around each other, like dogs more eager to bark than fight. Nevertheless, I could not doubt that Wild would relish this opportunity to see me destroyed. As he had made a career out of perjuring himself before any jury that would listen, I now only waited to discover the severity of his condemnation and the verve with which he delivered it.

Mr. Antsy hobbled toward the witness, hunched over to keep the frozen rain from his face. He looked to be anywhere between fifty and one hundred years of age—gaunt as death itself, with his skin hanging loose about his face like an empty wine bladder, and his head bobbing above the mass of his greatcoat. His peruke, limp from the rain, hung askew and was of such a horrible condition I could only suppose he had purchased it at the dip in Holborn, where a man might pay threepence for the chance to blindly pull a used wig from a box. Not having bothered to shave that morning, and perhaps the morning before, his face was fertile with strands of weedy white hair that poked from out the rugged earth of his face.

"Now, Mr. Wild," he said, in his shrill and quivering voice, "you have been called here to testify to the character of Mr. Weaver because you are widely regarded as something of an expert in criminal matters—a student of the philosophy of crime, if you will."

"I like to think so of myself," he said, his country accent so thick that the jury leaned in closer, as though proximity might help them to understand better. Wild, on whom the rain hardly dared to fall, held himself erect and smiled almost pityingly at Mr. Antsy. How could an old pettifogger like Antsy inspire anything but contempt in a man who routinely sent his own thieves to hang that he might retrieve the forty-pound bounty offered by the state?

"You are widely regarded, sir, as the metropolis's most effective agent in the sphere of thieftaking, is that not right?"

"It is," Wild said, with an easy pride. He was advancing into his middle years then, but he appeared nonetheless handsome and vibrant in his trim suit and wig. He had a deceptively kind face, too, with large eyes, rounded cheeks, and a warm and avuncular smile that made people like him and trust him at once. "I am known as the Thieftaker General, and it is a title I bear with both pride and honor."

"And in this capacity, you have come to know the many aspects of the criminal world, yes?"

"Precisely, Mr. Antsy. Most people understand that if they should lose an article of some importance, or wish to track down the perpetrator of a crime, no matter how heinous, I am the man to seek."

There was never a poor opportunity to enhance one's reputation, I thought. Wild intended to see me hang *and* get a few puffs in the newspapers at the same time.

"Then you think yourself privy to the criminal doings in our metropolis?" Antsy asked.

"I have applied myself to this trade for many years now," Wild answered. "There are few matters of criminality that escape my notice."

He neglected to mention that he noticed these matters of criminality because, in general, he or his agents orchestrated them.

"Tell us, if you will," Antsy said, "of Mr. Weaver's connection to the death of Walter Yate."

Wild paused for a moment. I glared at him. I did my utmost to say with silent words that he must know I would never be convicted, and if he crossed me in this I would not let the matter go. Proceed, I told him with my eyes, and you will be proceeding toward your own doom. Wild met my stare for a moment and nodded ever so slightly, conveying a significance I could not fathom. He then turned to Antsy.

"I can tell you almost nothing of that," he said.

Antsy opened his mouth, but it seemed to take him a moment to realize the answer he received was not the one he had been anticipating. He pressed the bridge of his nose with his thumb and forefinger, as though trying to squeeze Wild's answer from his flesh the way a cider maker wrings juice from an apple. "What do you mean, sir?" he asked, in a quivering voice more shrill than its usual.

Wild smiled slightly. "Only that I have no knowledge of the matters surrounding Yate's death or of Weaver's supposed involvement—only what I have read in the newspapers. It is my goal to discover the truth behind all horrific crimes, but I cannot learn everything. Though I do try, I promise you."

Every spectator at the King's Bench could see from the slackening of Antsy's face that the lawyer had expected something quite different from Wild. A lecture on the danger I posed to London, perhaps. A recounting of my former crimes. A list of atrocities in which he had long suspected my involvement. But Wild had a different game in mind—one that baffled me entirely.

Antsy looked up and grimaced. He took a deep breath that puffed out his chest nearly to the size of a normal man's and gritted his teeth into a deathly smile. "Do you not think Weaver a vicious man, quite capable of killing anyone, even a total stranger, without cause? And, accordingly, quite capable of killing Walter Yate? Is it not correct to say that you know with certainty that he *did* kill Walter Yate?"

"On the contrary," Wild answered blithely, like an anatomy instructor asked to discuss the mysteries of respiration. "I believe Weaver to be a man of honor. He and I are not friends; in truth, we often find ourselves opposed. If I may be so bold, I think

Weaver to be a rather miserable sort of thieftaker, who does the state and those who pay him a disservice. But being miserable in his trade does not make him necessarily a wicked man any more than a cobbler should be called wicked for making pinching shoes. I have no more reason to think Weaver guilty of this crime than I do any other man. To my knowing, you might be as guilty as he."

Antsy spun toward the judge, Piers Rowley, who stared at Wild with an astonishment equal to the lawyer's. "M'lord," Antsy complained, "this is not the testimony I had expected. Mr. Wild was to have spoken of Weaver's crimes and cruelties."

The judge turned to the witness. Like Antsy, he was well into his later years, but with his large face and ruddy complexion he wore his age far more comfortably than the lawyer. Antsy appeared starved for all nourishment, but the judge looked to receive more than his share. His enormous jowls were big with beer and roast beef and puffed like a fat infant's.

"Mr. Wild," Rowley said to the witness, "you will provide Mr. Antsy with the testimony he wishes."

I had not quite expected this reply. I did not know him well by any means, but I had observed Rowley in the past—when called to testify against men I had helped bring to justice—and I had always found in him as much fairness and honesty as one could hope for in a man of his profession. He took bribes sparingly, and then only to secure a ruling he had intended to make without financial incentive. I had ever noted that he took his role as protector of the defendant seriously, and I had felt a measure of relief when I learned he was to preside over my trial. Now it appeared that my optimism had been misplaced.

"Begging your pardon, m'lord," Wild answered, "but I cannot answer for his expectations. Having sworn an oath to speak the truth, I must do so."

Here was something comical. Wild had no more loyalty to oaths than a Frenchman does to clean linen. Still, he sat there, incurring the anger of the prosecuting lawyer and the judge, rather than speak ill of me. Wild, who spent far more time in the courts than I, surely knew Rowley's temperament. He could not but have known that the judge was a man who held himself with more than his share of gravity and would not let an insult to his authority pass lightly. By defending me as he did, Wild risked great injury to himself and his trade, for he must now expose himself to Rowley's hostility during future trials. As perjuring himself was among his most important sources of income, an adversarial judge could make his life most uncomfortable.

Antsy understood the situation no better than I. He brushed the rain off his face. "Given his reluctance to speak the truth, I have nothing more to hear from this witness," the old lawyer said. "You may go, Mr. Wild."

I rose to my feet. "Begging your pardon, m'lord, but I have not yet had a chance to cross-examine."

"No more questions to this witness." Rowley banged his gavel.

Wild stepped down and winked in my direction. I only stared blankly in return.

My pretty yellow-haired admirer wept into the sleeve of her coat, and she was not alone in her dismay. The spectators quickly answered with catcalls and hisses, and a few apple cores flew toward us. I was not such a popular figure with the mob that they would brook no insult to me, but they knew injustice when they saw it, and no rabble of this city will stand idly by while a fellow is mistreated by the law. Not in those days, when there was such little work to be had and bread was so dear. Rowley, however, had years of experience with such outbursts, and he banged his gavel once more, this time with an authority that brought down a veil of silence.

I was not so easily calmed. In our system of law, a defendant does not have a lawyer because it is presumed that the judge will act as his advocate. Often as not, however, a defendant finds himself with an unkind judge and thus with no protection whatsoever. I had never before had cause to lament the inequities of this system, for I was used to being in the position of wishing to see men convicted, that I might collect a bounty—and see justice served, of course. But now I found I could not call my own witnesses, question as I liked, or defend myself adequately. Judge Piers

Rowley, a man I knew only from a distance, seemed intent upon destroying me.

Antsy next called Spirit Spicer, a fellow of whom I had never heard—how should I forget so colorful a name? He was young, only a working lad, and clearly of the lower ranks. Spicer had dressed himself to the best of his ability, but his blouse was torn in several places and his breeches stained in a way that any man of a respectable station would find embarrassing, to say the least. He had cut his hair short for the trial, using, I would suspect, a dull blade, and he looked as though he had caught his head in a grain mill.

Through a needlessly protracted line of questioning (no doubt to help him regain his sense of order after the unfortunate business with Wild), Antsy revealed that Spicer had been upon the quays in Wapping the day of Yate's death and claimed to have witnessed the mayhem of that afternoon and the murder itself. "I saw that man there," Spicer said, pointing to me. "He killed the fellow, Yate. He struck him, he did. And then he killed him. By striking him."

"You are sure of this?" Antsy asked. His voice rang with triumph. His witness spoke as he wished. The rain had now let up somewhat. All was well in the world.

"I have never been so sure of very many things in some long while," Spicer assured him. "Weaver done it. That's for certain. I was close enough to see everything, and to hear it too. I heard what Weaver said before he done it. Heard his malicious and damning words, I did."

The old lawyer squinted in evident confusion but proceeded all the same. "And what did Mr. Weaver say?"

"He said, 'This is what happens to those who anger the man they call Johnson.' That's what he said. Clear as day. *Johnson*. That's the name he said."

I had no notion of who this Johnson was and neither, apparently, did Antsy. He opened his mouth to say something but then thought better of it and turned away, announcing that he had no more questions as he took his seat.

"Johnson," Spicer repeated.

Judge Rowley turned to me. "Mr. Weaver, would you care to ask the witness a question or two?"

"I'm delighted to learn that Mr. Spicer is on the list of witnesses that I may, indeed, question," I said. I regretted my words the instant I spoke them, but they drew a laugh from the gallery, and I took some comfort in that. Rowley had shown himself biased against me, but I was still foolish enough to believe his position would soon change. During my week in prison, I had been given little opportunity to inquire into Yate's death, but I had sent my good friend Elias Gordon about town, asking questions for me, and I was fully confident that what we had discovered would soon end this farce.

I glanced over to the part of the galleries where Elias sat, and he nodded eagerly, his thin face flushed with pleasure. It was time to strike a fatal blow against this disgrace to justice.

I rose from my seat, brushed the ice off my coat, and approached the witness. "Tell me, Mr. Spicer. Have you ever met a man named Arthur Groston?"

Perhaps I anticipated that Spirit Spicer would blush or blanch or tremble. He might bear down and deny knowing Groston, in which case I would have to badger him until he confessed. But Spicer thought neither to resist nor, if his face was any indication of his heart, feel a jot of shame. For all the world, his easy and open grin suggested a fellow interested only in pleasing anyone who might be so kind as to ask him a question or two. "Aye, I've met Mr. Groston. More than once."

The ease of this admission disoriented me, but I pressed on all the same. "In your time of knowing Mr. Groston, has he ever offered you any money to perform a service?"

"Aye, he has done so. Mr. Groston is extreme generous, he is, and he makes a point to look after me, on account of his cousin being a friend of my mother's, sir. He believes in looking after family, sir, as does my family, which is why he helped me out."

I smiled at the fellow. We were all friends here. "How would you describe the service that Mr. Groston asks of you?"

"I would describe it as generous and kind," Spicer said. Here the crowd laughed and Spicer grinned broadly, imagining himself the mob's darling rather than its clown.

"Allow me to ask that question another way," I said.

Antsy rose slowly to his feet. "M'lord, Mr. Weaver is wasting the court's time with this witness. I move you dismiss him."

Rowley spent an instant considering Antsy's request, and I believe he would have complied, but the crowd, sensing a bias, began to hiss. It began softly but soon swelled, so that the King's Bench sounded as though it were a court of serpents. No apple cores this time; perhaps that was what agitated the judge. The noise held the menace of a storm not yet broke. Unwilling to risk a riot, Rowley said I might continue but advised that I cease my leisurely approach, for there were other men awaiting trial this day.

I began again. "Let me be plain," I said to Spicer, "that the judge may not grow restless. Does Mr. Groston ever, to your knowledge, pay people to testify at trials?"

"For certain. He is an evidence broker. What else should he do?"

I smiled. "And did Arthur Groston provide you with money to say that you had seen me strike and kill Walter Yate?"

"Yes, sir," Spicer said, nodding eagerly. "He paid me before to say suchlike things on suchlike occasions as this one, but he never before paid so much as the half crown he give me for saying as I done just now."

The spectators murmured loudly. Here was drama they had never expected. In an instant I had completely devastated the prosecution. My aunt and uncle took each other's hands and nodded in triumph. Elias strained in his seat to avoid standing and taking a bow, for it was his dedication that had led us to this bit of knowledge. The woman with the yellow hair clapped her hands together with joy.

"So." I looked to the jury box, meeting the gaze of each man. "Do you now tell us, Mr. Spicer, that you never actually saw me harm Walter Yate, but that you said so only because you have been paid to say so by a notorious evidence broker?"

"That's it," Spicer said. "That's it on the oyster's shell, as they say."

I threw up my hands in mock exasperation. "Why," I demanded, "if you have been paid to say you saw me kill Mr. Yate, do you now admit that you never saw it at all?"

Spicer took a moment to puzzle over this question. "Well," he suggested, "I got paid to say I saw something, but I never got paid to say I didn't see it. So long as I said I saw it, I done what I was meant to have done."

Having spent some years performing for the public as a fighter, I knew a little about the rhythm of spectacle, so I let his words hang in the air for a moment before commencing once more. "Tell me, Mr. Spicer," I said, after I sensed a sufficient pause, "have you never heard of perjury?"

"For certain," he said brightly, pointing to the jury box. "That's them right there."

"*Perjury*," I explained, once the laughter diminished, "is a crime. It is the crime of swearing to speak the truth at a trial and then knowingly speaking false. Do you not think yourself guilty of this crime?"

"Oh, no." He waved a hand dismissively. "Mr. Groston explained it to me. He said it ain't no more a crime than it is blasphemy for an actor to speak out against God, if he do it while playing on the stage. That's all it is."

My having finished with the witness, Mr. Antsy moved to question Spicer once more. "Did you see Mr. Weaver kill Walter Yate?"

"Yes, I did!" he announced cheerfully. He then looked over to me, as though waiting for me to question him so he could tell me once more that he hadn't.

Antsy next brought out another eyewitness, a man of middle years named Clark, who also said he had seen me commit this crime. When I had the chance to examine him, he resisted a bit more than young Mr. Spicer, but he at last admitted that he had been paid by the evidence broker, Arthur Groston, to say he had seen what he had not. I had every reason to regret that the law does not permit a defendant to call witnesses, for I would have liked very much to know who paid Mr. Groston to secure this evidence. But the information I had obtained, I believed, more than answered my purposes, and there would be time enough for Groston later. The Crown had no evidence against me but two eyewitnesses, men who had admitted that they had seen nothing at all but the coin in their hands.

And so, as I gazed at the yellow-haired woman, I thought myself safe. Mr. Antsy had done his job admirably, proving that age need be no impediment to any man who maintained a youthful ambition, but the evidence against me had been exploded. Nevertheless, when it came time for the judge to direct the jury, I realized I had been overly optimistic and had put perhaps too much confidence in that phantasm called *truth*.

"You have heard many things," the honorable Piers Rowley told the jury, "and many things of a contradictory nature, too. You have heard witnesses say they have seen something and then, as though a trick done by Gypsy showman, you have heard them say they had not. You must decide how best to unravel this puzzle. As I cannot tell you which way to do so, I can only say that there is, perhaps, no more reason to believe a tale refuted than a tale spoken. You cannot know if these witnesses have been paid to say they saw something or paid to say they did not. I have no knowledge of evidence brokers, but I do know of villainous Jews and the tricks they will play to secure their freedom. I know that a race of liars might well pay honest coin to turn other men dishonest. I hope you will not be blinded by such petty cheats nor expose every Christian man, woman, and child in London to the ravages of a rapacious nation who might come to believe they can murder us with impunity."

And so the jury went off to make its decision.

This august body returned not half an hour later.

"How do you find?" Judge Rowley asked.

The foreman arose slowly. He removed his hat and ran his fingers through damp and thinning hair. "We find Mr. Weaver guilty of murder, just like you said, Your Honor." The man never once looked up.

The crowd let out a cry. I could not tell at first if it was of joy or outrage, but I soon saw to some small pleasure that the mob had taken my part. Rubbish once more took to the air. Men were on their feet in the back, shouting of injustice, popery, and absolutism.

"Have you anything to say before sentence is passed?" the judge asked me over the din. He appeared eager to press on with his business and depart as quickly as he could, without troubling himself to restore order. I must have thought on his question for an instant too long, for he banged his gavel and said, "Very well, then. Given the seriousness and cruelty of this crime, I can see no reason for leniency, not when there are so many Jews in this city. I cannot stand by and nod my approval, telling the members of your race that they may kill Christians as they see fit. I sentence you, Mr. Weaver, to be hanged for the most horrible crime of murder. This punishment shall be carried out at the next hanging day, six weeks hence." He again banged the gavel, stood up, and exited the courtroom, flanked by a quartet of bailiffs.

In an instant a pair of these worthies were at my side to lead me back to Newgate prison. Though my death had just now been ordered, my first thoughts were not on the terrors of facing eternity but on the indignity of being carted off by these roughs.

And then, in a flash, the enormity of what had happened pressed itself on me. I had been convicted of murder and sentenced to die. I had committed crimes in my time—and hanging crimes too—but the unfairness of this conviction made me dizzy with rage. In the benches my friend Elias Gordon shouted that this injustice would not stand. My uncle called to me, telling me that he would use all the influence he could muster to intervene on my behalf. But their words buzzed distantly in my ears. I heard them but did not hear them.

I felt the bailiffs pull me away, a firm grip on either arm. My muscles began to tighten, and for a moment I thought of attempting to break free. Why should I not? I could overpower these men. What rule had the law over me, now that it had so abused me?

But then there she was, directly in front of us, the woman with the yellow hair. Her pretty face was now red and raw. Tears poured from her eyes. "Oh, Benjamin," she screamed, "don't leave me! I'll die without you!"

This outcome seemed to me unlikely, since she had lived her entire life thus far without me, and that condition had done nothing but leave her hale and healthy. Nevertheless, there could be no easy refutation of the force of her emotion. She threw herself at me, wrapped her hands around my neck, and covered my face with kisses.

I should have been delighted to receive the attentions of so fine a woman under other circumstances—circumstances, let us say, that did not involve my death having just been mandated by law— but here I could only stare in confusion. The woman, now pushed back by the bailiffs, began to wail and cry of injustice. And then she turned just so, a masterfully natural turn that any tumbler or posturer at Bartholomew Fair might envy. Now the creaminess of her breasts, exposed to no small degree by the cheerful cut of her bodice, brushed against the hands of one of my keepers.

Distracted and delighted and perhaps discomfited too, the bailiff paused in mid motion, turning red in the face. The woman appeared to pause as well. She leaned forward just enough to press her skin against his hand. The bailiff stared at his hand and the flesh it touched. His companion bailiff stared as well, envious that fate had ordained this less deserving hand to find favor with the lady's bosoms. In that moment of confusion, she, with the dexterity of a cutpurse, slipped something into my hand. Some things, I should say, for I could tell in an instant that there were two objects, and I heard the clean note of their music as they clanked together—cold hand hard and sharp.

I did not need to look at them to know what they were. I had felt such things and, indeed, used them most villainously in my greener years when I had plied my trade outside the law: a lockpick and a file.

Events of the past few days had happened so quickly and so strangely, I felt I understood almost nothing, but I now knew two things with absolute certainty. I knew that someone desperately wanted to see me convicted and sentenced to hang, to which end the law had been cruelly abused.

And, just as surely, someone wanted me free.

CHAPTER 2

How had I found myself in so dire a condition? I could not even begin to fathom this upheaval, but I knew that my difficulties were in some way linked to the services I had engaged to render to Mr. Christopher Ufford, a priest of the Church of England, serving at St. John the Baptist Church in Wapping.

In the melancholy that had settled upon me since Miriam wedded herself to a Christian gentleman, I had left my business in a state of neglect. I hardly worked at all for some months, preferring to pass my time in drink and debauchery—or else sullen contemplation—and sometimes a combination of all. So when I received notice from this cleric the same day I received three urgent notes from my creditors, I thought it best to do as I had been promising myself I would do for some months—that is to say, shake off my stupor and resume my business. I therefore dressed myself neatly in a dark suit with a clean shirt. I splashed the sleep off my face, bound up my hair, which I wore in the style of a tie periwig, and traveled by hackney coach to York Street, at which address Mr. Ufford desired me to call upon him.

I set off that morning little thinking that I would, more than thirty-five years later, commit my actions to paper, but had I been so aware, I might have taken some additional notice of the disorderly men who surrounded me as soon as I exited my hackney in Westminster. Here were four fellows, made, unknown to them, to perform the literary act of foreshadowing. They took their positions at my four corners and sneered. I thought them nothing more than the countless thieves who haunted the streets since the South Sea Company had collapsed, taking the nation's wealth with it. But these were a different sort of criminal.

"Which be ye, Whig or Tory?" one of them, the largest—and very likely the drunkest—of them snarled at me.

I knew that the six-week-long election season was nearly upon us, and candidates would often canvass in advance by hosting riotous parties at taverns in which lowly men such as these, men who surely did not possess the vote, might drink their fill. The reason for the politicians' generosity was quite plain: They hoped their uncouth guests might go forth and behave just as these fellows now behaved, coarse advocates of their cause.

As it was quite early in the morning, I could only presume that these men had not yet taken their sleep. I stared at them, with their unshaved faces and ragged clothes, and attempted to measure their capacity to do me harm.

"Which be ye?" I asked in return.

The leader barked a laugh. "Why should I tell you?"

I took from my pocket one of the brace of pistols I always carried about me and pointed the firearm in this man's face. "Because you began the conversation, and I wish only to understand the level of your interest."

"Begging your pardon, sire," he said, grossly overestimating my position. He removed his hat and, placing it against his chest, began to bow like a Turk.

I'd have none of this groveling. "Which party are you?" I asked again.

"Whigs, if it please you, sir," another of the men said. "What should we be but Whigs, for we're only laboring men, you see, and not great lords, like your honor, to be Tories. We was at a tavern with drink paid for by Mr. Hertcomb, the Whig for Westminster. So we're Whigs now, and in his service. We meant you no harm."

I cared nothing, and knew less, for Whigs and Tories, though I understood enough to know that it was the Whigs, the party of new wealth and little church, that might be more willing to attract men such as these.

"Get gone," I said, waving my pistol. They ran off in one direction, I walked in the other. In an instant I had forgotten about the encounter, and my mind turned to my meeting with Mr. Ufford.

I have known very few priests in my day, but from my reading I harbored the idea of dignified little men living in neat but unremarkable cottages. I was surprised to see the lavish town house in which Mr. Ufford resided. Men who seek careers in the Church tend ever to be without prospects, either because their families have not much money or because they are younger brothers and excluded from inheritance by the strict laws and customs of the land. But here was a priest who had taken for himself the whole of a fine house on a fashionable street. I could not say how many rooms he possessed, or of what nature, but I soon found that the kitchen was of the finest quality. When I knocked upon the front door, a ruddy-faced manservant told me I could not enter thus.

"You must approach from the rear," he told me.

I rankled not a little at this treatment and thought to comment most unkindly on his orders, but his usage was, if not common, hardly unprecedented. Perhaps the excess of wine I'd consumed the night before inclined me to irritation. Nevertheless, I cast aside my annoyance and walked to the side entrance, where a stout woman with arms as thick as my calves directed me to a large table fixed in one corner. Sitting here already was a fellow of the meaner sort, not old but aging ungracefully, grizzled about the face, lacking a wig, with nothing on his balding and close-cut pate but a wide-brimmed straw hat. His clothes were of the plainer sort of undyed linens, though clearly new, and adorned only with his pewter porter's badge, which he wore pinned to his right breast. I could not say why, not knowing the man, but I had immediately the distinct impression that Mr. Ufford had bought the clothes for him, and recently too—perhaps for this very meeting.

Soon another man, wearing a black coat and a white cravat—a style I recognized as priestly—entered the kitchen tentatively, as though sneaking a look at a room in a house where he was a dinner guest. On meeting my eyes, he simpered briefly. "Benjamin," he cried with great warmth, though we had never before met. "Come in, come in. I am glad you could meet me as I requested, and at such short notice too." He was tall, inclined to be plump if not fat, and with a sunken face that resembled a crescent moon. He wore a tie wig, new and carefully powdered.

I bristled a little, I admit, at the unexpected use of my name. I had never met the man before and had no reason to expect such familiarity. I suspected that if I were to address him as Christopher, or perhaps even Kit, he would not take it kindly.

"I am honored to be able to attend you, sir," I said, with a shallow bow.

He gestured toward the table. "Come, sit down. Sit down. Oh, yes. Where have my manners gone? Benjamin, this fellow is John Littleton. He lives in my parish and has benefited from the kindness of the Church. More than that, however, he knows the parish and the sort of men who inhabit it. I have made much use of him in recent days, and I thought you might as well."

I turned to offer the *fellow*, as the priest would have it, my hand in friendship.

He took it with eagerness, perhaps relieved to see I was of a somewhat more open nature than our host. "How do ye," he said cheerfully. "Benjamin Weaver, I seen you fight, me spark. More than once, too. I seen you beat the tar out of that Irishman Fergus Doyle, and I seen you take out that French fellow too, but I don't recollect his name. But the best match I ever saw, let me tell you, sir, was the time you fought Elizabeth Stokes. Now, she was a great fighter of the female sort. They don't make the likes of her no more."

I sat next to Mr. Littleton. "The sad truth is that the art of pugilism has fallen on hard times among the ladies. Now it is all female sport, and they are made to hold coins in their fists when they fight so as to guarantee they don't scratch out each other's eyes. The first to unclench her fists so far as to drop the coin loses the match."

"A rotten thing. That Elizabeth Stokes, she could lay out a punch or two." He turned to Mr. Ufford. "A mean lass, she was— vicious as a legless rat and quick as an oiled Italian. I thought certain she would take Mr. Weaver here."

"She pummeled me something fierce," I told him cheerfully. "That's the difficulty I often felt when asked to fight with a lady. Were I to lose, I would be humiliated, but when I won, there was no glory in it, for I had done naught but beat a woman. I should have refused to do it entire, but such fights always generated a hearty take at the door. Those who arranged the battles could hardly shun something so lucrative, and neither could we fighters."

"I only wish them girls were made to strip to the waist like the men. That would make for good sport, I think, with their bubbies flying here and yon. Begging your pardon, Mr. Ufford," he added.

Ufford's pink skin reddened. "Well," he said, rubbing his hands together as though preparing to move a pile of lumber, "how about some refreshment before we cut into the meat of the matter. What say you, Mr. Weaver? Can I offer you a hearty dark ale? It's just the sort favored by hardworking men."

"I have not been used to work so hard as I ought of late," I told him, "but I should like an ale just the same." As it happened, my head ached somewhat furious from the wine of the night before and, short of a bowl of saloop, ale might be just the thing.

"I thought he'd never ask," Littleton told me quietly, as though passing along a secret. "I nearly died of thirst more than once as we awaited you."

Ufford rang the bell, and the serving girl with the massive arms entered the room. She was no more than sixteen, somewhat stooped of stature, and of her face I could only say that nature had not been her most generous. But she appeared a cheerful lass and smiled agreeably at all of us. She listened to Mr. Ufford's commands and then returned in an instant with pewter mugs filled with nearly foamless ale.

"Now," Mr. Ufford said, joining us at the table. He held out a fine-looking whalebone snuffbox. "Either of you care for a pinch?" he asked.

Littleton shook his head. "I prefer my pipe." He removed the mentioned device and began to pack it with weed from a small leather pouch.

"I'm afraid I'll have to ask you to refrain in my presence," Ufford said. "I cannot endure the smell of burning tobacco. It is both noxious and like to cause fires."

"Is it, now?" Littleton asked. "Well, I'll put it away then."

Perhaps to demonstrate his superiority, Ufford made an exaggerated show of his snuff-taking. He took a pinch of the dust between his forefinger and thumb and then proceeded to sniff with a great furor at each nostril. He then dabbed at his nose and sneezed three or four times. Finally he set his rag aside and beamed at us, as if to show that he had not a speck of snuff left upon his face.

I had always found the ritualized process of snuff-taking exceedingly tedious. Men would make great shows of who could sniff with the greatest strength, who could sneeze the most cleanly, who had the best-formed nostrils. Ufford had clearly made a good showing, but he found his audience not fit to appreciate his art.

He coughed nervously and then clutched a goblet of wine, its stem a shiny silver. "I suppose you are curious to learn what task you will perform for me, yes?"

"I am eager to hear your needs, certainly," I told him, trying mightily to demonstrate confidence. Having spent some months now in shirking my responsibilities, the wheels of my thieftaking mechanism were in need of grease.

I glanced over at Mr. Littleton. He had eyes only for his rapidly draining pot of ale, and his concentration allowed me to study him freely. I thought I knew him from some previous encounter, but I could not place the association, and that made me most uneasy.

"I fear I find myself in a bit of a situation, sir," Ufford began. "A very uncomfortable one that I cannot resolve without help, and not help to be got just anywhere, as you will see. I have preached many times in my church— Oh, I forget myself. As a Hebrew you may not be familiar with the doings of a church interior. You see, during our worship, it is common for the priest to give a long talk—well, not too long, I hope—in which he discourses on religious or moral issues he thinks relevant to his congregation."

"I am familiar, Mr. Ufford, with the concept of the sermon."

"Of course, of course," he said, seeming a bit disappointed that

I had diverted him from the task of definition. "I knew you would be. In any case, I have been used for the past months to preach on a subject very near to my heart, and very near to the hearts of my parish, for it is principally made up of hardworking men on the lowest echelon of the laboring ranks. Men, you understand, who live week to week on their wages and for whom the loss of even a few days' pay, or an unanticipated sickness that requires payment to a medical man, could bring utter ruin. I have taken their cause as my own, sir, and I have spoken out for them. I have spoken out, I say, for the rights of the laboring men of this metropolis, to earn a decent wage and to make enough to support their families. I have spoken out against the cruelty of those who would keep their workers so impoverished that the allure of quick earnings in heinous crime, the sin of whoredom, and the oblivion of gin all conspire to undo them, body and soul, yes, body and soul. I have spoken out against these things."

"I daresay you are speaking out against them now," I observed.

Again, Mr. Ufford surprised me by being so good-natured. He laughed and patted me amiably on the shoulder. "You must forgive me if I talk a bit much, Benjamin, but on the subject of the poor and their well-being I can hardly say enough."

"You are surely admirable in that regard, sir."

"It is only my Christian duty—and one that I should like to see others in my church embrace. But, as I say, I have taken on the poor as my cause and spoken of the injustices they face. I thought myself doing things for the good and right, but I find there are those who don't like my message, even among the lower orders, the very men whom I endeavor to aid."

Here Ufford reached into the lining of his coat and produced a ragged piece of paper.

"Shall I read this to you, Benjamin?" he asked pointedly.

"I have letters," I told him, as I concentrated with great intensity on concealing my irritation. I was not often thought to be quite so unschooled as to be illiterate.

"Of course. Your race is a very learned one, I know."

He handed me the note, which was written in a rough and uneven hand.

Mr. Youfurd,

Dam you and dam you and double dam you twice you black gard bich. No won cares to heer any of yore drivel so dam you and be silent or you will find that there ar those who will no how to make you silent by burning yore house down around yore ears or if stone wont burn by cutting yore throat so you bleed like the pig you ar. No more of yore speeches on the poor or you will no what the poor ar and what they can do and that will be the last thing you no before you go to hell you bich and pig. You have been warned wonce and wont again except in your being kilt. &

I set down the note. "I have, in my days, heard the men of my religion deliver discourses with which I was not in full agreement. This response, however, strikes me as excessive."

Ufford shook his head sadly. "I cannot tell you the shock I felt upon receiving this, Benjamin. That I, who have now decided to dedicate my life to aiding the poor, should be by any of them reviled—regardless of how small their numbers—is a great disappointment to me."

"And a bit of a scare too, I should think," Littleton suggested. "All that talk of burning and throat cutting. It's enough to put a man on edge, it is. Why, if it was me, I'd take to hiding in the cellar like a whipped child."

It was certainly enough to put Mr. Ufford on edge. The priest flushed and bit his lip. "Yes. You see, my first thought, Benjamin, was that if people object to my sermons so strongly, perhaps I ought not to continue speaking them. After all, I might have something to say, but I don't believe myself so original that I ought to put myself at risk for my ideas. But then, as I reflected further, I wondered if that was not a coward's way out. It would be far more honorable, I thought, to discover who is behind this note and bring him to justice. Needless to say, I will not be preaching on this subject until the matter is resolved. That would be, I think, imprudent."

At once, I began to feel the thaw in the frozen machinery of my trade. I thought of a dozen men of whom I might inquire. I thought of the taverns that wanted visiting, the beggars who wanted questioning. There was much to be done in the service of Mr. Ufford, and I found myself eager to perform—not for his sake but for my own.

"Properly handled, it should be no difficult thing to discover the author," I assured him. The certainty in my voice cheered us both.

"Oh, that is very good, sir, very good indeed. I am told you are the man to see in these affairs. If I knew who had sent it, and I merely wanted him apprehended, I am told I should go to Jonathan Wild. But they say you are the one who can find men when no one knows who they are."

"I am honored by your confidence." I took, I admit, some pleasure in his words, for the skills he attributed to me were hard-won. I had learned a thing or two during my difficulties in attempting to discover who had killed my father and how his death related to the great financial engines that drive this nation. Most of all, I had discovered that the philosophy behind their monstrous finance, called *probability theory,* had the most astonishing application for the thieftaker. Until I had learned of it, I had known of no way of detecting a villain other than by using witnesses or extracting a confession. Through the deployment of probability, I had discovered how to speculate based on who might have been likely to commit a crime, what might have been a likely motive, and how such a rogue might have attempted his misdeeds. With this new and wondrous way of thinking, I had been able to apprehend rascals who might otherwise have escaped the clutches of justice.

"You are perhaps wondering why I asked John to join us today," Ufford said.

"I have wondered," I agreed.

"John is someone I've met in my work with the poor in my parish. And he knows quite a bit, really, about the sort of people who might have sent this note. I thought he would be able to provide some guidance as you explore the lairs of the unfortunates who inhabit Wapping."

"I don't love to involve myself in suchlike things," Littleton told me, "but Mr. Ufford has done me some kindnesses, and I must return what I can."

"So." Ufford drained his glass and pushed away from the table. "I believe we are done. You will report back to me, of course, as you progress. And if you have any questions, I hope you will send me a note, and we will set up an appropriate time to discuss the matter."

"Do you not wonder," I asked, "about my fee for performing these services you request?"

Ufford laughed and fidgeted uneasily with one of his coat buttons. "Of course, I suppose you will require a little something. Well, when you are done, we will see to that."

Such was how men of Mr. Ufford's standing were used to paying tradesmen. Inquire of nothing until the work was done, and then pay what they liked when they liked—or perhaps never at all. How many hundreds of carpenters and silversmiths and tailors had gone to their graves paupers while the wealthy they served stole from them openly and legally? I knew better than to accept such treatment.

"I require five pounds, Mr. Ufford, to be paid immediately. If my labors take me more than a fortnight, I will require more, and at that time you can tell me if you are sufficiently satisfied to pay what I ask. It is my experience, however, that if I can't find this buck in a fortnight, I likely shan't find him ever."

Ufford let go of his button and cast a very severe frown at me. "Five pounds is a great deal of money."

"I know that," I said. "It is the reason I wish to possess it."

He cleared his throat. "I must inform you that I am not used to paying tradesmen for services before they are rendered, Benjamin. It is not very respectful of you to ask that I do so."

"I mean neither respect nor rudeness. It is merely the way I conduct my affairs."

He let out a sigh. "Very well. You may call here later today. I will have Barber, my man, give you a purse on your request. In the meantime, you boys surely have a lot to discuss, and you may use this room as long as you like, provided you do not stay more than an hour."

Littleton, who had been busy staring into his mug of ale, now looked up. "We ain't boys," he said.

"Pardon me, John?"

"I said, we ain't boys. You ain't much older than Weaver, and I know I'm old enough to be your father, provided I started my swiving young. Which I did, in case you're wondering. We ain't boys then, are we?"

Ufford answered with a thin smile, so condescending it was far crueler than any rebuke. "You are surely right, John." He then rose and left us alone in the room.

During the course of our conversation, I had recollected how it was I knew Littleton's name. Not ten years before, he had established some unwanted fame as the principal agitator among the laborers at the Deptford Naval Yard. The mayhem caused by his labor combination had produced no small number of pieces in the newspapers.

Workers in the yard had ever been used to taking home the unneeded chunks of wood remaining from their sawings, called by them *chips,* which they made use of by selling or trading. The value of the chips made up no small part of their wages. While Littleton had been working in the yard, the Naval Office had come to the conclusion that too many men were simply taking pieces of lumber, sawing them into chips, and walking off with them—this to the cost of a sizable fortune each year. At once the order was given: Workers could no longer remove chips from the yard, but they were offered no increase in wages to compensate for the loss. In a stroke designed to reduce fraud, the Naval Office dramatically reduced the income of their laborers and saved a great deal of money for themselves.

John Littleton had been among the most vocal in protesting this move. He formed a combination of workers in the yard, and together they declared that they would have their chips or the yard would have no workers. Defiantly they loaded up their wooden booty as they had been used to, piled it upon their backs, and departed, passing through a crowd of men from the Naval Office at whom they hooted and called foul names. It is for this reason that so many years later, when a worker is saucy with his betters, he is said to be *carrying a chip on his shoulder.*

The next day, when Littleton and his fellows attempted to leave with their riches, they met with more than a parcel of foul-tongued placemen. They found, instead, a group of ruffians, paid by the Naval Office to make the workers' defiance unprofitable. They were beaten and their chips taken for the ruffians to sell as they pleased. All escaped with little more than bruised bodies or broken heads—all but John Littleton, who was dragged back to the shipyards and beaten mercilessly before being tied to a pile of wood and left in desolation for nearly a week. Had it not rained before he was discovered, he would have died of thirst.

This incident was met with the greatest public outcry, but without consequence for Littleton's attackers—no consequence, that is, but that it brought to a period the rebellion against the Naval Yard, and it brought to a period Littleton's efforts as a labor agitator.

Littleton called the girl to refill his tankard and then drained it in an instant. "Now that he's gone, I'll tell you what you need to know, and the sooner you get the fellow and your five pounds, the more kindly you'll think on your friend John Littleton. With a bit of luck, you might have the matter in hand by the morrow, and you may then rest as comfortably as a housewife whose husband has been cured of the pox."

"Tell me what you know, then."

"First off, you have to understand that this here ain't Ufford's parish. He's at John the Baptist's Church in Wapping. He don't live there because it don't suit his style to live in such a shitten place that smells twice as beautiful as a Tom-turd man. He has a curate what he pays a few shillings a week to do most of the parish work, and this fellow is but a drudge, a mere slave to Ufford's whims. Until of late, he had the curate do the Sunday preaching too, but then Ufford took an interest in the plight of the poor, as he calls us, and so more of the tasks went to him."

"And how does this help me find the man who wrote the letter?" I asked.

"Well, you have to understand that there's a lot of grumbling going on with the dockworkers." He proudly tapped his porter's shield. "Old privileges are being taken away, and they ain't being replaced by anything. Men who sock a little tobacco in their trousers or stuff a few leaves of tea in their pockets—they're getting seven years' transportation and told they're lucky not to get the gallows. And now that they ain't allowed to take from the hogsheads, they ain't being given any wages in exchange. So they're angry, all of them, angry as a dog with a lighted taper up its arse."

"A *lighted* taper, you say?"

He grinned. "And dripping wax."

I could understand that Littleton did not much care for this situation, for it was remarkably like his troubles at the dockyards. Such was the nature of labor all over the island. Traditional compensations such as goods and materials were being wrested from workers, but no new wages were offered in place. What surprised me was that, in light of all he had suffered in his efforts to fight for the rights of workers, Littleton would allow himself to be drawn into Ufford's circle. But I knew that a man who is hungry will often forget his fears.

Nevertheless, the story Littleton told me made little sense. "If Mr. Ufford wants to help the laborers, why would they be angry with him?"

"That's the puzzle, ain't it? It used to be that all us porters caught what work we could, but then this big tobacco man—Dennis Dogmill by name—he put a stop to it. Said we should get together and come to him all at once so he could hire a crew instead of wasting his time hiring this man and that. So crews got formed, but somehow they turned from crews to gangs, and they hate one another more than they hate Dogmill, which I guess was the plan all along. You know him—Dogmill?"

"I'm afraid not."

"Ain't nothing to be afraid of in not knowing him. It's knowing him that's the trouble. He's the son of the biggest tobacco man this island's ever seen, but he ain't his father. No matter what he does, he can't sell as much as the family used to, and it makes him right furious. I saw him beat a porter near to death once for not working as hard as Dogmill reckoned he ought to. We stood there, Weaver, watching it, none of us willing to walk over and stop it, though we outnumbered him something severe, but that don't signify. You take a step toward him, and you lose your badge. You have a family, it will be without bread. And there was something more, too. I got the feeling—it's hard to say it, but it's so—that twenty of us would not quite have been a match for him. He's a big man and a strong man, but that ain't it. He's *angry*, if you know what I mean. And that anger is something vicious."

"And he is behind these gangs?" I asked.

"Not direct, but he knew what he was doing when he arranged that we should separate out as we done. There's a whole lot of gangs now, and we don't ever come together. Now, the biggest gangs are Walter Yate's and Billy Greenbill's, who they call Greenbill Billy on account of his funny lips."

"And not because of his name?"

Littleton removed his hat and scratched his nearly hairless head. "There is that, too. Howsomever, Greenbill Billy is a nasty fellow, and it's said he'd see the other men what want to lead the workers dead, and the workers dead too, rather than yield to another man—any man but Dogmill, that is. I suspect he don't want Ufford sticking his own bill into the mess, since it ain't none of his business, as he reckons it, and has no cause to jab his shitten stick in the porters' arse pot. The priest wants the gangs to form one big labor combination to fight Dogmill, and if that happens, Greenbill Billy goes from being the most powerful porter on the quays to no more than just another turd in the pile."

"Are the other gangs willing to set aside differences and become a combination?" I asked.

He shook his head. "Just the opposite. They compete with one another, for Dogmill's nearly got control of the whole dock now, and he don't let any one gang work unless it's outbid another. So our wages keep getting lower and lower, and we're fighting all the fiercer over these little scraps."

"And you suspect that Greenbill Billy is behind the notes?"

"Could as likely be as not. I'm in Yate's gang, and I know he don't go for that sort of thing. He's a good man, that Yate. Young he is, but smart as a pig running from Bartholomew Fair, and he seems to want to do right. And he's got the prettiest wife I ever saw. I wouldn't mind a wife like that, let me tell you. I've seen her look at me once or twice, too. I know I'm a bit older than Yate, but I still have some charms that the ladies glance to. Stripped to the waist, I look like a young man, and it wouldn't surprise me if so pretty a girl didn't sample the wares away from her husband, if you take my meaning."

Feeling we had somehow lost our way, I attempted to bring him back on course. "Perhaps I should have a word with Greenbill, then."

Littleton snapped his fingers. "That's the thing I propose. He likes to spend his time at a tavern called the Goose and Wheel, off Old Gravel Lane, near the timber yard. I ain't saying he's the one who sent the note, mind you, but there's a good chance that, if he didn't, he knows who did."

"Have you told all of this to Mr. Ufford?"

He winked at me. "Not so much of it."

"Why not?"

"Because," he said in a whisper, "Ufford is a horse's arse, that's why. And the less he knows and the scareder he is and the more he goes bum-firking from this place to that, the more he gives me ale and bread and a coin here and there. I'll be honest with you, since I don't want you hearing this elsewhere and thinking ill of me. I told him not to bring you in. I said it was because the Church don't need no Jews to do its business, but the real reason is that I don't want him to get his mind put at ease too quick. It's bad for my belly. This here is winter, and there ain't no work for the quays porters. I keep food and drink in me—and only just enough to keep off death—by catching rats off the docked ships. It's a disgrace that a porter with a badge like me is so reduced. Now, Ufford came to me and asked could I help him, and he offered me money and food, and these clothes he gave to me too. Milking his udders is a might better than catching rats, and I don't want to see that well dry up too fast, you understand, though he seems now to feel like he done for me all he need to and I should dance for him like a Mayfair puppet."

"I understand you." I reached into my purse and pulled out a shilling, which I handed to him.

"Well, now," he said, with a monkey's grin of strong yellow teeth, "this is as much as a fellow could ask for. I think you may have found yourself a friend, friend. If you're so inclined, I could take you to the Goose and Wheel myself and point out Greenbill to you. He ain't no friend of mine, and I wouldn't want him to see me there, but I can point you all the same. Provided you buy me something to drink once we're there."

This matter began to have the taste of something I could complete within a day or two, and that was exactly what I needed to help return me to the rhythms of my work. "I'd be most grateful," I told Littleton. "And if this Greenbill turns out to be our poet, or leads me to him, there will be another shilling in it for you, sure enough."

"That's what I want to hear," he told me. He then took his empty pewter mug and placed it in a small sack by the side of his chair. " 'Twere mine, once," he explained. "Or one like it."

I shrugged. "I can assure you I have no concern for any mugs you might take from Mr. Ufford's kitchen."

"Right kind of you," he said. He reached across the table to my half-full mug, drained it, and placed it with the other in his sack. "Right kind of you indeed."

CHAPTER 3

ONCE JUDGE ROWLEY had pronounced my conviction, I knew I would not be permitted to return to the relative comfort of my room on the Master's Side—a privilege that had cost dearly but had been worth the coin to keep me away from the dangerous masses of the prison. But no matter how much money he has at his command, any man condemned to hang must reside in the hold, the particular part of the prison designated for such unfortunates, whose ranks I had now joined. While I understood I would not be enjoying the most comfortable of accommodations, I had no reason to anticipate the gravity of the judge's intentions. When we arrived at the cell in the dark of Newgate's hellish cellar, one of the turnkeys ordered me to hold out my wrists for shackling.

"For what reason?" I demanded.

"For the reason of preventing escape. The judge has ordered it, so that's what gets done."

"For how long am I to be shackled?" I demanded.

"Until such time as you are hanged, I believe."

"That is six weeks away. Is it not cruel to shackle a man for six weeks without cause?"

"You should have thought of that before killing that spark," he told me.

"I didn't kill anyone."

"Then you should have thought of that before being nabbed for doing what you didn't do. Now, hold out your wrists. You needn't be what they call conscious, I might point out, or without a blow to the head, in order to be shackled right and proper. I've a mind to knock you if you don't do as I say, so I can tell my boys I exchanged blows with Ben Weaver."

"If trading blows is your plan," I offered, "then I shall take your offer willingly. But somehow I think you haven't a fair exchange in mind." With the gifts given by my pretty stranger clutched tightly in my palm, I held out my wrists and allowed this blackguard to shackle them together. Next, I was made to sit in a wooden chair in the center of the room. Here my legs were bound together in a manner similar to my wrists, but these shackles were attached by a chain to a staple rising from the floor. I had only a few feet of slack with which I might hobble about as best I could.

Once the turnkeys left me there, I had an opportunity to examine my surroundings. The room was not overly small, some five feet wide and ten feet long. It offered no more than the chair on which I sat, a rough mattress, barely in reach of the chain, a very large pot for my necessary business (its size suggesting that it would be emptied none too often), a table, and a small fireplace, now unlit despite the cold. At the very top of one wall was a small and exceedingly narrow window that just peeked above the ground layer. It permitted only a few rays of daylight to penetrate, but this was hardly an escape route, as a cat could not squeeze its way through those slits. There were two windows of a much larger kind that overlooked the hallway, though still not large enough to permit a man to pass.

I breathed in deeply to sigh, an act I regretted at once, for the air was exceedingly unwholesome and stank of condemned bodies nearby as well as those who had long since passed through. It smelled of chamber pots in need of emptying and those in need of being mopped. It smelled of vomit and blood and sweat.

The sounds were of no more comfort. I could hear the nearby clicking of rat claws on the stone floor and the scrape in my ear of the lice that had not given me a moment to adjust to my new surroundings before latching onto my person. Somewhere in the distance a woman sobbed, and perhaps a bit closer: drawn-out laughter, treacly with madness. My closet was, in short, a dark and desolate place, and the turnkeys had not left me alone for more than a minute or two before I began plotting my departure from it.

I am no master of escapes, but I had broken into a goodly number of houses in my younger days, after my career as a pugilist had been forced to a period by a leg injury. I therefore knew a thing or two about the use of a lockpick. I took the device that the pretty stranger had pressed into my hand and held it in my palm, as though its weight could tell me something of its utility. It did not, but I was determined that the lady's efforts should not be in vain. True, I had no ideas of who she might be or why she should have gone to such lengths to aid me, but I thought it better to address those matters after I was free.

I therefore set myself to the task of digging into the lock of my shackles. My wrists being manacled together, I had none of the dexterity a housebreaker enjoys, but I had not the fear of being happened upon either, so with careful application I was able to insert the pick into the lock and feel out the mechanisms. It took some time to be able to find the spring, and more time to activate it, but I managed to trigger the release, and in less than a quarter hour too. What a glorious sound, the muted snap of metal upon metal, and the musical slackening of the chains! My hands were now free, and after rubbing my wrists for the few moments that I indulged in this new liberty, I began work on my feet.

This was slightly more difficult because of the angle, because in just fifteen minutes what little light graced the room had begun to fade, and because my fingers had begun to grow tired from such precise labors. But soon enough I was entirely free of my chains.

There was little enough reason to rejoice, however. Though I could now move around my cell at liberty, I could go nowhere, and if my state of release was discovered I should find myself in a worse position than that in which I began. Now I would have to work quickly. I looked around my cell in the growing darkness. The onset of evening would be an advantage, of course, providing cover for my actions. It nevertheless increased my feeling of melancholy.

Why had such a thing happened to me? How could it be that I

was now condemned to hang for a crime I never committed? I sat down and put my face in my hands. I was on the verge of weeping, but then I at once chastised myself for giving in to despair. I was free of my chains, I had tools, and I had strength. This prison, I declared to myself with spurious determination, would not detain me long.

"Who's that over there, clanking around so?" I heard a voice, thick and distorted, through the walls of the prison.

"I'm new," I said.

"I know you're new. I heard you come in, didn't I? I asked who you were, not about your freshness. Are you a fish or a man? When your mama set a steaming cake before you, you wanted to know if it was seed or plum, not when she first started to bake it."

"My name's Weaver," I said.

"And what do they have you for?"

"For a killing in which I took no part."

"Oh, that is always the way, isn't it? Only the innocent end up here. Never been a man condemned who done what they said. Except me. I done it, and I'll say so like the honest man I am."

"And what do they have *you* for?"

"For refusing to live by the law of a foreign usurper, is what. That false king on the throne took away me livelihood, he did, and when a man tries to take it back, he finds himself thrown in prison and sentenced to hang."

"How did the king take away your livelihood?" I asked, without much real interest.

"I was in the army, don't you know, serving Queen Anne, but when the German stole the throne, he thought our company too Tory in its tone and had us disbanded. I never knew nothing but soldiering, so I couldn't think of how to make my living but by that, and when I couldn't do that no more, I had to find another way."

"That way being?"

"Riding out on the highway and stealing from those what support the Hanoverian."

"And were you always quite certain to rob only those who support King George?"

He laughed. "Perhaps not so careful as I might have been, but I know a Whiggish coach when I see one. And's not as though I never did try to make my living in honest ways. But there's no work to be found, and people are starving upon the street. I was not about to be one of those. Anyhow, they nabbed me with a stolen watch in me pocket, and now I'm to hang for certain."

"It is a small crime," I told him. "They may prove lenient."

"Not for me, they won't. I made the mistake of being taken in a little gin house, and the constable what took me heard me raise a toast to the true king just before he dragged me away."

"Perhaps that was unwise," I observed.

"And the gin house was called the White Rose."

The entire world knew that the white rose was a symbol of the Jacobites. It was a foolish place to be arrested, but men who broke the law were often foolish.

I knew that support for the Chevalier was common among thieves and the poor—I had many times been in the company of men of the lower sort who would gladly raise a bumper in the name of the deposed king's son—but such toasts were generally not taken very seriously. Men such as this, who had lost their army positions after the Tories had been purged, often took to robbing the highways and smuggling, joining gangs of other Jacobite thieves who told themselves that their crimes were but revolutionary justice.

As I write this memoir, so many years after the events I describe, I know I may find some readers too young to remember the rebellion of '45, when the grandson of the ousted monarch came close to marching upon London. Now the threat of Jacobites seems no more serious than the threat of bugbears or hobgoblins, but my young readers must recollect that, in the days of which I write, the Pretender was more than a tale to frighten children. He had launched a daring invasion in 1715, and there had been numerous plots since to return him to the throne or stir up rebellion against the king. As I sat in prison, a general election loomed upon us, the first to take place since George I acceded to the throne— so this election was widely seen as one that would determine how much the English had come to love or hate their German monarch.

It therefore seemed to us likely that at any time we might be subject to an invasion in which the Pretender would take up arms in order to reclaim his father's throne.

The Jacobites, those followers of the son of the deposed James II, saw this moment as their finest opportunity in seven years to retake the throne for their master. Outrage toward the ministry and, less openly, toward the king had been running hot ever since the collapse of the South Sea Company stock in the fall of 1720. As the Company sank, so too did the countless other projects that had taken root in the seemingly fertile soil of soaring stock prices. Not just a single company but an entire army of companies had been destroyed in an instant.

As wave after wave of financial ruin crashed upon our shores, as riot from food shortages and low wages kindled like dry straw in a drought, as men of great wealth lost their fortunes in a flash, discontent with our foreign king's government rose and overflowed. It was later said that in the months following the bursting of the Bubble, the Pretender might have ridden into London without an army and found himself crowned without the loss of a drop of blood. That may or may not be the case, but I can assure my readers that I have never before or since seen hatred toward the government as volatile as it was in those days. Greedy Parliamentarians scrambled to screen the South Sea Company directors—that they might better screen their own profits from the Company's stock fraud—and the crowds grew angrier and more vicious. In the summer of 1721 a mob descended upon the Parliament itself to demand justice, an unruly throng that dispersed only after three readings of the Riot Act. With an election imminent, the Whigs, who controlled the ministry, realized that their grasp on the government might be loosening, and it was widely believed that if the Tories could return a majority, King George would not remain our monarch long.

I write now with a political understanding I did not possess at the time, but I knew enough of the public resentment toward the king and his Whig ministers to understand why this thief's political inclinations should have reflected so ill on him. Thieves and smugglers and the impoverished tended to lean toward the cause of the Jacobites, whom they saw as dashing outcasts like themselves. After the Bubble burst, and more men than ever before were struggling for bread, thieves and brigands began to appear in unprecedented numbers.

"It is very hard," I told him, "that a man should be hanged for saying what men have always said."

"I think so too. It is not as though I've killed anyone. Not like you."

"I haven't killed anyone either," I said. "Not anyone for whose murder I've been charged, at any rate."

At this he laughed. "The name is Nate Lowth," he said. "What did you say your name was again?"

I stood up now. This Lowth, with all his chatter, seemed to help me find the fire I needed to act. I walked over to the windows that looked out on the hallway. There were bars, of course. I examined each one to see if it might be loose.

"Weaver," I called over. "Benjamin Weaver."

"Sod me!" he shouted. "Benjamin Weaver the fighter in the cell next to me. Isn't that the most rotten luck in the world?"

"How so?"

"Why, on hanging day, when a man can shine his brightest, no one will give a fig for poor Nate Lowth. They'll all be there to see Weaver swing. I'll just be a mere tidbit to whet their appetites."

"I intend not to make myself conspicuous," I told him.

"I appreciate your neighborly gesture, but it may not be in your hands. They've heard of you, and it's your end they'll want to gaze on."

None of the bars were so loose as I would like, so I picked up the file that the woman had given me and reexamined the metal that blocked my path. The bars were too thick to saw through. It would take me all night and more, and I had no intention of being in my cell when the sun came up. Instead, I began to chip at the stone around the bars. The metal of the file was strong enough that it did not bend or snap. I used a blanket to muffle the sound as best I could, but the icy crack of metal on stone still echoed through the hallway.

"What's that noise?" Nate Lowth asked.

"I don't know," I told him between blows. "I hear it too."

"You lying heathen," he said. "You're making a break for it, ain't you?"

"Of course not. I honor the law above all else. It is my duty to hang if told to do so." I had now removed an inch or two around one of the bars, and it was considerably loosened, though I could not yet tell how far it descended or how long I would have to continue my labors.

"You needn't worry about me," he said. "I won't raise the alarm. I told you—I'm of a frame of mind to prefer your not being in attendance for our hanging day."

"Well, I hope I *am* absent, but I don't see it as very likely."

"Now I know what all the clanking was for."

"You may believe what you like," I told him. "It does me no harm."

"Don't get sour with a fellow. I'm only making conversation."

I gave the bar a good pull, and the stone around the base began to crack. I pulled again, and rotated the bar in a circular motion, widening the area of its encasement. Dust rained from the upper portion, sticking to my hands, which were slick with sweat. I wiped my hands against my breeches and began to apply them once more.

"You still there, Weaver, or are you gone yet?"

"I'm still here," I said, grunting as I spoke. "Where would I go?" I gave the bar a good pull, and the stone at its base cracked fiercely. One or two more yanks, and it would be free.

"Can you send me something nice once you're outside? Some wine and oysters."

"I'm in here, just like you."

"Well, let us say that if you do happen to get out, I'd like you to send me something. After all, I'm not calling the guards, now, am I, as many a man would do for spite. Neither am I threatening you, mind you. I'm just pointing out that I'm a good friend to ye."

"Should I find myself outside these walls, I will send wine and oysters."

"And a whore," he said.

"And a whore." Another pull. More crumbling.

"A very eager whore, if you don't mind."

"I will be certain to review the candidates with great care," I said. "None but the most enthusiastic will meet my approval." I sucked in my breath and pulled with the sum of my strength. The stone cracked entirely at the base, and I was able to pull the bar free. It was a little more than two feet in length, and I knew what I would do with it.

"I'll make like I didn't hear that noise," Nate Lowth said.

I walked over to the fireplace and examined the chimney. It was narrow but, I thought, manageable. "I am going to sleep now," I shouted to Lowth. "Please, no more conversation."

"Sleep soundly, friend," he said. "And don't forget my whore."

I stooped over and crawled into the fireplace. It was cold and airless inside, and I immediately felt as though my lungs were coated with soot. I ducked out once more and, using the file, tore a piece of blanket from the bed, wrapped it around my nose and mouth, and then, once more, to the chimney.

Reaching skyward, I found enough of a ledge to grab on to, and I pulled myself up. No more than a foot or two, but still it was progress. The interior was tighter than I had first realized, and moving that little space took an interminable amount of time. My arms were now above me, one of them clutching the bar, and there was no room to lower them. I felt the pressure of stone against my chest, and the sharpness of a jagged edge as it cut through both skin and linen. The bit of blanket I had tied in place to protect my breathing now felt as though it were suffocating me.

What if I cannot get out? I thought. They will come in the morning and think me gone, while my body, lodged in the chimney, begins to rot.

I shook my head, in part against this notion, in part to loosen the mask I had made. Better to breathe in dust, I thought, than breathe in nothing. The little knot in the blanket soon wore thin, and the mask fell away. I immediately regretted it, for the dust filled my mouth and throat, and I felt I could breathe less well than before. I coughed something fierce so I thought I must vomit my lungs, and the sound echoed throughout the chimney and no doubt the prison.

Nevertheless, I knew I had no choice but to move forward. I reached up and found another ledge and pulled myself up a foot or two more. My sweat mixed with soot to make a nasty mud that caked my hands and face and lodged in my nose. A glob of it settled near my nostril, and I made the mistake of trying to set it loose by rubbing my nose against the wall. That only brought more dirt into my nose, and now I truly could not breathe.

I cannot do it, I thought, as a piece of rock pushed its way into an open wound on my chest. At least not now. Let me go back, clean myself as best I can, and rethink this route. But when I tried to move downward, I found the hope of retreat was now closed to me. I had no leverage to push myself down. Sharp pieces of brick, like spikes, seemed to materialize beneath me to jab at my arms and legs. I could not see why, or turn my head enough to examine the passage. I had no choice, I realized, but to move forward, but when I reached up, I found I could not do that either. My hand found a ledge, but I could not budge my body.

I was truly stuck.

The dizzying madness of panic began to descend on me. Swirls of terror flashed before my eyes like fireworks. This was my hideous fate, more hideous than even the one His Majesty's justice intended for me next hanging day. I squirmed and pushed and pulled and twisted, but I could still move only an inch or two.

There was nothing to do but apply the metal bar. It would make far more noise than I would desire, but I was now willing to accept rescue from my jailor as a pleasing outcome. With the little room afforded me, I began to strike at the wall of the chimney. Because my hand was above my head, dust and rock rained down into my face. I turned away as best I could and struck again. And again.

Did I strike five minutes or an hour or two? I could not have said. I was lost in a mad confusion of panic and urgency. I slammed the bar against brick, and I slammed again and again. I coughed out soot and mud and powdered brick. I pinched my eyes closed and slammed with my fist and felt the bar vibrate in my hand. I prayed I would not drop it into the abyss.

Finally, I felt the rush of cold air, and when I dared to open my eyes, I saw that I had made a small hole, only the size of an apple, but that was enough. The air tasted stale, but it seemed sweet enough to a man who had despaired of ever breathing more, and I swung more wildly.

Soon I had a hole large enough to crawl through, though I did this slowly, for the room I entered was as black as the chimney. As I squeezed from my hole, I discovered that I was but a foot higher than the floor. Had I applied my metal bar to the wall just a little lower, I would never have escaped.

Newgate is an old prison, with many sections in disuse. Clearly here was one of them. The room was fairly large, perhaps three times the size of my cell, and contained a great quantity of broken furnishings, piled in places almost to the ceiling. I stepped on old refuse, long since dried nearly to dust. My every move brought a new tangle of itchy spiderwebs into my eyes and mouth and nostrils.

After a moment, my vision adjusted to the darkness, and I saw that the windowless room had a door with a padlock, of which my now-cherished bar made short work. I came out in another room, this one barred from the other side, but after a few minutes of examining my chamber, I discovered a stairwell that led upward.

On the next level, I found my egress also barred from the outside. I broke through the door only to find another set of stairs. And so up again, and again after that. I could not rejoice that I made my way farther from the ground, but at least I also made my way farther from my cell.

At last I found myself in a large chamber, also dark and unused. Here, however, I saw a light in the far distance, and after carefully making my way toward it, I found a barred window. Normally such a thing would fill a man with despair, but I had come so far that to me a barred window might as well have been an open one, with a pretty girl nearby to help me through. The bars here were old and somewhat rusted, and within an hour I had smashed through them and was able to crawl through and drop down to the roof of a neighboring building.

A cold, nearly frozen rain was falling, and I shivered in the darkness as icy water pooled around my feet, but I delighted in the waters washing the mud from my body. I looked upward to the dark haze of cloud cover and rubbed my face in the rain until my skin was free of prison soot and my nostrils free of prison stench.

My flesh was indeed free. I had, however, no way to reach the street. After circling the roof several times, I found that there was no means of climbing down, and I could not hope to jump such a distance and live—or at the very least avoid breaking my legs. I had managed to escape from the fortress, but I could find no way to descend three stories to safety.

I knew I could not linger. Should my absence be discovered while I remained on the roof, I would be retaken without trouble. I therefore came to a rather unorthodox conclusion. Though I am, by nature, a modest person, I removed all my clothes and made a rope of them. Tying them to a nail that protruded from the roof, I managed to climb down most of the way, with only a drop of perhaps six feet or so. I landed hard on my feet (which still bore my shoes), and fell over into the icy sting of snow. My left leg in particular, which I had broken as a fighter, ached fiercely, but I was mostly unharmed and absolutely free.

Thus I limped naked into the cold London night.

CHAPTER 4

I AM WELL AWARE that it is unkind of me to leave my reader in suspense as I wander the streets of London, naked, cold, and pursued by the full might of the law, but I must once more take a step back if my reader is to understand precisely how it was that I found myself on trial for Yate's death.

I intended to avail myself of the obsequious John Littleton, the porter whom Ufford had provided to assist me, but before I followed that worthy's lead, I thought it wise first to strike out on my own. Littleton had spoken of Mr. Dennis Dogmill, the tobacco merchant whose greed had manipulated the porters into competitive gangs. If Ufford used his sermons to speak in favor of the porters and sought to stir up trouble on their behalf, it seemed to me only natural that Dogmill would know of it. While it was unlikely that he would pen any such note as the one I had seen, I presumed he would either have some hand in this extortion or have made a point to find out who did, that he might better protest his innocence.

I had discovered in my rambles around town that tobacco merchants were inclined to pass their time at Moore's Coffeehouse, down near the quays, and as I had rendered Mr. Moore some services in the past, I believed I could depend upon him to assist me in this matter. I sent him a note asking if Dogmill ever frequented his business. He informed me almost immediately that Dogmill did indeed make a habit of visiting, though he had not been by as often recently because he was the election agent for the Whig candidate for Westminster. Nevertheless, he knew that Dogmill would be in that afternoon for a meeting with some associates.

I therefore took myself to Moore's and approached the coffee-house owner, who was a very young man for a proprietor, having inherited the business from his father not two years before. No more than three or four and twenty, he nevertheless had a business acumen beyond his years and was most apt at subordinating his wishes and desires to those of his customers. He opened his doors early, closed them late, cleaned up spills with his own hand, and oversaw the brewing of the coffee, the buying of the beer, and the baking of the pastries. Though dressed in a fine dark suit that befitted a prosperous tradesman, his clothes were rumpled and stained, his face slick with perspiration.

"Hello, Mr. Weaver," he said, as he took my hand warmly. "Always happy to help you, I am—what with all you done for me."

All I had done for him was to find those who owed him money and force them to pay—while keeping a generous percentage for myself. I considered it not a favor, only business, but I was of no mind to explain that to Moore. "I know you've much to keep you busy, so if you will just point out the man, I'll leave you to your affairs."

"That's him there." Moore jabbed his finger in the direction of an enormous man sitting with his back to me. "The big one."

Describing him as "the big one" was like calling the Fleet Ditch "the smelly one." He was massive, and even with his back to me I could see his mass was of the muscular sort rather than the fat. The breadth of his back and his arms pushed at the fabric of his coat. His neck was as thick as my thigh.

I must remind my reader that I spent a number of years earning my living as a pugilist, fighting pitched battles for my bread. I was, in the days of which I write, retired from the fighting arts but yet no small man. Nevertheless, here was someone who made me feel consumptive and puny. He sat by himself, hunched over some papers, clenching his pen so tight I should have thought he sought to crush it.

I stood for a moment, waiting for him to notice me, but when he did not I cleared my throat. "Pardon the interruption, Mr. Dogmill. My name is Benjamin Weaver, and I wonder if I might speak with you for a moment regarding a matter of some porters at the Wapping quays."

Dogmill paused writing and raised his head only slightly, but he did not look up. I could see his face was broad and round. It was the look I'd seen in many men who produce prodigious strength through exercise, and therefore require enormous amounts of food to feed their appetites. While their bodies may be large with muscles, their faces are often pudgy and soft.

I knew not how to read his stiff silence, so I chose to plunge ahead. "My services have been secured by a priest, a Mr. Ufford, who has received a number of threatening notes for his words in favor of improving the conditions of the Wapping porters. As there are a number of these men in your employ, I thought perhaps you might have heard something of this incident."

Dogmill, without letting his eyes for an instant rest on mine, turned around. "Moore!" he called out, like a master wishing to scold a servant.

The proprietor, who had been in the process of polishing some dishes, dropped his rag and pewter and dashed over. "Yes, Mr. Dogmill."

"Here's a wretch troubling my quiet." He pushed a coin into Moore's hand. "Take him outside and teach him not to be so impertinent to his betters."

Dogmill returned to his papers. Moore remained for an instant with the coin in his palm, as though it were some beautiful butterfly he dare neither crush nor risk frightening. At last he clenched it and took me by the arm. "Let's go," he said and began to pull me along.

"Oh, and Moore," Dogmill said, without looking up, "please explain to this fellow that if he speaks to me again, I'll stomp upon his hands until they are broken beyond healing. Be sure to make certain he understands."

Moore, knowing that the speech was concluded, pulled me along once more. Though I wished to say to Dogmill that he might make an effort to stomp upon me any time he chose, I held my tongue instead. Doing so would gain me little, and I did not desire to put Moore in a bad position. He wished only to save face before his patron, and having to balance the risk of discommoding me and discommoding Dogmill, he had surely made the right choice. He could explain himself to me and know I would hold no grudge. Dogmill struck me as not the sort of man with whom one equivocates.

Once outside, I observed the redness of his face. "Truly, I am sorry, Mr. Weaver, but I hadn't any inkling that he would take a dislike to you. When Mr. Dogmill takes a dislike to someone, it can be terrible ugly."

"What with stomping on hands and such."

"It's no jest, I promise you. He did it once to a stockjobber who had pulled a trick upon him. That fellow can no more pick up a pen now than can a duck. And he does not always reserve his temper for those who do him deliberate harm. I observed once that he punched a whore in the face for meddling with his breeches when he announced he would be left alone. Punched her in the face; you saw those anvil hands of his. Poor little doxy. Died of it, you know."

"I ought to count myself lucky, I suppose."

He shook his head. "I wish you had told me you wanted to speak to him of a matter he would not like. I'd have advised you not to waste your time, or at the very least to conduct your business in someone else's coffeehouse. Dogmill is monstrous brutal, but he pays his debts in a timely way, and he brings business with him."

"I understand. I shall find some other time to speak with him, then."

Moore held out the coin. "I cannot in good conscience keep this."

I laughed. "You've earned it. I'll not take your coin."

"Certain, are ye?"

"Please, Moore. You did your best to serve me."

He nodded and then, eyeing a foul puddle of mud and filth, approached, squatted down, and took a handful, with which he splashed himself repeatedly. He stood and turned to me with a grin, his clothes now wet with refuse, his face smeared black and filthy. "I don't even know that he heard your name or looked upon your face, but presuming he did, I cannot very well expect him to believe that I vanquished Benjamin Weaver without looking the worse for it. Good day to you, sir."

I did not believe myself to be done with Dogmill, and indeed I was not, but I chose to pursue less obstinate methods for the nonce while I considered how I might reapply my efforts with the merchant. And so it was off to meet with John Littleton. Though I have ever been inclined to plain attire, I admit to a preference for superior materials and tailoring, but before we went in search of Greenbill Billy, Littleton suggested my usual clothing would generate too much notice down by the quays. I therefore dressed myself in worn trousers and a stained blouse with an old wool jacket. I pushed my hair under an old hat, wide in both brim and crown, and I even applied a bit of paint to further darken a complexion already somewhat dusky by pallid British standards. Examining myself in the mirror, I congratulated myself on looking almost unfamiliar—every bit the Wapping lascar.

I arranged to meet Littleton at his home, a decrepit room he rented on Bostwick Street, and from there we walked to the Goose and Wheel. I had only seen him before at Ufford's table, so when he met me at the door I was surprised to find him taller than I had imagined, and broader at the shoulder than I before noticed. I had thought of him as a frail fellow moving hard into the final portion of his life, but now he looked to me more rugged, one of those tough men who cling tenaciously to the strength of their youth.

"I ain't looking forward to this," Littleton said as we walked, making our way past the beggars and the gin drinkers sitting out in the cold. A man pushed past us selling newly baked meat pies that steamed madly in the cold afternoon.

Littleton held his shoulders tight, bunching them up toward his ears as though in a perpetual shrug. "I know it was my maggot at the start, but the Goose and Wheel is Greenbill's place, and if any of them blackguards recollect my face, they won't think too much of my being there. The end result will be to my prejudice, it seems."

"You needn't go in," I said. "You've proved as helpful as Mr. Ufford could have hoped. You've pointed me in the direction you think right, and I can proceed alone from here most assuredly."

He looked like a petulant child. "I'll go. I don't want you to have to fend for yourself. But I've been giving this matter some thought. You asked for five pounds from the priest. That is a great deal of bread from the baker, and all for one man too. Now when you get to thinking about it, all you done for this rhino is to ask me some questions and have me lead you to where I know you ought to go. A shilling here and a shilling there is mighty generous, but as I've been your friend all throughout, don't you think more like half of what you get is what's called for?"

"I think you ought to be happy with what you've been given and what you've been promised."

"And happy I am," he said, and grinned so as to prove it. "It's just that I'd be happier with what's fair."

"How can you say what is fair until the matter is resolved?"

"Well, if it goes smooth and all, I think I should get two and a half pounds. That's all."

"Let us say I speak to Greenbill and determine that he is our man. Then what shall we do? How will you earn your two and a half pounds then?"

Littleton let out a dismissive laugh—merely a method of disguising his confusion. "We shall see, I suppose."

At that moment we passed an alleyway hidden in shadows. I turned toward it and grabbed Littleton, pushing him two or three feet inside. As he stumbled, I took from my pocket a pistol and held it to him, not two inches from his face. "I am paid for what I do because, if called to do so, I will not hesitate to discharge my lead into Greenbill's body. I may have to strangle him or crush his feet or hold his hand in a fire. Will you do those things, Mr. Littleton?"

To my surprise, he appeared neither frightened nor horrified, only slightly bewildered. "I must say, Weaver, you know how to make yourself understood. I'll take my odd shilling and be happy that I am asked to set no one ablaze."

I returned my pistol to my pocket, and we resumed our walk. Littleton, in an instant, appeared to have entirely forgotten the whole exchange. He was like a dog who, a quarter hour after receiving a beating from its master, lies contentedly at the same man's feet.

"Ufford brung all this on himself, if you want my opinion," he said to me. "Him with his politics and suchlike."

I felt myself grow tense. "How do his politics come into play?"

"You don't think he's taken a sudden interest in the poor for no reason, do you? With the election nigh upon us, he's doing what he can for the Tories."

Here was a new twist. I had thought this was but a matter of a wellborn priest pecking his beak into matters none of his concern. If Ufford's troubles related to the election, however, I understood that things might be more complicated than I had at first realized.

"Tell me how these porters connect with the election," I said. I knew little enough of these things, only that the Whigs were the party of new wealth, men without titles or history, men who did not want the Church or the crown to rule over them. The Tories were the party of old families and the traditionalists, those who wanted to see the Church restored to its former strength, who wanted to see the power of the crown strengthened and Parliament weakened. The Tories claimed to want to destroy the corruption of the new wealth, but many believed they only wanted the new wealth to disappear so their money could be returned to the old families. I was apt to confuse the parties until my friend Elias explained to me, with his cynical wit, that the Whigs were worms and the Tories were tyrants.

It nevertheless always surprised me how strong was the support for the Tories among the poor and disaffected. The Whigs might offer the laboring man the better dream for improvement. The

Whigs had fought to remove restrictions to advancement by alter-
ing the oaths of loyalty men must swear to hold government or
municipal positions. Now any Protestant, not just a Church of England man, could hold such offices. They weakened the power of
the Church and Church courts so that religious men could no
longer hold back those merchants who grew too big for their
breeches—or their parish. But the Tories remained a bulwark of
tradition to stand against the tide of change. They promoted the
idea of a simpler and more benevolent time when men of power
protected those of little wealth. They winked at old beliefs like
magic and witchcraft and the power of the king's touch to cure
scrofula. The Whigs might make a man feel as though he could be
more than he was, but the Tories made him feel pleased to be an
Englishman.

From the look on Littleton's face, I wasn't sure he understood as
much as that. "Well, if I'm to be honest, I don't quite know of Ufford's interests," he told me. "You would think that porters are
porters and tobacco men are but tobacco men, but Ufford seems
to think it's all political. I heard him say that he wants to see the
Tories win Westminster and he'll face the devil himself before he
sees a Whig returned. You know how it is with these Church men.
The Tories promise them that they'll put them back in power, give
them the right to tell us when to piss and when to shit. There's
nothing quite so near to a priest's heart than the Tory cause."

I spat into the street. One of the Tories who stood to win Westminster was Griffin Melbury, Miriam's husband. I little troubled
myself about the details of politics, and not living within the
boundaries of Westminster, I cared less for that election, but I
understood one thing with certainty: I wished Melbury nothing
but failure. Why had Miriam married him? Why had she abandoned her nation—and me—for this man who would force her to
change her religion? If Ufford's effort to aid the laborers would get
Melbury elected, I would prefer to see Ufford hounded and the
porters pauperized.

I still winced when I thought of Miriam married to that man. I
had never met him or even set eyes upon him, but nonetheless I

had a clear image of Melbury in my mind: tall, handsomely proportioned, fine in the face, strong in the calf. He would be charming and easy in the English way. This much I did know of him: He came from an old Tory family of landed wealth, his father and uncles had always sat in Parliament, and he had two brothers in the priesthood. He had served before in a pocket borough, and because he was well connected with certain bishops in the Church of England whose power was strong in Westminster, he had been encouraged to run for a seat in that borough—perhaps the most important in the nation.

Melbury would have to be charming. He had succeeded in convincing Miriam to convert to the Church. She had been married very young to my Uncle Miguel's son, a dour lad who died at sea having hardly known his wife. I had come to be familiar with her during my efforts to discover the facts of my father's death, and in truth I believed that she felt the same love for me that I did for her. But despite what the novelists will tell us, we live in a world more inclined to pragmatic action than romantical ideals. We might sit about with neat little volumes and imagine the blissful love in a cottage, but such ideas are but phantasms. We cannot live them. Instead, we must eat and dress and comport ourselves with companions of our liking. And it is always preferable to live without fear of creditors.

Knowing all of these things to be true, I had nevertheless asked Miriam to marry me, but she had contended that our lives were not compatible. I understood that she had been right, but that did not stop me from asking her again. I stopped after three times, believing that more effort on my part would have only appeared foolish in her eyes and humiliating in mine.

Nevertheless, Miriam and I were ever used to be in each other's company. I had discontinued my requests for her hand, but my desire remained, unarticulated but palpable. She knew it—she could not but know it—and she sought my company all the same. Late one afternoon she had come to my uncle's house for the observance of Havdalah, the close of the Sabbath. I felt there was something more than usual in her attentiveness to me that evening, and by the light of the braided candle, with my head full of sweet scent of the spice box, I felt the heat of her gaze upon my face.

Miriam looked to me astonishing in her blue gown and matching hat, from which spilled ample dark ringlets. She was a finely proportioned woman and striking in her face, with her Iberian complexion and emerald eyes, but I should have been a fool if it were her looks alone that had rendered me her devotee, for London teemed with countless pretty and accessible women. No, I admired Miriam for her quick wit and lively humor and for her spirit. She had been treated shabbily by fate: married off as a young girl to an introverted boy she hardly knew and I daresay bore no love. Though he was gone within months of their wedding, she had remained the subject of my uncle's management, and benevolent as it was, she had longed for her freedom.

Through no error of her own, Miriam had found herself at the center of the South Sea Company stock mayhem to which I'd connected my father's death. She, however, fared much better than he, and the Company had paid her handsomely for her silence. That payment, in turn, secured her independence, though for a while she maintained a strong loyalty to her deceased husband's parents.

As we sat together that night, the room slowly emptied around us. My aunt, the guests, and finally my uncle too, who knew well what he was about and wanted to see me married to Miriam nearly as much as I did. He left us alone as though there were nothing unusual in his doing so. Miriam might have objected. She might have excused herself in confusion, but she did not. She remained. She called for more wine.

We had begun the evening on chairs at opposite ends of the room, but we had somehow come together on the same sofa. I say somehow, but I lie, for each incremental move closer to her represented the deepest strategy on my part. I would rise to get something and sit myself one position closer. I would drop a button, leave my seat to pick it up, and sit nearer to her. With each step I measured her reaction, and each time I saw no disapproval.

And it went so until we kissed. I had taken far too much to

drink that night, but I recall well how it started. We sat together, only inches apart, and she spoke of some book she had been reading and how it interested her, and I half listened as the wine and my desire rang heavily in my ears. At last, when I could endure no more of it, I reached out with my hand and placed it to her cheek.

She did not pull away from it but rather moved closer, nuzzling me as though she were a cat, and so I leaned in and kissed her.

It lasted but an instant before she rose and pushed herself backward. "What are you doing?" she asked, in the loudest whisper she could muster.

I chose to remain seated, that she might see her alarm was not universally felt. "I was kissing you."

"You mustn't. You know that. Why must I tell you that again?"

"Miriam," I said, "you all but put your request in writing."

She opened her mouth to sting me with some cruel retort but stopped herself, remaining motionless for what seemed an interminable amount of time. I listened to the sound of my own breath and the sound of rolling carriages outside the window as though they were the most interesting things in the world.

"You are right," she said in a whisper, now so soft I could not even be sure she had said what I thought. "You are right, and I am sorry. . . . I must go," she added abruptly and moved toward the door.

I darted out of my seat and grabbed her arm. Not hard, you understand, but I would not have her going. Not now. Not yet.

"Why are you running? You don't want to run, so why do you?"

She shook her head while looking down. It was clear she would not stay, so I let go of her.

"I run," she said at last, "because I don't want to run." She took a breath. "Benjamin, when was the last time someone tried to kill you?"

I had not expected this question, and I nearly laughed. "Only two weeks ago," I said, for a thief I had been tracking had turned on me with a knife. Had I not been alert, I should have been hardly cut—or worse.

"There are so many things I want for myself that you would give me," she told me. "I know you would not treat me as a thing, an object, an upper servant. I know what kind of a man you are, Benjamin. But you hurt and you kill and you are at risk of being hurt and killed."

She stopped but I had nothing to say in my defense, and we sat in silence for some long minutes.

"I can't live that kind of life," she said at last. "I can't live with a husband who might at any moment be murdered or hanged or transported. You want to marry me? To have children? A wife must have her husband. Children need a father, Benjamin. I cannot live so."

I could offer her no argument to make her believe she should.

Three weeks later, she sent me a note asking me to call on her at her home off Anne's Court. She had never sent such a communication to me before, and for a brief while I flattered myself that she intended to tell me by means of ladylike hints that she had changed her mind—that she had given the matter due consideration and had dismissed her earlier prejudices. Yet while I indulged my imagination, I never truly believed that she would tell me what I most wanted to hear.

Neither could I have anticipated that she would give me the intelligence I most dreaded. When her girl led me into her parlor, I saw her standing nervously, leafing through a volume whose name, I suspected, she would be unable to tell me if I put her to the question. She set the book down and smiled at me in the forced way of a surgeon preparing a painful operation. Her green eyes were more deeply sunk than I had recollected.

"A glass of wine?" she asked, knowing well I would take it. All illusions were now washed away by her anxious expression, and I took the wine from her shaking hand, eager to fortify myself.

"I have not yet informed your uncle," she said to me, once we were both seated, "as I wished to tell you first. I could not endure to think you would hear it from another."

I say now that I had no idea in my mind what she was about to say, yet I must have known, for I recall gripping the arms of the chair and half rising, before lowering myself once more.

"I am to be married," she announced. Her lips were parted, a pantomime's portrait of dread. Then, recollecting herself, she applied another forced smile. When I think of her married, I continue to think of her with that counterfeit grin.

I said nothing for some eternal minutes. I stared ahead and wondered. I wondered whom she had found to be more worthy than I. I thought of all the time we had spent together—as friends, of course—and the simple joy I had taken in her nearness, in the tingle of pleasure of being in her company. I thought of the thrill of possibility, as though every moment with her represented the chance that it might be the one that would change her mind. All that was now dashed.

"I wish you joy," I said at last. I kept my tone even and neutral, thinking it was the most dignified thing I could do—and the cruelest.

"I fear there may be some unpleasantness with your uncle," she said, her words coming out very quickly, as though she had rehearsed them. "You see, the man I am marrying is English, and his family has long been of the High Church disposition. For the sake of our ease, I have chosen to join the Church."

I took a sip of my wine and drank too fast. I felt myself growing slightly giddy. "You are converting?"

"Yes," she said.

I cannot say what she expected of me—that I might rail and lecture and rant, might demand to know what she knew of this man, and would use my thieftaking skills to learn all I could of him. I opened my mouth to speak, but I made only a humiliating, gurgling noise. I cleared my throat and began again. "Why?" I said quietly.

"How can you ask me that?"

"How? How can I not? Do you believe as he believes? Is his faith yours?"

"You have known me too long to think I would make this decision because of belief or faith. Had I wished to become a Christian out of devotion to Christian doctrine, I should have done so long before now."

"Then why do you convert?" I asked. My tone had grown louder and more violent than I had intended.

Miriam closed her eyes for a moment. "It is about happiness," she said.

Oh, how I would have rejoiced to have destroyed her argument, but what counter could I offer? What could I say of her happiness—the happiness provided by a man of whom I knew nothing? I should have left then, I know, but as I was about to torture myself for half a year, there was no good reason not to start at that moment.

"Do you love him?" I asked.

She looked away. "How can you ask me that? Why must you disquiet us both with these questions?"

"Because I must know. Do you love him?"

She still did not look at me. "Yes," she whispered, turning away.

I wanted to believe that she lied to me, but I could not do it. I could not say—I could never say—if my failure of belief came from her words or my heart. I knew only that there was nothing more for us to discuss. She had fired the fatal shot, the one that ends the battle, and there was nothing to do now but collect the dead.

I stood, drained my glass, and set it down. "I wish you joy," I said once more, and departed.

Only later did I learn the man's name: Griffin Melbury. They married some two weeks after our conversation in a private ceremony I was not asked to attend. I had not seen Miriam since. Upon hearing the news, my uncle rent his clothes. My aunt later whispered to me that her name must never again be spoken aloud to either of them. The world would be remade as though Miriam had never lived. Or such had been the plan.

A flawed plan, for I had begun to find that in this election season I could not go two steps without hearing of her husband, and I could not hear of the man without wishing for the chance to squeeze his throat until he hung limp in my hands.

The Goose and Wheel was larger than I anticipated, a long room with dozens of tables and a bar at the back. And it was full. Here were laborers of every species—Englishmen of course but also black Africans, swarthy East Indians, and lascars such as I pretended to be. The air reeked of gin and ale and boiled meat, of cheap tobacco and piss, and the noise was a raucous din of shouting, singing, and drunken laughter. I had wondered why Littleton was so willing to enter a tavern where he knew he would be unwelcome, but I saw that the risk he ran was minimal. The Goose and Wheel expended no more money on tallow than was absolutely necessary for the most basic functions of the business, and its proprietors kept it in a state of dusky gloom. With windows far outnumbered by pipes, the room was dark and smoky, and I could hardly see ten feet ahead of my face. The far end of the room, where men sat smoking, looked like a sky full of stars filtered through a thin veil of clouds.

Littleton let me know that a pint of gin was just the thing to blunt the edge of his anxiety. I thought it better he keep his wits about him, but I was not there to mother him, so I bought him the poison he desired—though to do so required stepping over the unconscious bodies of a few fellows who had taken too much. When I ordered a small beer for myself the tapman nearly laughed at me, as though no one had ever before asked him for so weak a brew. The best he could offer me was cock ale, that noxious soup of ale and fowl.

He slid me a pot of the drink and glared at me. "If it's too strong for your likes, blackbird, you can piss in it."

I thought to offer him a worthy response, but I held my tongue, wishing to remain inoffensive until I had conducted my business. Instead, I thanked him for his love and walked over to Littleton, who had pulled his hat down around his eyes for better anonymity.

"What else do you know about the political dimensions of this matter?" I asked him, as I handed him his pint. "No one spoke of politics and parties before, and I fear this might greatly complicate matters."

He shrugged. "As for that, I cannot say. I don't have the vote, and this party or that candidate don't mean much to my nugget. I'll go to the processions in the hopes of getting some bread or drink, and maybe a pretty girl will kiss me if she thinks I've got the franchise, but Tory or Whig, it don't signify. Both of them think they know best how to put the poor in their place. Neither know their own arses, if you ask me. We got other things to worry about."

"Such as."

"Such as it's February, and there ain't much loading to do. Nothing but coal barges this time of year, and no hope of anything more until spring. We are used to get paid better than most porters, and that's supposed to help us get through the lean months, but with the gangs at each other's throats, fighting for what little work there is, we're hardly making more than if we was lugging apples around for the grocers. And our work is more dangerous, too. Just last week a fellow I know got flattened to his death when a barrel of coal fell on him. Crushed his legs entire, it did. He died two days later and hardly stopped screaming the whole time."

"And how does Ufford hope to make things better?"

"That I don't rightly know. I heard his sermons, I but I don't understand them all proper, like. He says there was a time when the rich looked after the poor, and the poor worked hard but they made their living and were happy. He says these Whigs don't care nothing for the way things used to be, only for their money at the end of the day, and that they'll work the poor to death rather than give a good wage."

"So he wishes you to believe that Tories shall be kindly taskmasters because they are better used to lording it, while Whigs are poor taskmasters because they are new to their power?"

"That sounds about it."

"Is it true?"

Littleton shrugged. "Dennis Dogmill's a Whig, they say, and most of the work we do is for him. I can tell you that if every one of his men died after unloading he wouldn't give a fig if there were others to take their place next time. Does he have a black heart because he's a Whig or does he have a black heart because that's what he's got? I'm inclined to think his politics don't make much difference."

Littleton pulled down his hat even lower, a clear sign he wanted less talk and more gin. I therefore amused myself by looking about the tavern for the better part of an hour when a disturbance began near the back. Someone struck up a few candles while a figure stood upon a barrel. He was of middle height and wide of body, perhaps forty years of age, with a narrow face and wide-set eyes that gave him an appearance of surprise or perhaps confusion. He stomped his foot only a few times, and the din of the room began to wane.

Littleton roused himself from his gin stupor. "There he is. That's Billy."

The man on the barrel held up a tankard. "A drink," he called, "to Dingy Danny Roberts, dead last week from a barrel of coal that expostulated down upon his personhood. He was one of Yate's boys"—murmurs of disdain arose from the crowd, so Greenbill raised his voice—"he might have been one of Yate's boys, but he was a porter all the same, and we have somewhat in common with those boys, whatever imperative sort of fiend they might follow. A drink, then. May he be the last to go that way."

It does not take much encouragement for a roomful of porters to tip their glasses. After a moment of rumblings, I know not whether of agreement or discord, Greenbill began again.

"I called this here meeting of our gang because there's something you should know, boys. Shall I tell you what it is? There's a shipment of coal coming next week, and it's Yate and his boys that want to take it away from you."

Much grumbling and shouting here, so Greenbill had to take a moment to pause.

"See, there's this scoundrel called Dennis Dogmill, a tobacco man you might have heard named"—he waited for the laughter and hissing to die down—"and he had this idea to make the porters fight against one another. It worked so good that all the shipmen now do the same thing. 'Which one of you has the lowest price?' they all want to know. So I went to Yate and I said to him it would be best to work together. Let's not be different gangs. Let's be one gang to navigate and together raise up the wages of the porters. And Yate said—and I quote him now, boys—Yate said, 'I'd burn in hell before usurping with the likes of your rubbish. The men in your gang are nothing but cutpurses and mollies and buggerantos.' That's what he said, boys, and it was all I could do to keep from murdering him where he stood for speaking ill of the likes of you."

"That is a filthy lie, Billy, and you know it."

Halfway between where we sat and Billy stood, a man rose and stood on his table. He was in his early thirties but still youthful in his smooth face. He wore his natural hair, which was dark and cut with a short tail, and he was small of stature though clearly strong.

"Look at this, boys!" Greenbill exclaimed. "It's Walter Yate. He's gone mad to acuminate here. Either that or he's grown so fond of lies, he'll speak them where he can, regardless of who listens."

Littleton's mouth dropped open and he righted his posture. He reached up with one hand and pulled his hat back. "What's he up to?" he whispered, more to himself than to me. "He's like to get himself killed."

"Sit down!" a man shouted at Yate. "You've no business here."

"And Greenbill Billy's got no business telling these falsehoods to you," Yate said. "I'm not your enemy. It's Dennis Dogmill and the likes of him, who want to set us one against the other. We all have to eat, so we work for near nothing since that's better than nothing itself. Save your curses for Dogmill and his Whig friends, who want to work you to your deaths and then forget you ever lived. Instead of agitating against one another, we ought to do what we can to see Mr. Melbury gets his seat in Parliament. He'll do what he can to help us. He'll protect our traditional rights."

I felt my muscles tighten. Here was Melbury again, and I wanted him nowhere near me.

"What, did Melbury pay you to canvass here?" Greenbill asked. "None of us have the franchise, which you might know if you were one of our number, instead of thinking to lord it over us.

Griffin Melbury. Unless he's got a ship to unload, I don't care nothing for him *or* his whore mother's arse."

"You ought to care for him," Yate said. "He would help put Dogmill down and put food in your children's mouths."

"I'll put bum fodder in your mouth if you don't shut it," someone shouted at Yate.

"Your words smell prettier than a fen's cunny," another voice barked. "I'd reckon the pope himself sent you to tell us these lies."

And then someone threw a pint of gin at him. Yate stepped gracefully to one side, and the glass struck Greenbill in the chest.

Oh, the outrage! How dare he avoid a missile and allow it to muddy their beloved leader? There was an instant of silence, of stillness. And then someone grabbed Yate and pulled him off the table and he disappeared beneath a heaving sea of punches. I heard, over the shouting, the dull thud of fist on flesh. Some gathered around and kicked at their brethren who were closer to the victim. Some merely punched at the air in a troubling pantomime of the hidden violence. But these pleasures were limited, and while a few porters stayed to try to take their shot at Yate, others seemed to forget in an instant there was any cause to rally around but mayhem itself. These fanned out through the tavern, looking for aught to break or steal, or they dashed for the door that they might pursue a wider field of destruction.

And then I felt a hard pull on my arm. It was Littleton. "Time to go," he said. "Find your own way as best you can," he proposed, as he disappeared into the crowd.

I should well have taken his advice, but in the chaos of the moment my mind thought not so clearly. The tavern had mostly emptied out, but there were still a number of men who tore at the furnishings, the walls, the barrels of ale, and buckets of gin. The room was full of thuds and grunts and the clatter of pewter on stone. Broken oil lamps lay shattered on the floor where watered-down drink had mercifully doused their flames.

And then there was poor Walter Yate, sprawled upon the floor, propped on his back like an overturned turtle. One man held down his arms, while another lifted a chair over his head and prepared to lower it and crush the poor victim's skull. Three more stood by cheering, dividing their time between punching at the air in support for their brothers and glancing to the door in anticipation of the even greater acts of destruction that surely now took place outside.

It was true that these matters of what porter received which job were nothing to me, and it was even more true that a part of myself believed Yate deserved to have his head pushed in for speaking so favorably of Griffin Melbury, but I could nevertheless not stand by to murder. I ran forward and knocked aside the man who held Yate down and pulled the quarry out of the way in time so that the chair hit the floor, where it burst into pieces.

Seeing me come to their victim's aid, the porters scattered. I quickly pulled Yate to his feet. Though dazed and a bit scratched, he appeared to have escaped serious harm. "Thank you," he said, as he ushered me toward the door. "I thought to find no such friends here among Greenbill's boys."

"I'm not one of Greenbill's boys. And though I did not think to find you here, I would speak with you regardless. You're of little use to me with your head crushed." I pushed over a table near the door to provide us with some small shelter from the half dozen or so men who remained inside. Other than the two who had attempted to murder Yate, the remainder were exploring the wonders of a tavern without a tavernkeeper. That is to say, they were taking their fill of the bucket of gin and shoving their pockets full of knives and small dishes. In the next few minutes, they would be either asleep or more belligerent than ever.

The other two men eyed us as we crouched behind the overturned table. They eyed the men with the gin. They attempted to make up their minds.

"My name is Weaver," I said hastily to Yate. "I am in the employ of a priest called Ufford, who has hired me to find out the author of some threatening notes. He thinks you might know something of this—that it may be linked to your troubles with Dogmill."

"Dogmill should go to the devil, and Ufford too. I wish I'd

never involved myself in this business. It's nothing but plots and secrets and schemes. But it's the porters who pay the price."

I thought to ask what plots and secrets and schemes he meant,
but I observed that violence had defeated drink. Four men who
had taken their fill of gin now rushed toward us like angry bulls.

Yate saw at once that it was time to take our leave. As he pushed
open the door to the tavern, I knew that more talk would have to
wait, for there was no refuge to be found outside. There were dozens, perhaps hundreds of men in the street, fighting with one another and with strangers, pulling down doors and women. One man
had obtained a lantern and threw it at a building across the street.
It fortunately fell short of its mark and broke safely upon the stone
steps, setting on fire nothing more important than a fellow rioter.

We were not a foot from the tavern before two men descended
once more on Walter Yate, and it would have been a strange thing
to rescue him from one death and leave him for another, so I
stepped in and took a swing at one of the assailants. My fist landed
hard against the side of his head, and I took some pleasure in seeing him fall, but then there were two more who joined my first assailant, and I now found myself blocking and punching just to
keep the blows from my face.

At one instant I looked up and saw a brick, clutched hard by
white fingers, swinging toward my head. I don't know that I
would have evaded this blow—certainly fatal—if Yate had not
raised his arm, at the risk of exposing himself to violence from a
man he fought, and caused my assailant to drop his brick. I took
this brute down with a single jab to his face and grunted my thanks
to Yate, on whom I began to look now quite favorably. Though he
spoke glowingly of Miriam's husband—as grave an offense as I
could imagine—he and I were now bound in the brotherhood of
combat.

I still had the skills of a trained pugilist, though the leg injury
that had ended my fighting days began to ache as I pranced about,
defending myself and looking for an exit through which Yate and
I might escape. But no exit was to be found. Someone would present himself to me with his fists and I would fend him off or fell

him or sidestep him, only to find a new conflict. Yate, for his part, fought well, but like me could only keep his attackers away long enough to fend off more blows.

Occupied as I was in protecting my own life, I could see that the riot had taken a strangely political cast. Groups of porters were now chanting *No Jacobites! No Tories! No Papists!*—all being led by Yate's rival, Greenbill Billy. Riots were apt to take on convenient tones of protest, particularly in election times, but I was nevertheless curious that this should have happened so quickly.

I had, however, more pressing things with which to concern myself, for while many of the porters were busy with their chanting and window-breaking, many more showed a remarkable commitment to fighting—and to fighting us in particular. I cannot say how long we battled there. More than half an hour, I suppose. I punched and I took punches. My face grew heavy with sweat and blood. And still I fought. The instant I found an opening I stepped into it, only to be attacked once more. In the first few minutes I perpetually glanced over at my companion, but soon I lacked the energy. I could do no more than protect myself. At one point I did summon the strength to turn and see how the porter fared, and I was astonished to see he was gone. Either he had fled or the crowd had separated us without our knowing. I presumed it to be the second, and for reasons I cannot fully explain, this thought filled me with dread. I had saved Yate, and he had saved me. I now thought his well-being my concern. I shifted my position just enough to change my view, but still no sign. A strange sort of panic washed over me, as though I had lost a small child with whose care I had been charged. "Yate!" I called out, over the noise of grunting and cheering and the slap of fist on flesh. I received no answer to my calls.

And then it stopped. One moment I was fighting, shouting for Yate, and the next instant all had gone quiet, and I found myself swinging at air, spinning madly in search of the next anonymous opponent. A crowd formed around me with a good five feet of distance. I felt like a trapped animal, a thing dangerous and alien. I stood there breathing hard, half doubled over, waiting for the strength to inquire why I had become the subject of such scrutiny.

Then two constables stepped forward and took my arms.

I let them. I did not resist. I leaned forward to rest while they held me up, and in my exhaustion I heard a voice I did not recognize say, "That's him. That's the one. He's the dirty Gypsy what killed Walter Yate."

And with that I was taken to the magistrate's office.

CHAPTER 5

LONDON AFTER DARK is no place for the vulnerable, let alone the naked, but I had freed myself from the most dreaded prison in the kingdom, and I could rejoice that I still had shoes upon my feet. My state would otherwise be as unwholesome as it was humiliating, for in my journey I moved south and, consequently, near to the Fleet Ditch. On these streets a perambulator is likely to step in turds or bits of rotting dog or the discarded tumor of some surgeon's labors. A man who had just escaped prison and near death in a narrow tomb, however, had no business feeling squeamish about a bit of kennel or amputated flesh on his bare legs, particularly when there was an icy rain to wash him clean. As to the problem of my nakedness, it was, though cold and wet, also dark outside—surely the best condition under which to undertake a prison escape—and I had little doubt that, in this city I knew so well, I should be able to remain hidden in shadows.

But not forever. I would need clothing, and quickly too, for though the joy of having won my freedom coursed through my veins, making me feel as alert as though I'd had a dozen dishes of coffee, I felt dangerously cold, and my hands began to grow numb. My teeth chattered, and I shivered so hard I feared I should lose my balance and fall upon the ground. I was not happy with the prospect of taking from another what I so desired myself, but necessity outweighed whatever peccadilloes of morality troubled my thoughts. Besides, I had no intention of taking any man's clothes entire and leaving him in my own current state of nature. I merely wished to find someone who could be persuaded, one way or another, to share some small portion of his bounty.

There is something about having been in prison, and perhaps more so in having escaped from prison, that makes a man see the familiar as new. As I made my way to the west and south, I smelled the stench of the Fleet like some bumptious arrival from the country. I heard the strangeness of the cries of the pie sellers and the chicken men and the shrimp girls, "Shrimp shrimp shrimp shrimpers!" called out again and again like a bird of the tropics. The sloppy words scrawled on the walls that I would never before have noticed—*Walpole go ye to the devil* and *Jenny King is a hore and slut* and *Com and see Misus Rose at the sine of the Too Biships for sheepskins*—now seemed to me the outlandish scrawl of a mysterious alphabet. But the renewed strangeness of the city took little of my attention from the discomfort of being cold and wet and hungry—hungry to dizziness—and the cries of pies and pickled fish and roast turnips distracted me something immense.

My ramble through this unsavory part of town took on the grim, disjointed tone of a nightmare. Once or twice a linkboy or mendicant spotted me and hooted, but, for good or ill, in a metropolis such as this one, where poverty is so rampant, it is not so unusual to spy an unfortunate without raiment, and I was merely taken for some desperate victim of the current poverty weighing upon the nation. I passed by more than my share of beggars, who refrained from asking me for money, but I could see by the empty looks in their eyes that they knew me to be well fed and therefore more fortunate than they. A few ladies of pleasure offered their services to me, but I explained that I had, at that moment, no money about me.

Off Holborn, I saw a man of precisely the species I wanted. He was a drunkard of the middling sort who had abandoned his friends in an alehouse somewhere and gone in search of cheap flesh. For a staggering inebriant—that is to say, a man who is not overly particular—cheap flesh is easily found, all the more so because a man in his state might prove an easy mark for a woman with an eye toward his purse or watch or wig.

This fellow, bloated, soaked to the bone, and somewhat past the middle point in life, swayed toward a dark-haired woman who could be described in sadly similar terms. In some ways, I thought,

I would be doing him a favor by preventing him from an intimacy with a creature far inferior to what he would desire in a state of sobriety—one who would almost certainly take what had not been offered and leave in return that which was not desired. I emerged from the shadows, lashed out at him with a hand on each shoulder, and pulled him into the alley where I had been hiding.

"Gracious God, help me!" he cried, before I could put a hand over his mouth.

"Be silent, you drunk fool," I whispered. "Can you not see I am trying to help you?"

My words had the effect I had intended, for he paused to consider their meaning and how this naked stranger might be trying to lend him aid. While he drunkenly measured my intentions, I was able to help myself to his coat, hat, and wig.

"Just a moment!" he shouted, but it afforded him nothing. He stood up, perhaps to chase me, but slipped in some slick filth and fell back into the alley. Still naked, but with my booty tucked under my arm, I dashed off into the night. I would be using those things but a short time, however, for I had it in my head to steal the clothing off another man next, and that would be to far more purpose.

Half an hour later, I was at last under a roof and near a gloriously hot stove, conducting a conversation marred with violence. "You can either do as I ask you, or you can be bludgeoned senseless," I said to the footman, a strapping lad of hardly more than eighteen years.

He glanced to the other side of the kitchen where the body of the butler lay facedown and slumped, a bit of blood trickling out of his ear. I had made the butler the same offer, and his choice had been none the wisest.

"I haven't worked here more than two weeks," he said, in a thick northern accent. "They told me ruffians have been known to break in without a by-your-leave. There's been hungry men at the door, begging for scraps, begging awful fierce, but I never thought to see a housebreaker till now."

I am certain I looked a frightful sight, wearing nothing but an outer coat, a periwig that hardly covered my own hair, and a hat propped haphazardly on top—all of which were drenched. I had thought to take the wig because I believed that if my escape had been discovered, the search might be for a man of dark natural hair, not a bewigged gentleman, but I looked no more a gentleman than did a chained African just arrived in Liverpool.

"You'll see nothing but the back of your eyelids, lad, if you don't do as I tell you." I ought to have moved closer to him that I might appear menacing. Instead I backed up to feel the warmth of the stove.

He noticed nothing of my movements, however. "I've no cause for getting myself hurt in his service," the footman said, gesturing with his head toward another room in the house.

"Then give me your clothes," I said.

"But I'm wearing them."

"Then perhaps you should remove them first," I proposed.

He stared at me, awaiting further clarification, but when he saw none was forthcoming, he let out a confused sigh, mumbled to himself as though I were his father and had asked him to slop the pigs, and began to unfasten his buttons and unlace his laces. His teeth petulantly dug into his lower lip, he stripped down to all but his shirt and tossed his clothes toward me so they landed in a pile. I gave him in exchange my recently got coat, heavy with wet, and I then donned his livery—agreeably dry, though thicker with lice than I should have desired.

My goal was not to trick his master; I would not do so for more than an instant. I believed, however, that seeing me in his servant's garb would prove disorienting enough to make him more pliable. I also knew that, once I left the house, the livery would make a fine disguise.

After the footman had put on my coat, I tied him with some rope I found in the kitchen. "Are there any other servants in the house?" I asked him, as I grabbed a half loaf of bread and bit into it violently. It was a day old, and hard, but it tasted wonderful to me.

"Just the lass what does the cleaning," he said, "but she's virtuous, she is, and I haven't done nothing with her that would harm her honor."

I raised an eyebrow. "Where is she now?" I asked, my mouth full of bread.

"This is her night off. She's gone to see her mother, who tends children for a great lady what lives near St. James's. She won't be back for two hours at least."

I considered the possibility that he was lying—about the time of the girl's return, not her virtue—and concluded that he had not the guile to deceive me. Unwilling to set down my bread, I held it between my teeth while I took a kitchen rag and wrapped it around his mouth to keep him silent. I then told him that over the next few days he might review the daily papers to see if anyone advertised for the coat and wig and hat. The kind thing would be to return them to their owner.

I quickly finished the bread, found a pair of apples—one of which I ate, the other dropped into my pocket—and then thought it time to set out upon my business. The town house was not so large nor laid out in an unusual manner, and it was no difficult thing to seek out my man.

I found Judge Piers Rowley in a brightly lit study of red curtains, red cushions, and a red Turkey rug. Rowley himself wore a matching red dressing gown and cap and was hardly recognizable to me without the full regalia of his judge's costume. I took this as a good sign. I would, perhaps, be equally unrecognizable in my own disguise—at least for the length of time I wished to effect a surprise. He sat with his back mostly to me, angled to get the most light possible from the blazing fireplace that illuminated a writing desk scattered with papers. Around the room a number of other candles burned, and a tray of apples and pears had been set out, along with a decanter of a brilliantly red wine—port by the smell of it. I could have used a glass or two myself, but I could not risk disordering my senses with drink.

As I drew closer, I saw that Rowley clutched a thick volume to his chest. He had fallen asleep. I was tempted, I confess, to take my revenge there. To grab him by his throat and allow him to wake to the nightmare of his own death. The cruelty of so mad an experience appealed to me, and certainly he deserved no less. But no matter how satisfying, I understood that the crime would accomplish little.

I stood before him and made coughing noises until he stirred sufficiently. His fleshy eyelids flickered and fluttered, and his jowls danced a rousing dance. He wiped the drool off his lips with the back of his sleeve and reached out for his wine goblet.

"What is it, Daws?" he asked absently, but when the silver rim of the goblet met his lips, his eyes, for the first time, focused upon my face, and he knew I was not Daws. He sat up straight, forgetting about the wine, which fell into his lap. "Weaver," he whispered.

"Mr. Daws is incapacitated," I told him, "and your butler, whose name I did not learn, has broken his head."

He pushed himself backward into the chair. "You've got yourself out," he noted, with the slightest of smiles.

I saw no point in confirming the obvious. "You were determined to see the jury convict me," I said. "Why?"

"You must take that up with the jury," he shot back, now attempting to escape by pushing himself through the back of the chair. The pressure forced his jowls out like wings, and he looked more like a costume mask than a man.

"No, I must take that up with you. You showed no interest in learning the truth of Yate's death. You concerned yourself with nothing more than seeing me convicted, and then you did not hesitate to sentence me to hang. I want to know why."

"Murder is a dreadful crime," he said, very softly. "It must be punished."

"So must be the attempt at murder, for I cannot regard your treatment of me as anything but."

Rowley stopped squirming, as though he had decided all at once to be bold rather than timid. "You may regard what you like. Your opinions are your own, so you must not make me accountable for them."

I took a step closer. "Allow me to state a fairly obvious fact, sir:

I can be hanged but once. The verdict has been pronounced. If I am retaken into custody, I shall surely meet that most terrible of fates regardless of what transpires between us. You must understand that the law cannot now restrain my actions." I leaned in toward him. "In your efforts to see me punished by the law, you have placed me beyond the law, and I have little to lose by acting upon every violent impulse. So let me ask the question once more. Why did you choose to see me convicted?"

"Because I thought you guilty," he said, turning his face away from mine.

"I cannot for an instant believe that. You heard those witnesses confess that they had been paid to say they saw what they never saw, what they never could have seen, since it did not happen. You chose to ignore the falseness of the testimony. You all but ordered the jury to ignore the falseness of the testimony. I demand to know why." Because I had anticipated a reluctance on his honor's part, I had taken a carving knife with me from the kitchen. I now presented it and, rather than wait for him to decide whether or not I meant to use it, jabbed it quickly into the flesh under his left eye. I meant to do no serious harm, only show him that I was not one of those men who will speak but not act.

His hands shot up at once to cover the wound, which I must say was rather inconsequential. It bled some, but I've had more urgent injuries inflicted upon my face by my barber.

"You've blinded me!" he cried.

"No, I haven't," I answered, "but I see now that the idea of being blinded offers you some distress. I'll not hesitate to slice your eye if you don't tell me what you know. It may not have occurred to you that I am a man with little time to spare. I hope you will forgive me if I grow impatient."

"The devil take you, Weaver. I had no choice. I did what I could for you." He remained curled over, pressing both hands to the cut as though he might bleed to his death if he did not press all ten digits into service.

"Why did you have no choice?"

"Damn you," he murmured, but not to me. He seemed to be

speaking to the air itself. Then he faced me once more. "Look, Weaver, you've got yourself out. That ought to be enough. If you're wise, you'll not dawdle but get gone as best you can. You don't want to anger these people."

"What people? Who told you to sway the jury against me?" I demanded.

Silence. But I held up the carving knife, and he reconsidered his reticence.

"Oh, bother it! I'll not be mutilated on his behalf. I hardly bear that much love for the man, and I curse that I ever involved myself in this. But there is a general election upon us, and no man can afford to remain neutral."

I felt myself tense. "What? The election again? What does the election have to do with this?"

"It was Griffin Melbury," he said. "Griffin Melbury told me to do it, but I must beg you not to say I've told you. The man is a dangerous enemy, and I won't have him set his cap at me."

His words so surprised me I nearly dropped my knife. I checked the loosening of my grip, however, and found that my hold grew tighter—so tight that my fingers turned white.

Griffin Melbury. The Tory candidate standing for Westminster. The man who had married my Miriam.

"Explain it all to me," I said. "Omit nothing."

"Melbury called me to meet him the instant I drew your trial. He said it was imperative that you be found guilty, that you hang. All the Tory values—a strong Church, a strong monarchy, controlling the new wealth and the liberal thinkers—all of it was to depend upon my taking this action. He made it quite clear that should I not do my duty in this matter I would find that, following the election, there would be by far more Tories in power than necessary to see me lose my place."

I knew that most judges were political creatures and owed their loyalty to one of the two parties. I also knew well that these men thought nothing of allowing their affiliations to influence their rulings. I could not, however, imagine why the Tories should wish to see me convicted for this crime. How could my fate be bound up with the Tory cause? Unless, of course, Melbury only fabricated the urgency of the situation, and for him it was a matter of honor. But having never met Griffin Melbury, having never crossed him or angered him, I could hardly believe that he would hold so powerful a grudge against me simply because I had once courted the woman who became his wife.

"Why?" I asked.

"I don't know," he snapped, as though I were his child and had asked him why the sky is blue. "I don't know. He did not say; he would not say. I demanded an answer, but he only offered me threats. You must believe I had no satisfaction in doing as I did. I had no choice."

"What have I to do with this? How can I have anything to say of the Tory cause?"

"How should I know when Melbury would tell me nothing? I would think that you might answer that question better than I. If I could have avoided the scene in the court today, I would have. I have no love of seeing my reputation weakened on your account— or on his, for that matter. I acted as I did because there was nothing else for me to do."

I remained still for a long while, hearing nothing—not the crackling of the fire or the ticking of the clock or the deep breathing of Piers Rowley, whose hands had ceased their stanching of his long-clotted wound and had instead commenced to hold his teary face.

I found him nothing but risible. "Show me your banknotes," I said.

Rowley removed his hands from his face. He had been content to cower and shake when I merely threatened his life, but now that I sought his wealth, I had roused the lion in him. "I thought you had more honor in you than to turn thief," he said steadily. His voice had gained some composure, and I thought that either the man truly loved his money or the cowardice he had displayed had merely been a bit of mummery meant to stave off more brutal punishment.

"I have been convicted of a felony," I said. "The court, I am certain, wasted no time in descending upon my rooms and confiscating my belongings. I now have no home and no money, but since you have been the architect of that conviction, I think it only just that you compensate me for my losses. Now, where are your banknotes?"

"I won't tell you, Weaver. I'll not be robbed. Not by you."

I won't tell you? Surely he had lost his wits. Better to say he had no notes. I brandished the carving knife, but Rowley remained defiant.

"I think this little wound you've given me proves that you are not a man of senseless violence," he said. "You might have done worse, but you haven't."

At that moment, I heard a scuffle emanating from the kitchen. And then I heard a woman's shriek. The serving girl, whose virtue was safe with the footman, had returned early and found her fellow domestics in a dire condition. I had not much time to dally in the judge's house.

"The banknotes," I said. "Now."

He ventured the slightest of smiles. "I think not." I could see his eyes go wide as he concentrated to find the courage to defy me. "You see, Weaver, your reputation has done you some harm. You may brandish sword and pistols, and even use them when threatened or facing dangerous rogues, but I am but an aging man of the law, defenseless in his own home. I doubt you will hurt so powerless a creature as I am, and I say that I have had enough of your threats. I've told you what you wanted and put myself at great risk in doing so. Now get out if you still can, for I won't give you a penny, not one farthing. If you believe yourself entitled to compensation, you must take up the matter with Griffin Melbury."

I considered his words for a moment and then reached out with a speed that even I found remarkable. With one hand I grabbed his right ear, and with the other I used my knife to sever a substantial part of it. I held the bloody thing in my fingers and showed it to him before tossing it onto his writing desk, where it landed on a pile of correspondence with a heavy slap. Too astonished to cry out or even to move, Rowley only stared at the little pieces of flesh.

"Where do you keep your banknotes?" I asked again.

To my delight, I discovered that Mr. Rowley had more than four hundred pounds' worth of negotiable notes on his person—in addition to another twenty-odd pounds in cash—and I was able to gather them up and quit the house before the girl had returned with whomever it was she had gone to fetch. Although it was small recompense for the harm he had done me, it was nevertheless satisfying to relieve him of so large an amount and reassuring to have it in my possession.

I had no clear idea of how best to use the information that Rowley had provided me, what course of action I would pursue, or where I should find myself a safe hiding place. I knew, however, where I would go next.

CHAPTER 6

I HAD NEVER before imagined the life of a footman, but in my travels toward Bloomsbury Square I found myself greeted by whores, jeered by other men in livery who observed something lacking in my presentment, taunted by linkboys, and offered drinks by apprentices. A footman walks the thinnest of boundaries between privilege and powerlessness, living in both camps and mocked by each if he dares to step too far into the territory of one or the other.

I avoided these tormentors as best I could, for I had no idea how convincing I might appear should anyone get too close. Most footmen were somewhat younger than I, though not all, and my age would not prove the most treacherous of my features. My ill-fitting wig did far more damage, for though I had taken some pains to tuck my own locks underneath, it sat oddly and bulging on my head, and I knew it would answer poorly to any extended scrutiny.

I approached my friend Elias Gordon's lodgings with some trepidation. I could only presume that my escape had, by now, been discovered, and anyone familiar with my habits would know that Elias, who often lent his assistance in my inquiries, might well be the first man from whom I sought refuge. If his house was being watched, I could presume that my uncle's was as well, along with those of a half dozen or so of my closest friends and relations. But of all the people I knew, I believed I could most trust Elias, not only to protect my safety but to consider the problems I faced with a clear and open mind.

Elias, though a surgeon by trade, was something of a philosopher. During my efforts to unravel the knot of secrecy surrounding my father's death, it had been Elias who introduced me to the mysterious workings of the great financial institutions of this kingdom. More important, it had been he who taught me to understand the theory of probability—the very philosophical engine that ran the machinery of finance—and to use it to solve a crime without witnesses or evidence. My troubles now seemed far more dire than they had then, but I had hope that Elias might see what I could not.

I therefore chose to take the chance in visiting him, relying on my disguise, my quickness of mind, and—somewhat diminished but nevertheless dependable—strength of body. Unless a small army awaited me, I convinced myself I should dispatch easily enough any man who interfered.

The rain had eased since my escape from Newgate, though not let up entirely, and the streets were dark and slick with muck. As I approached Elias's lodgings, I saw two men posted guard outside, hunched over to protect themselves from the drizzle. They were both of about my years, neither particularly dominating of body. They wore dark clothes of the respectable middling sort, short wigs, and small hats, all of which were heavy with water. Not quite a livery, but near enough to one. I could not guess who they were, though I could see most clearly that they were neither constables nor soldiers. They were, however, quite well armed. I saw each clutched a pistol in one hand, and their pockets were heavy, surely well loaded with spares. I, on the other hand, had no weapons upon me but the carving knife, which I had hidden in the interior of my coat.

I thought to go around these men and enter through the back way, but one of them sighted me and called me to him.

"Ho, there, fellow," he said. "What business have you?"

"I'm come to see Mr. Jacob Monck, what lives here," I said, using the name of a lodger I knew to dwell within. I also affected a heavy Yorkshire accent, hoping this would put them off my scent.

The two men approached. "What's your business with this Monck?" asked the one who had called out to me.

"The delivering of a message." I took a step closer.

"Whose message?" He wiped the cold rain off his face.

I did not pause for an instant. "Me lady's," I told him, hoping he had not done his business so well that he knew Monck to be septuagenarian and little likely to be involved in intrigues.

"Who is your lady?"

I smirked at him and rolled my eyes as I had seen saucy footmen do a hundred times before. "That ain't none of your business, nor for you to know neither. Who might you be, who stand in my way like insolent fellows?"

"These fart catchers think themselves great gentlemen," one of the centuries announced. "We're Riding Officers, that's who we be, and you are but a bootlick. You oughtn't to forget that."

"Go and deliver the message, me lord," the other one said. "And I beg you pardon our disturbing you as you carry out your important task. I should hate to think I had stood between Mr. Monck and your lady's cunny."

I offered a sneer to the one who had spoken and then knocked upon the door; despite my haughty performance, I'd grown restless with alarm. Riding Officers: the agents who enforced the laws of customs and excise. Why would men whose role was to search for smugglers and customs evaders come in search of a supposed murderer who had broken his way out of Newgate? It made no sense, but it suggested that there was even more to the matter of my prosecution than I had yet supposed.

When I heard the doorknob turn, I had further cause for alarm, for Elias's landlady, Mrs. Henry, would surely recognize me, and I did not know if I could depend on her silence. She had always looked upon me more kindly than is perhaps ordinary, but I was now generally believed to be a murderer, and I knew well that there would be those who might interpret my actions at Mr. Rowley's house in none the best light.

Fortunately, I had little cause for alarm. Mrs. Henry opened the door, glanced at my face, and, as though she had no idea who I was, asked me my business. I simply repeated what I had told the centuries, and she invited me inside.

I thought she might have questions for me, or pleading words about how I must return myself to prison and have faith in the law and the Lord, but she offered none of that, only a warm smile and a gesture of her head. "Go upstairs, then. He's there."

Elias opened the door almost immediately upon my knocking. His eyes went wide for a moment, and then he grabbed me by the arm and pulled me inside. "Are you mad coming here? There are men downstairs looking for you."

"I know," I said. "Riding Officers."

"Customs men? What business can they have with this?" He began to say something on the peculiarity of my pursuers, but changed his mind and instead approached a sideboard with a bottle of wine and some unwashed glasses upon it. Elias's rooms were pleasant enough, but none the neatest, and old clothes, books, papers, and dirty dishes were spread throughout. He had several candles burning upon his writing table, and he appeared to have been at work on some project or another when I called. Though a surgeon of some reputation, Elias preferred the literary arts to the medical ones and had tried his hand already at playwriting and poetry. He was now, he had told me, at work upon a fictional memoir of a dashing Scottish surgeon making his way through the social labyrinth of London.

"Obviously, you have been through a great deal," he said, "but before we discuss it, I must urge you to take an enema." He held a cylinder the size of my index finger. It was brown and looked as hard as a stone.

"Pardon me?"

"An enema," he explained with great earnestness. "It is a purging of the bowels."

"Yes, I'm familiar with the concept. But having escaped from the most dreaded prison in the kingdom, I haven't the inclination to celebrate my freedom by shitting in your pot while you stand by, ready to examine the goods."

"No one relishes an enema, but that is hardly the point. I've been doing a great deal of studying of the matter, and I have come to the conclusion that it is the best thing for you—better even than bleeding. Ideally, you would combine it with a diuretic and a purging, but I suspect you're not quite willing to subject yourself to all three."

"It is amazing how well our friends know us," I observed. "You see my innermost soul as no stranger could, and you perceive that I am in no mood to shit, piss, and vomit all at once."

He held up his hand. "Let us set the matter aside for the nonce. I have only your health in mind, you know, but I see I cannot force good medicine upon you. I suppose you shan't object to a glass of wine, however."

"For reasons I cannot fully articulate, that offer appeals to me more than your other."

"There's no need to be sour," he said, while he poured a glass of pale red wine. As he turned to hand it to me, he seemed, for the first time, to notice my livery. "Service becomes you," he said.

"It has proved, thus far, an adequate costume."

"Where did you get it?"

"From Piers Rowley's footman."

His eyes widened. "Weaver, you didn't go there, did you?"

I shrugged. "It seemed like the best course at the time."

He put a hand to his face, as though I had ruined some great plan of his. He then stood up straight and breathed in deeply. "I trust you engaged in no foolish actions."

"Of course not," I said. "I did, however, cut off one of the judge's ears and take four hundred of his pounds."

Somehow, the extremity of this revelation calmed him. He cleared a pair of wine-stained breeches from a chair and sat. "You'll have to get out of the country as quickly as possible, of course. Perhaps the United Provinces. You have a brother there, do you not? Or you could go to France."

"I'm not leaving the country," I said, as I lifted what appeared to be a lady's stays from the chair nearest to me. "I'll not run away and let the world believe me a murderer." I tossed the article of clothing on top of the breeches and took my seat.

"What do you care what the world believes? Even if you could prove you did not kill this Yate fellow, you will still be hanged for cutting the ear off a judge of the King's Bench and then taking four hundred pounds. The law frowns upon that sort of thing."

"It frowns upon judicial corruption too. I am certain that once the world is made to understand that, in his corruption of his office, Rowley left me no choice, any charges against me will be dropped."

"You've gone mad," he said. "Of course the charges won't be dropped. You can't trample upon the law, no matter how just your motivation or logical your reasoning. There's no fair play to be had. This is the government."

"We shall see what I can do and what I can't," I said, with a confidence I did not possess.

He paused for a moment. "Four hundred pounds is a great deal of money," he said. "Do you think you'll need it all?"

"Elias, please."

"Well, you do owe me thirty pounds, you know, and as you are about to be carted off to the gallows, I think it only right that I bring this up. If I am to finish this little work of fiction I'm composing, I'll need all the help I can get."

"Listen to me," I said. "I can't stay here long for I told the Riding Officers outside that I was merely here to deliver a billet-doux to your fellow lodger. I will leave now and meet you in one hour at an inn called the Turk and Sun on Charles Street. Do you know of it?"

"Yes, but I've never been inside."

"Neither have I, which is why it will be a good place to meet. And make certain you are not followed."

"How would I do that?"

"I don't know. Call upon your writerly muse for inspiration. Take multiple hackneys, perhaps."

"Very well," he agreed. "The Turk and Sun in an hour."

I stood and set my glass down on his writing table.

"How did you get out, anyhow?" he asked me.

"Did you see that woman who embraced me after sentence was pronounced?"

"Truly, I did. A fine-looking creature. Who is she?"

"I don't know, but she pressed a lockpick into my hand."

He raised an eyebrow. "How very good-natured of her. You don't know who she was at all?"

"I can only guess that, following his performance, she might belong to Jonathan Wild. Only the Thieftaker General would have a stable of pick-wielding beauties at his command. However, I won't even speculate as to why he would wish to see me free, but then I could not suppose why he would have testified so kindly on my behalf."

"I wondered that myself. When he took the stand, I felt certain he would do all in his power to destroy a rival. He's treated you mighty shabbily in the past, what with sending his roughs after you to knock you down and stomp upon you. And now he pretends to admire you. It is the confusingest thing in the world, but I don't expect you care to ask him, do you?"

I laughed. "Not likely. I have no intention of showing up in his tavern while there is a bounty on my head, to ask him if, having done me one good turn, he was responsible for doing me another. Should the answer prove to be no, I would find myself in a bit of trouble."

Elias nodded. "Even so, if he is responsible for sending that lass to you, it would behoove you to learn why."

"I will. In the end, I'll know."

"As you are no longer inside Newgate, I can only suppose that you put the lockpick to good use."

"I put it to the best use I could. I picked the locks of my chains," I said, "tore a bar from the window, which I used to smash through the wall of a chimney I climbed. I then broke through a few more locks, made my way up a series of stairways, and smashed through a barred window and, finally, climbed down a rope made of my own clothes, leaving me naked in the street."

He stared at me. "An hour," he repeated, "in the Turk and Sun."

I had passed by this inn a hundred times and never entered, for it always looked unremarkable. This unremarkable quality, however, was now precisely what I sought. Inside, the tables were filled with nondescript men of the middling sort, with their rough wool clothes and their coarse laughter. They did what men do in such places—drank, mostly, but also ate their chops, smoked their pipes, and grabbed at the whores who drifted in, looking to earn a few shillings.

I took the most poorly lit table I could find and called for a plate of whatever was warm and a pot of ale. When a boiled fowl in raisin sauce was set before me, I dug at the bird with carnivorous ferocity until my face was slick with grease.

I suppose liveried footmen were not part of the usual patronage of the inn, and for that reason I received my share of curious glances, but I endured no more molestation than that. After I finished eating, I drank my ale and, perhaps for the first time, contemplated in all seriousness how I might go about extricating myself from this terrible situation, surely the worst I had ever faced in a life full of terrible situations. I had reached very few conclusions by the time Elias showed himself. He joined me at the table, hunching over as though afraid someone might toss an apple at his head. I called for ale, which cheered him not a little.

Once the drink had moistened his lips, he found himself ready to begin addressing the matter at hand. "Explain to me again why you will not flee."

"Had I truly murdered Yate," I said, "I would flee gladly, with all my heart. I would adopt the role of a fugitive. But I have not murdered anyone, and I won't live the rest of my life as a renegado, afraid to enter the country that has always been my home, because someone has wished to see such a thing happen."

"What someone has wished is to see you dead. While you live, you surely have defeated your enemies."

"I cannot accept that. I must have justice. At the very least, I must understand why all of this has happened, and I will risk my life by remaining in London to find out. And I owe it to Yate."

"To Yate? I thought you'd never met the man until an hour before his death."

"It's true, but in that hour we formed a friendship of sorts. At one instant in the fighting, he saved my life, and I won't let his death go unpunished if I can help it."

He sighed and rubbed his hands down along his face. "Tell me what you know thus far."

I had already recounted to him of my early meetings with Mr. Ufford and Mr. Littleton, though I recalled those events to him and spoke also of my meeting that night with Rowley.

Elias was no less astonished than I had been. "Why would Griffin Melbury want to see you hang?" he asked. "Good Lord, Weaver. You are not cuckolding the man, are you? For if this is merely a matter of bedding another man's wife, I will be very disappointed."

"No, I am not bedding another man's wife. I have not seen Miriam for nearly half a year."

"You have not *seen* her, you say. Have you carried on some sort of intrigue by letter?"

I shook my head. "Nothing of the sort. I've had no contact with her. I would be surprised that Melbury even knew I had ever asked his wife for her hand. I cannot believe she would speak to him of his former rivals, and certainly not in a way that would be intended to spark his jealousy."

"You can never be certain with women, you know. They will do the most astonishing things. After all, did Mrs. Melbury not surprise you entire by becoming a Christian?"

I looked away. Miriam *had* surprised me—to a degree that I could not entirely understand. Since I had resumed contact with my relations, most notably my uncle and his family, and returned to our neighborhood, Dukes Place, I had found myself drawn—as much by habit as by inclination—deeper into the community of my coreligionists. I attended Sabbath worship on a regular basis, said my prayers at the synagogue for nearly all major holy days, and increasingly found it difficult to violate the ancient dietary laws. I had not yet determined to observe these laws to the letter, but I had come to get a queasy feeling when I contemplated eating pig flesh or oysters or meat stewed in milk—or even the bird given to me at this tavern. I had begun to dislike keeping my head uncovered; I begged off business on Friday night or Saturday if it could be postponed; from time to time I would sit in my uncle's study looking through his Hebrew Bible, struggling to recall the slippery language I had studied for so many years as a child.

I do not claim to have been inching toward anything a true devotee would consider full observance of the Jewish laws, but I found myself more at ease if I inclined myself toward several of them. And perhaps because, like all men, I tend to look inward and easily presume the rest of the world thinks the way I do, I believed Miriam would be so inclined as well. After all, she attended the synagogue, she assisted my aunt with holiday preparations, she never, that I could see, blatantly violated Sabbath or dietary law— not even after she moved from my uncle's house. So why had she joined the Church?

At first I presumed it had merely been to appease this Melbury, whom I imagined as oily and unctuous, a handsome spark of better breeding than means. But later, as I contemplated Miriam's choice, another thought occurred to me. More than once she had told me that she envied me for my ability to be like the English. I knew it was something she desired, but it was made impossible by her being a Jewess. There was an irony here, for as a Hebrew man, I could never be English, I could only be *like* the English. As a Hebrew woman, the opposite was true of Miriam.

Only look at the works of the poets, and you will see it. There is always the *Jew,* and there is the *Jew's daughter* or the *Jew's wife.* This truism is perhaps most blatant in Mr. Granville's famous *Jew of Venice,* in which the pretty daughter, Jessica, need only leave her villainous Jew father and embrace her Christian lover in order to shed all vestiges of her Hebrew past. Miriam, to deploy the terminology of the natural scientists, as a woman was but a body in the orbit of the most powerful man to whom she attached herself. Marrying a Christian allowed her to become English; more than that, it necessitated it. It has happened that Jewish men marry English women, and each partner maintains the erstwhile religion. It cannot happen with a Jewish woman, and so it did not.

Elias, however, was far more interested in why Melbury would wish me harm. "If you have done him no wrong, and presuming that you are right and that his wife has not incited a hatred, why would he wish to destroy you? And perhaps more important, how could he possibly tell Piers Rowley how to conduct himself?"

"As for the latter, I presume that Rowley owes some sort of allegiance to the Tories, and that Melbury is a patron of one kind or another. The judge made it clear that in anticipation of the upcoming election, men must gravitate as their loyalties demand and act accordingly."

"Indeed they must." Elias cocked his head. "I had forgotten that you were no politician, Weaver, which is why the story is utter nonsense. Rowley owes nothing to the Tories. He is a Whig, sir. A Whig, and one known to be aligned with Albert Hertcomb, Melbury's opponent in the upcoming race."

"I know who Hertcomb is," I said sullenly, as I took a sip of my drink, though I had only learned of the fellow because I had heard a newspaper story about him read aloud at a tavern a few days before my arrest. "Rowley insisted that my arrest and hanging were somehow vital to the Tory cause, so why—?" I stifled my own question as I recalled the nature of the story to which I had listened. "Wait a moment. Is there not some connection between the Whig candidate, Hertcomb, and Dennis Dogmill, the tobacco merchant these porters hate so much?"

Elias nodded. "I am surprised you know that. Yes, Dogmill is Hertcomb's patron and, as such, Hertcomb has been instrumental in the passage of several bills that favor the tobacco trade in general and Dogmill in particular. He is also Hertcomb's election agent."

I slammed my hand upon the table. "Let us use your wondrous ideas of probability and see what we know. A priest spoke up for the rights of the porters who unload Dogmill's tobacco and then received a threat, warning him to cease his actions. Next, a leader of the labor agitators is killed, and I am arrested for the crime. The judge at my trial, a Whig, does all in his power to convict me, but when his feet are to the fire, he blames a great Tory. When I approach a location where any searcher might hope to find me, it is guarded by men of the Riding Office, who ought to concern themselves with smuggled cargo rather than escaped murderers. Given the generally acknowledged corruption of customs officers, who are said to be in the pockets of the most powerful merchants, I believe I can deploy the mechanisms of probability and determine the identity of the villain."

"Dennis Dogmill," Elias breathed.

"Precisely. I should love to see him swing after the rude treatment he meted out when I tried to speak with him. He must be the man. There is no other person who would want to see Walter Yate dead, have the power to make another man hang for the crime, *and* want to set me against Griffin Melbury."

Elias studied my face. "You must be disappointed," he said, "to discover that Melbury is very likely not your foe."

I admitted to myself that he was right, but I would not give him the satisfaction of saying so. "Why should I be?"

"Come now, Weaver, you have been out of sorts this last half year, ever since you learned that that pretty cousin of yours had joined the Church and married Melbury. I cannot but think you would take some delight in the thought of exposing him for a villain. After all, if Melbury were hanged, Mrs. Melbury might marry once more."

"I have more things to concern myself than affairs of the heart," I said weakly. "For now I shall content myself in almost certain knowledge that Dennis Dogmill is my enemy." I was not so content at all, and I had not yet entirely abandoned the notion that Melbury might not be somehow involved—or perhaps that I could involve him.

"Dogmill is well known to be cruel and sour," Elias agreed, "but if he did have Yate killed, why should he seek to harm you of all men? The docks are swarming with the lowest fellows on earth, men who would hardly know how to speak a word on their own behalf, who would offer no worthwhile defense of themselves, and who would certainly not have the mettle to break from New-gate. Why assign blame to a man whom he must know would fiercely resist this usage?"

I shook my head. "I agree that it does not seem wise. I had little chance to learn anything of the matter of the threatening notes. I was arrested at the very beginning of my inquiry, so it cannot be that Dogmill wished to silence me, for I have nothing yet to say. I believe this question must be the key. If I can learn why Dogmill wished to punish me, I can discover some way to prove myself innocent."

He frowned skeptically. "And how will you do this?"

"Tomorrow I shall go to Ufford and see if he can offer me any more information. And there are a few others I must seek out. For now, I must get my sleep."

"I will leave you then." He rose and replaced his hat, and then turned to me. "One more question. Who is this Johnson fellow the witnesses against you were speaking of?"

I shook my head. "I'd forgotten about that. The name means nothing to me."

"Very strange. That young fellow, Spicer, appeared particularly eager that the world should associate you with this Johnson."

"I thought so too, yet I know no one by that name."

"I suspect you may yet," he prophesied—and, as it turned out, quite correctly too.

We then determined another tavern where we might meet the next night. As he prepared to leave, however, Elias hesitated for a moment and then extracted a small purse from his coat.

"I've brought you an enema and an emetic. I hope you will be wise enough to use them."

"I really must get some sleep."

"You'll sleep better if you cleanse yourself. You must trust me, Weaver. I am, after all, a medical man." With that, he departed, leaving me to stare at his generous gift.

CHAPTER 7

THERE WERE some curious glances at the Turk and Sun when I took a room there that night. From my livery they must have concluded that I had run away from an unkind master, but as I paid my reckoning in advance with ready cash, there were no questions put to me, and I was shown to my room with reasonable cheer.

I intended to do nothing with Elias's medicine, but in a fit of restlessness I chose to administer the dosages, and though I spent an hour or more in the greatest discomfort, I confess I felt mightily cleansed thereafter and slept longer and deeper than I likely should have otherwise, though my dreams were a wild and incoherent jumble of prisons and hangings and escapes. After I had voided my body I called for a hot bath, that I might wash away the vermin of the prison, but they were soon enough replaced by the vermin of the tavern.

The purges had the effect of leaving me enormous hungry, however, and in the morning I ate my breakfast of bread and warm milk with great relish. Then, still in my footman's disguise, I began my journey to the home of Mr. Ufford, who I hoped would be able to shed some light on my troubles. As I walked the street, now in the light of day, I felt the most unusual sensation. I was at liberty but not free at all. I had to remain in disguise until . . . until I hardly knew what. I would have thought that I must prove my innocence, but I had already done that.

I could not dwell upon these difficulties fully, for they made me far too uneasy. I wanted only to keep occupied, and I believed that

Ufford might well have information to aid me. I found, however, that when I presented myself at his door, the priest's serving man showed no sign of granting me admittance. To a third party, our encounter would have appeared very much like two dogs evaluating each other, each wishing nothing but the worst for the other lest his rival receive too many caresses from their master.

"I must speak with Mr. Ufford," I told this fellow.

"And who are you, that you must speak with him?"

I certainly could not tell him that. "Never mind who I am," I said. "Let me speak to him, and I promise you your master will tell you that you've done right."

"As to that, I shan't allow you to enter based on that promise of someone when I don't know who it is," he said. "You will give me your name or you will go. Indeed, I think it very likely you will do both."

I could not allow a meeting of such vital importance to be prevented by this fine fellow's sense of duty. "You will find that I'll do neither," I said, and shoved him aside and forced my way past him. Having not previously been in any room but the kitchens, I had no idea where I might find Mr. Ufford, but I fortunately heard voices coming from down a hallway, so I made my way there, with the servant all the while close behind me and pulling at my shoulder the way an untrained lapdog nips at its keeper.

I burst into the room where Ufford was sitting and sipping wine with a young man of not more than five and twenty. This fellow was also dressed in the humorless blacks of a churchman, but his clothes were of an inferior cut. Both men looked up in surprise as I forced the door open. Perhaps Ufford's expression might be more fairly characterized as fear. He leaped from his chair, splashing wine upon his breeches, and took three steps backward.

"What is this?" he demanded of me.

"I beg your pardon, sir," the servant said. "This rogue pushed his way past me before I could stop him."

"I am sorry that doing so was necessary," I said to Ufford, "but I am afraid I need to speak with you urgently, and the normal channels are not open to me just now."

Ufford stared at me with disbelief until something seemed to slide into place inside his brain, and he recognized me despite my costume. "Oh, yes. Of course." He coughed like a stage actor and brushed at the stain. "You will excuse me, Mr. North," he said to his guest. "We will have to continue speaking of our business another time. I will call on you tomorrow, perhaps."

"Certainly," the other murmured, rising to his feet. He looked harshly at me, as though I had arranged this little scene for no purpose but to embarrass him, and then he glared at Ufford. I make no special claims to know the secrets of the human heart, but I could not doubt that this Mr. North hated Ufford, and violently so.

Once he and the servant had left, Ufford came over to me, tiptoeing as though to perform the degree of stealth this meeting required. He took my hand most gingerly and hunched over. "Benjamin," he said in a hushed voice, "I'm glad you've come."

"I don't know that such precautions as whispering are strictly required," I said in something short of my normal volume—for quiet is contagious—"unless your servant is listening at the door."

"I hardly think so," Ufford said in a now very loud voice, all the while skulking toward the door with his arms stretched out like a bird's wings. "I know I can count on Barber to conduct himself as befits his station. I need not even check on him." With that he threw the door wide open to reveal an empty hallway. "Ah," he said, when he'd once more pressed the door shut. "You see? Safe after all. No need to worry. Though I suppose there is every reason for you to worry, isn't there. But let us not worry for now. Come, a glass of wine, to restore your spirits. You do drink wine, I hope? I know many men of the lower sort never take it."

"I drink wine," I assured him, believing I should have to take a great deal of it to endure this interview. Once he had handed me the glass and I took my seat (he never invited me, and appeared a bit out of sorts when I lowered myself unbidden, but I could not trouble myself for such niceties now), I gestured toward the door with my head. "Who was that man?"

"Oh, that was just Mr. North. He is the curate who serves in my parish in Wapping. He's resumed his preaching duties since I've started receiving those notes. Have you made any progress in discovering the author?"

I stared at him. "You do understand, sir, that I have been otherwise absorbed."

"Oh, yes. I understand that. But I also understand that you made a promise to me, and a promise remains a promise though the fulfilling is more difficult than we anticipated. How shall you ever raise yourself if you are deterred from performing the services you have contracted to perform?"

"At this particular moment, I am much more concerned with avoiding swinging from a halter than I am in raising myself. But as it happens, I am now prepared to return to your affairs, as I believe that the discovery of the author of those notes will shed some light on my own predicament."

"I hardly think that a fit reason to pursue the work I paid you to perform. Is not the satisfaction of a job performed incentive enough? In any case, I should like to know what predicament you refer to."

"The predicament of my having been convicted of a murder I did not commit," I said very slowly, as though the sluggishness of my speech might help him to understand me better. "I cannot but suspect I was tried for that man's death because I intended to discover the author of those notes."

"Oh, ho!" he cried. "Very good, sir. Very good. A murder you did not commit. We shall play that little game if you like. You will find me agreeable in that."

"There is no game, sir. I did not harm Walter Yate, and I have no idea who did."

"Was he perhaps the author of those terrible notes? Could that be why some unknown person—and who could say who this person might be?—meted out justice upon his lowly skull?"

"To my knowledge, Mr. Ufford, Walter Yate had nothing to do with those notes."

"Then why on earth would you have abused him so cruelly?"

"I've told you, it was not me. But if I find out who did kill him, then I believe I shall find out who sent you those notes."

Ufford scratched at his chin, contemplating my strange words.

"Hmm. Well, if you believe that this inquiry of yours will discover my harasser, then I suppose it is an acceptable use of your time. I think it is quite all right if you proceed thus, so long as you don't lose sight of your true aims."

I had, by this time, reached the conclusion that responding directly to Ufford's words was a waste of time, so I thought it best to attempt to set the agenda myself. "Have you received any more such notes?"

"No, but as I have not been preaching, I have tricked the writer into believing he has got what he wanted."

I don't know that I could have distinguished between the trick and the genuine article, but perhaps that was my own weakness. "Mr. Ufford, did you have any particular encounters with Walter Yate, or have any reason to believe that there might be some link between this man and the notes you had received?"

"Yate was by far the most agreeable of those fellows. I met with him once or twice, you know, and though he rejoiced in my benevolent interest in the porters, he never seemed to believe that my words would do him any good. You see, such men have no idea of the power of speech, and for them to believe in rhetoric is like believing in magic, for it is something they cannot hold in their hands. But he and I shared no particular intimacy, if that is what you mean."

"And what of Billy Greenbill?"

"That fellow was far less likable. He would not meet with me, and he called my man names when I sent him."

"Tell me," I said at last, "about your interest in the current election."

He looked at me curiously. "I could hardly have thought it any concern of yours. Jews don't have the vote, you know."

"I am aware that Jews don't vote, and never do we vote less than when we are escaped felons. I ask about your interest, not mine."

"I am a great admirer of the Tories. That is all. I believe that the porters will be far better off under the Tories than the Whigs, for these Whigs care only to use men like rags and wring them out when they are done."

"And you want the porters to understand that and support Mr. Melbury?" I asked.

"That's right. Melbury is a good man. He believes in a strong Church and in the power of the landed families."

"But what good will the support of Wapping laborers do him? They cannot vote. And even if they could, Wapping is nowhere near Westminster. It is the other side of the metropolis."

He smiled. "They hardly need to vote to make their presence felt, sir. If I can deliver these boys for Melbury, I will not only have done some good for the Tories, I will have robbed the Whigs of a weapon."

I understood now. The porters were to be roughs for Melbury. That, at any rate, was what Ufford desired. They could intimidate voters at the polling station. If need be, they could riot. Ufford's desire to help them was only to make sure that when they were used, they were used for the Tories.

I thought little of this plan, but I had small incentive to lecture him on his ethics—nor to inform him that upon the docks I had heard these same porters chanting against *Jacobites, Papists, and Tories*—all of which suggested that his efforts, thus far, had failed. Instead, I returned to matters more pressing.

"Sir, has it occurred to you that the letters you received might have come from Dennis Dogmill himself? This tobacco man, after all, has the most to gain from seeing any labor combination fail. I met with him but once, and briefly at that, but he seemed to me not above any sort of threat of violence."

Ufford chuckled softly. "I do not love Mr. Dogmill, who is a notorious Whig, but I must bring to your attention that he is a John's man."

I had no idea of his meaning. "A John's man?"

"That is to say, he attended Saint John's College at Cambridge, which I attended myself, though at an earlier date. You may not have observed the many ways in which that letter I showed you bespoke a lack of education, but the flaws were painfully obvious to me, and I can promise you no man from Saint John's would write thus."

I let out a sigh. "It might well be that he wrote thus in order to deceive you, or that he had the letters written for him by a man who had not the honor of attending your college."

He shook his head. "I am certain I heard that Dogmill was a John's man, and so what you say is unthinkable." He held up a hand. "Wait a moment. Now that I think on it, I recall that he was cast out of Saint John's. Yes, indeed he was. He was cast out for some act of violence or another. You may be right about him after all."

"What was the act of violence?"

"I don't know, precisely. I understand he was hard with one of his tutors."

"Any man who is hard with a tutor could certainly pen a threatening note with poor spelling," I said, by way of encouragement.

"It is certainly possible," he agreed.

"And as I presume he does not dirty his own hands with things like killing porters, have you any knowledge of who his brutal instrument might be? Does he have any particular relationship with one rough or another? A man who might always be by his side?"

"I hardly know the man enough to answer your question. Or any of your questions. Do you think the law might persecute me for allowing you into my home?"

I could see he had begun to grow uneasy and thought it time to change subjects. "What of your Mr. North?" I asked, by way of concluding.

"Oh, he is also a John's man. That was the reason I took him on as my curate. I can always rely on a John's man."

"I meant something else entirely. Do you think he might have some notion of who I am and, if so, can be depended upon to say nothing of having seen me?"

"As for knowing you, I cannot say. Did he know you before your current troubles? I did not first recognize you in your new clothes, but I cannot speak for another man. As to his remaining quiet, I can make my demands of him and he will certainly obey my orders. I do not give him thirty-five pounds a year to no effect, and a man with four children shan't discommode his source of income."

"I must ask you one more thing. During my trial, one of the false witnesses who spoke against me mentioned a Mr. Johnson. Do you know anyone of that name?"

He shook his head with an urgent violence. "I've never heard of anyone with that name. Indeed, I have not. It is a very common name, and there is no telling how many thousands of men may answer to it."

"I was hoping you might know of a Mr. Johnson with some particular connection to the matter of your notes or of Mr. Yate."

He shook his head again. "I do not. Did I not just now say it?"

I cannot say that I believed him to be lying, but neither was I entirely convinced he told me the truth. My uncertainty was such that I thought it best not to burn my bridges, as the saying goes, over this enigma, which as yet meant nothing to me. I had no way of knowing how largely Mr. Johnson would figure in these events. I merely stood and thanked the priest for his time. "If I have further news or questions, I will call on you again. Please ask your man to be less rigid with me in the future."

"I do not know that my parlor is the best place for us to meet," he said. "And as to my servants, it would be very hard if I could not ask that they approve my visitors for me."

"Then it will be very hard," I said.

As for Ufford's hired curate, Mr. North, I thought there might be some good in talking to him immediately. Ufford thought fit to make his speeches from his church in Wapping, but North lived there, and he would have a far better knowledge of the goings-on among the porters. I therefore took a hackney to his neighborhood, hoping he would have arrived home by that time. It took some inquiring to learn of the location of Mr. North, but I received directions soon enough and was on my way.

And a sad way it was. Here were unpaved streets full of refuse that flowed like a great brown river. The stench of rot and filth was everywhere, but children played in this soil all the same. Men staggered about in a gin stupor, and women too, some clutching babies with utter carelessness. And should an infant dare to cry out, it got but a few drops of its mother's gin for its trouble.

Liveried footmen did not visit regularly in that neighborhood, so my appearance generated a fair amount of notice from gawking children in tattered clothes and wizened women who pursed their mouths and squinted at me. But like a haughty footman, I paid these folk no mind and continued about my business, dusting off the dirt and dung that the lowlies flung in my direction.

I learned something far more interesting while rooting around those streets, however. My escape from Newgate had now become generally known, and had grown into something of a celebrated tale. I did not believe that the daily newspapers had been granted enough time to publicize the event, but already wandering peddlers shouted out their broadsides and ballads recounting my adventures. I learned of this in the most astonishing way—by hearing a ballad singer calling out "Old Ben Weaver's Got Away" to the tune of "A Bonny Lass to a Friar Came." I grabbed a copy at once and read the lyrics—the most wretched drivel, I assure you. They were accompanied by a woodcut depicting a man—who resembled me only in that he had arms and legs and a head—leaping naked from the roof of Newgate as though he were a great cat who could safely land from any distance. How had the tale of my nakedness circulated? I could not say, but information flows through the veins of London, and there is no stopping it once it starts.

My encounter with Mr. Rowley was spoken of as well, but these broadsheets, which were composed for the poor and lowly, celebrated my acts as the revenge of the repressed against his ill users. I took no small satisfaction in this, and in the way in which my escape was described, with much admiration and wonder. Benjamin Weaver, these articles said, smashed through two dozen doors, singlehandedly defeated a score of guards—using only his fists against their firearms and blades. He leaped from (and to!) great heights. No lock could hold him. No constable could defeat him. He was a strong man, a master of escapes, and an acrobat all combined. These accounts sometimes veered toward the fantastical and depicted me fighting armies of villainous Whigs and corrupt Parliamentarians—not to mention violent Rome-inspired Papists.

Though these versions of my adventures were fantastically exaggerated, I now flatter myself that had not a celebrated prison-breaker by the name of Jack Sheppard emerged a bit later, escaping from prison half a dozen times in a variety of extravagant fashions, my own acomplishment would be far better recalled than it is today.

Yet, while I delighted in my name being spoken of with such admiration, I saw that there can be no good without a touch of bad. My championship came with a steep price, for the ballad seller informed me—without ever once suspecting to whom he spoke—that a hundred and fifty pounds had been placed on my head. I was somewhat gratified that I should fetch so mighty a sum, but I would have traded that gratification for a greater hope of being left to my own devices.

Mr. North lived in one of the better houses on Queen Street, though even the best house on Queen Street was a mighty poor house. The edifice was cracked and crumbling, the stairs so damaged as to be almost impassable, and most of the front windows had been bricked to avoid the window tax. The landlady showed me to his chambers—two rooms on the third floor of this feeble building—and I found him at home with his wife and four small children, who made the most appalling noises. Mr. North greeted me at the door. I now had the opportunity to study him more closely than I had before, and I saw that his black coat was worn and patched, his white cravat stained, his wig unpowdered and disordered. He appeared, in short, a meager representative of his church.

"You were just with Ufford. What do you want?" he asked me, treating me in a surly fashion no doubt because of my livery. I thought it mighty unkind of him to look down upon a man of my supposed station, but I was not there to become his friend.

"I beg a moment of your time," I said to him. "In private, if you please."

"On what business?" His impatience made him appear older than his relatively meager years. He knit his brow and bared his teeth like a cur.

"On business of the utmost importance, which can only be discussed in privacy, and not with your landlady lurking just out of sight, listening to us." I repressed a smile at the sound of her shuffling a few steps down.

"You must tell me more than that," he insisted, "if I am to grant you audience."

"It concerns Mr. Ufford and his connection to a great crime."

I don't believe I could have said anything else half so effective. He ushered me into the back room, a small sleeping chamber that he evidently shared with the entirety of his family. There was but a large mattress on the floor, piles of clothes, a few chairs cobbled together of broken things. He stepped out, said a few words to his wife I could not hear, and then rejoined me and shut the door. With the door shut I felt ill at ease in that poorly lit room, smelling of sweat and fatigue.

"Speak your business, then."

"What do you know of Mr. Ufford's relations with Walter Yate and a tobacco man called Dennis Dogmill?"

He narrowed his gaze. "What is this?"

"Can you not answer the question?"

He blinked at me a few times, and then his eyes widened to the size of apples. "You're Weaver, aren't you?"

"My name is immaterial. Please answer the questions."

He took a step back, as though I might attack him. I could hardly blame him, what with the press full of accounts of my prison breaking and ear severing. "Ufford told me he had hired you to find out who was sending him those notes. You must be very dedicated to continue your inquiry even though you are fleeing from the law."

"I am fleeing from the law because of that inquiry," I said. "I have killed no one, and I believe that if I can find out who sent those notes, I may discover the true killer and so unsully my name."

"I am afraid I don't see how I might be of use to you. I have never been invited to concern myself in Mr. Ufford's projects, and I have never wished to be invited either, for his ideas are fantastical and his thinking inept. He would have you believe, I am sure, that he is out to help the laboring man because he is a Christian, but Mr. Ufford cares to help the poor because he believes that the poor, if content, are more easily herded."

"You do not agree."

"I am not in a position to agree or disagree," he said, "being of the poor myself. An education at one of our nation's universities may confer knowledge, but it does not confer wealth—and certainly not wisdom." He paused for a moment. "Can I offer you something to drink? I haven't much of quality, but a man on the run for his life must build a powerful thirst."

I declined the offer, preferring to continue with my inquiry.

He cleared his throat. "Then allow me to take a drink for myself, for I find this conversation not a little disordering, and it leaves my throat uncommon dry." He stepped out of the room, took a pewter mug of ale from his wife, whom he kissed on the cheek and murmured to affectionately. He then smiled thinly, returned to the sleeping chamber, and closed the door.

"Do you know," I asked, "if Mr. Ufford had any dealings with Griffin Melbury?"

"Melbury," he repeated. He took a sip from his mug. "The Tory standing for Parliament? I suppose he may have. They are both Tories, so it is possible they may have had some business together, but I could say nothing of its exact nature. Though I must inform you that my understanding of Mr. Melbury is that he has honorable intentions, if you understand my meaning, and that might not appeal to Mr. Ufford."

"I'm afraid I don't understand you at all."

"Oh, just that Ufford is rather, shall we say, dissatisfied with our current monarch."

I admit freely that I did not understand politics so well that I could be absolutely certain of North's implication. "Please don't be coy, sir. Say precisely what you mean, so there will be no misunderstanding."

He smirked. "I don't know how much clearer I might be. Mr.

Ufford is, in all likelihood, a Jacobite. He supports the old king. Do you understand?"

"As he is a Tory, that should be no surprise. I was under the impression that Tories and Jacobites were mere variants of the same thing."

"Ha," he said. "That is what the Whigs want you to believe. In reality, they are quite different. Tories are High Church men who want to see the Church restored to its great days of power. They tend to represent old money, old power, privilege, that sort of thing. In general, they are counter to the Whigs, with their Low Church ways, all latitudes and laxness. Jacobites, on the other hand, want to restore the son of James the Second to the throne. You do know that James the Second was forced to flee for his life some thirty-five years ago?"

"I'd heard something about that," I said sheepishly.

"Yes. James was a Catholic, and the Parliament would not stand for a Catholic to take over the throne. So James fled, and now there are those who wish to see his line returned to power. Mr. Ufford is very likely among them."

"But if Ufford is a Jacobite, and Jacobites are not one with the Tories, why does he support Melbury, the Tory candidate?"

"These Jacobites always masquerade as Tories. And if the Tories win the upcoming election, the Jacobites will almost certainly see this as a sign that the people are tired of Whigs and our current king. Westminster is a particularly important election, since it has the largest popular franchise in the country. What happens in Westminster may well determine the fate of the kingdom, and it seems as though Ufford wants to have a say in that."

"And does this connect with his interest in the porters?"

"I believe it has occurred to him that all these laborers are selling their life's blood to a pack of heartless Whigs. He therefore believes their anger could be turned against these Whigs and harvested for a Jacobite invasion. These porters, in his mind, could be turned into ready soldiers for the Pretender."

"And if Mr. Ufford's Jacobitical project were discovered," I observed, "this parish would need a new appointee."

North shrugged. "That is true, but I would not fabricate a story of treason because of the distant chance I should find myself in Ufford's post. Were he arrested, more like than not I should be wanting employment entirely. I merely tell you what I believe to be true—that Ufford wishes to fire up the porters to the cause of the Pretender."

"From what I have seen, with their riotous cheers against Papists and Tories, they have not shown themselves to be Jacobitically inclined."

"I don't believe Ufford has won them over sufficiently to learn of their politics or discover just how malleable they might be. I'm sure you are well aware that the poor, the suffering, and the hopeless are inclined to Jacobite sympathies—not because they have any notion of how the Chevalier is supposed to make a better king than George, but because George is the king now and they are unhappy. It therefore makes perfect sense to them that they would be better with a different monarch. I believe it is this inclination that Mr. Ufford intends to draw upon. But I will thank you to say that you have not heard as much from me."

"Come now. You cannot fear these men. They have been trying to regain the throne for nearly thirty-five years and have nothing to show for it. How fearsome can they be?"

"They may not have regained the throne, but in thirty-five years I promise you they have learned a thing or two, mostly about how to operate in secret and how to protect themselves. They're everywhere, you know, hidden from sight, operating with secret codes and passwords and signs. And you must recollect that these are men who can be hanged for their beliefs. They have survived this long only by their skill in concealing themselves from peering eyes. Take my advice, Weaver. Stay clear of them."

"Or what shall happen to me? What have I to fear that has not already transpired?"

He laughed. "Your point is well taken."

"And what of Melbury? You say he has no knowledge of this scheme?"

"I cannot speak to what he knows or does not know. I cannot

even say for certain that Ufford is a Jacobite; it could be no more than a rumor that dogs him. I can only say that I find it hard to believe, from what little I know of him, that Melbury would countenance such a plot. He strikes me as the perfect species of an opposition politician, not a man who plots treason. Of course, I am only guessing, but my rather limited experience of Melbury is that he is an ardent defender of the Church and would not relish seeing the country fall into Romish hands."

"Of course. Are you a Tory yourself?"

"I am not a party man of any stripe," he said. "Politics is for men who make their living in such activities or who have no living to make. I am not so lucky as to belong to either category. I minister to a large parish and do so for thirty-five pounds a year. I haven't the time to concern myself with who is in Parliament and who opposes the king. And I don't possess the franchise, so my opinion is immaterial. But I do support the idea of a strong Church, so I would most likely be drawn to the Tory party."

"Have you ever heard of a man called Johnson?" I asked. "Perhaps in association with Mr. Ufford, perhaps not."

"I had a neighbor named Johnson when I was a boy in Kent, but he was killed in a fire some fifteen years ago."

"I don't think that is who I mean."

He shrugged. "It is a common name, but it means nothing in particular to me—and I can think of no Johnson in Ufford's circle."

I could see that my questions here would yield little bounty, so I thanked Mr. North for his time and began to excuse myself.

"Are you certain," he said, "you would not care for a drink?"

"I am certain," I told him.

"Perhaps something to eat, then. I imagine it must be difficult for you to find the time to take a meal in your current crisis. My wife and I have not much, but we would be glad to share with you what little is on our table."

"I would not think of so presuming upon you," I said. And then I paused, for I could see no good reason why a man of such little money would insist on giving food and drink to a stranger wanted by the law. There was, however, one ill reason he might do so. It suddenly occurred to me that they might not have been words of love he had whispered in his wife's ear.

For an instant I thought to strike North hard in the face for his treachery, but that would prove a waste of my time. More than that, I understood it was no treachery to his way of thinking. He did not know me and owed me no loyalty. I was but an escaped murderer to him, and if a man with four children and a painfully meager salary sees an opportunity to secure four times his yearly income by doing his duty as a British subject, he cannot be called to account for acting as most any man would.

I merely turned from him, threw open the door, and rushed through the front room, terrifying Mr. North's wife and children as I pushed my way past. The priest's lady must have known what was at issue, for she stood before me and attempted to block the hasty departure from her home of 150 pounds' worth of escaped felon. Having no time for genteel respect for the softer sex, I merely shoved her aside and began to make my way down the stairs, taking them two or three at a time.

As I approached the landing, I could see a pair of constables just entering the house, pistols drawn. They only had time to look up before I threw myself at them and knocked both down like pins on a bowling green. Somewhere the landlady screamed, but I could not devote any attention to her and could only hope that she did not take it in her mind to do something heroic like strike me on the head with a kitchen pot.

The two constables were momentarily dazed, so I took advantage of their confusion, and of their wearing hair rather than wigs. That is to say, I grabbed each by his locks and knocked their heads together soundly and with enough force to render them useless to the world and to themselves. With the two men agreeably slumped, I helped myself to their pistols and dashed out into the street.

A cold rain had begun to fall in thick sheets, blown by a hard and cruel wind. The weather worked well to my advantage, for it limited visibility. Still, I thought, as I tucked away my newly got pistols, my footman's disguise was no longer of any use.

I could only hope my next excursion would be more profitable than my last. During my trial, both witnesses against me had admitted to condemning me only because they were in the employ of Arthur Groston, so I thought I would see what the man had to say for himself.

After my arrest, I had sent Elias out to learn what he could from his ample connections among the legal men of the metropolis. Though he was no ruffian and feared to question low men, he nevertheless screwed up his courage and discovered it was widely believed that there would be eyewitnesses who could provide proof of my guilt. We both found this passing odd, since there could hardly be witnesses to an event that had never taken place. I could only conclude that these witnesses had been paid for, and I sent Elias to treat with the dozen or so most notorious purveyors of false testimony.

The method I devised was simple. Elias would inquire of the possibility of hiring witnesses to speak in my defense. We knew that if any of these men had already paid witnesses to appear against me, they would be forced to decline, lest the gentleman face the wrath of those who hired him. Of the men to whom Elias spoke, only Groston demurred, and so we knew at once that he was our man.

This worthy kept a stationer's store off Chick Lane that offered a variety of pens and papers and blank books, in addition to a few lurid pamphlets and romances. The bulk of his income surely came from his alternate trade, and it was one he was in no way embarrassed to promote. A painted sign hung in the window: EVIDENCE.

I approached cautiously, for I thought it entirely possible that the Riding Officers might have anticipated this move on my part, but I have long since discovered that very few men truly understand the nimble art of the inquiry. The deft thieftaker must anticipate his prey's movements, but most of these fellows know only how to react once the prey is found.

The interior was a small shop, crowded with clutter and detritus and dusty sheaves of paper. The space was quite small—only ten feet in length, five in width—in which a customer might move without facing a counter that separated the proprietor from the rest of the store.

I had seen Groston about town, though he and I had never met. He was a younger man than was usual in his trade, not yet into his middle twenties, and of lean but strong build. He wore his natural hair, which hung down in stringy clumps, and there was a half-week's growth of beard on his pointy face. Though not generally of a physiognomic temperament, I had never once set eyes on this weaselly fellow without feeling a strong dislike.

"Good afternoon," he said, not bothering to raise himself from where he sat, at table with a glass of thin red wine. "How can I be of service to you? Are you interested in goods material or immaterial?"

"I am in need of evidence," I said, "and the sign in your window suggested that I might procure it here."

"That you can. Tell me what plagues you, and you will find that I am in all ways prepared to provide you with the assistance you crave."

I approached the counter and, in doing so, advanced upon a rather unpleasant scent. Mr. Groston himself smelled unwashed, and there was a chamber pot nearby that was so recently used it fairly gave off heat like a stove. None of this made me more inclined to be gentle with the fellow.

"There has been a death," I said. "A murder."

He shrugged. "These things are apt to happen now and again, sir. It is better that we not trouble ourselves more than we have to."

"You and I are of a similar way of thinking," I assured him. "But I require witnesses to clear my associate."

"You would be surprised," Mr. Groston told me, "how easily a man of my talents might find those who suddenly recall having seen what no one might have before suspected they had seen. You need only provide me with the details, and I shall find these witnesses for you."

"Very good," I said. "The man in question is named—um, Elias Gordon, and he is accused of having killed a man called Benjamin Weaver."

Groston raised his eyebrows. "Oh, ho. Weaver's dead, is he? Well, that is the best news I've heard in epochs." For the first time he looked up at me and met my eyes. I could only assume that he knew my face from about town as well as I knew his, and at once he realized the error he had made. "Oh," he said.

"Yes. Now, let us talk, Mr. Groston. We must begin with your telling me who hired you to provide the witnesses at my trial."

He moved to back up, but I lashed out quickly and grabbed his wrist.

"I won't answer any of your questions."

"Do you think you might reconsider," I asked, "if I held your head in that chamber pot long enough that you risked drowning in your own kennel?"

Rather than await his mulling over this hypothetical, I moved around to his side of the counter, grabbed him by his greasy hair with one hand, and forced him downward with my other, that I might try the experiment. This was a tricky business, you understand, because I did not wish to have any of his refuse splash on me, but it was not a terribly difficult thing to shove his head in the pot and keep him there for more than two minutes—all without a drop of his nastiness tarnishing my costume.

When I felt his struggling diminish to a dangerous degree, I pulled him out and tossed him on the floor. I took a step back, lest he shake himself off like a dog and send his refuse flying. But Groston only lay there panting and coughing and wiping at his eyes.

"You blackguard," he wheezed. "Are you mad to use me so?"

"Perhaps it is a shitten way to treat a man, but as I have already used you thus once, I do not it think it so outrageous that I do so again. Now, let me ask you again: Who is it that bought those witnesses?"

He stared at me, not sure what to do, but when I took a step toward him he reasoned that he had better tell me all. "Damn you for a dog!" he shouted. "I don't know who he was. Just a fellow, and one I ain't seen before."

"I don't believe you," I told him. I reached out, grabbed his hair, and held him down for another dunk. This time I kept him contained a bit longer than was wise. He thrashed and shuddered and pushed against my hand, but I did not relent until I felt the fight begin to die out of him. Then I yanked him free and tossed him on the floor.

He stared at me with wide eyes while he hacked a filthy mucus. His first efforts at speech were aborted by a heaving cough, and he nearly vomited but somehow did not. This time he managed to find his voice. "Go to the devil's arse, Weaver. You nearly drowned me."

"If you disoblige me by refusing to answer my questions," I explained, "it hardly matters to me if you be living or dead."

He shook his head. "I told you, I don't know him. I never saw him before. He was just a fellow, you know. Not tall nor short. Not young nor old. Neither mean nor great. I hardly remember nothing about him but that he handed me a fat purse, and that was enough for me."

I grabbed him once more by the hair and began to drag him toward the chamber pot. "You'll not be coming out so soon this time."

"Stop!" he shrieked. "Stop it! I told you! I told you everything! You want me to make up a name? I'll do it, if you just leave me be."

I let go of him and sighed, for I had begun to suspect that he had spoken the truth. Perhaps I had suspected so all along but had only relished the opportunity to punish him. "Who is Johnson? The witnesses both said I used that name."

He shook his sad and beshatted head. "I don't know who he is. The man what hired me only said that the witnesses must say you spoke that name to suggest that you were his agent."

I took a step nearer to him and he shrieked again. "Leave me," he cried. "That's all I know. It is all I know, I tell you. I don't know no more. Except—"

"Except what?"

"He told me that should you come looking for him, to give you something."

I stared in disbelief. "What do you mean?"

"Just that." Groston stood up and wiped the kennel from his face and over his head, so it ran down the back of his neck. "I thought it most strange. I asked him why you should come here; was it not more like the case that you should be hanged? He said there was always a chance, and if you did come by I was to give you something. They kept on dying, but he give me money to buy a fresh one every day, just in case."

"What are you talking about? Dying? A fresh one?"

He held up his hands. "I told you, I don't know no more than that. I don't want to regret telling you so much as this, but it's what he said to do, and I don't know no more than it."

"What is it? What did he tell you to give me?"

He fumbled behind his counter, looking for something, muttering to himself that he hadn't bought a fresh one today or the day before either, but there was surely one here. I kept a close eye on Groston for fear that he would produce a weapon, but none was forthcoming. At last he found what he sought and presented it to me with a shaking hand.

"Here," he said. "Take it."

I did not have to take it. Taking it was immaterial. It was the thing itself that mattered, the message of it. What had been left for me was a white rose. This one was wilted and drying, but it lost none of its potency for all that. A white rose.

The symbol of the Jacobites.

CHAPTER 8

ELIAS FOUND ME none the most cheerful that night. We sat in yet another tavern neither of us had ever before entered. It was a louder place than I would have preferred, full of boisterous drunkards—mostly grocers, it would seem—who loved to laugh loudly at nothing, sing without tune, and pull the plump and aging innkeeper's wife into manic jigs. Elias and I hunched over our tables, as though trying to keep below the cloud of tobacco that hovered in the room.

"The white rose," he said. "That cannot be good."

"Why should the Jacobites wish to taunt me?"

"I doubt they would. It seems to me far more likely that someone else *wishes* you to believe that they taunt you. The Jacobites are not interested in playing games. They move silently and strike from quiet cover. I detect a deception."

"Unless it *is* the Jacobites, and they have left the rose precisely so I will think it is a deception and not suspect them."

He nodded. "There is always that possibility."

"Then I have learned nothing except that there is nothing to learn."

He shook his head. "And what if there were something to learn?" he asked. "Would that do you any good?"

"Perhaps I should go back to Rowley. If I remove his other ear, he may tell me the truth this time."

"That is a most dangerous proposition," he said, "and one that is fortunately barred to you. I have heard that, for purposes of convalescence, he has retired to his country estate. Rowley has placed himself out of your hands."

"And I'm sure he is well protected now."

"Without a doubt. What chaos this all is. I wish, by gad, we'd known this Ufford of yours was a Jacobite from the start. I'd have told you never to involve yourself with him."

I shrugged. "White rose or no, I hardly see what it signifies. Half the people in the country, I am led to believe, are Jacobites. One more or less can make no difference."

"I'm not talking about some housebreaker who raises his cup to the king—" and here he waved his hand over his glass, the Scottish code Jacobites used to toast the Pretender when they feared Hanoverian spies might lurk near. It signified *the king over the water.* "Ufford is a priest of the Church of England, Weaver. If he is a Jacobite, there is a good chance that he is a well-connected operative, one working with the inner circle."

"How can there be Jacobites within the Church? Is not the great fear of the English resistance to the Pretender that he will turn the nation Catholic?"

"Yes, but there are those within the Church who are Romish in their leanings, those who do not think they have a right to pick and choose a monarch. There were many who refused to swear allegiance to the new king after the Pretender's father fled the throne. They have a powerful legacy within the Church, and they believe that the Pretender alone can restore their power."

"North seems to think that Ufford, despite his sympathies, has nothing to offer but hot air. It seems unlikely that the Jacobites would trust such a man."

"It is hard to say. He may have something they need. Or Mr. North may have such dislike for Ufford that he sees only weakness where there may lie hidden strength. Jacobites have not survived by advertising themselves, you know. That's why I mistrust your rose. These men are like Jesuits. They disguise themselves. They move silently. They infiltrate."

I laughed. "I have enough with which to concern myself. There is no need to start looking over my shoulder in search of shadowy Jesuits."

"That may well be your chief concern, for all we know."

"No, my chief concern is clearing my name, not worrying about who plots against whom or who will be king next year. And I am finding the project increasingly frustrating."

He shook his head. "Well, look, if you want to discuss that we can, but you won't like what I have to say. I've been giving this a great deal of thought, and I don't believe you can win out, the way you are proceeding."

"No?" I asked dryly. He had found me bloodied and chosen to administer salt to my wounds.

A raised eyebrow told me he saw my displeasure, but he was in no mood to indulge me. "Listen to me, Weaver. You are used to perusing matters with the hope of learning the truth. You wish to know who stole this item or who harmed this person, and when you know it—when you can prove what you know—then you are done. But the truth will not serve you here. Let us say you can prove that Dennis Dogmill is behind the death of Yate. Then what? The courts have already shown they will not answer to the truth. Do you tell your story to the papers? Only the Tory papers will print your tale, and no one who is not inclined to believe it will credit your account because a political paper says so. You have walked the streets all day in the hopes of learning something that will serve you no good. You have only endangered your life, nothing more."

I shook my head. "If you are to suggest, once again, that I flee, I must tell you that I shall not."

"I *would* suggest that, but I know it would do no good. Instead, I think you must consider a unique approach. Since discovering and proving truth, in this case, will not be enough for you, you must determine a way to *use* what you discover. You cannot win by simply proving you did not kill Yate, for you have already done that in court and it served you little. You cannot win by showing who *did* kill Yate, for those in power have demonstrated that they don't give a fig for the truth. Instead, you must make Dennis Dogmill *want* to see you exonerated, and you may then depend on him to order things to your liking."

I was loath to abandon my foul mood, but I confess that Elias's words intrigued me. "How would I do that?"

"By finding out what he does not want found out and then coming to an understanding with him."

Here was something positive; I liked the sound of it. "You mean extort him."

"I should not have put it that way myself, but yes, that is what I mean. You must give him the choice of undoing what he has done to you or facing ruin."

"You propose I threaten his person?"

"You've met him. I don't know that cutting off his ear will make so violent a man comply with your wishes. I think you must discover what he is afraid of. You must worry less about proving who killed Yate and more about why Dogmill should wish to have you punished for the crime. You know something, or he thinks you know something, that can do him harm. He has obviously risked a great deal to see you destroyed for it. You must now learn what it is and use it against him."

"I don't think what you are suggesting is so different from what I am already doing."

"Perhaps not. But your methods put you in great danger. How long can you continue to wear that footman's livery? Surely Mr. North will report what he has seen."

"I will have to obtain new clothes."

"Agreed," he said pointedly. "But what sort of clothes shall they be?"

I sighed impatiently. "I suspect you already have an answer to that question."

"I suppose my tones suggest as much," he said happily. "You see, I fear that as you go about your business now, it is only a matter of time before you are recognized and apprehended. I believe I may have discovered a way to avoid so unhappy an outcome." He paused for a dramatic sip. "Do you recall how last year at Bartholomew Fair we saw the show of that man Isaac Watt?"

I thought back to that boozy day as we stood thick in the malodorous crowd, watching a most dextrous little man perform wondrous trickery before an eager and bibulous crowd. "The fellow who made coins disappear and fowl appear and that sort of thing? What of it? Who cares for a fair showman now?"

"Just listen to me for a moment. After we observed his performance, I became interested in learning the mysteries of legerde-
main. I wished not so much to know the secrets behind his various
tricks—I had no desire to perform wonders myself. Rather, I was
curious as to what principles allowed for the tricks to work. From
my reading, I have learned that much of what happens is based on
the principle of *misdirection*. Mr. Watt comports himself such that
you cannot help but watch what his right hand does. By doing so,
he may use his left hand with impunity. Because no one is looking
for or at the *left* hand, it may engage in all kinds of mischief unseen, even though it operates in the open."

"All very interesting, and if the might of the king of England
were not seeking to end my life, I might share your passion for this
subject. But right now I fail to see how it will help me," I said.

"I believe we should hide you using the principle of misdirection. We will use these four hundred pounds you've stolen to obtain for you new clothes, wigs, and a fine place to live. You will
choose a new name, and you may then walk among the elite of
this city unmolested, for no one will ever think to look there for
Benjamin Weaver. You may greet a man who has seen you in the
flesh a dozen times, and he will think nothing more of you than
that you look somewhat familiar."

"And if I need to engage in some rough questioning? Would
not this foppish version of me hesitate to slap a man until his eyes
bleed?"

"I should think he would. That is why you—the true you—will
also appear from time to time but in Smithfield and St. Giles and
Covent Garden and Wapping, all the most wretched parts of the
city. Precisely the sorts of places, you understand, where a desperate man would be *expected* to hide himself."

I admit I had begun to lose interest in what I thought was nothing more than another of Elias's philosophical maggots, but here
my eyes went wide. "They will be so busy looking for my right
hand, they won't think to watch what mischief my left hand per-
forms."

He nodded sagely. "I see you understand."

"Ha!" I shouted, and slapped the table. "Elias, you have earned your drink," I told him, as I took his hand and shook it with great enthusiasm. "I think you have come up with the very thing."

"Ah, well, I thought so too, but I'm glad to hear you say it. How will you proceed?"

"For now, I will take a room here."

I then called for a pen and piece of paper, and together we made a list of a dozen or so inns with which we were familiar but where we were unknown. We agreed we would meet every third day at this time at these taverns, moving down the list one at a time. Elias, of course, would be certain to see to it that no one tracked him through the streets.

"As for tomorrow," I said, "meet me at the sign of the Sleeping Lamb on Little Carter Lane."

"What is there?" he asked.

"Why, the right hand is there. And we shall see what sort of glove to put upon it."

I had asked Elias to meet me at a shop where a tailor named Swan plied his trade. I had long found him sufficiently competent and good-natured (which is to say, no more than necessarily pressing about my credit) for some years when he approached me—perhaps a year and a half prior to these events—to tell me that he now required *my* services. It would seem that his son had been making merry with some friends in none the best part of the metropolis—namely, Wapping, near the wharves—and he had taken himself too much to drink. For that reason he had not been so nimble as his companions when the press-gang came upon them, and Swan's son had been taken into service in His Majesty's Navy.

As my reader knows, a boy of the middling ranks, apprenticed to a tradesman, is not the sort usually preyed upon by the press-gangs, so Mr. Swan made every effort to have his son found and released, but at each step he received only denials and dismissals; nothing could be done, they said. Such assertions are never true. These men only mean to say that nothing could be done that was worth the trouble of saving a tailor's son from serving his king—

dom at sea. Had Swan been a gentleman of five or six hundred a year, quite a bit could have been done. As it was, they turned him away impatiently and assured him that the lad could not be found but that surely he would only be better off for his time aboard ship.

When tapped by the grieving father, however, I found there was much to be done, including contacting a gentleman I knew in the Naval Office who had once hired me to retrieve some silver stolen from his house. He was good enough to make inquiries, and the boy was discovered and released only hours before his ship was to have left port.

Some six months later I visited Mr. Swan to have a new suit made and found him more fawning than usual. He applied considerable care and attention to measuring me, insisted upon only the finest of materials, and made certain I had my fill to eat and drink while he waited upon me. When I returned to retrieve the suit, he announced that there would be no charge.

"This generosity is hardly necessary," I told him. "You paid me for the services I rendered, and there is no further obligation between us."

"But there is," Swan said, "for the ship my boy would have served on, I have recently learned, was lost in a storm with all hands. So, you see, our debt to you is greater than you knew."

This gratitude he felt toward me made me inclined to put my faith in him. I could not but assume that Mr. Swan, like all men, would prefer to have an additional hundred and fifty pounds—such as my head might now bring—to his name, but he had shown me already that he valued loyalty more than money and believed himself in my debt. As much as I could trust any man, I could trust him.

I had sent Swan a note to advise him of my arrival, so he met me at the door and ushered me inside. My tailor was a short man approaching hard on the elderly, thin, with long eyelashes and large lips that looked to have been flattened by a lifetime of pressing pins between them. Though his skills were above reproach, he had no interest in finery for himself and wore instead old coats and torn breeches, caring only for the appearance of his customers.

"Your friend is already here," he said. "You'll ask him to stop talking to my daughter."

I nodded and suppressed a smile. "I must thank you again, sir, for agreeing to offer me assistance in this matter. I cannot say what I would have done if you had refused me."

"I would never do anything so treacherous. I will do anything in my power to help you restore your good name, Mr. Weaver. You need only ask it. Times are hard, I won't deny it. Since the South Sea sunk, men aren't buying clothes like they used to, but times are never too hard to help out a true friend."

"You are too good."

"But for now, sir, there is the matter of my own girl."

We arrived in his shop, where Elias was seated at a table, drinking a glass of wine and chatting about the opera with Swan's pretty fifteen-year-old daughter, a girl of dark hair and dark eyes and a face as round and red as an apple.

"Such a marvelous spectacle," he was saying. "The Italian singers warbling, the momentous stage, the marvelous costumes. Oh, you must see it some day."

"I'm sure she will," I told him, "and I would hate for you to ruin the surprise of it, so you'll tell her no more of operas, Elias."

He flashed me a pout, but he took my meaning well enough and I knew he would not make himself difficult. "Good, then." He rubbed his hands together. "We are all here, and we may begin."

Swan sent away the daughter and closed the door. "You need only direct me, and I will do as you say." He began picking with distaste at my footman's livery with his long, unusually narrow fingers.

"Here is what we want," Elias began. He rose to his feet and started to pace about the room. "Having given the matter a great deal of thought, I have decided that Mr. Weaver must take on the persona of a man of means, one recently returned to this island from the West Indies, where he owns a plantation. His father, let us say, was always active in politics, and now that he is come to his homeland, of which he knows nearly nothing, he has decided he too would like to become a political creature."

I nodded my approbation. "It seems a fair disguise," I said, thinking that this persona's newness to the isle would conceal my own awkwardness in society. "As to the clothes?"

Elias clapped his hands together. "That's the thing, Weaver. Our worthy Mr. Swan must manage it very carefully. If you do this right, Swan, I can promise you my own business in future."

"I can think of no greater incentive to give the man," I observed, "than the business of a gentleman who never pays his bills."

Elias pursed his lips but otherwise ignored me. "If Weaver is not to be recognized, there must be as little about him as we can manage that draws attention to his identity. His clothes, then, must be fashionable and bespeak his supposed station, but they must not make themselves conspicuous in any way. I want that when a man looks at Weaver, he merely thinks he has seen that kind a hundred times before and looks no further. Do you understand my meaning, Swan?"

"Perfectly, sir. I am your man."

"I am delighted to hear it," Elias exclaimed. "We can use the very principles of a performing trickster to hide Mr. Weaver in plain sight. Why, I believe anyone might look upon him who had seen him countless times before, and not know him for who he is. And as for the rest of the world, which seeks him out from a description of his general personage—why, these strangers will never look at him twice."

Swan nodded. "You are right in that, sir. Very right, for in my trade I have long come to know that when we meet each other, we see the clothes and the wig and the grooming, and we form our opinions with only a glance or two at the face. But as to choosing the clothes to do what we wish, that shall not be easy. Or, rather, it shall not be easy to hit it just on target. We must be most cautious, I think."

And here they entered into a conversation I could hardly even begin to understand. They spoke of fabrics and cuts and weaves and buttons. Swan pulled out samples of cloth, which Elias waved away with contempt until he found what he liked. He examined threads and lace and buckles; he dug through buckets of buttons. Elias proved himself as much an expert on these matters as Swan, and they spoke in their particular argot for near an hour before the course of my wardrobe was determined. Would a coat of silk or wool be more fitting? A dye of blue or black? Blue, of course, but how deep a shade? Velvet, but not *this* velvet! Of course, they could not use *this* velvet (which looked to me indistinguishable from the one they could use quite happily). And as for the embroidery—well, that would have to be just so. I believe Elias took as much pleasure from ordering my new clothes as he did his own.

"Now, regarding your wigs," Elias announced, when he had ordered clothing to their mutual liking. "That is another matter requiring particular attention."

"My wife's brother is a peruke maker, sir," Swan said. "He can do the business."

"Can he be trusted?"

"Entire, sir. He can be trusted entire, but there is no need for him to be trusted at all. He need not know who Mr. Weaver is or that there is aught unusual about him."

"I fear he must, for we need wigs with a singular design—that of concealing Mr. Weaver's own hair."

"Would it not be easier for me simply to shave my head?" I asked. Though no Samson, I admit to an attachment to my locks, which I thought rather manly. However, I was more attached to my life, and I saw no reason to burden myself with the hangman's noose if I could squeak by with the barber's shears.

"That cannot be," Elias said, "for you are to make appearances still as Benjamin Weaver, and if you show yourself with a wig or a shaved head, the world will know that you are otherwise disguising yourself, and those who seek you out will look for a man in a wig. Far better for you to be blatant in your exposure so that no one even thinks to peek under the hat of a West Indian planter."

I accepted his point, and we agreed that there was no choice but to put our faith in Swan's brother-in-law.

Mr. Swan began to take my measurements while Elias continued to chat about how I would carry out his plan. "You will need to choose a name, of course. You want something Christian sounding, but not too Christian."

"Michael?" I suggested, thinking of the English version of my uncle's name.

"Too Hebrew," Elias said, waving his hand. "There's a Michael in your Jewish scriptures."

"How about Jesus," I suggested. "That should be sufficiently un-Hebrew."

"I thought perhaps Matthew. Matthew Evans. There is a name neither unusual nor common. Just the very thing we need."

I had no objections, so at that moment my identity as Matthew Evans pushed its way into the world through the womb of Elias's mind. Not a particularly pleasant way to be born, but the alternatives were surely worse.

Swan informed me that it would be some days before my first suit was ready, but he was able, while I waited, to provide me with a plain and unpretentious costume of the kind I normally wore (he was working on such a one for another customer and merely altered it to fit my frame). I could now safely dispose of my footman disguise, but in doing so I also ran the risk of being recognized, for in these clothes I looked far more like myself than I would have preferred.

The tailor then took us to his brother-in-law's shop, where I ordered two fashionable wigs. The peruke maker offered to trim my hair somewhat to make the fit easier, but not so much that a casual observer might notice my hair had been altered. This fellow, too, said that he would work night and day to make certain my wares were ready as quickly as possible. Matthew Evans would have to wait only a little while before making his first appearance in the world.

In the meantime I had to procure for myself a place to stay, for I thought it best not to linger at a single inn or another for more than a day or two. I therefore found new lodgings, and though the innkeeper appeared suspicious of my lack of belongings, I bespoke a fiction of relocation and lost baggage that he found satisfying enough once I promised to pay for my stay each night in advance and for my meals as I ate them.

Thus, with a tolerable roof over my head once more, I commenced my political studies, a program that began with a visit to Fleet Street to buy several of the common newspapers. I learned less of politics than I did of myself, for I discovered that there was no more celebrated topic than Benjamin Weaver. Our British papers love nothing so well as a notable cause, and no hack writer wishes to be so unoriginal as to have the same thought as any other writer in the land, so I could not be utterly astonished at seeing my name so used. I had seen these journalistic eruptions many times in the past. Nevertheless, it was somewhat disorienting to see one's name used so freely, with so little regard for the truth. It is a very strange thing to be transformed into metaphor.

I stood to each writer as a mere representation of his own political beliefs. The Whiggish papers lamented that so horrific a criminal as myself might have escaped, and they cursed the wicked Jacobites and Papists who aided me. The Whigs painted me a rebel who conspired with the Pretender to murder the king, though the mechanics of this plot were mentioned only in the vaguest of terms. Even I, a political naïf if one had ever been born, could see that the Whigs merely wished to turn a potential embarrassment into a political tool.

The same held for the Tories, whose papers suggested that I was a hero, having attempted to prove my innocence in a crooked Whig court. I must be commended for taking matters into my own hands when the government had betrayed me. And as Whigs were known for their relative tolerance toward Jews (a mere side effect to a greater laxity in matters of religion), and Tories for their intolerance, I thought it interesting that neither camp made reference to my being of the Hebrew nation.

None of this, however, was as interesting as an advertisement I found in the *Postboy*. It read:

Mr. Jonathan Wild announces that he has found himself in possession of a box of missing *linen* and should very much like to return it to its wayward owner. If that gentleman will present himself at the Blue Boar tavern this Monday at five o'clock, being sure to stick to the *right-hand* side, he will find many of his most pressing questions answered.

Here was surely a hidden message, for my true family name, Lienzo, signifies *linen* in the Spanish tongue, and my first name, in the Hebrew language, means *son of the right hand*. I understood the code at once. Wild, my old enemy, the greatest criminal in the history of the metropolis and the man who had defied all expectations by defending me at my trial—this man wished to meet with me.

I would find out his intentions sure enough, but I had no intentions of walking blithely into his lair. No, I would take quite another route.

CHAPTER 9

JONATHAN WILD'S secret message indicated that he wished me to call on him come Monday, but I found his note on a Thursday, and I had no intention of waiting so long for my answers. I continued to believe that the pretty girl with the yellow hair and the deftly hidden tools of escape had been his creature, but I could not know that with any certainty. I only had a hunch and the knowledge that Wild was inclined to send off pretty girls in disguise to do his bidding. But even if he had helped to orchestrate my freedom, I did not for an instant believe that he would be immune to the lure of a hundred-and-fifty-pound bounty. He could not truly expect that I would walk into his offices in the Blue Boar—a tavern located across from the Little Old Bailey, just a few paces from where my death had been mandated by law—and present myself to be disposed of as he saw fit. Wild had used me ill in the past, and even his kind words at my trial could not entice me to trust him now.

Instead, I thought to learn more of his interest in me through quite different means. I visited a butcher in a part of town where I was unknown and there took for myself some choice cuts of beef, which I noticed were wrapped in newspapers featuring a story about the notorious villain Benjamin Weaver. From there, I sat in a tavern until dark and then made my way to Dukes Place, my own neighborhood, where I had not been now in more than two weeks. It was an odd thing, being back in such familiar surroundings, hearing the chatter in Portuguese and accented English and occasionally the tongue of the Tudescos from eastern Europe. The streets smelled of food now being prepared for the Sabbath, to begin at nightfall the next day, and the air was ripe with cinnamon and ginger and, less appealingly, cabbage. Ragmen and trinket peddlers and fruit sellers cried out their wares. It was all too familiar, for I was only a few streets from my own rooms, rooms that had surely been picked clean by the state in compensation for my having been convicted of a felony. I felt a strange urge to go there, to see what had been done, but I knew better than to indulge such a feeling.

Instead, I found the house I sought, which was none the best guarded, and it was no difficult thing to slip inside a window that faced an alley and climb the stairs to my desired chamber. The locked door proved no great obstacle, for, as my reader already knows, I have in the past proved myself handy with a lockpick.

The barking and growling on the other side of the door, however, would present more of a challenge. Nevertheless, I had always heard that the man I sought made a habit of coddling his dogs, feeding them sweetmeats and fondling them like children. Here, surely, were beasts who had never tasted human flesh. That, at any rate, was the wager I had made.

I opened the door, and the creatures lunged at me—two enormous mastiffs the color of day-old chocolate—but I was ready and held out my package from the butcher. Whatever urge to protect their territory that drove them they now set aside, as they tore at the little package, devouring flesh and paper all. I, in turn, closed the door and took a place in a chair I found convenient, acting all the while as though there were nothing more natural than for me to be in this room with them. It is the trick with dogs, I had long since discovered. They are strangely canny at discovering your mood and responding to it. Act with fear, and they will lunge at you. But toward a calm and relaxed man they will show indifference.

By the time I took my seat, the meat I had purchased was gone, and now I faced no greater challenge than managing the affection of the creatures. One showed me its belly and demanded that it be rubbed. The other set its head in my lap and stared at me until I agreed to scratch its ears.

I had a trying two hours to wait in this unlikely state, breathing in the pungent scent of pampered beast, and then I heard the turn of the door handle. I could not tell if he detected that the door had been meddled with or no, but he entered the room, a candle held before him, calling out warm greetings to the dogs, who had now abandoned me that they might leap up upon their master.

The instant he shut the door behind him, I had a pistol to the back of his neck. "Don't move."

I heard a heavy exhalation, perhaps a laugh. "If that pistol misfires, you'll have to face both me and the dogs."

I shoved a second pistol into his ribs. "I am willing to gamble they'll not both misfire. Are you?"

"Shoot me if you like. You'll still have the dogs at your throat, and you'll never get out of here alive," said Abraham Mendes, Wild's most trusted lieutenant. He, like me, was a Jew of Dukes Place and we had grown up together. While this accident of geography hardly made us friends, there was something of a begrudging understanding between us, and I was far more inclined to treat with him than his master.

"I've already faced down the ferocity of your beasts."

"Look, Weaver, you may have lost all fear of my dogs, but though they do not tear you apart at this moment, rest assured that they will not hesitate to do so if I give the command or if you hurt me. Nevertheless, this show of strength is hardly necessary. One word out my mouth would have you dead and ripped to pieces. That I haven't spoken this word should tell you I want you alive and healthy. Surely you must know after Wild's performance at your trial that we will not go after you. You've nothing to fear from him or from me."

"There wasn't a hundred and fifty pounds to be had at my trial."

"He has no interest in pursuing that bounty and neither do I," he said. "I give you my word."

I was reluctant to take the word of a man who made a good deal of his income through perjury, but I felt I had little choice, so I set aside my weapons. "Apologies," I muttered. "But I'm sure you understand the need."

"Of course. I'd have done the same." Mendes lit two lamps and called over his dogs. If they felt any guilt at having betrayed their master, they showed none of it. Neither did Mendes show any resentment to the animals for their gullibility. He pulled from his pocket some dried beef, which surely paled in comparison to their earlier fare, but they made no complaint.

It was odd for me to see this man, large and ugly, with hands that appeared strong enough to crush these dogs' skulls if he chose, engaged in such a warm display toward mere beasts. But I had long since learned that people are not the uniform creatures the novelists would have us believe but, rather, a series of contradictory impulses. Mendes might love these beasts with all his heart and still coolly unload a pistol into the skull of a man whose only crime was to be disliked by Jonathan Wild. And Mendes alone would see the consistency in such behavior.

"Some port?" he asked.

"Thank you." I only briefly considered the possibility that he might poison the drink. But poison did not seem Mendes's way. Seeing me ripped to pieces by his dogs was more in his line, and as he had not done this I could assume the drink to be safe.

He moved to hand me my pewter cup, but it slipped from his hand. As it landed on the wooden floor with a light tap, I understood that it was empty—and I understood that it had been a distraction.

Mendes now stood over me with a blade to my throat—a long knife of remarkable sharpness. He pushed with the sharp blade, and I backed up, feeling it cut into my skin. He pressed forward, however, and soon I was against the wall.

"Guard," he said quietly. I did not understand his meaning until I realized it was a command to his dogs. They approached and stood at my feet, legs wide apart. They looked at me and growled but did nothing more, awaiting Mendes's command.

The blade moved just a quarter inch, and I felt the skin on my neck slide. Not deeply, but enough that there should be blood. "I thought to let the insult go," Mendes said. I felt his breath on my face, hot and pungent. "I understood that you believed you needed to put a gun to me, that you could take no chances until you were certain. I am not unaware of all of that, and so I thought to forget the matter. But I cannot forget it, Weaver. You put a gun to me and you threatened me, and now there must be retribution."

"What sort of retribution do you envision?" I asked. I spoke slowly to keep the skin from moving too much against the blade.

"An apology," he said.

"I apologized before," I observed.

"Before you apologized to be courteous. Now you must apologize out of fear." He stared hard into my eyes, refusing to turn away. "Are you afraid?"

Of course I was afraid. I knew Mendes to be unpredictable and violent, two qualities I did not desire from a man holding a knife to my throat. On the other hand, there was such challenge in his voice that I could not capitulate—not like he wished me to.

"I'm uneasy," I said.

"Uneasy is not enough. I want to hear that you are afraid."

"I'm concerned."

He blinked. "How concerned?"

"Quite."

He let out a breath. "And sorry?"

"Certainly," I said. "Very sorry to have had to hold a pistol to you."

He took away the blade and backed off. "I suppose that will have to do. You with your irrational pride—we'd have been here all day." He turned away—to show his confidence, I suppose—and found a rag, which he tossed to me, presumably for the purpose of dabbing up the blood on my neck.

"Now," he said, as he picked up the fallen pewter cup, "shall we take that port?"

Soon we sat in chairs across from each other, faces red from the fire, chatting as though we were old friends.

"I told Wild you would never come to meet him," Mendes said, his scarred face erupting into a satisfied grin, "but he insisted the advertisement, assuming you saw it, would have the desired effect. And now it seems he was correct, for in truth he only wanted to pass some information along to you, and in your current state you are a difficult man to seek out."

I could not regret that it was so. In the past, Wild's efforts to seek me out had involved sending his men to attack me and drag me to his house against my will. "And what information would that be?"

Mendes leaned back in his chair, as satisfied as a country squire who had just finished his evening fowl. "The name of the man who has brought all this trouble down on your head."

"Dennis Dogmill," I said flatly, in hopes of seeing him perhaps a bit less puffed up.

He leaned forward, unable to hide his disappointment. "You are cleverer than Wild would have believed."

"Wild thinks no one clever but himself, so I cannot bristle at his underestimating me. Nevertheless, I wish you would tell me what you know."

He shrugged. "Not very much, I'm afraid. We learned that you had been meddling around with the porters at Wapping. Dogmill has been wrestling with the labor combinations for months, even while he sets them against one another. This fellow Yate was causing him no small amount of grief, and it's easier to kill a porter than it is a rat."

"That much I know. Why would he choose to blame me for the crime?"

"Wild had hoped," Mendes said, "that you would tell us that."

I felt the sad tug of disappointment. Nevertheless, that Wild had known to blame Dennis Dogmill for my woes suggested to me that he might have more information as well. "I wish I could. I believe that is the very key to all of this."

Mendes gazed at me skeptically. "Come, Weaver. The truth."

"Why should I not speak the truth?"

"There have been some suggestions in the paper that your loyalties are not to His present Majesty."

I laughed aloud. "The Whigs are merely trying to turn an embarrassment into political capital. It was one of their judges who so blatantly condemned me against the evidence. You are not so foolish as to believe what you read in the political papers, I hope."

"I don't believe it, but I wonder about it. You have not involved yourself in some Jacobite plot, have you, Weaver?"

"Of course not. Do you really think me mad enough to indulge in treason? Why should I want to see any James the Third on the throne?"

"I admit it seemed to me unlikely, but these are strange times and there are plots everywhere."

"I cannot speak for that. Until recently, I could have hardly told you the difference between a Tory and a Whig—or a Tory and a Jacobite, for that matter. I am far more interested in saving my skin than restoring a dethroned monarch—and I should be loath to see a change in a government that has treated our race so kindly."

"I should think you would look favorably on the Whigs when the man who married your cousin's pretty widow runs as a Tory. You once took it into your head to marry her, did you not?"

I glared at him. "Don't think to take liberties with me, Mendes."

He held up a massive hand. "Stay your temper, friend. I meant nothing by it."

"No, you did mean something. You meant to prod me to see how I should react. Prod me again on this matter, and you'll know—dogs or not—I am not to be made sport of."

He nodded solemnly, a look—almost of remorse, I must say, settling onto his misshapen face. "Then let us go back to the matter at hand. Why have you been singled out to hang for Yate's death?"

"I cannot even speculate. It seems there would be countless other men who would have made more convenient victims, so I can only conclude that Dogmill chose me for some purpose relating to my inquiry." Here I told him of my service to Mr. Ufford.

"Ufford has been making trouble with the porters," Mendes said, "and he is a known Jacobite, but that hardly seems reason enough for Dogmill to wish you to hang. You say you learned nothing about these notes, but it would be reasonable to suspect that Dogmill thinks you've learned something—and he would rather see you dead than reveal it."

I shook my head. "Then why not slip a blade into my back when I am not looking? Why not have my food in prison poisoned as I awaited trial or have a guard smother me in my sleep?

There are a hundred ways to kill a man, Mendes. You know that. A thousand, if he is in Newgate. Arranging for a trial and bribing a judge to misdirect a jury hardly seem the most effective. I am not convinced that what has happened to me is a mere effort to keep me silent."

He gazed into his glass thoughtfully. "You may be right, but it is nevertheless true that Dogmill wished that these things should befall you. Wild believes you must be dangerous to Dogmill in some way, and he is willing to offer you protection in exchange for learning the truth. But now you tell me you don't know. That's bad news, Weaver, because if you cannot hold something over Dogmill, you will be on the run for the rest of your life, and with a hundred and fifty pounds on your head, the rest of your life may prove to be a sadly short period of time."

"Why would Wild offer me protection? What is Dogmill to him?" I asked.

"Well, that is another matter. Wild supports the Whigs in general, but not this one. Dogmill has had the quays under his thumb for some time now. A lot of business can be conducted on the quays, but it is impossible to move in with Dogmill there. He has too many Parliamentarians working for him, and he has the Customs in his pocket."

"Yes, I've already had to dodge a pair of Riding Officers who were on my trail. Is it not a bit of a contradiction for customs men to be working for an importer?"

"A rather convenient one. Half the men employed by the customs office receive bribes from him. When his ships arrive in port, these fellows remove a significant measure from his hold before the true inspector comes to assess the value. This is a fine practice they call *hickory pucker*. Dogmill then pays duties based on only a fraction of his cargo."

"A little bribery is one thing, but to use the armed constabulary of the Customs is quite another. How can I hope to act undetected?"

Mendes shrugged. "It's brazen, but unsurprising. Dogmill has the wealth to bribe whom he likes, including many open-handed fellows in the Commons. His slaves in Parliament recently pushed through legislation that allows significantly lower duties for tobacco men who pay all their assessments within six months, meaning that, because he is wealthy in the first place, he pays far fewer taxes than merchants who have to borrow their wealth and then sell their goods before paying their duties. So he cheats the government at both ends."

"Is it not a little sanctimonious for Wild to look down upon such cheating?"

"I don't know that he looks down on it. I suppose he admires it. I merely meant to inform you of the sort of enemy you face. Dogmill is a bad man, Weaver, you may be sure of that; it is not every scoundrel that Wild hesitates to cross. It is not merely his power that Wild fears, it's his rage. The man was cast from his school at Cambridge for torturing his tutor. One day Dogmill could no longer accept the tutor's demands of a Latin memorization or some such nonsense, so he horsewhipped him as though he were a servant. I have heard of three instances in which he's beaten men to death with his fists. Each time, the magistrate dismissed the matter as self-defense, for Dogmill insisted that he had been attacked. But I know from a reliable witness that, in one of these attacks, Dogmill was accosted by a beggar looking for a bit of copper for bread. Dogmill spun around and beat the fellow in the skull until his head was quite broken."

"I believe myself equal to a man who beats down beggars."

"I have no doubt you are. I only warn you that he is vicious and unpredictable. All the more reason why Wild should like to see him gone."

"I suppose, with Wild's own smuggling vessels, he wants Dogmill out of the way to gain a better grasp on the quays."

"That is it exactly. A few years ago, I made some inquiries on Wild's behalf with a few of the more powerful men on the parish boards. It soon became clear that no one dared to cross Dogmill in this regard. And he let us know that if we tried to interfere with his business, things would go hard for us."

"So Wild testified in my favor because he could do so while

pretending to know nothing of Dogmill's involvement in Yate's death."

"Precisely."

"And that is why he sent the woman with the lockpick."

Mendes leaned in. "Wild told me about the woman. He said you must have set it up. Her technique, he reported, was rough but adequate."

"Come, Mendes. Am I to believe that you and your master were not behind this woman?"

"Wild is a man who loves to boast, and I am one of the few people to whom he can boast freely. If he did not commend himself for that action, I can promise you he was not behind it."

"I don't believe you," I said.

He shrugged. "Believe what you will. I cannot make you see the truth of it, but surely you must admit that if Wild had done you this favor, there would be nothing gained by refusing to acknowledge it."

I could not but see his logic. "Then who?"

"I don't know. I would suggest that finding this woman, or finding who sent her, may help you discover what it is that Dogmill thinks you know."

I took a moment to consider his words. "What do you know of a man called Johnson? One of the false witnesses at my trial said that I announced myself to be in his service."

Mendes shook his head. "It means nothing to me."

"And what of Dogmill's roughs? I find it hard to believe that the foremost tobacco merchant in the city goes about murdering porters on his own. He must have fellows he deploys for his dirty work."

Mendes shook his head again. "I would think so myself, but I have never heard of any such men. Surprising though it may be, I have concluded that he does indeed go about murdering porters himself. Dogmill has no fear of violence. He relishes it, and if he was of a disposition not to entrust his crimes to the silence of some ruffian or other, he might well have killed Yate with his own hands."

"And he might not have," I observed.

He grinned wickedly. "True enough. I suppose I don't know very much at all."

A moment of silence passed between us, for it seemed as though there was little more to say.

"Very well." I drained my glass and stood. "Thank you for your time."

"Thank you for feeding my beasts," he said.

"Just one more thing." I turned to him. "The metropolis is crawling with men who want that bounty on my head. Is there some way Wild could call off his men?"

"No," he said. "Wild won't appear to support you publicly. He might have hazarded it if you supplied information to help destroy Dogmill, but he will not risk the notice of the law on the one hand and Dogmill on the other. It will have to be enough that he is not actively seeking you out. You should be more than a match for the brutish fellows who might attempt to outwit you."

"One would think that if I remove this great enemy of Wild's, he would be in my debt."

"You are already in his debt."

"And why is that?"

"Because he has decided not to capture you for the bounty."

"Do you really think he could?"

"I could," Mendes said, without a hint of good-natured teasing. "But you need not fear. And I might add that I am willing to go where Wild is not. This must remain between us, but if you do find yourself in need, you may safely call on me."

I studied his deep-set eyes. "And why is that?"

He took a breath. "I told you that when we first began to inquire into Dogmill's doings, I was the one who went forth to learn the lay of the land. It would seem that, because I engaged in the reconnoiter, I became the target of Dogmill's anger. I had a dog back then, a wondrous beast called Blackie. These two are very fine dogs, make no mistake of it." He paused to pet them, that they might not feel neglected. "Yes, these are good animals, but Blackie was a great friend. I was used to taking him to the tavern with me and on my way. Though he had the heart of a lamb, the sight of him drove fear into the hearts of all who opposed us. And then one day he was gone."

"You think taken by Dogmill."

"I know it. I received a note not a week later in which the anonymous writer detailed how poorly Blackie had acquitted himself in the dogfighting pits of Smithfield. Dogmill was not mentioned, but he is known to have a taste for blood sport, and there was no misunderstanding the message. Dogmill meant for us to keep away from him and his business. He made a point of discovering what he could about us and so learned of my fondness for my dog. It took all of Wild's protestations and a dozen men to hold me down, to convince me not to murder the blackguard. But Wild promised me Dogmill's time would come, so I will do what I can for you, Weaver, to make that time come the sooner."

"How did he get the dog out from under your nose?"

"Do you remember a fellow that used to travel with Wild, a funny-looking Irishman called Onionhead O'Neil?"

"Yes, a peculiar fellow with orange whiskers. What ever became of him?" I asked, but then I knew the answer at once. "I suppose nothing good."

"Onionhead thought it worth a few shillings to side with Dogmill against a helpless beast. I had no mercy on such a one as he. And I can have no mercy on Dogmill. If you want my help, Weaver, you need but let me know."

CHAPTER 10

O<small>N THE AGREED-UPON</small> day, I visited Mr. Swan, who had my first suit, with an assortment of shirts and hose and linen ready for me. Swan had taken the liberty of collecting the wigs from his brother-in-law, and he assured me that he would have two more suits for me by the end of the week. I could only imagine that he had been working through the nights and would continue to do without sleep.

I suppose I should have donned these clothes with a certain sense of wonder, but the truth is I dressed with no more ceremony than I usually reserved for so mundane an act. All, however, was much to my liking. I examined with pleasure my dark-blue velvet coat with large silver buttons. The shirt was well laced, the breeches finely shaped. I tried on the first wig, which was of a bob variety, different enough from my own hair, which I wore in the style of a tie wig. Only when I looked in the mirror did I feel anything new. I must admit, I hardly knew myself.

I turned to Swan and inquired of the good tailor what monies I owed him.

"Not a thing, Mr. Weaver. Not a thing," he said.

"You go too far," I told him. "You have obliged me by doing this work. I cannot ask you to shun payment as well."

Swan shook his head. "You are not a man in a state of luxury to offer payment where none is required," he said. "When you put these difficulties behind you, perhaps then you might come see me and we will discuss a bill."

"At least," I proposed, "allow me to reimburse you for the raw materials. I should hate to see you lose so much money on my be-half."

Mr. Swan was a kindly man, but he could not deny the justice of this offer, so he took some of my money, though he did so with a heavy heart.

With my costume in place, I went out into the city to begin ordering Matthew Evans's affairs. I have disguised myself as a gentleman before, so this was no new experience to me, but I now thought myself on an entirely new footing, a new level of deception. On previous occasions I had masqueraded as a man of quality for an hour or two and usually in dark places such as coffee shops or taverns. Never before had I attempted a fraud of this nature in broad daylight and for a period that, if I was honest with myself, could last weeks—even months.

Now that I could perpetuate the fraud of my new self, I knew it was time to find a place to lodge. After reading through the papers and examining a number of prospects, I settled on an only slightly less than fashionable house on Vine Street. The space was adequately comfortable, but I required more than comfort. I looked for rooms with at least one window that overlooked an alley or blind street. This window should not be very high up, and it should be accessible to a man climbing in, just as the street should be accessible to a man climbing out. In a word, I wished to be able to get in and out of my lodgings without anyone's knowing it.

The house I found had a set of three rooms one flight above the ground floor. One window did indeed overlook a blind alley, and the brickwork was ragged enough that I should have little trouble making my way to and fro.

Much like the innkeeper where I had been staying, my landlady thought it quite strange that I had no belongings, but I explained that I had recently arrived from the West Indies and had arranged for my effects to be sent ahead of me. Much to my dismay, they had not yet arrived, and I was getting by as best I could in the meantime. This aroused both her sympathy and her sense of narrative, and she told me three separate stories of former tenants who had been separated from their trunks.

I admit the rooms on Vine Street were none the most pleasant, and if my single desire had been to gain as much enjoyment from my masquerade as I might, I should have looked for housing elsewhere. The rooms themselves were shabby and thick with dust. The rags stuffed by the windows did little to stanch the cruel draft that came in from outside; the snow had melted through and then frozen the rags solid. The furnishings were old, often broken or breaking, and the Turkey rugs throughout the house were all worn to the threads in one or two places.

Nevertheless, since location and convenience were more pressing concerns for me, I was willing to live with these shabby rooms. More to the point, I don't believe my landlady knew her rooms were run-down. When she showed me the space, she spoke of it as though she truly believed there to be no finer house in London—and I was perfectly willing to allow her to continue in her beliefs.

This lady, Mrs. Sears, was a thoroughly reprehensible Frenchwoman. I am not subject to the common prejudice that all the French are disagreeable, but here was someone who made a poor ambassador of her race. She was as short as a child, shaped like an egg, and her ruddy cheeks and poor balance suggested to me that she was a bit overly fond of her drink. None of this would have troubled me had she not demonstrated a horrific urge to converse with me. When I first discussed terms with her, she lured me in part by announcing that her house had a small collection of books, which her tenants were welcome to peruse so long as they were careful not to harm them and replaced them promptly. Now that I found myself, for the first time in days, in a comfortable place, I thought nothing would be more gratifying than to pass an hour or two in a relaxed state with an engaging volume. Sadly, to retrieve the treasure, I first had to slay the dragon of chatter.

"Oh, Mr. Evans," she called out to me, in the unflattering accent with which her nation is afflicted, "I see you are a lover of words, as I am. Allow me to walk you through my little library."

"I would not so impose on your time," I assured her.

"It is no imposition," she said, and had the audacity to take me by the arm and lead me forward. "You must tell me first, though, about life on Jamaica. I hear it is a very strange place. I have a cousin who lives in Martinique, and she tells me it is very hot. Is Jamaica hot? I think it must be."

"Quite hot," I assured her, calling upon the memory of what I had read and heard of those lands. "The air there is most unwholesome."

"I have known it. I have." Though we now stood before her bookcases, she still did not let go of me. If anything, she dug in even deeper with her thick fingers. "It is no place for a handsome man to live. It is much better here. My husband, you know, was an Englishman just like you, but now he is dead. He is dead some ten years."

I thought to propose that they must have been his most satisfying ten years since he was born, but I held my tongue.

"And they say you are a bachelor, yes? I have heard you are worth a thousand a year."

Where had she heard I was worth so absurdly large an amount? Still, the rumor could do me no harm, and I saw no reason to deny it. "Madam, I do not discuss such matters."

She now released my arm and instead took my hand. "Oh, you need not be shy with me, Mr. Evans. I will not think the less of you for your fortune. No, I won't. I know a girl or two, very agreeable girls, I might add, and with no small fortunes of their own, who might make you a very pretty adornment. And what if they are my cousins? What if they are?"

I hardly knew how to answer this question, but I thought that if I was to be entrenched in intercourse with this lady, I might as well put her to some use.

"What," I asked her, "do you know of this Weaver fellow, who appears to have created such a stir?"

"Oh, he is a very bad man," she said. "A very bad man. A Jew, so it is no surprise he is full of murder and rage. I have a picture of him here," she said, and quickly retrieved from the next room a broadside that depicted my prison escape. I had not seen this one before, but its likeness was no better than the ones I had examined.

She would no more recognize me from that image than she would from her own reflection.

"From what I have read," I ventured, "opinions of his goodness or badness seem to be marked along political lines."

"I care nothing for politics," she said. "I understand nothing of these English parties. These names—Whigs and Tories—make my head spin. I only know I wish he would be catched soon, or he might attack again. And not just men, you know."

"Oh?"

"Oh, yes. He is very cruel to the ladies. I do not feel safe walking the streets with him out there. He might very well grab me and throw me down."

I looked her up and down. "He very well might," I ventured, which effectively put an end to our conversation.

As planned, I met Elias at the next tavern on our list. He was there when I arrived, and perhaps he was merely flattering me, but he appeared not to notice me when I walked through the door and approached him. Only as I grew very close did his gaze pause on me for a moment, and his eyes narrowed before he offered me an enormous grin.

"Matthew Evans," he said, with no little joy. "It is good to see you." He looked me up and down, as though I were an expensive strumpet, and grinned so broadly he verged on metamorphosing into a grotesque. "I must say, you've fine taste in clothing."

"You are kind to say so."

"Really, we must take a moment to celebrate my cleverness. Your appearance could not be more perfect. I am quite convinced that I am the greatest thinker of our time."

"To know you is to feel the same," I assured him.

"You mock me, but I must inform you that I have this very day shown the first portion of my manuscript, 'The Lively Adventures of Alexander Claren, Surgeon,' to a very notable bookseller in Grub Street, and he thinks it may answer quite nicely. He sees no reason that it should not be every bit as popular as the tales of *Robinson Crusoe* or *Moll Flanders*."

"I wish you luck of it," I said, "but you will forgive me if your literary adventures are not foremost on my mind."

"Of course, of course. You are ever preoccupied with yourself, I know. If you wish to talk about *your* interests instead of mine—all this running from the law and such—I will certainly understand."

We called for drink and food, and after a few minutes Elias ceased his simpering over my appearance. "Well," he said, "if we are to talk about you, let us do so. It is time we began the business."

"And how do we do this?"

"There are a number of things that I've been pondering. First of all, I imagine you have seen the political news."

"I have. I wanted your opinion on that."

"Nothing but what might have been anticipated. Your escape has become celebrated, and now each side wishes to use it for its own ends. You must let it ride its course and see what happens. In the meantime, I believe Matthew Evans must make his appearance in society."

"To what end?" I asked.

Elias looked most dismayed. "I thought we had reached some agreement on this matter," he said. "Is that not why we went to the trouble of having your clothes made?"

"It is, but as I have contemplated this plan, I confess I have come to understand less and less of it. I am to be Matthew Evans so that I may act unmolested."

"Precisely."

"But what acts am I to perform? I can hardly inquire into my own affairs when I pretend to be another man. What will Matthew Evans do with himself?"

"I thought you understood that. You will get close to Dennis Dogmill and learn enough about him to threaten him. And then you will act."

"Is that not rather naïve? Do you think, if I can convince him to invite me to his parlor for a glass of claret, I shall be in a position to learn his secrets?"

"Of course not. You'll do the sorts of thing you usually do—speak to his servants, sneak a look at his papers, all that sort of inquiring business. And in the meantime, as your true self you will be able to search the quays for answers there."

Elias's plan had seemed enticing when he had first suggested it, but now it struck me as less than useless, and no matter how he endorsed it I could not believe it would meet with success. "What about Griffin Melbury?" I said at last.

Elias raised an eyebrow. "What of him?"

"Should I not also get to know him better?"

"Surely you recognize that you are being absurd. If you are disguising yourself as a Whiggish West Indian, why should you seek out Griffin Melbury? And even more to the point, what would you gain by doing so? It is clear that Dogmill is your enemy, not Melbury."

"Rowley tried to point me toward Melbury. Perhaps Melbury would be able to help me if he thought we sought the same thing—the undoing of Dogmill."

"I understand you too well, Weaver. All you want is a way to get close to Mrs. Melbury. Don't think I can't see it."

"You're mistaken. I would prefer that this matter involve no one connected with her, but I have not set out the terms of this conflict and I must use them as best I can. If I can resolve my troubles without setting eyes on her, I should be the happier for it." Did I believe my own words? Even now, I cannot say.

"Very well, I'll indulge you for the moment. I beg you continue."

"You must know that I feel no fondness for Melbury, but I have come to the conclusion that he must succeed if I am to succeed. I wish to see him elected to Parliament, to aid him in his election. Once in office, he will have the power to expose the wrongs of my trial and to demonstrate the influence of Dogmill."

"And why should he do so?"

"Because he can have no love for Dogmill. Besides which, he and I will become friends," I said smugly.

"You make it sound so uncomplicated."

"I believe you were the one who, not long ago, advocated I become friends with a monster like Dogmill. But in my brief encounter with the man, and from all I've heard of him, attempting to attach myself to him will only incur his displeasure, something surely best avoided by a would-be toadeater. On the other hand, all state that Melbury is a reasonable man. His friendship should be far more easily secured. If I help him, if I work against Dogmill as a common enemy, should he not, in return, show me his gratitude? Even more than that, by exonerating a man cruelly used by the Whigs, he advances his own career, his own party. Once I am able to prove my case to him, I don't know that he could be dissuaded from helping me."

"Perhaps," he said quietly. I could not tell if his hesitation stemmed from a weakness of the plan or from petulance that it was not he who had devised it.

"I want to meet Melbury," I said again. "He will be my friend, and Dogmill my foe. Can you think how I might do so?"

"I don't believe that you can set aside your feelings for his wife. Meeting with him, trying to earn his friendship, would be a mistake."

"It is my mistake to make," I said.

Elias sighed deeply and rolled his eyes for effect. "Well, I just now read that there is a breakfast for supporters of Mr. Melbury at the Ulysses Tavern near Covent Garden the day after tomorrow at eight in the morning. Frightfully early, I know, but you could attend if you were intent on doing so."

"No, that's no good. I would hardly know what to say, and I would reveal myself as an impostor in moments."

"Do you think everyone who attends these things is full of canny observations? Most are merely windbags who want to feel important. If you are at a loss for what to speak of, you may complain about Whig corruption or the Whig oligarchy. You may talk of the Church in danger or of villainous Whig latitudinarians who are little better than atheists. Rail against the South Sea scheme and the screening of the Company directors. If you wish to be a Tory, you must be a curmudgeon, just as if you wish to be a Whig, you must be an opportunist. All the rest is mere posturing."

I considered my strong but ultimately limited resources. "How much will I have to pay to attend?"

He laughed. "*You* pay? You know nothing of politics, I see. It is

Mr. Melbury who pays. You pay, indeed! Politics is corrupt enough without asking the voters to pay for the campaigning. But I suppose that is one of the reasons why elections have become so expensive of late. I'm told that a hundred years ago a man could win Westminster with five pounds out of pocket. Today he will count himself lucky if his bill does not exceed a thousand."

"Why does it cost so much?"

"Because there is a great deal of money to be made, and because the other fellow will spend if you don't. The man who wishes to sit in Parliament must offer food and drink and entertainment and pretty girls. And the Septennial Act has only made things more dear. When a man ran every three years, he could ill afford to expend a fortune on an election, but now that terms run seven years, he can ill afford *not* to. The prize is of too much value."

"And given the dear cost of elections, can any man go to this Tory breakfast and announce that he likes Mr. Melbury and would enjoy some beer and sausage?"

"Some events do work that way. Particularly in the provinces, a candidate might well rent out an inn for the day and give food and drink to anyone who comes by. But this breakfast is for supporters only. We need only write to his election agent and let him know that you wish to follow the banner of Melbury. But in doing so you will declare yourself a Tory and thus destroy any ability to befriend Dogmill—and, very possibly, any chance to interact with him at all on friendly terms. You had better think about this carefully, Weaver. If you truly believe you may advance your ends best by befriending Melbury, that is one thing—but do you wish to risk the gallows so that you might eat some buttered bread with Miriam's husband?"

"I have told you my reasons. Can you deny them?"

"Of course I can deny them. Look at you, Weaver. You've been courting this woman for years and drinking yourself numb in her name for months. And never once has she given you a word of encouragement."

"She has," I told him, feeling myself angering.

"Words then, but no more. She is not available to you now. She is another man's wife. Though the truth is, she was never available to you. She was never going to leave her life of comfort and ease to marry a thieftaker, and you know it. You've always known it. That's why her being married is no impediment to your love for her. It should only make you feel it more deeply."

Elias was the greatest friend I had, so I chose not to strike him. I even bit back the bitter words that came to mind—that he, with his whores and serving girls, was no one to lecture on love—but I knew, angry though I was, that he said what he did because he wished to help. And he knew the risk. I saw his hands trembling.

"My interest in Melbury has nothing to do with his wife," I said again. "I want only to use him for my purposes."

He shook his head. "No doubt, but you gamble a great deal with poor odds. You must become friends with Melbury *and* he must win the election *and* he must then agree to use his newly got powers to rescue you. He may consider it a great deal to ask from a man who once courted his wife."

"In truth, befriending Melbury is only part of my plan."

"Am I to hear the rest?" he asked, like a jealous wife.

I took a deep breath. "We know that Dogmill is of a violent disposition. My plan then is not only to befriend Melbury but also to make Dogmill my enemy. If he hates me, despises me, he will attempt to act on his feelings, and in doing so I may be able to discover something of his operations. Between these two approaches, I can only hope one will lead me to victory."

"You are mad." Elias's eyes went big. "Just a moment ago you were speaking of the danger of incurring his displeasure. Why do you now say you wish to do all in your power to secure it?"

"Because," I said, "if he comes after me, he will be off balance, and that is when I will have the greatest opportunity to discover his secrets. If he plans and plots against me, I will learn how he plans and plots."

Elias studied me for a moment. "You may be correct, but you may also be on the path to destruction."

"We shall see who has more to put forth in the ring, me or Dogmill. Now, the first step will be for me to befriend Melbury."

"I hate your scheme, but I must admit there is some logic in it. Very well, we'll try it your way. I suppose I will have to do some extra work, for I have already made it known that Mr. Evans is a Whig—seen to it that a few lines are planted in the papers and all that. But the damage can be undone, and it should hardly be the first time the papers have made such a mistake."

"Have you made anything else known about Mr. Evans?"

"Oh, a thing or two. For you to prosper in this disguise, people must have some idea of who you are, so I have gone to work in that regard. I should be a poor surgeon in this metropolis if I were incapable of spreading gossip. The hero of my little romance, Alexander Claren, is also quite gifted at the game of gossip. A whisper here and there, you know. I have just this evening penned a rather amusing scene in which he is attending the wife of a barrister who turns out to be the sister of the very woman he once—"

"Elias," I said, "when I am no longer in danger of execution, I should be very happy to learn of Mr. Claren's whimsical doings. Until then, let me hear no more."

"I hope, if I am ever convicted of murder and then on the run for my life, I won't be so dour about it. Very well then, Weaver. I've let it be known that you are recently arrived and have been in the process of establishing your household, but you are now prepared to enter the world. You are an unmarried man of singular success in the West Indies, and you are worth a thousand a year. Perhaps more."

"You do good work. My landlady has already announced my worth to me."

"Gossip is but one of my talents, sir, in addition to penning clever tales. But I shan't tell you about them."

"Unmarried and a thousand a year. I shall find myself using my pugilist's skills to keep the young ladies away."

"It should prove quite diverting, but you would do well to recall that your goal is to return to being Benjamin Weaver, and you should not like to sour your reputation before you do so. Now, if you are going to fulfill this role, you must know something of your background. Here is a bit of authorial musing I believe you won't object to learning of."

He handed me an envelope, which I opened to find three pieces of paper scribbled over in Elias's neat, impossibly compact hand. At the very top he had written *The History of Matthew Evans, Esq.*

"I suggest you study what I have written. You may make what changes you like, of course, but it would be in your best interests to learn the details of your alleged life. If you are intent on making Dogmill your enemy, you may alter all the Whig bits to Tory, but otherwise it should hold. It is far less amusing than the adventures of Mr. Alexander Claren, but it will serve. Learn it well."

"I shall." I examined the first page, which began, "After five years of barren matrimony, Mrs. Evans prayed to the Lord to grant her a son, and her prayers were rewarded one chill December evening with the birth of twin boys, Matthew and James, though James died of a fever before his first birthday." I could see these pages contained perhaps more information than I required, but flipping ahead I found rich detail of Evans's involvement in the tobacco trade. For all its literary indulgences, this document would prove invaluable.

"I thank you for this."

"No need, no need." He cleared his throat. "You might also wish to be advised that I have made certain that word of your presence on our isle will reach men of a journalistic stamp, so you ought not to be surprised if you read of yourself in the papers. All of this should make for a delightful debut at Hampstead."

"Hampstead?"

"The Hampstead assembly will be held in four days." He reached into his jacket and produced a ticket, which he then slapped on the table. "If you wish to reveal yourself to the bon ton, then this will be the place to do so. There is no more agreeable or vivacious event in London society this week."

"The event of the week. How can I refuse?"

"You may laugh if you like, but this is what you must do if Mr. Evans is to meet the sort of people he needs to meet in order to proceed."

"Surely some attendee will have set eyes on Benjamin Weaver at some time or other."

"It is possible. I can only say that had I not known it was you, I should not have recognized you—at least not right away. I suppose I might have thought you looked familiar, but that is all. Remember, this is misdirection. No one is looking for you, so they will not see you. They will see what they expect to see."

"Will you be there?"

"Under normal circumstances I would not have thought of missing it, but I might serve as the agent to make someone recognize you, and we cannot have that. I have, in fact, volunteered my own ticket."

"You are very generous."

"I am," he said. "Though I should point out that I require of you the two shillings that the ticket cost me."

CHAPTER 11

I HAD FAILED to mention to Elias my plans for the following morning because I knew he would have told me I was taking too great a risk. Perhaps I did not want to argue with him, and perhaps I did not want to risk his argument's prevailing over mine. I therefore went back to my rooms, studied the biography he had written for the persona of Matthew Evans, made some adjustments, and contemplated my strategy.

I arrived at Mr. Dogmill's fine house at Cleveland Street just after ten in the morning. Though anxious in the extreme, I did my utmost to conceal my concern. I merely knocked upon the door and presented my card to his unusually tall manservant. The fellow held it in his gloved hands and studied it for a moment the way a pawnbroker gazes at a piece of jewelry offered for evaluation.

"I promise you, he will want to speak with me," I said.

"Any man may make a promise," he said. "Mr. Dogmill is very busy."

"I am certain he has time to speak with a brother of the tobacco trade," I proposed.

The mention of my fabulous business appeared to turn the tide. Donning the slouch of a man surrendering to the inevitable, the servant showed me to a pleasant little room where I was invited to sit in a high-backed soft chair, clearly of French construction. The fellow knew not how long Mr. Dogmill should be nor how much time he might be able to spare for me. I nodded and folded my hands agreeably and gazed down at the intricate Turkey rug on the floor to lose myself for a moment in the swirl of its blue and red patterns. Across from where I sat, over the marbled fireplace, I studied a picture of an aging plump man and his aging plump wife. Dogmill's father, perhaps?

After more than half an hour, I rose from my chair and began to pace. I have never loved being made to cool my heels, as the saying goes, and I found the experience to be, if anything, far more trying when I was in disguise and visiting the very man I believed responsible for every difficulty I faced in the world. How could I know that Dogmill would not recognize me at once? I hardly thought it likely. He might well have orchestrated my ruin, but he and I were not acquainted. He could not know me so well as to spot me in this disguise—at least, so I told myself.

At last the door opened and pulled me from a reverie of exposure and ruin. I turned, perhaps too quickly, but instead of seeing the imperious servant come to lead me to his master, a pretty young lady faced me. She was unusually tall, nearly my height, but neither gangling nor overly plump, as tall women tend to be. Rather, she was most striking in appearance, with dark, almost wine-colored hair and very pale orange eyes. The features of her face were regular and finely formed, though her nose was strong— possessing a rugged beauty perhaps better suited for a man's face than a woman's. I found her appearance most charming, however, and I bowed to her at once. "Good morning, madam," I said.

"George informs me that you have been in here for some time. I thought you might wish for something to make the wait pass more easily." She reached out with a graceful arm and presented an octavo volume. A quick glance showed it to be the plays of William Congreve. How ought I to interpret her giving me a book of plays by so naughty an author? She might easily have offered me a volume of Otway.

"My name is Matthew Evans," I told her, still feeling the tug of doubt at using this nom de guerre.

"I am pleased to meet you, sir. I am Grace Dogmill, Mr. Dogmill's sister."

"Please come sit with me and make my wait more pleasant. I very much like Mr. Congreve, but I think I might like talking with you more."

I had meant to be forward, perhaps even a bit rude. I hardly expected her to comply, but she did just that. Like a proper lady, she left the door behind her open and came and took a chair across from me.

"Thank you for your company," I said, now somewhat softened. My first impulse had been to make Dogmill dislike me by insulting his sister. I now had other ideas.

"I must confess, sir, to something of a wicked tendency to review my brother's appointments when I can. He is cruelly inconsistent in speaking of his business to me—sometimes he will seek my advice earnestly, other times he will refuse to speak to me at all. In those times, I must discover his affairs as best I can on my own."

"I see nothing wicked in your offering conversation to a man with no other diversion. Particularly when he is a man new to the city, and with very little acquaintance as yet."

"Oh?" she said. Her lips curled into a delightful little smile. "Where do you come from, Mr. Evans?"

"I am just this month arrived from Jamaica," I told her. "My father purchased a plantation on that island when I was but a boy, and now that it is grown to self-sufficient status, I have returned to this island from where I come, but of which I have so little memory."

"I hope someone will show you all the interesting sights," she said.

"I hope so too."

"I am blessed with a large circle of acquaintance," she said. "Perhaps we might impose upon you to join us for one excursion or another."

"I should be delighted," I told her. And I spoke the truth. Miss Dogmill was turning out to be a curious creature—strangely forward without seeming improper. I knew I would have to be careful lest I find myself liking her more than would be prudent.

"You are in the tobacco trade in Jamaica?" she asked me.

I raised my eyebrows. "How could you know that?"

She laughed. "You are newly arrived in London and know no one, but you call on my brother. It seemed to me a likely prospect."

"And you are right, Miss Dogmill. I am in the tobacco trade. It is the principal crop of my plantation."

She bit her lower lip. "Mr. Dogmill will be certain to inform you, and perhaps in none the politest way, that he believes Jamaica tobacco inferior to the Virginia that he principally imports."

"Mayhap your brother's opinion is sound, madam, but even the poor must have their tobacco, and they cannot always afford that of Virginia or Maryland."

She laughed. "You are a philosopher, I see."

"No, not a philosopher. Only a man who grew weary of the limitations of island life and sought the fine scenery of London."

"And do you like what you see, Mr. Evans?"

I could not mistake her meaning, so I met her eyes. "Indeed, I do, Miss Dogmill."

"I thank you for entertaining my visitor, Grace," said a voice from behind me, "but you may now return to your affairs."

It was Dogmill standing in the doorway, looking even more massive than he had when sitting in Mr. Moore's coffeehouse. I had thought him huge then, but now I caught sight of his hands, which were so large as to be almost absurd. His neck was wider than my skull. I had spoken manfully with Elias about who would persevere in the ring, but I knew in an instant that I should never want to try my luck with this colossus.

Yet I took some delight in Dogmill's blank and impatient gaze. The contempt he had shown me at the coffeehouse now worked in my favor, for it was clear he had no recollection of having seen me before. Nevertheless, the leg injury that ended my career as a pugilist now began to ache, as if to remind me that I was but a frail thing in comparison to this Hercules.

"I am Dennis Dogmill, sir," he said to me. "You have some business that I presume does not include my sister."

I rose to bow at Mr. Dogmill, all the while keeping my eyes upon his cold face. Here, I had good reason to believe, was the man responsible for every trouble I had in the world. Here was the man who had murdered Walter Yate and made certain the blame fell upon me. Here was the man who had convinced a judge to rule against me at my trial, that I might hang for what he had done himself. I suppose—despite his size and apparent strength—I ought to have wanted to strike him, to knock him from his feet and kick him senseless, but instead I felt a strangely cool dispassion, like a medical man studying some new disease for the first time.

"At this moment, sir, I regret to announce that I do have such business with you, but I can always remain optimistic that the future will hold some more inclusive affairs."

He stared at me for a moment, as though he could not credit his ears. His face was wide and boyish, but for the heaviness and the darkness about the eyes. He possessed what would certainly be called a handsome appearance, but I would have guessed that women were not quick to give him second or third glances. There are some men, no matter how pleasing their countenance or shape, who announce their hardness and cruelty in inexplicable and silent ways. Dogmill was such a man, and I admit I felt a queasy urge to discontinue my plan.

"Follow me, if you please," he said to me curtly.

I offered Miss Dogmill one more bow and smile and followed her brother into an adjoining room, where another gentleman sat reading through papers and drinking from a silver-stemmed goblet. Dogmill took a moment to study this man with disgust.

"I thought we had concluded our business," Dogmill said.

The gentleman looked up. He was young, perhaps in his mid-twenties, with a slightly feminine appearance and an air of confusion I could not judge whether situational or permanent. He smiled broadly, but his eyes would not focus. "Oh, I was just looking through some things," he said, clearly ill at ease. "I had not thought you would be back so soon." The fellow now noticed me and rose to bow, as though he believed I might save him from some awkwardness. "Albert Hertcomb at your service."

I knew from my readings in the political papers that Hertcomb was the incumbent in Westminster, a Whig who would face Melbury in his race for the seat. The Tories decried him for a simpleton, a mere puppet of Dogmill's whims. There was nothing in his easy and open face to contradict those accusations.

I returned the bow. "Matthew Evans," I said. "You are, I believe, running once more for the House under the Whig banner."

He bowed again. "I am honored enough for that to be so," he said. "I hope I may count on your vote, sir."

"You may not count on anything from him," Dogmill said. "He's just returned from the West Indies and has no property here. He won't have the franchise for this election."

"Then perhaps the next election, seven years hence," he said, and laughed as though at the greatest joke in the world.

"We shall see how we are all feeling then," I said merrily.

"Very good, very good."

"Perhaps, Mr. Hertcomb, you might leave me and Mr. Evans alone," Dogmill suggested, not a little irritated.

"Oh, certainly, certainly," he said, oblivious to Dogmill's impatience. "I just wanted to talk a bit about this speech you've handed to me. It's grand, you know. Quite the picture of grandness. Grandeur, I suppose, really. But there is a point or two about which I'm not quite clear, you know. And, well—faith!—it should be a devilish business if I am to give speeches the meaning of which is lost on me."

Dogmill stared at Hertcomb as though he spoke some mysterious language of the American interior. "You are not to give that speech for nearly two weeks," he said at last. "I think in that time you will puzzle out the meaning. If not, we may talk later. As we have been in the habit of speaking every day for the past month, it is a likely prospect that we shall do so again."

Hertcomb laughed. "Oh, very likely, I should think. There's no need to be so sour with a fellow, you know, Dogmill. I just wanted to ask you a question or two."

"Then you may ask me tomorrow," Dogmill said, now with a massive hand on Hertcomb's shoulder. In movements forceful without exactly being rough, he began to shove the Parliamentarian out of the room, but then he stopped and pulled Hertcomb back. "One moment." He let go and pointed a finger—long and thick and unnaturally flat, like a cricket bat—toward an empty decanter of wine. "Did you finish that?"

Hertcomb seemed like a child caught stealing pies. "No," he said meekly.

"Damn you to the devil," he swore, though not at Hertcomb— nor anyone I could see. He then rang a bell, and in almost an instant the same servant who had answered the door appeared.

"George, did I not tell you to fill that decanter?"

The servant nodded. "Yes, Mr. Dogmill. You did tell me so, but there was a bit of confusion in the kitchens with a collapsing rack of pots, and I thought to assist Miss Betty in collecting the mess, who had been slightly hurt, sir, when the pots came a-tumbling."

"You may conspire to get under Betty's skirts on your own time, not mine," Dogmill said. "Get me what I ask for when I ask for it, or you'll know my displeasure." He then turned and, with the same ease that you and I might demonstrate in closing a door or lifting a volume from a desk, he kicked the poor servant in his arse.

I mean that quite literally. The thing of it is, we often talk of kicking this fellow or that in the arse, and it is but a figure of speech. No one ever does such a thing. I have even seen the operation performed in comical stage plays, and part of the humor is the very absurdity of the act. But let me assure my readers that there was nothing comic here. Dogmill kicked the man quite soundly, deploying his toe as a weapon, and the servant's face collapsed into itself in pain. Perhaps because it is something we do not think of happening literally, there was a raw brutality about the act, a cruelty one associates with nasty little boys who torment cats and puppies.

The servant himself let out a cry and stumbled, but I knew that the pain must be more in his heart than his posterior. He had been utterly humiliated before stranger and familiar alike. Me, he might never see again; Hertcomb he must see every day. Every day he would face the Parliamentarian, whose gaze, no matter how kind or placid, would remind him of this utter degradation. I understood well that if he should live another forty years, he would always cringe to think of this moment.

I have seen men abuse their servants, treat them no better than animals, but there was a cruelty here that made me wish to strike back. What have I set in motion? I wondered, as I glanced over at Dogmill's hard face. But I never once considered changing my plans. Dogmill, in all likelihood, had murdered Walter Yate and ordered matters so I would hang for his crime. He might kick every servant in the kingdom before I would run away from him.

"Well, then," Hertcomb said, "I'll be off, shall I?"

Dogmill waved a hand dismissively and shut the door behind him. He then gestured for me to sit with an impatient flick of the hand. "As to my sister," he said, as though we had been before in the midst of a conversation, "do not think to take her prattlings as anything but silly nonsense got from reading too many romances. She speaks thus to everyone and creates all manner of mischief in doing so, but she is a good girl all the same. She is a very good girl, and a man ought never to be caught by me in a mistaken notion concerning her. If you think that because you're a gentleman I'll treat you better than my manservant, you shall be unpleasantly surprised. I spare nothing to propriety where the welfare of my sister is concerned."

There was a tenderness in his voice I found surprising, and though I liked Miss Dogmill, I thought that her brother's affection for her might be a means of exploitation. "I promise your foot shall have no need to seek my arse," I said. "I found Miss Dogmill to be delightful company and nothing more."

He smacked his lips together. "I never asked that you evaluate my sister's company, and your opinion of it cannot be relevant to whatever business you bring here. Now, what is it I can help you with, Mr. Evans?"

I told him what I had told his sister—viz., that I was newly arrived and in the tobacco trade.

"Jamaica tobacco is not fit for a dog. And I have never heard your name before, even in the context of foul Jamaica weed. Who is your purchasing agent?"

"Mr. Archibald Laidlaw in Glasgow," I told him promptly, making use of the name Elias had provided in the fictitious biography he had penned. I was grateful both that he had produced a document of such detail and that I had taken the trouble to read it carefully. I cannot say how I would have hummed and hawed otherwise. "I do not know if his reputation has extended so far south, but I am told he is of some importance in North Britain."

Dogmill turned as red as a Norfolk apple. "Laidlaw!" he cried. "The man is nothing but a pirate. He sends his own cutters to meet his ships when they are still at sea and unloads them there— all to escape the Customs."

Strong words, I thought, considering what Mendes had told me of Dogmill's own practices. Yet I knew well that men can see the faults in others far more easily than they can in themselves.

"I have never met him and know nothing of his practices. I am merely used to selling him my goods."

"You ought," he said, "to sell your goods to a better man, and you ought to make a habit of learning the nature of the men with whom you trade." Here was something else. Though I sat more than six feet away from him, I realized that I felt a sudden and unexpected flash of fear for my safety. I was not used to being afraid of other men, but there was something about the way he sat, his muscles gone taut, that made him seem like a barrel of gunpowder on the verge of ignition.

I should not get what I wanted from him if he sensed my anxiety, so I offered a warm smile, the smile of a merchant who cares only for his trade. "You are certainly right, sir. I have often found it hard to find a purchasing agent in London, where the docks are full of the tobaccos of Virginia and Maryland. It is for that reason, now I am arrived here, that I thought of setting myself upon such a trade. As you are well known as the most respected purchasing agent in the city for tobacco, I had hoped I might impose on you for some advice on navigating the waters of such a business."

Dogmill had begun to redden again. "Mr. Evans, I cannot say how affairs are conducted in Jamaica or in any of His Majesty's other primitive domains, but I can assure you that in London it is no common thing for a man to provide the secrets of his business to a competitor. Did you believe you would walk in here and I would instruct you on how to take money from my own pocket?"

"I had not thought of it in those terms," I said. "I know you do not trade in Jamaica tobacco, so I did not consider myself a competitor."

"I do not trade in Jamaica tobacco because it is ghastly, and I do my utmost to keep it from the ports of London because it is so devilish cheap. I am afraid you will get no help here."

"If you will but give me a moment to explain myself further," I began.

"I have given you too many minutes. Perhaps you are unaware of it, but in this country we have a regular institution known as Parliamentary elections, and as I am the election agent for Mr. Hertcomb, whom you have just met, my time is shorter than that to which even I am used. I must therefore bid you a good day."

I rose and bowed very slightly. "I thank you for what time you have granted me," I said.

"Yes, yes," he answered, and turned to some pages on his desk.

"I should add, sir, that your words are not offered in the spirit of brotherhood. You say that you don't know how we do business in Jamaica, so I will take one more instant of your time to inform you that in Jamaica men of a particular trade, even those whom we might regard as competitors, as you so style it, know the value of the trade itself over the interests of any one man in it."

This was all rubbish, of course. I knew no more how men conducted business in Jamaica than how they conduct business in the most hidden depths of Abyssinia, but I found myself warming to my performance and was of no mind to do anything but indulge myself.

"We work together to strengthen the trade before we work apart to line our pockets," I continued, "and this manner of doing business has served us very well."

"Yes, yes," he said once more. His pen scratched away at his paper.

"I have heard that your trade has dropped off somewhat since your father's time, sir. I wonder if perhaps a more open disposition might not help you to restore your family to the pinnacle of its glory."

Dogmill did not look up, but he ceased his writing. I could see that I had stuck him in his tenderest part, and I could hardly keep from smiling at the trueness of my aim. I might have left then, but I was not quite ready.

"Can it be that there is something else, Mr. Evans?" he asked.

"One more thing," I admitted. "Would you have any objections to my calling upon your sister?"

He studied me for a moment. "Yes," he said at last. "I would object most assuredly."

CHAPTER 12

THAT EVENING, I met briefly with Abraham Mendes and secured two favors from him before returning home for the night. The first was a bit of charity I dared not execute myself. I had not forgotten the good-natured Nate Lowth, whose cell had been adjacent to mine and who had graciously refrained from calling the guard during my departure from Newgate. I therefore gave Mendes a few coins and asked that he provide Lowth with food and drink as well as the companionship he had requested. The second request I made of Mendes I shall speak of more anon.

After returning to my rooms, I spent a few hours before sleep reviewing the political newspapers I'd bought that day, hoping to familiarize myself with the Tory cant. Despite Elias's assurances, I had little confidence that a man as ignorant of politics as I could pass for an interested Tory. On the other hand, I knew well that my standing as a wealthy West Indian would compensate for any flaws I might display, and at least my ignorance was part of the character I was to portray. They might look at me and sneer and think, Who is this fellow to come here and pretend he can simply join our ranks? It is unlikely they would look at me and conclude that I was an escaped felon disguising himself to find evidence of his unjust ruin.

I arrived at the inn shortly before eight in the morning. It was on the east side of Covent Garden, and it afforded me a fine view of the electoral camp set up in the piazza. Though the election was not to commence for more than another week, already the grounds were astir as though it were a great fair, featuring all but fire-eaters and rope dancers. Men in the green and white colors of Melbury or the blue and orange of his opponent, Albert Hertcomb, paraded about, carrying placards and handing out leaflets. Pretty girls strolled to and fro, eager to canvass for this candidate or that. Peddlers pushed their carts through the crowds, and of course there was no shortage of the pickpockets and cutpurses that these gatherings attracted. The cold air smelled of roast pig flesh and oysters just turning foul.

I entered the inn and gave my name to a gentleman who sat by the door. He examined a roster that had been written in a neat hand and then urged me inside. I seated myself at an empty table, but it was soon filled as men of the prosperous sort filed in. Many seemed to know one another, but others were alone as I was. After the first few pots of small beer were served and some fresh loaves of white bread passed around, I began to feel myself warming to the proceedings.

The fellow who sat on my left was a corpulent man, an importer of oriental curiosities, he told me. He praised Melbury for his fairness, his dedication to the Church, and his willingness to speak out against Whig corruption. Indeed, I was able to hear these things for myself, for not long after we ate I noticed a handsome gentleman making his way toward the front of the room, greeting this man and that as he walked. I could not doubt but that this was Melbury, and I felt a kind of panic stir within me. Here was the man who had bested me in the contest I had considered most important. I had never laid eyes on him before, and while he struck me as somewhat ordinary in appearance, lacking any radiance or hint of the divine about him, he also struck me as inexplicably— *worthy* was the word that came to mind—and I felt small and insignificant by comparison.

I hardly even listened to his words as he first spoke, so intent was I on examining his shape and face and the way he held himself. But as I realized his talk was coming to a period, I forced myself out of my reverie that I might at least hear some of his remarks.

"I cannot say that all of the electors of Westminster should vote for me," the candidate announced, by way of conclusion, "only those who disdain corruption. If any of you gentlemen relish that the House should take your money to line the pockets of thieving members and their creatures, if you take pleasure in seeing the Church gutted and weakened, and if you think small men of petty ambition should determine the course of this nation based on their own greed and acquisitiveness, then by all means vote for Mr. Hertcomb. No one here will resent you for it. I thank my Maker that I live in a land of liberty where each man may make this decision for himself. But if, on the other hand, you prefer someone who will fight corruption and Godless deism, someone who will do his utmost to restore the former glory of this kingdom to the days before stockjobbers and debt and disgrace, then I invite you to cast your vote for me. And if you are so inclined to vote that way, I will also invite you to have another glass of beer and to toast this great kingdom."

After the speech, my importer friend lauded his words as though Melbury were a second Cicero. I admit that he proved himself eloquent and had a charismatic quality to him, but I was as yet unmoved to anything but envy.

"You must know," said my companion, "he is ever more personable in conversation. It is a shame that each voter in Westminster cannot have five minutes with Mr. Melbury. I am sure the affair would be most easily decided that way, for if you have ever heard Mr. Hertcomb speak, you know he is little more than a blockhead. Melbury, on the other hand, cannot but show his wit and intelligence."

"I will have to take your word for it," I said, "for I have never met him."

The fellow took most quickly to my hint and promised to secure me an introduction before the breakfast ended. And not a moment later he pulled me to my feet and led me to the far end of the tavern, where Mr. Melbury sat in close conversation with a very grim-looking young man.

"Excuse me, Mr. Melbury, sir, but there is someone I very much wish for you to meet."

Melbury looked up and offered us his politician's smile. I admit he managed it astonishingly well, for—if only for a single instant when I was off my guard—I found him an appealing man with strong cheekbones, a nose that was manly without being large, and vibrant blue eyes. Some men know themselves to be attractive and wear their looks with a sort of arrogance, but Melbury seemed at ease with himself and the world, and that comfort gave him a powerful charm. He had a fashionable bob wig and a handsome blue suit, but, more impressively, he had a fine white smile that radiated a friendship I resented most fervently. I admit that even I began to feel my loathing of the man recede, though I fought hard against these benevolent sentiments.

"Why, hello, sir," he said to the importer, clearly having forgotten this man. No doubt they had once met in very much the fashion he was now to meet me.

"Wonderful speech, Mr. Melbury. Wonderful. Ah, yes. This, sir, is Mr. Matthew Evans, lately returned to this island from the West Indies, and he has now taken a most fervent interest in the Tory cause."

Melbury embraced my right hand in both of his and shook it. "I am heartily glad to hear that, Mr. Evans. It seems to me that your name is now bandied about town, and I am happy to meet so celebrated a personage, particularly when he is a supporter of our party. The returned West Indian is nearly always a Whig, but I am glad to find you otherwise inclined."

There was something of a coolness in his manner that I had noticed at first. His winsome smile and handsome face masked well a hint of reserve that I rejoiced in, for upon it I could place some measure of dislike and resentment. But my role was not to find fault with Melbury nor to delight in exposing a hidden stiffness in his manner—a stiffness not uncommon in members of old families. I was there to make him like me, to make him my ally, and to use his support when he won his election.

"My father was a Tory, and my grandfather fought in the war for the king." Nothing wrong, I thought, in suggesting some Royalist blood. Just the sort of thing to make him take a liking to me. "As

I have been in Jamaica most of my life, I have not, until now, had much opportunity to participate in politics."

He smiled, though I knew a false smile when I saw one. "When did you arrive in England?"

"Only last month."

"Then I must welcome you here with all my heart. And what was your business in Jamaica, Mr. Evans?"

"My father established a plantation there, and I had been involved in running it ever since I was a boy, but as it has become prosperous I have turned the matter over to a trustworthy nephew. Now I am determined to reap the rewards of many years' labor by returning to the land of my ancestors. Though I can hardly recall a time I did not live there, the West Indies offer a most unwholesome climate, and I have discovered that I am, by nature, more inclined to British temperateness."

"Quite understandable. There is something remarkably British about you, if I may say so. The West Indian, I'm sure you know, has the reputation of being without social graces, as he has not had the advantage of our public schools and society. I am delighted to see you explode that myth."

I bowed in response. Here I was, trading pleasant chatter with the man who had taken from me the woman I loved: he with his banalities, me with my falseness.

"I am afraid I must make my way to another appointment just now," he told me, "but I am pleased to meet you, sir, and I hope our paths will cross once more." With that, he stepped out of the tavern into the light of day.

I followed him closely. "If I might have one more moment of your time, sir. Perhaps a private moment."

"I beg you to excuse me for now," he said, as he and his agent quickened their pace. I could only imagine that he must have found himself perpetually hounded by such men as me, and he had clearly grown skillful at dodging their advances.

However, his own advances were suddenly halted by a trio of very rough-looking fellows in undyed clothes and caps pulled down along their faces. One of them carried a blue-and-orange banner.

"Vote for Hertcomb or be damned!" the tallest of them shouted in Melbury's face.

The Tory rose up to his full height and puffed out his chest. "I fear I cannot do that," he said, "for I am Griffin Melbury."

I understood his pride well enough, but this was hardly the most efficacious of all available approaches. Better for his own safety to have agreed to vote for Hertcomb, but Melbury would not swallow medicine so bitter, not for an instant. I admired him for it—a begrudging and resentful sort of admiration, you understand—foolish though it was.

"My arse you're Melbury," another of the ruffians said. "Melbury is a Jacobite devil, and I know a Jacobite devil when I see one."

"I am Melbury, and neither a Jacobite nor a devil, which leads me to question your ability to recognize either on sight. What you ought to recognize, however, is that you have been listening to Whig lies, my friend, and you have been hardly used by men who do not wish you well."

"You're the liar," the large fellow said, "and what you'll be listening to is my fist against your ear."

I suppose I cannot blame Melbury or curse him for a coward because he cringed and held up his arms for protection. Here, after all, were three uncouth ruffians who appeared for all the world to have lost their minds to the fervor of an election not yet commenced and in which they were surely too poor to participate. How could he have defended himself? On the other hand, he might have drawn his hanger and put the blade to the tallest man's throat.

I certainly found that such a course did my business very well. My blade flashed in the sun as I drew it out and pressed it against his flesh, using just enough pressure to keep the skin from breaking. There would be no blood drawn, I was determined.

The lead ruffian remained motionless, his faced pointed upward, the skin of his throat taut. The others took a step back.

"You three don't look like electors to me," I said, "though I honor your desire to participate in this election despite your lacking the franchise. But I must tell you that beating up on one of the candidates will make a poor showing for your cause." I pulled back the blade an inch. "Flee," I said.

They were most obliging. They fled.

Melbury stood nearly motionless, his eyes unfocused, his limp hands trembling. I suggested he might wish to return to the tavern and take a drink before continuing to his next appointment. Melbury nodded his agreement. He sent his agent ahead to his next appointment, and I opened the door to usher the candidate inside. We took a dark table in the tavern, and I approached the barman and insisted that he send over a bottle of strong port without delay.

Once I rejoined him, I knew that the result of the preceding events would be revealed. Melbury might resent me for having shown my mettle while he had shown none, or he might bear me the friendship I deserved for having saved him from harm. To my great relief, he opted for the latter.

"Mr. Evans, I am grateful your business was urgent enough that you chose to follow." He rubbed his hand along the rough surface of the table. "I should have been most vulnerable without your help."

In the thrill of my success I found my resentment of the man, if not quite melting away, then at least receding as excitement of conquest took its place. I had acted boldly, and boldness had been rewarded. That I had been a man of valor while he had cringed was but an added pleasure. "I suspect those fellows were more of the chattering than the pummeling kind, but I am delighted to have been able to serve you in any way, no matter how trivial."

Our bottle arrived, and I filled his glass to the brim.

"I shall certainly do you the kindness of listening to whatever you wished to say before, Mr. Evans." Melbury lifted his glass with a shaking hand.

"I shall be direct with you, then, for I know you have many demands on your time," I began. "We have an enemy in common, and his name is Dennis Dogmill. As Hertcomb's agent, and the mastermind of Hertcomb's efforts to maintain his seat, Dogmill would stand between you and a seat in the House. As a near monopolist in London's tobacco trade, he would stand between me and my business."

"I can only imagine how difficult it must be to conduct your business in a city where a villain like Dogmill reigns supreme as he does," Melbury said. "Have you something to propose that might rectify this situation? I cannot abide the man, and I should love to help you take him down a peg."

I sensed that there was more to Melbury's feelings about Dogmill than he told me. "I propose only that he is a criminal of the worst sort. I am made to understand that he bribes the Customs freely—nay, that the Customs attend more to his business than they do to the Crown's. Inspectors report to him, and the Riding Officers are little more than his personal guard."

"What you are made to understand is well known," said Melbury. "The world is aware of that brute Mr. Dogmill and the Customs, and it knows that Hertcomb has done all in his power in the House to keep the Customs in Dogmill's pocket."

"But can nothing be done about this?" I asked. "Surely the Tory papers could make known this criminal behavior. If the electors of Westminster knew—"

"The electors of Westminster know and don't care," Melbury said, with a note of exasperation. "You saw those men who threatened me. Why would they do such a thing? Is it because they are Whigs in their hearts? I don't think it so. They could probably not tell you the difference between a Whig or a Tory to save their lives—or for a pot of ale, whichever they value more. For them—even for most electors—it is all a kind of elaborate theater, a spectacle. Who has more villains? Whose villains are stronger? Who has prettier girls to kiss the voters? This election is but a spectacle of corruption, and you cannot be surprised that men like Hertcomb are willing to turn the Parliament into yet another stage. Meanwhile, politics becomes a sordid game, the Church and the Crown are made the butt of jokes, and the kingdom becomes more wretched for it."

"Yes, the kingdom becomes more wretched," I agreed, knowing this to be the heart of the Tory concern, "and ought we not to stop that? There is a great difference between hiring pretty girls to kiss voters and Hertcomb's coddling of the South Sea directors. Nothing enrages the public more than the fact that their purses are empty because the South Sea scheme brought a crash to the market, and the Whigs were the ones who protected the men responsible. Is it not incumbent upon prominent Tories to expose how Hertcomb continues to favor these corrupt men—men like Dogmill, who would turn the Customs, the very body meant to regulate his excesses—into his private army?"

Melbury took a breath. "Here's the thing of it, Evans. There's more than one Tory man in the House who looks to be returned there and who has a friendship, shall we say, with importers in London or Liverpool or Bristol. You see, the Whigs may not, precisely, be the only ones who have an arrangement with the Customs, and if a man begins making enemies in one place, he might soon find he has made enemies in another."

"You claim to fight corruption, and yet you countenance it!" I cried, with a vehemence that surprised even me.

I feared I might have angered Melbury, but the candidate took no offense. He only patted me on the shoulder and smiled. "I shall never condone it, and in private I must condemn it, but I may not condemn it too heartily in public and still maintain the friends I need to win this seat. Take heart, my friend. Our cause will prevail, and we shall kick the Dennis Dogmills of the world soundly, very soundly. But this is not the field on which to begin the battle. We have much to do, we Tories. If we win this election, if we can retake the House, I see no reason why we cannot restore the position of the Church in this country. Think only of all the crimes that were once tried in Church courts, that are now tried in civil courts, if they are tried at all."

"It is repulsive," I said, with a creditable amount of feeling.

"These filthy Whigs with their new money and their nonconformists and Jews—they wish to buy and sell this bit of the kingdom or that for whoever has the fattest purse. That Dutchman wants to buy; give him the treasury. There's an Irishman who's amassed some wealth in 'Change Alley; let him buy our laws. All this must stop. We must take power away from sordid greedy men and return it to the Crown, where it belongs."

"I agree entirely, sir. Which is why I wish to see Dogmill restrained. Without him, Hertcomb cannot win."

"He will be restrained, I promise you, he and his corrupting Whig friends. I am grateful that you brought this matter to me, and if you learn anything else of our enemy, I hope you will come see me again. Perhaps the next thing you find will be something we can declare publicly."

"Thank you, Mr. Melbury," I said, rising from my seat.

"It is I who must thank you, Evans," he said to me. "I like you, sir. I like you tremendous, and you may depend that I will not forget the service you have rendered me today. You will discover that it is a fine thing to be my friend."

I bowed in response.

"However," he added, "to be my friend may mean incurring the anger of Dogmill. You must ask yourself if that is a price you are willing to pay."

"You may be sure I shall not shrink from him," I said.

An hour later, I met with the three ruffians as I had done earlier that morning in a filthy Smithfield inn. Mr. Mendes had proved as good as his word and had found these fellows for me—petty thieves and footpads in Wild's service.

"As promised," I said to the leader, "here is the second shilling for your labors."

"You never spoke of blades to me throat," he complained. "You just said you would step in and prevent me from doing harm to that Melbury spark. You never said aught about blades. I thought you was like one of these highborn sparks you hear of who likes to have fun with the likes of us, and you would cut me for certain. I nearly pissed meself."

I knew a plea for more money when I heard one, and though I thought his claims poorly justified, I also knew it never hurts to show generosity. "Here is an extra half shilling then," I said, reaching into my purse. "Had you truly pissed yourself, that would have been worth far more."

He pocketed the coin. "I wish to Christ I'd knowed that. I'd have swallowed a pot before doing the business."

CHAPTER 13

W<small>HEN I NEXT MET</small> with Elias, I told him of my adventures with Dogmill. He shook his head and drank wine with equal verve.

"You must be mad," he said. "I still think it pure destruction to antagonize a man of his stripe."

"He antagonized me first," I observed.

"And now what will you do, set his house on fire?"

"If I thought it would advance my cause, I would not hesitate. But as it might not resolve my problems, I believe I will hold off on that course for the moment. Instead, I think it is time to let Mr. Dogmill know that Matthew Evans will tolerate no ill treatment."

While Elias did not much care for my visiting Dogmill in his home, he would have heartily objected to what I planned next, but I could not defeat my enemy by gentle means. I had already learned enough of Dogmill to know he was not a gentle man, and he brooked disagreement and challenge poorly. It seemed to me most obvious, then, that if I wished to provoke him I would have to challenge him, and I could think of no better place to do so than in public.

I had begun to make it a habit to review the newspapers most frequently, and in one of the Whig organs I noted that Mr. Hertcomb was to host a goose pull at St. James's Park. I did not doubt that Mr. Dogmill would be in attendance and saw this event as a fine opportunity for me to further develop our antipathy.

I regretted that I would have to pay my visit in the same set of clothes that I wore to his house, but as they were not particularly conspicuous in their design, I could only hope he would not notice that I had not changed my suit. I checked my appearance in the mirror and soon convinced myself that I was every bit the English gentleman. I therefore hired a coach to the park and soon found myself milling about with a few dozen Whiggish electors.

Despite an unseasonably warm afternoon with a welcome respite from the rain, only a very few of them were engaged in the advertised event. Most, like myself, had not come dressed for riding, but there were a few men who made eager sport. I must admit that I have never had much of a taste for the kind of cruel games the English play with animals, and a goose pull was among the most base of these diversions. A plump goose was tied by its foot from a high branch of a tree, its neck well greased. Each participant had to ride at top speed under the goose and grab it by its neck. The fellow who could successfully hold on to the bird and wrench it free—or as was often the case, pull its very head off—came home with the prize.

As I approached the crowd, I saw that there were a few ladies in their number who cheered as a fellow rode hard under the goose and made a hearty grab for it. Alas, his might was no equal to the grease of the creature's neck, and though it cried out most pitiably, it would yet receive no mercy.

As another fellow prepared to take his turn, I saw that both Dogmill and Hertcomb were among the men not riding, though Dogmill looked over most wistfully from time to time, as though hungrily gazing at a steaming pie set out to cool.

It was, however, Hertcomb who saw me first and, recognizing me from Dogmill's house, he must have thought me a great friend of his election agent. "Why, it is Mr. Evans, I believe," he said, shaking my hand eagerly. "Very good to see you again, sir, very good, indeed. I hear you are something of a tobacco man, like our Mr. Dogmill."

"Jamaica tobacco, to be sure. And I hear you are a friend to the tobacco man in Parliament."

He blushed, as though I had called him handsome or brave. "Oh, I have done a little of value to the tobacco men. I fought quite hard, I assure you, against that wretched bill that would have forbidden the inclusion of wood and dirt and suchlike into the weed. Imagine the increase in cost if merchants such as yourself had to ensure that every pound of tobacco was nothing but the thing itself."

"Terrible," I said.

"And when they wished to classify tobacco as a luxury item and so subject to taxation, I fought that like a wild cur, I promise you. Tobacco is not a luxury but a necessity, I cried, for do not men spend their silver on weed before bread—and sometimes even before beer? And as it has the qualities of keeping our workingmen healthy and stout, it would be a horrible drug on the nation if these men could no longer afford it in quantity."

"You have quite convinced me, I promise you."

He laughed warmly. "I thank you, sir. I flatter myself I have a certain something with words in the chamber." He looked around the field. "Are you enjoying the pull, sir?"

"If I may be bold, Mr. Hertcomb, I never love sports so cruel to nature's creatures."

He laughed. "Oh, it is only a goose, you know, good only for eating, not petting like a lapdog."

"But does that mean it must be tied from a tree and tormented?"

"I had never thought of it," he admitted. "I don't suppose it means that it must or mustn't. But surely a goose is made for man's pleasure, not the other way around. I should hate to live in a world in which we do things because they are convenient for geese."

"Surely," I proposed good-naturedly, "there is a space between conducting ourselves for the benefit of fowl and conducting ourselves in a way that revels in cruelty."

"Well, I'll be deuced if I know it." He laughed. "I think you would rather vote a goose into Parliament than me, sir."

"I think he would as well," said Mr. Dogmill, who now approached us, jostling aside any man who got in his way. "I have heard that Mr. Evans is a Tory. His being so makes his appearance at my home inexplicable, but not nearly so much as his appearance here."

"I read in the papers, Mr. Dogmill, that all were invited to attend this event."

"Nevertheless, it is generally understood that these events are for electors, and electors who intend to support the party. That is how business is conducted in His Majesty's civilized domains. In short, sir, your presence is not required."

"Faith!" Hertcomb said. "I rather like Mr. Evans. I would hate to see him run off so unkindly."

Dogmill muttered something under his breath but did not trouble himself to address the candidate. Instead he turned to me. "Again, sir, I cannot think what it is you do here, unless you visit in the capacity of a spy."

"An event that shall be written of in the papers hardly requires a spy," I said. "I had heard of these cruel games with animals, but I have never witnessed one for myself and only wished to gaze with my own eyes upon the depths to which an idle mind will sink."

"I suppose you have no blood sport in the West Indies."

I neither knew nor cared if there was blood sport in the West Indies, but such matters were hardly my concern. "Life there is troublesome enough. We require no added brutality for our amusement."

"I suspect a little amusement would help you to ease the brutality. There is nothing quite so pleasing as watching two beasts have at it. And I value my pleasure as a man over the beast's suffering."

"It seems to me," I said, "a rather sad thing to brutalize a creature simply because one can and to call it sport."

"If you Tories had your way," Dogmill said, "the Church courts would be invited to condemn us for our amusements."

"If amusements be condemned," I answered, rather pleased with the quickness of my wit, "it matters little if the court be religious or civil. I see nothing wrong with immoral behavior being judged by the very institution that helps us to remain moral."

"Only a fool or a Tory would condemn amusement as immorality."

"It depends upon the amusement," I said. "It seems to me that the foolishness is to condone any behavior, no matter how much anguish it causes, because someone, somewhere, finds it pleasurable."

I suppose Dogmill might have answered my criticism with little more than his contempt had not a lady with pretty gold ringlets and a wide hat full of feathers not overheard our conversation. She studied me for a moment and then my rival and then fanned herself as she raised expectations as to what comment she might have for us.

"I own," she said to Dogmill, "that I must agree with this gentleman. I find these sorts of gatherings monstrous inhumane. The poor creature, to be teased so before its death!"

Dogmill's face flushed red, and he appeared to feel the greatest confusion. I could not but doubt that a man of his strength and his temperament should find this sort of verbal confrontation unbearable, particularly since his role as election agent precluded taking a more physical stance against me. It was for that reason that I meant to press on.

"You are clearly a lady of great sense," I said with a bow, "to recognize the lowness of this entertainment. I hope you share my horror."

She smiled at me. "Indeed I do, sir."

"I beg you consider that Mr. Griffin Melbury also shares my horror," I added, strongly suspecting that my words would further inflame Dogmill.

They did. "Sir," he said to me. "Walk over this way with me for a moment."

The gentlemanly thing would have been to comply, but the provoking thing was to refuse. Accordingly, I refused. "I think I should prefer to speak of these matters here," I said. "I cannot imagine that there is anything in the treatment of geese that cannot be discussed openly. It is hardly a matter of love or money that requires privacy."

Dogmill could hardly have been more astonished. I do not know that anyone had ever teased him so much in his life. "Sir, I wish to speak with you in private."

"And I wish to speak with you in public. It is a terrible puzzle, for I hardly know how our different designs can be reconciled. Perhaps a state of semi-privacy shall answer our needs."

The lady with the golden hair let out a shrill titter, and the noise was to Dogmill like a blade in his back. Had she been a man, I believe he would have set aside the demands of his public role and struck her in the face without a moment's hesitation.

"Mr. Evans," he said at last, "this is a gathering for supporters of Mr. Hertcomb. As you are not among that number, and as you have done the rudeness of canvassing for a Tory, I must beg you to vacate."

"I am no supporter of the Whigs, but I like Mr. Hertcomb tremendously and support him with all my heart in his other endeavors. And as for speaking kindly of the Tory candidate, I hardly think it so offensive. I would not hesitate to attend one of Mr. Melbury's events and mention how amiable I find Mr. Hertcomb."

Hertcomb smiled and nearly bowed at me, but he thought better of it. He had seen enough to know that he could offer no more public support of me.

"I have heard," I continued, "that you are a man of a violent temperament. And I have seen you behave barbarously toward your servant. You are reputed to be unkind to the indigent and the needy. I see now that you are also unkind to brute creatures, and that may be, for all I know, even worse, for they have not the power to choose their paths. One might look at a beggar and wonder to what degree he elected to eschew a life that would have been more productive, but what choice did that bird ever make to end in such terror?"

"No one," Dogmill said in a coarse whisper, "has ever spoke to me thus."

"I cannot account for what others have done or not done," I said calmly. "I can only account for myself, and I should be ashamed to call myself a Tory and an Englishman if I were to hold my tongue in the sight of this behavior."

Dogmill's face now found heretofore-never-known shades of red. He clenched his fists and kicked at the ground. A crowd had gathered around us as though we fought a boxing match, and I fairly believed that such an outcome was perhaps likely.

"Who called you here?" he demanded at last. "By whose invitation did you come here to disturb our recreation? Has anyone asked for your opinion on the treatment of livestock? I have never before encountered such rudeness, and I can only believe that it is your rusticated ignorance that leads you to speak thus. If any man dared to speak to me in this manner while I was not an election agent in an important campaign, I would not hesitate to treat him as he deserves, but I see what you are about, sir. You have come to provoke me so that the Tory papers will have something to say. They will have no such satisfaction from me."

I glanced at Mr. Dogmill and then to the crowd and back once more at Dogmill. "You have grown marvelous hot," I said calmly. "I had thought we were only having a conversation, and now I see that you insult me in the rudest manner. It is easy for a man to speak of what he would do if he could, but it is perhaps less easy for him to speak of what he will do just now. You say you would call me out if you could, and I say you would call me out if you were a man. If you wish to apologize to me, sir, you may send for me at my lodgings at Vine Street. Until then, I wish you good day, and I hope you may find yourself some superior manners."

I did not look back to witness his perturbation, but I can only imagine it manifested itself in some extreme fashion, for I heard the woman with the golden hair gasp in astonishment, or perhaps terror.

Having had the pleasure of advancing my interests as Mr. Evans, I thought it high time that Benjamin Weaver involve himself in the affair of his own ruin. Elias's idea that I make myself conspicuous in the less seemly parts of town had struck me, in the relative safety of a tavern, as a fine idea. Once trudging through the streets of Wapping, however, I wondered if I had been a fool to attempt so dangerous an endeavor. Any group of eager villains could set upon me in an instant and drag me off to the nearest magistrate, but to do so they would have to know my face and recognize it when they saw it. I hoped the darkness of the streets and a hat pulled low would protect me well enough, at least until I was ready to be seen.

Besides, what choice did I have? There were tasks to be performed, and they could not be performed by a man of Matthew Evans's stripe. So I strode boldly to the house I needed to visit, knocked upon the door, and asked for Mrs. Yate. I kept my eyes cast downward when I spoke to the landlady, but this withered creature, with hardly the strength to turn the doorknob, barely noticed. She inquired of me no name or that I state my business, but only sent me upstairs when I asked for the woman. I could not but suspect that she had some experience in sending men to those rooms. Perhaps, in the absence of her husband's earnings, Mrs. Yate had been forced to turn whore. I wondered, too, how she would react to seeing me come for her. If I could but ask her my questions and leave, I had no doubt that the story of my visit would circulate widely, and so Elias's plan would be executed without my risking my life.

The stairs of the house were broken and treacherous, and those parts remaining intact were often covered with old clothes or piles of newspapers or empty beer buckets. I should hate to have to make a hasty exit from such a place.

The door I sought was on the third landing, and when I knocked a distractingly pretty woman, small in stature but finely shaped, answered without hesitation. She wore a loose-fitting gown that did little to conceal the treasures of her form. Her hair, which tumbled out beneath her bonnet, was so pale as to be almost white, and the features of her face were rounded and delicate. She looked as much a doll as a breathing woman.

"Do I know you?" she asked me. Her voice was sweet and soothing, but it quivered, too, when she spoke. Her eyes, of a gray so dark as to be on the cusp of black, focused on nothing in particular, as though she were afraid to look too much at my face.

"I beg you, allow me in and we shall talk of it," I answered. I had expected her to want more persuading than that, but to my surprise she stood back and let me step inside.

The room was dark, with one lamp lit, but there was enough light for me to see that it was cluttered and ill kept. I could smell old beer and sour wine, and older and more sour clothes. I stumbled my way to an old chair, whose originary legs had all been replaced with mismatched wood, and sat in response to a lazy flick of her hand.

"You do not recognize me now?" I asked her, as I stepped into the light of her single flame. She stared at me while lowering herself into an old barrel that had been adapted into a chair.

"I do," she said. "I do now, and I'm not surprised to see you, for I believed you must come at last."

"I did not kill your husband," I said, holding my palms upward in a gesture of—I don't know what. Something benevolent, I suppose. "I had never met him before, and I had no reason to wish him harm."

"I know it," she said softly. She looked to the floor. "I never thought you had done. I was at your trial and heard all."

"I am glad that you say so, for I would be very grieved if you thought me guilty. You must know that we are all of a single purpose. We both want justice for your husband."

She shook her head. "There can be no justice. The world ain't right, Mr. Weaver. I see that now. I once reckoned it was, but that was just foolishness. A woman like me don't have a chance, and Walter never had a chance neither. I thought he did before. I thought that Judge Rowley was a kindly man to do Walter such a turn, but I see he is no less wicked than the rest of us."

I leaned forward. "I don't understand you, madam. What good turn had Rowley ever done your husband?"

"What good turn? Why, he saved him from the gallows is what he done. Not a year and a half ago, sir, when Walter stood before Rowley on charges of socking tobacco. That Dogmill said Walter took two shillings' worth, though he never done no more than what every man who worked his ships done: collect the gold dust, as they call the loose leaves that fall out of the hogshead. And maybe now and again he'd dip in with his hand, but what of it? That's the way it's always been done—since time immemorial, he always said. But then Dogmill has Walter taken by the constables, and a month later he is facing trial for his life. They wanted to hang him, they did, for two shillings' worth of tobacco scraped from the deck of a ship."

I blinked hard, as though to banish the confusion. "But Rowley sided with Mr. Yate?"

"He did, sir. Dogmill sent a thousand witnesses to lie, sir, saying that Walter was a bad man who wanted nothing but to steal so he could be lazy, but Rowley looked after Walter, the way the law says he should have done for you—but he didn't."

It would appear that Rowley once took his responsibilities as a judge more seriously than he had at my trial, all the more surprising because, in the case of Walter Yate, he sided against a Whig like Dogmill—particularly when it appeared he had sided against me *because* of Dogmill. Could it be that he was less of a political creature then, or that now the imminent election made his obligations to party stronger than his obligations to the law? "Do you have any idea why the judge behaved toward me as he did?"

"I don't have no ideas at all. Not anymore. When Walter got set free by the jury, I thought all was right in the world. We had two little boys then, and my husband was at liberty and clear of the law. But that don't last. Now both those boys is dead and our new baby has no true father, for Walter's been struck down and no one cares who done it."

"I care," I promised her.

"Only because you want to save your own flesh. No, don't make a protest. There's no harm in it. Walter was nothing to you while he yet lived. There's no reason you should trouble yourself of his death but that his death has troubled you."

I looked into her coal-gray eyes. "Walter Yate saved my life. Had he not acted valiantly in his last minutes, I should be dead now too. Finding the man who killed him is more to me than my own safety."

She nodded slowly, as though the news that her husband had saved my life were the sort of thing she heard all the time.

I took the blank look upon her face as permission to proceed with my inquiry. "Did Mr. Yate ever say why he thought Dogmill had decided to pursue him in particular in this charge of socking? It is, as you say, something done by nearly all porters."

She laughed. "It were obvious, weren't it? Walter wanted to rally the men so that Dogmill couldn't abuse them no more. He wanted to make his peace with Greenbill Billy and try to get the wages to rise, but Dogmill wouldn't have none of it. I said to him it were better he worried about his family than the porters, but he said he had to do his duty, and so he put them before us, and he ended up the way I always knew he would. There are things made for great men, and small men oughtn't to bother with them."

"Such things as labor combinations?"

She nodded.

"Did he trouble himself with other affairs of great men? For example, had you ever known your husband to demonstrate an interest in political matters?"

"He said once that he would have liked to have made enough money to pay his scot and lot and then vote in an election."

"But was he involved in any way in the election that has only now commenced?"

She looked down so that I could not see her face. "Not that I ever heard of."

I took a moment to collect my thoughts. "Do you know what has happened to his gang of porters since his death? Have those men joined with Greenbill, or have they found a new leader?"

Mrs. Yate looked up once more, and even in the dim light of the room I could see the blood rush to her face. She opened her mouth but could not speak.

"They will never join with Greenbill," a man called out, answering in her stead, "and so they have a new leader."

I nearly started from my chair. In the darkness of the threshold stood a tall figure, ruggedly built, silhouetted by the cheap tallow that burned behind him. It took only a moment for me to recognize him as John Littleton, looking far more self-assured than he had in Ufford's kitchen.

I half rose and bowed in greeting.

He nodded at me. "Rest assured," he said, rather jauntily, "that Yate's boys will stand firm against Greenbill Billy—and against Dogmill too."

"And whose boys are they now?"

He laughed with an easy confidence. "Why, they're Littleton's boys now. There's one or two other things what were Yate's that are now Littleton's. We do what we can to honor the man." He winked at me with evident humor. Whatever had happened to make him the gang's leader, it had turned Littleton into a new man.

Mrs. Yate met my eyes for an instant, a silent pleading for my understanding. I attempted, by means of my facial expression, to show her compassion, though I fear I only showed indifference.

"Go to the other room, lass," Littleton told the widow. "The baby is stirring and wants its mother."

She nodded and retreated, softly closing the door behind her.

"Good to see you looking so healthy," Littleton told me as he lowered himself into his chair. Behind him, I noticed, were a series of wicker cages that appeared, as I squinted in the dusk of the room, to hold rats. Littleton, I recalled, had mentioned that he earned some coin as a rat catcher. I knew now that he employed that all too common trick of unleashing his own rats that he might be employed to remove them, which a skilled ratman could do with little more than a whistle. Such men could earn a nice bit of silver catching the same rats dozens of times over.

"Good to see you looking so prosperous," I said dryly.

"Aye," he answered. "There are those what would call me callous, taking up Water Yate's place among the men, taking his place with his pretty wife. But someone had to step in, do you see? I couldn't let Greenbill Billy have his way with those boys. Would Yate have wanted that? I don't think so. And I could not let any cruel bastard have his way with Anne."

"You are surely generous," I said dryly.

"I see what's happening behind those shifty Jew eyes of yours, Weaver. You think maybe I helped in getting rid of Yate so I could have his woman and his place too—that I'm a wicked godgel-gut who would take what isn't his any way he can get it. Well, you were there, and you know it ain't true. I had nothing against Yate but that I thought his wife was pretty, and I never fancied myself as leader of the gang until the boys insisted I become so. It was right moving. We sat in a little gin house down by the quays and talked about what would happen next. One fellow stood and suggested we throw our lot in with Greenbill, but he was answered with many fine blows to the face, I can tell you. Then another stood and said that I should lead them, that of all the men there only John Littleton knew aught about labor combinations. I tell you, Weaver, I had a tear in my eye."

"It sounds very stirring."

"Oh, you may mock if you like, but it was powerful touching. And you think it were easy for me? I was beat nearly to death once for standing at the head of a labor combination, and I vowed never again. All I wanted was to earn my shillings so I could eat my dinner and drink my pot. But this is bigger than me. I'll be beat to my death this time if I have to. That's my resolve, so you had better say nothing to me of your suspicions."

"I did not say I suspected anything of you."

"Well, I would if I was you," he said, with a devilish grin. "I'd think me a bastardly stallion, out to get the doxy and the socket. But you oughtn't to, 'cause I had nothing to do with what happened with poor Yate, the Lord rest him."

"Do you, by any chance, know who did?"

"Of course I know who bloody well did. It was Dennis Dogmill, who else? Meantime, Greenbill Billy stands by and laughs because now his gang will be in better shape for the next job, or at least that is what he hopes. But the two of them will run afoul of each other before long, I promise you. It's only a matter of time before Dogmill gives Greenbill what Yate got."

"It may be that Dennis Dogmill had Yate killed; he surely did not come down to the quays and beat the fellow with a metal pipe. Who did?"

"I would not put anything past that one. It could well be he did the work himself, though I haven't heard about it this way or that."

"What about this Greenbill? Might he have thrown his lot in with Dogmill?"

Littleton let out a snorting sort of laugh. "Not likely, friend. They may both of them rejoice to see Yate dead, but they could hardly have come to terms on the execution of such a monstrous deed. Of course, anything is possible, isn't it. And now that I think on it, I haven't heard of Greenbill showing his poxy marketplace in the past couple of weeks."

"It seems as though he may be hiding, then."

"He might be doing just that."

"Any thoughts on where a fellow like that would hide?"

"Might be anywhere, you know. This basement or that garret. So long as he has a punk to fetch his food and drink for him, he don't need to see the light of day for a while, now, does he?"

"And if he is not guilty of killing Yate, why should he fear to see the light of day?"

"He might be guilty of far more—or far less, for that matter. Just different, is all. Most likely, if you ask my opinion, he's afraid that what killed Yate will get him next. Dogmill, he might reckon, will want to do away with the both of them, and the gangs be damned."

"I think perhaps I shall go looking for him. If he suspects Dogmill is after him, he might have good reason for thinking so. Any thoughts on where to begin looking?"

"Well, you might try asking around the Goose and Wheel. Those are Greenbill's boys there. They won't be too happy to give you much information about him, though, not if he don't want to be found. They will, however, be happy to beat you over the head and take you to the magistrate for the bounty. But you know your business."

"I do."

"Well, if I hear anything of Greenbill, I'll be sure to let you know. Where can I get a message to you?"

I laughed. "I will find you in a little while. You can tell me what you know then."

He returned the laugh. "You can trust me more than you think."

I nodded, but I had not lived so long by believing anyone who spoke such words.

CHAPTER 14

I HOPED I could find this Greenbill Billy, who was surely the creature of my true enemy. For the moment I assumed that person to be Dennis Dogmill, but as I could not pursue that line of inquiry, I chose the only one available to me.

I waited until nightfall and then headed to the docks and to the Goose and Wheel tavern. The space was fortunately lit with few candles, and the interior was a stew of filthy bodies and foul breath. The sick, sterile smell of gin had permeated the tables, the benches, the dirt floor, and even the walls. Only the wholesome scent of tobacco made the air breathable.

I approached the barman, an unreasonably tall fellow with narrow shoulders and a nose that looked as if it had been broken once for each year of his life. Though I have no love for the drink, I ordered a gin lest I draw more attention to myself, and sipped it cautiously when the pewter pot was set before me. At a penny a pint, the barman had still chosen to water it down.

Sliding over a coin for my liquor, I nodded at the barman. "You know Greenbill Billy?"

He stared at me hard. "Everyone knows Billy. Except you, which means you got no business with him."

"I don't think he would say as much. He'd thank you for pointing me in his direction. You know where I can find him?"

He sneered. "Nowhere, for the likes of you. What do you want anyhow, coming in here with your questions? You with the constable's office? You want to make us look fools?"

"Yes," I said. "That is why I came here. Particularly, I wanted to make *you* look the fool. I believe I am succeeding quite admirably."

He narrowed his eyes. "Well, you ain't no coward, I'll say that for you. How about you tell me your name and where you can be reached, and if I see Billy, which I may or may not, I'll tell him you was looking for him. How does that sound to you?"

"That sounds to me like I'll never find Billy." I dropped a pair of shillings into my pint of gin and slid it back toward him. "Surely you can think of some way I might reach him."

"Hmm. Well, I don't know precisely. He's been scarce the last week or so. I heard he's hiding out, that the law or some like is after him. But maybe his woman knows."

"Where do I find her?"

"On her back, most like," he said, and guffawed heartily at his own joke. After a moment, he contained his mirth. "Lucy Green-bill is her name. Has a room in the cellar of a house over on the corner of Pearl and Silver streets. It ain't where Billy lives, but they ain't truly married in the more legal sense of these things, though she took his name as if she were. But she'll know where he is as well as anyone and better than some."

"Better than you, to be sure." I said.

"I done my best. What's your name, anyhow, in case he comes looking for you?"

I thought of what Elias had said, of the advantage of being seen in such places. "My name is Benjamin Weaver," I said.

"I heard that name somewhere before," he said.

I shrugged and began to take my leave, a bit disappointed that my fame was not sufficient for him to have known the name at once.

"Sod me!" I heard him shout after a moment. "That's Weaver the Jew. Weaver the Jew's here!"

I don't know if anyone heard him over the din, but I was outside and three streets over before I dared to slow down.

Keeping to dark and snowy streets as best I could, I made my way to the house where the barman had told me I might find Lucy

Greenbill. I did not bother to knock on the door, in no small part because I doubted that it would withstand so forceful an effort on my part. Here was one of those old houses, rushed into standing after the great fire of 1666, that year of wonders. These buildings, thrown together so awkwardly, now appeared perpetually on the verge of toppling. The pedestrian passed them at his own risk, for they shed bricks the way a dog sheds fleas.

I pushed open the door and found a foul space, cluttered with the bones of long-ago meals, a full chamber pot, and rubbish of all sorts strewn about. There was but one lamp lit, and I heard naught but silence except for the rustle of rats among the refuse. I could only guess that no one was home, but I wished to take no chances. For that reason, and to give my eyes a moment to adapt properly to the darkness, I moved with deliberate slowness. Soon I found the stairs, and I began to make my way downward.

Here my best efforts at stealth were squandered, for I could do nothing to keep silent as I moved down these old and creaky boards. I could with more ease have descended a set of stairs made of dry bread crusts, and as I feared, my movements betrayed me. Someone stirred down there. I saw a small light and smelled the smoke of cheap oil.

"Is that you?" I heard a woman's voice cry out from below.

"Mmm," I agreed.

As I descended, I could see that the decor of the upper rooms was shared by those below. Trash everywhere, torn broadsheets, a pile of soiled linen.

The cellar was but a single room, not particularly large. The floor was of dirt, and there was little enough on it: an old straw mattress, a single chair, a table with no legs on which the oil lamp sat. Mrs. Lucy Greenbill lay on the mattress, wearing, I might add, nothing at all.

Lest my reader think this tale about to turn as salacious as the scandalous works of Mr. Cleland, I should observe that she was none the most attractive of women—far too thin, with bones jutting out this way and that from her flesh, which, despite her lean frame, hung loosely in those places it was not stretched. Her eyes were enormous, such as might have been stunning on a more vibrant face, but she had the look of a gin drinker, so they were sunken deep into her skull. This pitiable creature had all the signs of those made slaves to that vile liquor: Her nose appeared shriveled and flat, her skin dry and lifeless, so she looked more the death's-head than the temptress. But even if her shape been more pleasing to the eye, I believe her actions might have undone nature's good works, for she lay there picking over clothes, piled off to one side of her naked form, and plucking off lice. She then proceeded to put them in her mouth, snap them between her teeth, and spit out the bloody skins.

"Don't be too long now, Timmy," she said.

"Timmy," I repeated. "Surely Mr. Greenbill would be surprised to hear of you lying without clothes and awaiting someone called Timmy."

Lucy bolted upright and prepared to scream, but I knew better than to let her. I leaped over from the stairs and, with a quick hop, found myself on the floor next to her with one hand over her mouth. A flash of pain shot through the old wound in my leg, but I bit my lip and determined to show no weakness.

"I realize this is an awkward position for you," I said, trying to sound more menacing than distressed, "and I will allow you to dress yourself, but you must promise not to make noise. You've seen I move quickly, and I will be upon you in an instant if you defy me. Before you decide to utter another sound, you must choose whether you would prefer to conduct our business, which I promise will do you no harm, with or without clothing on your body."

I did not wait for her to respond. I merely let go and allowed her to back up hurriedly and toss her gown over her head, which she wiggled into most quickly. Now that we were both more comfortable, she moved over to her legless table and reached out with one shaking hand for a pewter cup, which from the sharp scent of it was filled with gin.

"What do you want?" she asked me, as she took a swig hearty enough to fell a man of my size. In the light of the oil lamp I could see her face more clearly. Her cheekbones were pronounced but her jaw slack, giving the impression that the lower part of her face was but an empty bladder that hung upon the upper. When she spoke I could see she had but few teeth in her head, and those were broken or filed down almost to the root. And there was a deep scar on her left cheek, which had been hidden from me upon my entry to her room—a massive *H,* carved by a thick blade.

"Who did that to you?" I asked.

"My husband," she said defiantly, as though daring me to find some fault with a man who would carve letters into his wife's flesh.

"Why would he do such a thing?"

"To mark me for a whore," she said proudly. "Now tell me what you want."

"I want to know where I might visit this honorable husband of yours." I discovered myself unwittingly rubbing a hand against my aching shin and stopped at once. "He is proving a difficult man to find."

"He'll kill you for coming in here, and he'll do worse if you think to do me injury. And for all that, who are you?"

"My name is Benjamin Weaver," I said.

"Oh, Jesus save me!" she cried, and took another step back. She clutched her pewter gin cup to her breast as though for a moment confusing one savior with another. "You'll kill him, won't you?"

I took a step forward to match her retreat. "Why should I do that?"

"That's what you do, ain't it? You kill porters. Everyone says you are Dennis Dogmill's man, and you come to kill those who stand against him."

"You would be wise not to listen to everyone. They are none the most truthful sources. If Billy wishes to resist Dogmill, he will find no better friend than me."

"Then what do you want with him? You ain't looking for him to become a friend."

"I want to ask him some questions."

"What if he don't want to answer?"

"I find that most men I put to the question choose to answer sooner or later."

"Like Arthur Groston?"

I felt a chill run through my body. I forgot at once about the pain in my leg. Why should Billy Greenbill's wife have heard of my dealings with the evidence broker? "What do you know of him?"

"That he's dead. That you killed him."

I struggled to control my surprise. "Last I saw Groston, he was healthy enough. Who told you I killed him?"

"Marry come up, everyone says it's true. They say you held his head in a pot of sir-reverence until he drowned."

"I did not drown him, but I did stick his head in a shit pot."

"You tell me that and you think I'll let you know where Billy is?"

"I'll find him in the end," I said. "You may depend on it. If you are the one who tells me where to find him, I'll make certain you are compensated for your efforts."

She took a more restrained drink from her mug. "How is that, compensated?"

"For one thing," I said, "I won't mention Timmy to him. For the other, I will give you some silver."

She blinked at me. "How much silver?"

Why quibble? I thought. It was, after all, the judge's money, and I knew it would take a mighty sum for her to overcome her fear of angering Greenbill. "Five shillings," I said.

I might as well have offered her the kingdom of the Incas. She put a hand to her mouth and pressed the other against the wall for support. "Show me," she whispered.

I reached into my purse and retrieved the coins, which I held out in my hand for her. And so she traded her lord for my silver. If she noticed any parallels to the behavior of certain figures in her scriptures, she did not choose to mention them to me.

Billy Greenbill, she had told me, was staying in the garret of a house only a few blocks away on King Street. I thought it sound to wait until it was much later, for I had no intention of walking in on Billy and his friends while they were awake. Therefore, I found a quiet spot by the river and merely sat, with one hand on a pistol at all times. No one disturbed me, though I heard the rustling of footsteps once or twice.

When it was far into the small hours of the morning, closer to dawn than not, I returned to the house Lucy had indicated and quietly forced open the lock. All was quiet and dark, as I had hoped, and I made my way up the stairs as soundlessly as I could manage. At the very top, the entrance to the garret, I made ready with my blade and gently tested the door. It was, mercifully, unlocked, so I gently turned and forced open the door.

There was but one candle burning. Had there been more, I should have been alerted to the scene that awaited me. But I had the door open and I had taken preliminary steps before I realized what lay there for me. A half dozen men, each with blades and pistols, were awake and sitting on chairs. And grinning.

The door shut behind me.

"Weaver," one of them said. "I wondered what was taking you so long."

I glanced at him. He was my age or older, with an unshaved face and thick lips that made him look the result of an unholy union between a laborer and a duck. "Greenbill Billy," I said.

"At your service, or I should say that you are at mine." One of his men rose and took from me my sword and both my pistols. None the most thorough, these fellows did not think to examine my legs for any extra blades I might have on my person.

"I presume," I said, "that Lucy was advised to tell me to come here."

"Exactly. We've been waiting for you for some days now, and I can tell you that we're glad you've come, for we've been getting as mad as shitters from sitting in this room."

"And now you plan to capture me and collect your reward?"

"That would be preferable, but if we have to kill you we'll do that too."

"Why?" I asked. "What am I to you that you would have to go to such lengths to harm me?"

Greenbill grinned, and even in the dark I could see his teeth were a horror. "Why, what you are to me is a hundred and fifty pounds, that's what. Now, what are the condolences that you'll come with us all quiet-like while we bring you to the magistrate and collect our booty?"

"And what shall pass if I don't?"

"If you don't, we can take you there with blood coming out of your head as much as not. Now, do you think you'll come along nice and easy?"

I shrugged. "I made my way from Newgate before. I don't doubt I will do so again."

He laughed. "You're mighty sure of yourself, ain't you? But that's their problem, not mine, so let's be on our way, shall we?"

It is a poor thieftaker, I have found, who requires weapons to defend himself. Weapons are always preferable, but if a man must use his fists to save his life, he ought not to hesitate to do so. Two of his men approached me, no doubt with the intention of each taking an arm. I allowed them to think I would submit, but when they were positioned just as I liked, I caught the arm of each under my own armpits and pressed down and then jabbed upward sharply with my elbows. I caught both in the face, and they reeled backward.

Billy wasted no time. He raised his pistol at me, so I reached out for one of his compatriots who, having realized that the situation was not to his liking, had just begun a dash for the door. I grabbed him by his shoulders and spun him toward Billy that I might turn this coward to a human shield. Billy either had not the time to check his fire or did not care to do so, for he sent a ball into his friend's shoulder.

Certainly it boded well that in the space of a few seconds I had dispensed with three of the six men. I could only hope the next few seconds would unfold so favorably. With his pistol fired, Billy, for the moment, was without protection, so I rushed at him, but one of his attendants jumped on my back to pull me down. It was not the most effective technique to use in a deadly fight, but it served the purpose of allowing Billy to dash for the door. My assailant was now riding atop my back, one arm crooked across my throat to suffocate me. I backed up hard into the wall, but he was still not dislodged. If anything, he strangled me with added fury, so I repeated the same move, trying hard to hit his head. I did so with ample force this time, for the fellow slid off me and to the floor, where he joined the ranks of his wounded comrades.

Billy and his remaining unharmed companion were nowhere to be seen. They had either fled for their lives or gone to fetch reinforcements. I could hardly afford to wait around if they were to raise the hue and cry, but I did not dare let so ripe an opportunity pass without learning what I could. One of the men whose faces I had smashed lay on his side, curled and whimpering. I gave him a nudge with my foot to let him know that I was now interested in having a discussion.

"What is Billy's interest in me?" I asked.

He said nothing, and having little time to misuse, I attempted to find some more persuasive method of questioning. I placed my foot on his throat and repeated the question.

"I don't know," this fellow said in a raspy voice, full of bubble and froth. I could only guess that I had done some damage to his teeth, perhaps his tongue too. "The money."

"The money? The reward money?"

"Yes."

"Did Billy kill Yate?"

"No, you done that."

"Who is Johnson?" I had asked this question so many times, I despaired of ever receiving any sort of answer, but here I found myself quite surprised.

"I don't know his real name," he told me.

"But you know who he is?"

"Of course I know who he is. Everyone knows who he is."

"Not everyone. Tell me."

"Why, he's an agent for the Pretender, of course. No one knows his real name, but that's what they call him."

"Who calls him that? Who?"

"In the gin houses. When they drink to the true king's health, they drink to his health too."

"And what's he to do with me?"

"How should I know your business better than you do?"

I could not but allow that it was a good question.

Below I heard the scuffle of feet, and a watchman's whistle blow. I could ill afford to waste more time with this fellow, so I hurried down the stairs as best I could while making certain that Billy did not lie in wait for me. But he had gone to look for safety. I would have to find some other way of tracking him down. And I had other things to concern myself with as well. For example, I wished to know why, at my trial, whoever had hired Arthur Groston to produce witnesses against me had wanted to establish that I was an agent of the Pretender. It seemed clear to me now that my conviction for killing Yate was but one part of a much larger scheme in which my name and my life were to be destroyed forever.

Having narrowly escaped with my life and liberty, I was in no mood that night for more ill news, but I discovered upon returning to my rooms that my day was not yet done. A note awaited me, and it indicated the most urgent revelation.

I had not thought anything of Greenbill's wife's words, but it would seem I was remiss in my dismissal. The note I received was from Elias, who had received word from a fellow surgeon. Apparently Elias's friend had been asked by the coroner to examine the body of Arthur Groston, who had been found murdered— presumably by Benjamin Weaver.

CHAPTER 15

Eᴌɪᴀꜱ'ꜱ ɴᴏᴛᴇ proposed a meet-
ing for breakfast. I knew he believed the situation dire if he
thought it worth his while to rise early in the morning, so I was
prompt in meeting him at the agreed-upon time. He, alas, was not
quite so punctual, and I was drinking my third or fourth dish of
coffee by the time he arrived.

"I'm sorry to have kept you waiting," he said, "but I was up
frightfully late last night."

"So was I," I said. "I had a rather inconveniently timed ambush."

"Oh. Well. That does sound unpleasant. But look here—er,
Evans—there's something of a situation with this Groston business. He was murdered, you know, and the whole world is aware
that you—which is to say that Weaver fellow—had something
against him."

"I had less against him than whoever hired him—and I will
surely find it difficult to learn who that was now. How was he
murdered? He was not drowned in a privy pot, was he?"

Elias looked at me doubtfully. "I must say, in all my years as a
surgeon, I have never before had that particular question put to
me. As it happens, no, he was not drowned in shit. Is there some
reason for thinking he might have been?"

I decided not to illuminate him. "How did he die, then?"

"Well, I've a friend who is often tapped by the coroners of London and Westminster to examine bodies that may have been mur-
ders. When he came across Groston, he thought it best to contact
me, knowing of our friendship. The body had been sitting for

some days before discovery, so it was in none the best shape for examination. Nonetheless, the surgeon had determined that someone struck Groston repeatedly in the face with a heavy object, and then, once the fellow was down, strangled him for good measure. It was a bit brutal."

"And your friend thought you should know simply because I spoke of Groston at my trial?"

"No, there was more. You see, a note was found by the body. He was good enough to copy it for me."

He handed over a piece of paper on which was written: *I bin jimin weever the jew done this god bless king james and the pope and grifin melbrey.* I handed it back to Elias. "You must be certain to thank your friend for having corrected so much of my spelling."

"Gad, can you not be serious? This is all rather grave."

I shrugged. "I don't believe Groston had any more information for me, so I cannot claim to be sad at his death. As to the note, I hardly imagine that anyone might believe me to have authored this gibberish. Whoever wrote this must be remarkably dull."

"Or?" Elias said.

I shifted in my seat as his point became clear to me. The note was *too* dull, *too* absurd to convince anyone. "Or remarkably clever, I suppose. You are suggesting that it might as well be a clever Tory as a brutish Whig."

"No one but the most excitable roughs will ever believe that you would write a note blessing the pope. No real plotter, certainly no real Romish plotter, would do such a thing. But what if Groston was killed in order to create the illusion of a conspiracy?"

"So the Tories kill him, and make it look like the Whigs killed him in an effort to harm the Tories. That is a mighty deep game."

"Probably too deep for the Tories. They are, after all, but a political party, and not the sort of men to engage in this level of mischief."

I understood his meaning. "The Jacobites?"

"Hush," he snapped at me. "Don't speak that word so loudly in my presence. I'm a Scot, don't forget, and easily a target for accusations. But yes, I do believe they may be behind this. Whigs and

Tories may well do a bit of rioting and wrecking, and things may get ugly when they get angry with one another, but cold-blooded murder is, as yet, not a party tool—not even in election time. Some of these Jacobites schemers, however, are a bit bolder. If they believe that causing the Whigs to lose a seat in Westminster might inspire the French enough to fund an invasion, you may be sure there is no shortage of men willing to bash the faces of a hundred Grostons rather than let the opportunity slide."

"Why mention me at all? Jacobites are no friends of the Jews. Do you not find all this a bit unusual? The Whigs have always been criticized for their excessive toleration of Jews and nonconformists, and the Tories have always railed against Jews and dissenters gaining too much power."

"I don't think it signifies anything but opportunism," he said. "Piers Rowley, a Whig appointee, unjustly made certain of your prosecution, and you defied him by escaping. No one could have predicted it, but you have become an anti-Whig rallying cry whether you wish to be or no. And you know how the English are. If they decide they want to hate Jews one minute and embrace them the next, they will do so and never notice their hypocrisy."

"Damn these plottings," I murmured. "First the white rose that Groston gave me, and now there is more." I told Elias about my encounter with Greenbill and his gang, and of one of the porter's underlings informing me that Johnson was a well-known Jacobite.

"It would seem," Elias said thoughtfully, "that someone sought to implicate an alliance between you and the Jacobites even before your trial became a political cause. Who would want to do so? Not the Jacobites, surely."

"No," I said. "My enemy must be someone who hates me and Jacobites equally."

"Once again, we must turn to Dennis Dogmill," he observed. "And once again, we cannot even say why he should wish you ill, nor can we say who the woman who aided your escape might be. There are still far too many questions, Weaver, and no answers."

"I like it no more than you. I cannot even think what I must do next."

He shrugged. "You might hope they don't kill anyone else in your name."

"But they will," I said. "And I know whom they will kill too."

His eyes widened. "The witnesses against you from the trial?"

I nodded.

"But why? What harm can they do?"

"I don't know, but they can be killed without disturbing anyone of note, and their deaths can easily be blamed on me."

"Weaver, you seem to be facing far more than you can handle. This is by several degrees more severe than the death of a laborer. There is something at work here that smells of a genuine assault against the nation. The Jacobites are gathering their forces, and they are using you to screen themselves. You must go to the ministry and tell all. They will protect you."

"Are you mad? It was the government's party that condemned me to death and set all this in motion. For all I know, it is the government itself that wanted to link me with the Jacobites. And even if there are not powerful Whigs behind all of this, if I should choose to go to them now, how can I know they won't pin the conspiracy on me? They might happily hang me at Tyburn and count their votes without troubling themselves to wonder who is guilty and who is not. You know full well they might prefer to take advantage of the moment than actually see justice served."

"Yes, yes. You are right, there. They would gladly string you up so they could point to you and say, *Here is a Jacobite plotter. We've proven the threat is real.* So what will you do now?"

"Find the witnesses first and be there when the killer comes for them."

I hated once more to call on Mendes, but circumstances were such that I had no choice, and as there were lives other than my own in the balance, I thought it improper to stand upon ceremony. I therefore wrote to him, asking that he meet me at his rooms that night—with the request that he send his reply to a coffeehouse I had previously designated. When I went to retrieve my messages I found that Mendes had written back, indicating that he did not believe it would be safe for us to meet at his home, and instead asked me to lease a room in the back of a tavern of my choosing, and then let him know when and where. I took care of this task immediately and sent him the information, though I was now on edge, for I could not think why his rooms would not be safe. Had someone discovered our previous meetings? Did an enemy of mine keep Mendes under surveillance?

I would have to wait to learn. At the appropriate time I changed out of my Matthew Evans costume and then slipped out the window into the alley. It would have been far easier, and far safer, simply to stroll there like a gentleman, particularly since the papers reported that Weaver had been seen in some of the more unpleasant parts of town. But even though Mendes had proved himself a most worthwhile ally, I could never think of confiding all my secrets to him.

I was glad I had taken the precaution, for I soon discovered I had trusted Mr. Mendes perhaps more than I ought. When I walked into the room I had rented, I found him waiting for me, but he was not alone.

Jonathan Wild was by his side.

Until the time he met his fate at the end of a hangman's noose, I don't know that Wild ever came as close to death as he did at that moment—and I include in my reckoning the incident in which Blueskin Blake famously stabbed him in the throat. In an instant I had kicked closed the door and withdrawn a pistol from my pocket. I came within an inch of discharging it directly into his head.

But I paused. I believe it was the look on Wild's face: one of utter composure. It suggested to me that either Wild had not come to harm me or he had come so fully prepared to harm me that he had nothing to fear. In either case, I was eager enough to avoid adding another charge of murder to my troubles that I hesitated.

"Put it away," he said to me, as he drank from his pot of ale. "If

I wanted you taken, you'd have been taken by now. As it is, you're of far more use to me free than you would be in chains. And you're sadly mistaken if you think a hundred and fifty pounds is enough to turn my head."

I lowered my pistol and approached the table. Mendes had already produced me an ale. "You've nothing to fear," he said.

"Then why didn't you tell me you were bringing him here?" I asked Mendes, still not ready to sit.

Mendes remained impassive. With Wild around, he was no longer his own man but the thieftaker's puppet. I would get nothing from him. "He did not tell you," Wild said, "because you would not have come."

It was true enough, but it did not, in my mind, excuse the deception. Still, I had no one to blame but myself. As much as I should have liked to have trusted Mendes, I knew he was Wild's creature, and I could not be surprised that he would bring his master to meet me. The only question remaining was why.

Wild had about him a manner that was so comfortable and at ease that any man who showed himself to be anxious must think himself pitiable. This great thief had the strange ability to make every man believe in his corrupt authority, and I found that, though I knew what he was, I believed it too if I was not careful. I therefore clenched every muscle in my body in resolve to resist his strange charms.

"Let us not trouble ourselves with these niceties." I held myself straight in the effort to create a false authority of my own, but the thin smile on the thieftaker's lips told me that I had not done a very good job. "I have been uneasy with your involvement in my troubles since your appearance at my trial."

"Have you?" he asked. His features were so sharp and angular, I thought they should shatter under the pressure of his smile. "Would you be easier if I had spoken ill of you, as you had no doubt anticipated?"

"I should have been less surprised, certainly."

"I am sorry to have surprised you, but I should think you would be more grateful. I set aside whatever differences we might have had in order to do you a good turn. You and I are used to scrambling after the same prize—or, worse, being opposed to each other. But in this matter I am your greatest friend."

"I am under no illusions that you did so for any reason but to serve yourself. Mr. Mendes has made me aware that you have no love for Dennis Dogmill, and you relish the idea of my doing him harm."

"True enough. I suspected his involvement the moment I heard Yate was dead. And Mendes tells me you have no knowledge of the woman who passed you the housebreaking tools. Is that right?"

"I still believe it was your doing," I said, though I was not sure I did.

He laughed. "You may believe it if you like. It must certainly make you angry to think me that much involved in your rescue. But I had no hand in that little scheme."

I shook my head. "Then what is it you want? Why have you come here?"

"Only to offer you assistance, Weaver. Faith, I am no friend of the Tories, any man can see that, but this Dogmill and his lapdog Hertcomb are a plague upon my business. I should support Cardinal Wolsey if he ran against Hertcomb and made Dogmill his enemy. I thought for certain that this race was all sewn up for those villains, but then you come along and make the situation far more interesting. So long as you are running about town, knocking over ruffians and searching for the truth, it is good news for me. For that reason I am happy to assist you."

I spat out a bitter laugh. "And if I should fail, good riddance to me. If I should succeed, you imagine I will be in your debt."

He tilted his head just slightly, a mild gesture of agreement. "You have always shown yourself a reasonable man, Weaver. I have no doubt that a good turn done now might yield some fruit in the future. So I have come to see what I can do for you. Some money, perhaps?"

I scowled in contempt. I would not have Wild offering me money like a generous uncle. "I have no need of your money."

"It spends quite as well as another man's, I promise you. But as to your means, your judge-thieving methods seem to work out quite nicely for you. Though I must say that Rowley has always been a pliable fellow. I am sorry to see you've driven him into convalescent retirement."

"I'd always believed him reliable as well. Why should he turn on me as he did?"

"It is an election season," Wild said complaisantly. "They were dangerous enough when elections were held every three years. Now that they are every seven, the prize is worth a great deal more, and men will go to far greater lengths in support of their party or, I should say, their interests. Rowley only did what was required of him by Dogmill. There is no more to it than that."

"I don't know," I said.

Wild turned to Mendes. "It appears that our friend has been corrupted by his encounters with the South Sea men. Now he believes everything deeper than the appearance. You'll never clear your name if you look for hidden plots and intrigues. The answer is on the surface, I promise you. It is but Dogmill's greed."

"And what can I do about it? Dogmill has power over every judge in Westminster."

"I hardly know what to say," Wild said, with a mischievous grin. "What are you doing about it now?" When I said nothing he added, "Other than killing fellows like Groston, I mean."

I shifted uneasily. "That's why I wished to see Mendes. I didn't kill Groston."

"Never laid a hand upon him, I suppose."

"I gave him what he deserved, but no more than that. But whoever is behind Groston's death will surely move against the two witnesses who testified against me at my trial."

He nodded. "Mendes should be able to track them down without difficulty. Would you like to speak to them when we find them?"

I nodded. "Yes. I won't have these sods killed just so that my enemies can pin more deaths upon my chest. And there is always the chance they might have information that could be of use."

"Then we shall find them straightaway," Wild assured me. We

next took a moment to figure a means whereby they could contact me. "Is there any other way we might serve you?" he then asked.

I was now full of regret that I had trusted these men so far as I had, but these were trying times and I would resolve the tangles I made in the future. "No," I said. "If you do that, it should suffice."

CHAPTER 16

As ELIAS had promised, news of Matthew Evans's alleged arrival appeared in the *London Gazette* and a few other papers of note, so even while the Whig papers condemned Benjamin Weaver as a murderer and the Tories defended him as a maligned victim, the Tory Tobacco Man was making his glorious debut. While villains murdered men in my name, I remained a fugitive, and it struck me as almost frivolous that I had to see to the obligations of my private masquerade.

Nevertheless, this was the path I had chosen and I had no choice but to proceed. That night I arrived at the Hampstead assembly promptly at ten o'clock. I was a bit early, but I thought it best to be so that I might be noticed.

The room itself was gorgeous, a great domed assembly hall full of sparkling gilt chandeliers, bright red furnishings, tables of food, and a sparkling white-tiled floor. Already the space was filled by enough people that my presence would not prove conspicuous. Near one end, the musicians played adequately and dancers moved gaily across the floor. A crowd gathered around the banquet table, on which raisin cakes and sliced pears, shrimps pickled with prunes, and other dainties had been set out with great care. At a more crowded table, men gathered to collect punch for themselves and their ladies. Over on the far side of the hall was the entrance to the card room, where older women, chaperoning their daughters and wards, retired to amuse themselves while the young frolicked. No such closeting was required for older men, who were there as much as the younger to seek matrimonial companionship or, at the very least, to pretend to be engaged in such a quest.

I had circled the room twice before I heard my name called out—or at least my false name. It was called two or three times before I responded, not yet having grown used to the sound of it, and then I found myself surprised. Who, after all, knew me to call that name? But when I turned I saw none other than Griffin Melbury, who was standing with a small group of people.

"Ah, Mr. Evans," Melbury said, taking my hand warmly. He continued to radiate the patrician reserve I had detected at our last meeting, but it seemed to me that I had earned his trust with my little ruse. I returned his embrace and forced myself to wear a mask of pleasure.

And forced it was. I felt a clammy revulsion as I touched him. Here was the hand that touched Miriam—touched her as only a husband can. For an instant I thought of crushing his flesh, of pounding upon him, but I knew this urge was both irrational and impolitic. So I maintained my smile instead, though the falseness of it made my flesh feel heavy and doughy.

"I'm glad to see you again, Melbury."

"I wondered if you might not be here. I know you are new to town, so there are some people I should like you to meet." He then began a dizzying array of introductions—to priests and old monied men and the sons of earls and dukes. I would have found it a challenge to repeat these names moments after they were given, let alone so many years later. But there were a few of these people whom I found remarkable at once.

First, he pulled me off to one far side and introduced me to a man I had already met. "This," Melbury told me, "is my great enemy, Mr. Albert Hertcomb."

I shook Hertcomb's hand, and he smiled agreeably at me. "Mr. Evans and I have already met. Sir, you must not look so surprised," he told me. "You must not think Mr. Melbury and I need be uncivil because we compete for the same seat in Parliament. After all, you and I can be friendly with each other, and we are of different parties."

"I own that party need not rule all things or men, but I confess that I am surprised to see you on such merry terms."

Melbury laughed. "I rejoice that things are not so grim that I must hate a man simply because he vies for the same prize I do."

"Faith," said Hertcomb, "I have never felt animosity toward any man, even if he be what is termed a political *enemy*. To my mind, an enemy is but a man who is opposed to me, and nothing more."

"How would another man define the word?" I asked.

"Oh, much more harshly than I do, I am sure. But I don't care to trouble myself with this word or that. A political man is, after all, not a doctor of rhetoric."

"But you must make speeches," I proposed.

"Of course. The speeches are the very thing in the House, but they're not about words, you know. They're about the ideas behind the words. That's what matters."

"It is good advice," Melbury said. "I shall be certain to remember it when I assume my seat. Ha-ha."

Melbury then excused us, and he pulled me with a little too much force to one side. "What a fool," he whispered to me, as we moved away. "I cannot say that I've ever met such a dunderhead above the station of shoeblack. It takes an idiot like that to have Dogmill as a sponsor."

"You presented a very different opinion to the man himself," I said, taking some delight in my unveiling of his hypocrisy.

"In truth, I have something of a fondness for Mr. Hertcomb. He is a simple man, and in all likelihood he means no harm. It is Mr. Dogmill, his agent, I object to."

I could not have asked for a better introduction to a topic of such import. "I get the impression he has no love for Dogmill himself."

"It shouldn't surprise me. I have never met a man less deserving to be loved. I tell you, I cannot abide that man. I long to serve the House in Westminster, I don't deny it. I am a patriot, Mr. Evans, in the truest sense of the word. I want only to do good for my kingdom and my Church. I want only to see the men whose families have built up this island—old families like ours, whose fathers have bled in defense of the realm—retain their rightful place. I cannot love to look upon true Englishmen robbed of their influence by a pack of Jews and stockjobbers and atheists. But when I win my seat, I will relish it all the more for taking the power away from Dogmill. I want to destroy him, to grind him into the dust."

I did not try to hide my surprise. "I honor your competitive spirit, sir, but are these sentiments not beyond the normal bounds of politics?"

"Perhaps so. I confess to you that I am prone to hatreds. I do not hate many men in this world, but those I do I hate with passion—some with good reason and some, I admit, for little reason at all. But Dogmill—he is a species unto himself. I lost a bit of money in that South Sea Company confidence game; many of us did, of course. But there were some friends of Dogmill's family on the board, and he directed Hertcomb to shelter them, to use all the influence he could muster in the House to protect these criminals. I ask you, sir. Is it not contemptible for a man to use the full power of the government merely to look after the business of his friends?"

"I admire the strength of your feeling," I said, though I felt certain there must be more to this animosity than Dogmill's wade into the Whiggish pool of corruption.

"You know nothing of the strength of my feeling. I tell you, there are some days when I am exhausted from my work, but the thought of dashing Dogmill's hopes invigorates me and makes me feel like a man who has slept ten hours."

"Is there nothing more to this rage than that he directed Hertcomb to shelter South Sea men?" I found this hard to believe. There had to be some other root to this anger, and discovering it might well aid my cause.

"Why, is not that enough? He is a villain, sir, one of the worst kind. I believe I would rather die than lose to him."

After a moment, I said, "I honor your determination, sir, and promise you that I shall do all in my power to see that you take your rightful place."

"I appreciate that, Mr. Evans, I do indeed. For the moment, I shall only inform you that the most expedient thing you can do in my cause is to cast your vote for me."

"I fear I cannot. I must remind you of how recently I am arrived on this island."

"It appears to me," he said, "you have forgotten that you established a residence here long before you arrived, and as you have paid all sufficient taxes on that residence, I think you will find your name is in the register of voters, as it should be."

Clearly Melbury had used his influence to add my name to the books. I could not imagine that I was the only voter he had illegally added. If he had managed to insert so many as a hundred men into the register, it could make the difference in a tight race.

"How can you manage such a thing?" I asked.

"As for that, it is nothing. I have more than my share of contacts with the men who order these matters, and I may owe one or two of them a few pounds incurred at play. If I owe a man a small debt, he is more inclined to make things go my way, as it shall make me more inclined to pay him. It is nothing more complicated than that."

"I have never before heard that debts of honor could be deployed so effectively," I told him, "but you will have my vote with all my heart."

He smiled and shook my hand and led me back to his party. Hertcomb had been joined by Dennis Dogmill and his sister, and the three of them made some small chatter together. I flatter myself that Miss Dogmill's face brightened upon seeing me.

"Why, it's Mr. Evans, the Tobacco Tory," she said.

"The lover of geese," Dogmill said, with a kind of ease only to be found among those born with wealth. He sounded both furious and calm at the same moment. "For a Tory, you seem to find yourself in Whiggish company often enough."

"In Jamaica, we never fretted so about party," I explained.

"All those years in the sun," Dogmill proposed, "explain your swarthy complexion."

I laughed agreeably, for I thought doing so would anger more than a show of irritation. I even felt an undesired kinship with Melbury in our mutual dislike of this brute. "Yes, in that clime, one cannot be squeamish about the sun or working under it.

Many's the day I had to inspect my fields and my laborers in heat that you of this temperate land cannot even imagine."

"Did you not cover yourself," Miss Dogmill asked, "as I have heard men do?"

"The ladies always keep themselves covered," I said, "and so do many men, but I found the feel of the sun on one's body one of the few pleasures the island's clime had to offer, and some days I would strip to my breeches as I made my way about my lands."

I would not have my reader think I spoke so boldly always to ladies, but she had asked her question with an unmistakable twinkle in her eye, and I knew at once that she wished me to further tease her brother. I hardly needed more encouragement, and though she now blushed, she clandestinely winked to show that she had taken no offense.

"Did you also put a bone in your nose like the natives?" Dogmill asked me. "I've been to the colonies many times, to find that in a place where it is often hot enough to cook an egg on the sands of the beach, English rules of propriety often don't apply. But as they apply here, I should inform Mr. Evans, lest he embarrass himself further for his ignorance, that it is not considered polite to speak of stripping to your breeches in the company of ladies."

"Don't be such a blockhead," Miss Dogmill said sweetly.

Her brother, however, turned a bright red, and his massive neck began to stiffen with anger. I thought for a moment that he would strike out—at me, at her, I hardly knew. Instead he smiled at her. "A brother can never be said to be a blockhead if he acts out of concern for a sister. I may know a thing or two more things than you, my dear, regarding the rules of propriety—if only because I have been alive for more years than you."

I found that when I stood in Dogmill's company, my mind raced to think of the most stinging reply to anything that ventured from his mouth, but here I could only keep quiet. There was an unexpected kindness in his voice, and I understood that no matter the harshness of his behavior, no matter what crimes with which he had dirtied his hands, no matter the cruelty with which he had struck down Walter Yate and caused me to stand in his stead before the law, he truly cared for his sister. I should have been busy attempting to determine how best to put this weakness to use were I not under the impression that I cared for his sister too.

The band now struck up a new piece. Miss Dogmill looked over my shoulder and observed that the floor was now crowded with dancers, and unless I was mistaken there was a gleam of yearning in her eyes.

"Perhaps, then, I might invite you to dance with me," I proposed.

She did not even look to her brother. She offered me her hand, and I led her out to the dance floor.

"I am afraid Mr. Dogmill is not overly fond of you," she said, as we glided along to a pleasing bit of music.

"I hope that does not make *you* disinclined to be overly fond of me," I said.

"It hasn't yet," she said merrily.

"I am glad to hear that, for I am fond of you already."

"We have only just met. I hope you will not begin your protestations of love before our dance is complete."

"I have said nothing of love. I hardly even know you well enough to like you. But I think I know you well enough to be fond of you."

"What an unusual response. But I must say that I like it. You're very honest, Mr. Evans."

"I endeavor always to be honest," I said guiltily, for I do not believe I had ever in my life been so false to a woman I admired than I was to her, pretending to be a man I was not with means I did not have.

"That may not always serve you well. There has been much talk of you among the ladies, you know. It is far enough along into the season that the arrival of a new man with a fortune to his name is bound to excite interest. If you are honest with all of them, you will not make many friends."

"I think a man can be honest without being unkind."

"I have known very few who were capable of it," she said.

"I think your brother has yet to master that skill."

"You are certainly right there. I don't know why he dislikes you, sir, but I must tell you his behavior toward you is mortifying."

"If that mortification played any role in your agreeing to dance with me, I would gladly endure the barbs of a thousand brothers."

"You are beginning to sound like an untruthful man, sir."

"A dozen brothers, then. No more."

"I do believe you would be more than a match for them, sir."

"Have you lived with your brother alone for long?" I asked, in an effort to change our subject to something more material.

"Oh, yes. My mother died when I was but six years of age, and my father some two years later."

"I am sorry to hear of your early losses. I can only imagine the grief you must have endured."

"At the risk of sounding unfeeling, I must tell you that it occasioned far less grief than you might suppose. My parents were of the habit of sending me off to school from the earliest age and, before that, of leaving me in the care of my nurse night and day. Upon their deaths, I understood that people materially close to me had been taken, but I hardly knew either better, sir, than I know you now."

"Your brother seems some years older than you. I hope he proved a more tender parent."

"Tenderness is not his great strength, but he has been good to me always. I knew nothing of a home life until after our parents died. He continued the practice of keeping me away at school until the school pronounced me too old to keep, but I was welcome home during holidays, and Denny was always happy to see me. He even came to visit me at school three or four times a year. After I completed my education, he told me he would set me up with my own home if I wished, but he would prefer that I lived with him. In truth, he was very kind to me once, and I shan't ever forget it."

"Just once?" I asked.

"Well, once particularly. Many times, I suppose, for, if I may be honest with you, I was when I was younger inclined to be fat. Very much so, in fact, and the other girls at my school were cruel to me."

I could scarce believe it, for she had now a shape of very pleasing proportions. "Surely it is now you who is being hurtful to Miss Dogmill."

"No, I was an enormous girl until I was sixteen. Then I became very sick with a fever that put me to bed for more than a month. Every day the doctor despaired of my life, and every day Denny sat by my side and held my hand. He could hardly bring himself to speak, even on those occasions when I spoke to him, but he was there all the same."

I could not join her in admiring a man whose greatest contribution to the world has been to sit in silence by a sister he presumed to be dying, but I did not tell her as much. "Such events can often yield a great closeness," I said dutifully.

"Well, I recovered after some time, and I suppose it was all for the best. I have found I like being of a smaller frame more than I like seedcake. And Denny has been very protective of me ever since. I don't know if I would have chosen to live in the same house with him, had it not been for that dreadful month."

"And have you found sharing a house with him an agreeable arrangement?"

"Oh, mightily agreeable. It is a large enough house that we need not see each other but when we want to. And though Denny may be a fiend in the world of business and a cruel opponent in politics, he is a kind and indulgent brother."

"He is not, then, one of those brothers who wishes to marry off his sister as early as he might conveniently do so?"

"Oh, no. My domestic affairs would be far too much trouble for him to attend. He did make a halfhearted effort to see me married to Mr. Hertcomb, but my brother better than most men knows what a simpleton he is, and though he thought the match might make good political sense, he chose not to force the issue."

"I cannot but feel sorry for Mr. Hertcomb to see so great a prize slip through his fingers."

"I don't believe the prize was ever close to his fingers, but he fancies himself to be quite in love with me, and will occasionally mortify me by making amorous protests that are both absurd and embarrassing. I cannot see why men continue to press their case when a lady has made her position clear. It is the most troublesome thing in the world."

I winced at the memory of my many proposals of marriage to Miriam. "Perhaps a gentleman must ask many times because it is the habit of ladies to be coy."

"Mr. Evans, I believe I have stung you," she said. "Is there some lady who has refused your many proposals? Some mulatto beauty, perhaps, who rebuffed you under a coco tree?"

"I only defend my sex in the face of cruel assault," I said. "Where shall we men be if we do not offer to take up for one another?"

The music ended, and I saw she was smiling at my quip. "Before I return you to your friends," I ventured, "I must ask you if you would be willing to allow me to call on you at your home."

"You are welcome to call on me, and I will do my best to make you feel at your ease, but I remind you that it is Mr. Dogmill's home too, and he may not be so happy to see you as I."

"I may change his opinion of me yet," I said to her.

She shook her head, and something like sadness darkened her face. "No," she said. "You won't. There is no changing his mind. Not ever, and not for an instant. His stubbornness is the greatest curse of his life."

When we returned to the little gathering, I saw that Mr. Melbury was facing away from me in close conversation with a woman who was blocked almost entirely from my view. I thought nothing of it, but when I grew closer, Melbury turned to me and put a hand on my shoulder.

"Ah, Evans. Here is someone I want you to meet. This is my wife."

When I considered the matter later, I was unable to say why it had never occurred to me that Miriam would be at the assembly. Certainly it seemed to make sense that she would be there with her husband. But the thought never once came into my head. I had grown so used to not seeing her that the idea of a face-to-face encounter would have struck me as being on the verge of an absurdity.

Miriam held out her hand to me, but she hardly even looked me full in the face and by no means recognized me. She might never have done so—she would have given my face a casual glance and forgotten it even before she had seen it—had I not stared most inappropriately, almost daring her to meet my eyes. Why should I have done such a thing? Why would I not have allowed us to pass and be done with it? I cannot say for certain. In part, it was surely because I wanted her to see me. I wanted her to face what had become of me. But there were more practical reasons too, I believe. It was far better that she recognize me now and that I be there to monitor her reaction. What if she should wake up in the middle of the night and suddenly realize who this man was who had been deceiving her husband? Once out of my sight and out of my control, she might become the greatest threat imaginable to my masquerade.

So I looked at her hard and without blinking until she looked back. She appeared to notice nothing unusual but then, after an instant, her lips quivered and then parted. She began to say something, but then she merely smiled crookedly. "How nice to meet you, Mr. Evans. My husband tells me you are very capable of handling the Whig ruffians."

I nearly blushed at her reference to my little fiction. No doubt she now believed I had brought all of my pugilist's skills to bear in the rescue of her husband, though she was perhaps curious about the coincidence. Nevertheless, I assured myself, Miriam had more than once seen me act quickly when the London streets turned dangerous, and I did not believe she could have suspected the truth behind that incident. "I merely encouraged some low fellows to move along," I said.

"How—" She stopped and stared at me for a moment, as though imploring me for help. But she must have seen that there would be none coming, so she began again. "How are you liking England?"

"I like it very much," I assured her.

"Mr. Evans is that rarest of creatures," her husband said to her with a happy little smile, "a Tory tobacco man." It was the warm, syrupy smile of a man who loves his wife. I should have liked to have struck him in the face with a hammer.

"A Tory tobacco man," Miriam repeated. "I should never have known."

An awkward pause formed and I knew not what to do, so I did perhaps the most incorrect thing imaginable. I turned to Melbury. "Sir," I said, "might I impose upon your good nature and ask your wife to dance with me?"

He stared at me in astonishment, but he could not very well deny my request. "Of course," he said, "if she is feeling up to it. She did not feel well earlier." He turned to her. "Do you feel like dancing, Mary?"

I suspected that Melbury had made up this lie on the spot to give Miriam a way out, but I knew she would not take it. "I am well," she said quietly.

He smiled his politician's smile. "Then by all means."

And so we were off on the dance floor.

We danced I don't know how long before either of us found the courage to speak. I could not say what the dance meant to her, but I found it the strangest thing to hold her in my arms, to smell her scent, to hear her breath. I could, for a mere instant at a time, convince myself that this was not a fleeting moment but my real life and that Miriam was mine. Suddenly, Elias's proposal that I flee the country appealed to me. I could take Miriam with me. We would go to the United Provinces where my brother lived quite well as a merchant. And then Miriam and I could dance every day if we wished.

But I could not entertain this fantastical notion for long. I would not flee from this country. And I knew Miriam would not flee with me.

I felt the pain of not being able to cling to my illusion for more than an instant, so I said perhaps not the kindest thing in the world. I said, "Mary?"

She did not look up. "It is what he calls me."

"I suppose the name *Miriam* sounds too Hebrew for his taste."

"I cannot endure to have you judge me," she hissed. And then, in a somewhat kinder voice, "What are you doing here?"

"I am attempting to restore my good name," I said.

"By insinuating yourself into my husband's life? Why?"

"It is complicated. It is best I don't say more."

"You won't say more?" she repeated. "You must know that I will have to tell all of this to him."

It took all of my strength to keep dancing, to keep acting as though nothing had changed. "You cannot tell him."

"Can you imagine I have a choice in it? He is standing for Parliament. I had thought it passing odd that your name should begin to be associated with his party in the papers, but now I understand it is but some scheme of yours. You may plot what you like, but if your deception should be revealed, the scandal will ruin him, and I will not permit it. Can you think to involve him in your business of mutilating judges and murdering evidence brokers?"

"I did with that judge no more than I had to and no more than he deserved. And I hope you know me well enough to understand that I've murdered no one. As for my connection to your husband's party, if you think I have arranged to become a Tory hero, you give me more credit than I deserve. I have become so because the judge who sentenced me against reason is a Whig of some importance. I have done nothing to encourage the notoriety that now follows me but decline to remain in prison."

"That will hardly help Mr. Melbury if it is learned that he has become the particular friend of an outlaw."

"I don't give a fig for Mr. Melbury or his scandal. If you tell him who I am, do you know what will happen? He will be obliged to turn me in to the courts. I did not escape from Newgate because the accommodations were not to my liking. I escaped because they intended to hang me by my neck until I died, and if I am recaptured that is precisely what will happen. You seem mightily concerned about Mr. Melbury's reputation and not nearly concerned enough about my life."

She said nothing for a few minutes. "I had not thought of that," she said. "Why have you put me in this position? Why did you have to come here?"

"I promise you I never intended to make things awkward for you. All I want is to find out who killed Walter Yate and who arranged for the judge to all but order the jury to find me guilty. Once I learn these things and can prove them, I can have my life returned to me. Until then, I will do what I must."

"I don't understand why what you must do involves passing the time with Griffin Melbury."

"You needn't understand," I said.

"If you are working against him, I shall never forgive you."

"Do you think you might cease thinking of me so skeptically? I will tell you this much, if it will put your mind at ease. My true enemy is Dennis Dogmill—I know that with near certainty. If I can use your husband to get what I want from Dogmill, I will do so. That he will surely benefit from my efforts is but a consequence. I tell you, I mean him no harm."

"I believe you. I wish I could believe, however, that your meaning him no harm means that you will allow no harm to come to him."

"I will not value his well-being over my own, Miriam, even though he be important to you."

"Do not call me that. It is not proper."

"Mary, then."

She let out a sigh. "You must call me Mrs. Melbury."

"I will call you no such thing," I said. "Not so long as I am in love with you."

She began to pull away, and if I had not gripped her tight, she would have left me on the dance floor. I could hardly permit that to happen, and after her initial struggle she seemed to understand that abandoning me in anger might well ruin me forever.

She therefore took a different approach. "If you say that to me again, I shall leave here at once and let you offer what explanation you may. I am married now, sir, and not a fit object of your affection. If you have regard for me at all, you will recall that."

"I do recall it, and I will not speak of the depth of my regard so long as you understand it."

"I am told that there is some depth to your regard for Miss Grace Dogmill as well."

Here I could not but laugh. "I did not expect jealousy."

"It is hardly jealousy," she said coolly. "I merely think it unkind to court a young woman, regardless of her reputation, if you are not serious in your regard."

I decided not to pursue her barb regarding Miss Dogmill's reputation. Perhaps because I knew she was right: It *was* unkind of me to pursue her, regardless of how frivolous the pursuit. How could I be fair to the lady when I was unable to tell her so much as my name? "Miss Dogmill and I understand each other very well," I said, in an effort to make myself seem less cruel.

"I have heard something of her ability to reach understandings with gentlemen."

The music being over, I had no choice but to end our dance. Miriam and I had exchanged some hard words. We had fought and we had each said unkind things. Though she was yet married, I somehow could not but rejoice in what I believed to be a considerable success.

CHAPTER 17

THE NEXT DAY I made my way to a local coffeehouse and began my now-usual ritual of scanning the papers to learn what they had to say of me. The Whig papers were full of tales of Benjamin Weaver and his murder of Arthur Groston—murdered, it was suggested, as part of a plot orchestrated by both the Pretender and the pope. I should have found the accusation laughable had I not understood that most of the Englishmen who heard these claims did not find them so very absurd. There was no bugbear as frightening as the pope and his schemes to take away British liberties and replace them with an absolute and totalitarian regime, such as that which governed France.

The Tory papers, however, cried out with rage. No one but a Whig or a fool—which is much the same thing, they said—could believe that this note was authentic, that Weaver would leave a penned confession with the body. The anonymous author claimed to have corresponded with me in the past—certainly possible—and could assert that both my spelling and style were superior to those found in the murderous epistle. Someone, he claimed, though he stopped short of saying who, wished the world to believe this was a plot against the king when it was truly a plot against Tories.

It is, in general, an odd thing to reach some measure of fame and see one's name bandied about in the newspapers. It is quite another to see oneself turned into a chess piece in a political match. I should call myself a pawn, but I feel that does some disservice to the obliqueness of my movements. I was a bishop, perhaps, sliding at odd angles, or a knight, jumping from one spot to another. I did not much like the feel of unseen fingers pinching me as I was moved from this square to that. It was in some ways flattering that this party or that might want to make me its ally or even its enemy. It was quite another that men, even unsavory men, might be killed in my name.

Such were my thoughts when I noticed that a boy of eleven or twelve years called out a name Mendes and I had chosen to use. "I ain't to ask your true name," he told me when I tipped him, "but to ask you if you might be expecting something from Mr. Mendes."

"I am."

He handed me the paper, I handed him a coin, and our transaction was finished. I opened the note, which said the following:

> B.W.,
>
> As you requested, I've made some inquiries, and I'm told you may find both men living in the same house, one belonging to a Mrs. Vintner on Cow Cross in Smithfield. Such is what I have heard, though I must tell you that my source all but came to me and struck me as overeager to provide the information. In short, you may find yourself being lured to this location. I leave it to your management. Yrs., &c,
>
> Mendes

I stared at the note for some minutes, all the while suspecting that the person who was luring me to this location was Wild himself. Nevertheless, I felt confident that with a bit of caution I might be equal to whatever trap was laid for me. Consequently, I returned to Mrs. Sears's house and transformed myself once more from Evans to Weaver. I then took myself to Smithfield and, after making an inquiry or two along Cow Cross, found the home of Mrs. Vintner.

I spent some time circling the premises to determine if anyone might have it under a watchful eye. I saw no sign of this. Certainly, enemies might lurk inside, but I would cross that bridge, as it is said, when I came to it.

I knocked upon the door and was greeted by an elderly lady who appeared both cheerful and frail. After a moment of conversation in which I ascertained that the two men, Spicer and Clark, were within doors, I felt confident that if ruffians or constables lay in wait for me, this lady knew nothing of it. She struck me as a simple, kindly woman incapable of duplicity.

I therefore followed her instructions to the fourth floor and waited for a moment before knocking upon the door. I heard no creaking of the floors, no shuffling of bodies. I smelled no amassing of bodies. Again, I felt confident that I might walk into the room without fear of attack. I therefore knocked and was told to enter.

When I did, I found Greenbill Billy waiting for me.

"Don't run," he said quickly, holding out a hand as though to stay my fleeing. "There's none here but me, and after the pummeling you gave my boys last time, I don't have any inkling to try to take you myself. I only want a convocation with you, is all."

I looked at Greenbill and tried to read his expression, but his face was so thin, his eyes so far apart, that nature had already affixed upon him a permanent countenance of astonishment. I knew I could not determine any more on top of that. I also knew, however, that if he wished to speak with me, it would be on my terms.

"If you want to talk to me, we'll go somewhere else."

He shrugged. "It's all analogous to me. Where shall we go, then?"

"I'll tell you when we get there. Speak not another word until I address you." I grabbed his arm and pulled him to his feet. He was very wide in his frame but surprisingly light, and he resisted me not at all. With him in advance that I might monitor his motions, I marched him down the stairs and through Mrs. Vintner's kitchen, which smelled of boiled cabbage and prunes, exiting at the back of the house, which opened onto a little lane. There were no signs here that anyone watched us or planned to move against me, so I pushed Greenbill out to Cow Cross. My charge went merrily, with a silly grin upon his face, but he said nothing and questioned nothing.

I took him to John's Street, where we hired a hackney with relative ease. In the coach, we continued on in silence, and the hackney soon brought us to a coffeehouse on Hatton Garden, where I shoved Greenbill inside and immediately hired a private room. Once we were secured with our drink—I never even entertained the idea of trying to obtain information from him without providing for his thirst—I chose to continue our chatter.

"Where are Spicer and Clark?" I asked.

He grinned like a simpleton. "That's the thing, Weaver. They're dead unto mortification. I heard it this morning from one of me boys. They're lying in the upstairs of a bawd's house in Covent Garden, with notes about their bodies saying you done it."

I remained quiet for a moment. It could be that Greenbill had concocted this story, though I could not imagine why. The question was how he knew and why he cared to tell me of it. "Go on."

"Well, word come down that Wild put it out that the two of them were to be found, and it didn't take no clever thinking to realize who it was what wanted to see them. So after I heard they got killed, I thought I'd sit up in their rooms and wait for you myself. Not to take you for the bounty; I won't try that again, I promise. No, though I tried to play you a decrepit turn before, I hoped I might now ask for your help."

"My help in what?"

"In not getting killed, mostly. Don't you see, Weaver? Folks you don't much care for or who done you wrong since your trial are getting killed so as it can be blamed on you. As I laid ambush on you, it seemed to me I'm next."

There was a certain logic to what he said. "And you want what of me? That I should protect you?"

"Nothing suchlike, I promise. I don't know that you and I could much endure the confabulation of the other. I only want to hear what you know and think and see if that will keep me alive—or if I'll have to leave London to effect that end."

"You seem to know a great deal about all of this already. How were Spicer and Clark killed?"

He shook his head. "I hadn't got those details. Only that they was killed and you were meant to have done the killing. No more than that. Except—" He looked off into the distance.

"By gad, Greenbill, this is not a stage play. Don't think to be dramatic with me, or I'll show you your bowels."

"Now there's no need for longitude. I was getting to it. With the bodies and the note they found a single white rose. If you know what I mean."

"I know what you mean. What I don't know is how you have all this information if you did not kill them—or Groston and Yate."

"I got ears with which to be licentious, don't I? I got loyal boys who tell me what they think I ought to know."

I smiled. "How can you be so certain I didn't do what these notes claim?"

"It don't make sense, is all. You come hunting me down before to see what I know about it. Hardly seems to me that you done it."

"And who do you think *has* done it?"

He shook his head again. "I haven't any ideas whatsoever. That's what I wanted to ask you."

I studied his face in an effort to measure the degree of his dishonesty, for I could not believe that he was entirely honest in his claims. And yet I saw no reason not to proceed. "I cannot prove what I say, but it is my belief that the man behind the death of Yate, and therefore the other deaths, must be Dennis Dogmill. To my reckoning, there can be no other man who would want to see Yate dead and who would want to create havoc to be blamed upon the Jacobites—and the Tories by extension. Dogmill gets to remove Yate and promote the election of his man, Hertcomb."

"Ha!" He slapped his hands together. "I knew it had to be that villain. He's had it out for us gang leaders all along, you know. I ain't surprised he went for Yate. But don't it seem strange that he didn't go after me first, what with my being more powerful and such?"

"I hardly know his reasoning. It seems to me that you must keep yourself apprised of Dogmill's doings. Have you heard aught of this?"

"Not a word," he told me. "It's as quiet as can be. I ain't heard nothing, which is why what you say surprises me. Believe me, I spend more than a share of my time keeping an eye on him and his doings. I can't claim to have loved Yate, but he was a porter's man like me, and if Dogmill goes about killing us, I want to know."

"Would he have some reason for wishing an ill to Yate and not to you?"

"Yate was but a girl in pants, you know. He hardly knew how to press back against Dogmill. As for me, I held my ground with that fiend. I told him *no* when I meant *no,* and he understood the words when they come from my mouth and into his ear. I'm the man on the quays, Weaver. I'm the man who looks after the porters and tells Dogmill to heave to when he says there's to be no more picking up the loose tobacco or no more taking a moment to catch the breath. I can't see him going for Yate and not for me."

I could little determine if Greenbill's objection merely reflected his pride or if he had something of value to offer. "You cannot think of any reason for Dogmill to harbor a particular anger toward Yate?"

He shook his head. "It don't make sense. Yate gave way under pressure, he did. Dogmill would've liked to have seen all the porters under Yate. Now he has to worry about them all working with me, and he can't much like that. Besides, how would he have done it? Yate was killed in the midst of my boys. None of us saw him do it. None of us saw Dogmill—and you can best believe we'd have seen that villain in all his vapidity."

"Surely he must have an agent to do his violent work."

"None that I ever saw," Greenbill said. "Believe me, we've had many a dealing with him that felt sour as a lemon, and he never once presented a rough or a Swiss to do his bidding. He thinks himself man enough to pummel and punch, and if there was any killing to be had, he'd have it for himself. Anything otherwise don't come in line, to my thinking."

I thought it well that my life did not depend on his thinking. I found it hard to believe that Dogmill would risk being seen about on such murderous errands, but it did seem odd to me that he never hired roughs on his own.

"And how is it you have Wild asking questions for you and such?" Greenbill now demanded to know. "I heard he put in a word on your behest at your trial, too. Have you and he come to be friends?"

"That would overstate the case. Wild and I are not friends, but he seems to bear some dislike for Dogmill. He offered to help me find Clark and Spicer, but I shall not seek his assistance again."

"Quite wise, that. You don't want him turning you in for the bounty."

"Only a scoundrel would do that," I agreed.

"An unkind characterization, but I shan't dispute it. The posthumous question is what you will do now. Will you take out Dogmill?" he asked eagerly. "That should be a pretty piece of revenge. If he done what you say, cutting his throat should answer."

It would seem that Greenbill wanted to turn me into his private assassin. I would exact my revenge on Dogmill, and Greenbill would be left with no real rival and no central authority in the tobacco trade. "I have neither the means to do so nor the desire."

"But you can't let him ruin you and go about sullying your name."

I saw no reason to perpetuate this conversation. Greenbill clearly had no information for me, and I should gain nothing by entertaining his encouragement for murder. I thought for a moment to urge him to do the job himself, but then I thought he might take me up on it, and Dogmill would be of no use to me dead. I therefore stood and invited Greenbill to finish his ale and depart at his leisure.

"That's it, then? You won't do the manly thing with Dogmill?"

"I'll not do as you suggest, no."

"And what about me? Do I stay in London or flee?"

I had by now reached the door. "I see no reason for you to flee."

"If I stay, don't you think Dogmill might kill me?"

"He might," I conceded, "but that is no concern of mine."

I had no love for the two men who had testified against me at my trial, but neither did I take pleasure in the news of their deaths. That the murderer should think fit to put the blame on my shoulders provided me with more reason for worry. And while I was reluctant to credit the words of a man like Greenbill, I found troubling his belief that Dogmill could not be my man.

There was but one person I knew of who might be of some small use to me. I therefore waited until darkness had just fallen and then, dressed as myself rather than as Mr. Evans, I slipped, via the window and alley, out of Mrs. Sears's house and made my way to visit Mr. Ufford.

This time Barber, the manservant, admitted me at once, and gave me such a cold look that I determined I could not prolong this stay, for if he knew my true identity I cannot believe he would have hesitated to inform the nearest magistrate—whether in accordance with or in defiance of his master's wishes, I could not say.

Ufford was in his parlor with a glass of port by his side and a book upon his lap. I could not believe but that he had just now been awakened to visit with me.

"Benjamin," he said, setting aside his thin volume, "have you discovered the author of those notes? Is that why you've come?"

"I am afraid I have not obtained any new information in that matter."

"What are you doing with your time? I have tried to be patient with you, but you seem to be acting with the most unrestrained frivolity."

I handed him a news sheet, folded to the story of Groston's murder. "What do you know of this?" I asked.

"Less than you, it would seem; I never trouble myself with these sordid crimes. Perhaps if you were more interested in finding the author of those notes instead of going about killing all these low sorts of people, we would both be better off."

I paced for only a few steps and then turned to him once more. "Let us be honest with each other, Mr. Ufford. Was Groston killed as part of a Jacobite scheme?"

He blushed and turned away from me. "How should I know the answer to that question?"

"Come, sir, it is well known that you have Jacobitical sympathies. I have heard tell that the men who are truly powerful in that movement eschew you, but I do not believe it. It would be of some use if you can illuminate this matter for me."

"Eschew me, indeed. What makes you think I have anything to do with that noble and justified movement?"

"I haven't an interest in games, I promise you. If you know something, I'll thank you to tell me."

"I can tell you nothing," he said with a simper, clearly meant to imply that he knew more than he would say.

What to do next? He surely thought he played at a great game, but it was one whose rules he hardly knew. I had in my time faced thieves and murderers, wealthy landowners and men of influence. But Jacobites seemed to me another species altogether. These were not men who knew how to deceive when necessary; they were men who lived in a web of deception, who hid in dark spaces, disguised themselves, came and went unseen. That they knew how to do these things was proved by the fact that they yet lived. I hardly believed myself an equal to their cleverness. However, I believed myself more than an equal to Ufford, and my patience with him was running thin. I therefore thought it wise to educate him, if only a little, as to the consequence of my impatience. That is to say, I slapped his face.

I did not slap him particularly hard. Still, from the look in his eye, one might think I had struck him with an ax. He reddened and his eyes moistened. I thought he would cry.

"What do you do?" he asked me, holding up his hands as though such a gesture could deflect another blow.

"I slap you, Mr. Ufford, and I shall do so again and with far more force if you don't begin being honest with me. You must understand that the world wishes me dead, and it wishes me dead because of a business in which you involved me. If you know more than you have said, you had better tell me now, because you have awoken my anger."

"Don't hit me again," he said, still cringing like a beaten dog. "I'll tell you what you want to know—as best I can. Jesus, save me! I hardly know anything at all. Look at me, Benjamin. Do I seem like a master of espionage? Do I seem like a man who has the ear of powerful plotters?"

I could not but admit that he did not.

He must have sensed my acknowledgment of his ineptitude, because he took a deep breath and lowered his arms. "I know a few things," he said with a nod, as though convincing himself to move forward. With one hand he reached up and gingerly touched the slightly red flesh of his face. "I know a bit, it is true, because I may have some sympathies that—well, it is best not spoken of. Not even here. But there is a coffeehouse near the Fleet where men of that way of thinking are like to congregate."

"Mr. Ufford, I am led to believe that there are coffeehouses on every street where men of that way of thinking are like to congregate. You will have to do better, I'm afraid."

"You don't understand," he said. "This is not some gin house where bricklayers go to besot themselves with drink and pretend to know something of politics. This place, the Sleeping Bear, is where men of import go. What you want to know—well, someone there will surely be able to tell you."

"Can you give me a name? Someone with whom I may speak?"

He shook his head. "I have never been there myself. It is not for the likes of me. I have only heard of its centrality to the cause. You will have to make do on your own, Benjamin. And please, for mercy's sake, leave me alone. I've done all I can for you. You must ask no more of me, bother me no more."

"You have done all you can for me?" I demanded. "Why, you have all but put my head in the noose, involving me as you have with your Jacobitical intrigues."

"I could never have imagined you would come to such harm!"

he shouted. "I could not have known that these men threatened me because of my political interests."

"Perhaps not," I said, "but neither did you offer to help me. I think you nothing but a fool—one who dabbles in things too great for him. Such men always expose themselves before the world."

"Of course, of course," he muttered.

I could not but doubt that Barber, his man, had gone to get some sort of assistance for his master, so I made my way from that house as quickly as I could.

Night was full upon me as I found my way to the Sleeping Bear, located on the first floor of a handsome little house in the shadow of St. Paul's. The interior was well lit and lively. Nearly every table was occupied, and some were quite crowded. Here were men of the middle ranks, some perhaps of a better station, who sat with food and drink and lively conversations. I saw no representatives of the softer sex except for a gaunt woman hard on old age who served them.

My plain style of dress fit in as well as I could hope, but I nevertheless found all eyes upon me in an instant, staring at me with near murderous intent. Never one to shrink from a cool welcome, I strode at once to the barman, an unusually tall old fellow, and asked him for a pot of something refreshing.

He glared at me and offered me my drink, though I was certain he had thought I said a pot of something *wretched,* for the drink he gave me was old and warm and tasted like the leavings of yesterday's patrons. I turned to the man and, setting aside the unpleasantness of his drink, thought to engage him in some other conversation, but I saw from the hard look in his eyes that he was not of a conversational nature, so I took my pint and found one of the few empty tables.

I sat there, holding my pot but hardly daring, for the sake of my health, to drink from it. Some of the men around me resumed their conversations in hushed whispers, though I sensed that the talk now centered around me. Others merely stared malevolently.

I remained in that state for but a quarter of an hour before a fellow came and joined me. He was perhaps ten years older than I, well dressed, with thick white eyebrows and a matching wig—overly long and of the sort already out of fashion in those days.

"Are you waiting for someone then, friend?" he asked me, in the thick accent of an Irishman.

"I came in from the street to take the chill off," I said.

He flashed a warm grin in my direction and raised the bushy shelf of his brow. "Well, there are a number of places hereabouts where a fellow might do that, but, as I imagine you've already noticed, there's something of a chill in here, if you get my meaning. I recollect that at the Three Welshmen down the street they serve a fine mutton stew and have a mulled wine wondrous for this cold. Certainly you'd be welcome there."

I looked around. "I believe the owner of the Three Welshmen would thank you for your praise, but this is no private place. The sign outside advertises it as a public coffeehouse. How can it be that I cannot take refreshment here?"

"The men who come here—well, they come here all the time, and there's none that come here that don't do so regular."

"But surely each of these men must have come here for the first time once. Were they all used as I am?"

"Perhaps they came with a friend, one already in the habit of visiting," he said cheerfully. "Come, now, you've surely heard of coffeehouses that are the province of this group or that. No one here wishes you ill, but it's best that you finish up your drink and find a place more suited to you. That mutton stew must sound pleasing."

I did not think to accomplish much by simply leaving, nor would it do much good to remain and be ignored. I could only think that this fellow was my one hope of learning something of value. "In truth," I said to him, "I came here because I heard that this was the place to go if I was of a particular frame of mind. Which is to say, if I was looking for men who thought like I did, in a political way."

He smiled again, but this time it seemed far more forced. "I can't imagine how you might have heard such a thing. There are countless taverns the city over for any number of political dispositions. This one—well, we don't go much for strangers here, if you take my meaning, and we don't talk politics with them. I don't know what you are looking for, friend, but you won't find it in this place. No one is going to talk to you or answer your questions or invite you in on their chat. It may be, as you say, that you are here because you are like-minded. If that's the case, I wish you happiness, and perhaps our paths will cross again. It may also be that you're a spy, sir, and you don't want to be found out as such a one in this place. No, you surely don't."

"Tell me," I said, feeling I now had little to lose, "is there a man called Johnson who comes here? I should very much like to meet with him."

I had meant to speak quietly, but my voice carried more than I anticipated, and at the next table a fellow half rose until his companion reached out and, with a hand on his shoulder, forced him down again.

"I don't know any Johnson," my Irish friend said, as though neither of us had witnessed this man's alarm. "You've come to the wrong place. Now I suggest you take your leave, sir. There's nothing more to be gained by your bringing confusion to my friends."

There was surely nothing more to be gained by finishing my drink, so I rose and departed with as much dignity as I could, though I have rarely made a more ignominious exit.

I could hardly have been more frustrated. Surely something should have come of this venture, but I had been rebuffed most coolly and I learned nothing of value. I cursed myself and my foul luck as I walked along Paternoster Row. It was foolishness for me not to have been more vigilant, but my anger overtook my emotions, so I did not see the two men who stepped out to the alley to grab me, each by one arm. I recognized them at once—the Riding Officers who had been standing outside of Elias's house.

"Well, then, here he is," one of them said. "It's our Jew, sure enough."

"This is our lucky night, I think," the other one answered.

I attempted to break free, but their grips were firm, and I knew I would have to wait for a better chance, provided one came. There were, after all, only two of them, and they would have to remain firm in their grip every second as we traveled to wherever it was they wished to take me. The streets of London at night afforded countless obstacles that might prove just the distraction I needed. It would only be a matter of time before they were put off their guard by a linkboy or a footpad or a whore. One of them might slip in horse kennel or trip over a dead dog.

My hopes were soon dashed, however, as two more of their allies emerged from the shadows. While two of the Riding Officers held me firmly in place, a third grabbed my arms and pulled them behind my back while the fourth began to tie my wrists together with a piece of cord selected for its abrasiveness.

I should surely have been undone had not a most unexpected event transpired. The Irishman, with a band of more than a dozen of the surly men from inside the coffeehouse, stepped forth from the darkness.

"What is the trouble here, gentlemen?" the Irishman asked.

"It's no concern of yours, Dear Joy," said one of the Riding Officers, using that name so insulting to Irishmen. "Get you gone."

"It *is* my concern, I'll have you know. Leave that fellow be, for no one is taken on this street but by our leave."

"You'll be taken too, fellow, if you don't step away," the Riding Officer said.

Here was brave talk, for each man was outnumbered three or four to one, and none of them looked particularly competent in a fight. The Irishman's little army, sensing the weakness of the Riding Officers, drew blades, all at once. The Customs men, very wisely in my opinion, chose to flee.

As did I. I spun into the darkness of the alley and turned and turned again until I was far enough away that I could no longer hear the shouts of the Riding Officers. I was surely grateful for the timely rescue, but I had no desire to stay and learn if they had chosen to liberate me because they recognized me after I left and wished the bounty for themselves. It might have been that, or it might have been that they hated the Customs more than they hated a stranger. I was not curious enough to risk learning the truth.

It had now been weeks since my escape from Newgate, and other than my encounter with the Riding Officers outside of Elias's house that first night, I had not faced a single other confrontation from men in authority. I could only conclude that they had no effective means of tracking me. I had hidden my identity and my movements sufficiently that unless one of their number became astonishingly fortunate and simply happened upon me by chance, I had little to fear from the government.

Yet the Riding Officers had been lying in wait outside the Sleeping Bear. I was inside the coffeehouse, in total, for less than half of an hour, which meant it was very unlikely that one of the patrons could have recognized me and sent a note to the Riding Officers in time for them to have arrived and awaited my departure. Indeed, even more unlikely since it was the patrons themselves who rescued me from those worthies. It could only be, then, that Mr. Ufford, on sending me to the Sleeping Bear, took pains that I should not emerge from my visit a free man. Though shaken by my encounter with the Customs men, I knew I must act, and act quickly. There was more to Ufford than I yet understood, and I would learn what I could that night.

I waited until two or three in the morning, when no one was on the street and all the houses were dark. I then betook myself to Mr. Ufford's house and forced open a window in the kitchen through which I quickly climbed. The drop down was greater than I anticipated, but I landed safely, if not quietly. I remained motionless for some minutes to see if my clumsiness aroused any suspicion. As I waited I felt the warm brush of two or three cats against my leg, so I could only hope that if anyone heard the noise they might blame these creatures rather than an intruder.

Once a safe amount of time had passed—or, perhaps more accurately, once I had grown too impatient to wait any longer—I moved from my crouched position, bid a silent farewell to my new feline companions, and made my way through the dark. I recalled well enough where Ufford kept his study, so it took no great amount of time to locate the room, though the darkness was close to absolute.

I made certain the door was shut behind me and found a pair of good wax tapers to light. The room was now sufficiently illuminated that I might search it, though I had no idea what it was I sought. Nevertheless, I began to go through papers in his books, in his drawers, and on his shelves, and it did not take long to find that I was on the right path. Within minutes I found numerous letters written in an indecipherable jumble of letters—most obviously a code, though I had not the slightest ability to decipher such a thing. Nevertheless, the mere presence of this sort of writing informed me of a great deal. Who but a spy would require the use of code? The discovery ignited my resolve, and I dove in with a new vigor.

This new enthusiasm paid off well. I had been in the room for near an hour when, having gone through all the papers, files, and ledgers I could find and not having discovered anything of immediate use, I thought to leaf through some of the large volumes that crowded Ufford's shelves. This project proved of little worth, and I was near to abandoning it when I came across a tome that felt much lighter than its size suggested. It was hollowed out, and when I opened it I found a dozen or so pieces of paper on which had been written the following damnable text, signed in the most ostentatious hand:

> I acknowledge to have received from_____the sum of_____which I promise to repay, with an interest for it, at the rate of_____per annum.
>
> James R.

James Rex, the Pretender himself. Ufford had set for himself the task of raising monies for a Jacobite rebellion and had done so with the knowledge of the Pretender. These receipts, signed by the would-be monarch, were left to the priest's management, that he might secure what lenders he could. I picked up the papers and examined them closely. Of course, they could be forgeries, but why would a man pretend to the ownership of documents that could lead easily to his execution? I could only conclude that Ufford was in fact an agent of the Pretender and, more than that, he was not the hapless self-aggrandizer the world believed him to be. No, the keeper of these receipts would be a well-trusted member of the Chevalier's circle. Ufford's foolishness and blundering were but a disguise to hide a cunning and capable agent.

I held these receipts tightly in my hand, and the most fanciful thought occurred to me. No one knew how highly placed among the Jacobites sat Mr. Ufford—no one but me. This information would surely be of great interest to the administration, of far more interest than persecuting a simple thieftaker for a murder the world knew he did not commit. Could I not trade the information I now had for my freedom? The thought sat ill with me, for no man likes a traitor, but I owed Ufford no devotion—not when his schemes had landed me in this position in the first place. Surely I owed more loyalty to my monarch. It could be argued that failing to report what I knew was an unforgivable act of negligence.

"Or perhaps one of loyalty to the true king."

I must have spoken aloud, so transfixed was I by the evidence I had discovered. I had neither seen nor heard the men enter the room. I had been foolish and careless, seduced by the possibilities of my discoveries. Now I turned around and found myself facing three men: Ufford, the Irishman from the Sleeping Bear, and a third man. I had never before met him, but I thought at once there was something familiar in his angular face, sunken cheeks, and beaky nose. He looked in his thirties, perhaps a bit older, and though he dressed in unremarkable clothes and wore an inexpensive bob wig, there was something imposing about his stance.

"Surely," the Irishman said, "you would not trade another man's life for your own comfort."

"It appears that the question is but a hypothetical one," Ufford observed. He stepped forward and took the receipts from my hand. "Benjamin shan't have the opportunity to share what he knows with anyone."

The Irishman shook his head. "Well, he won't be able to share the evidence, that much is certain. I would not have him believe that we mean to do him any harm, however."

"Oh, no," said the third man, in a patrician voice. He emphasized each syllable he spoke. "No, I am too much of an admirer of Mr. Weaver to even think of acting against his interests."

And then I knew his face, for I had seen it a hundred times—on posters, on broadsheets, on pamphlets. Standing in the room with me, not fifteen feet away, was the Pretender himself, the son of the deposed James II, the man who would be James III. I knew little about the planning of revolutions and usurpations, but I could not but believe, if he dared to step foot in England, that the situation for His (present) Majesty King George was dire indeed.

I was in a private house with the Pretender himself and what had to be two very highly placed Jacobites. No one knew I was there. My throat might easily be slit, my body hauled away in a crate. And yet my foremost concern was not for my safety but for decorum: That is to say, I did not know the correct protocol for addressing the Pretender. On the other hand, I decided that I might be far safer if I acted as though I did not recognize him.

Ufford, however, would not let me take that route. "Are you mad? He's seen His Majesty. We can't let him leave."

The Irishman closed his eyes for a moment as though considering some great mystery. "Mr. Ufford, I must ask you to wait outside and leave us alone here for now."

"I should remind you whose house this is," he answered.

"Please step outside, Christopher," the Pretender said.

Ufford bowed and retreated.

Once he closed the door, the Irishman offered me an amused smile.

"I have come to believe," I said, "that you are the man they call Johnson."

"It is a name I use," he said. He poured three glasses of Mr. Ufford's Madeira and, after delivering the Pretender his glass, he placed one in my hand and then stood across from me. "I am certain you have already surmised that with us is His Majesty, King James the Third."

Without any training in this sort of thing, I bowed to the Pretender. "It is an honor, Your Grace."

He nodded slightly, as though approving of my performance. "I have heard many good things about you, sir. Mr. Johnson has kept me informed of your actions. He tells me that you have fallen victim to the government of a fat German pig of a usurper."

"I am a victim of something, that much is certain." I thought it best not to say that I had come to believe I might well be the victim of his own machinations. It is the sort of thing that does not win friends.

He shook his head. "I detect some suspicions on your part. Let me assure you, they are unfounded."

"I had thought better of you, Mr. Weaver," Johnson said. "The Whigs want you to believe that we plot against you, and you are so foolish as to believe it. Surely you recall that the witnesses hired against you at your trial tried to link you with a mysterious stranger called *Johnson*. Do you need more evidence that the Whigs were trying to turn you into a Jacobite agent to scapegoat before the world? Only your clever escape prevented it."

There could be no denying what he suggested. Someone certainly had wished to paint me the Jacobite.

"I have followed your trials with some interest," Johnson continued, "as I always follow with interest when a useful and productive—dare I say heroic?—member of our society is trampled to paste by a corrupt ministry and its servants. I can assure you that it has never been the aim of His Majesty or his agents to see you come to any harm. What you have witnessed is a Whig conspiracy, meant to remove its enemies, cast blame on its rivals, and sway an election by distracting the voters from a financial scandal engineered at the highest levels of Whiggery."

I looked at the Pretender. "I do not know that I have the liberty to speak freely," I said.

He laughed a condescending kingly laugh. "You may speak as you like. I have been at this end or the other of plots my entire life. Hearing of one more will not harm me."

I nodded. "Then I must say that it seemed to me most likely that it had been Jacobite agents who had a hand in the death of that fellow Groston and the false witnesses he hired for my trial."

He laughed softly. "What sort of men do you take us for? Why should we wish those men ill—or you, for that matter? The notes left upon the scene were a carefully constructed farce. They claim that you committed these unspeakable acts in the name of the true King but are written so as to give the lie to that claim, thus making it *appear* that it is a Jacobite plot meant to expose the Whigs. In reality it is a Whig plot. The world suspects us of this sort of deception, but the world is wrong. What have you ever done, Mr. Weaver, that we should know of you or care enough to murder three—no, four!—men for the purpose of seeing you suffer?"

"I cannot answer that question, but neither can I say why the Whigs would pursue the same course."

"Then shall I tell you?" Johnson asked.

I took a hearty drink of my goblet and leaned forward. "If you can, I beg you do so."

"Mr. Ufford hired you to discover the men who sought to disturb his quiet and the exercise of his traditional liberties as a priest of the Church of England. He did not intend you to find yourself caught in such a nest of vipers, but that is inconsequential, for caught you are. But those who wished to silence Mr. Ufford are the very ones who want you destroyed—namely, one Dennis Dogmill and his lapdog, Albert Hertcomb."

"But why? I have found myself returning again and again to this man, but I have not yet discovered a reason why Dogmill should go to such trouble."

"Is not the answer obvious? You were attempting to learn who sent the notes to Mr. Ufford. If you were to discover that they originated with Dogmill, he would have been ruined, Hertcomb discredited, and the Westminster election lost for the Whigs. Instead, he cleverly arranged that he could remove an obstacle, this poor Yate, and blame the crime on an enemy. I own that the matter has taken on political dimensions it might not have had otherwise because of my efforts to keep you in the public eye, but that is the extent of our involvement in your affairs. And if I have encouraged sympathetic newspapers to praise your efforts—which are indeed praiseworthy—and to point to the dangers you face from the Whigs—which are quite real—I can hardly be blamed."

"If the Jacobites are my friends, why did Ufford attempt to have me destroyed tonight?"

The Pretender shook his head. "That was a regrettable mistake. He feared you grew too close to learning what he would not have you know, so he took action himself. When I received word, telling me what he had done, I instructed Mr. Johnson to make certain you did not fall into Whiggish hands."

"And I did as much as could be asked," Johnson said.

I nodded, for I had to admit to the justice of what he claimed.

"Then you must trust me enough to believe my interpretation of the facts before us," Johnson continued.

Johnson's theory withstood the assault of logical inquiry, but it still failed to convince. Could Dogmill have been foolish enough to believe I would go blindly to the gallows? All I knew of the man suggested that, though he might be violent and impulsive, he was also a calculating planner, and he would have known better than to hope I should cooperate with my own destruction.

"I feel there must be more to it than that," I said.

Johnson shook his head. "Perhaps you are not familiar with the principle called Occam's razor, which tells us that the simplest theory is almost always the correct one. You may spend the rest of your life searching for the truth, if you like, but I have set it out before you."

"It may well be as you say—you cannot but know that I have come back to those same conclusions many times—but I must be able to prove it in order to accept the truth of it and to sway others."

"It is pitiable, but you may never be able to do so. Dogmill is a treacherous beast, and he will not surrender damning evidence easily. You have already made your case to the law, and the law has been proved to care nothing for justice. In light of that, I fear you have set yourself upon a course, no matter how honorable, that will ultimately end with your destruction." He paused to sip his wine. "But there is another way available to you."

"Oh?"

"I should like to offer you a post in my service," the Pretender said to me. "I will have you spirited out of the country before nightfall tomorrow. There is much to be done on the continent, and you will be able to act without fear of the law. What say you? Is it not time that you ceased your noble efforts to make a corrupt system acknowledge justice? Would it not be better to help usher in a new order of fairness and honesty?"

"Please do not take this as an insult, Your Grace, but I cannot act against the current government," I said, very coolly.

"I have heard this sentiment before," he said, "and I am ever astonished that even a man like you, who suffers at the whim of evil men, can be so reluctant to turn away from those same men."

"You fear being called a traitor," Johnson said. "How can it be treachery to serve the man who is your true sovereign? I am sure you know the history of this kingdom too well to require a lecture, but I shall only point out that our right monarch was driven from his throne by a pack of bloodthirsty Whigs who would have served him with the same sauce they served his father when they beheaded that great king. Now, out of a bigoted hatred of the way the king chooses to worship—a bigotry that must be particularly odious to you Jews—they have conferred the crown on a German princeling with no connection to these islands, no knowledge of the English language, and nothing more to recommend him than that he is not of the Roman religion. Are not the supporters of the Whigs the true traitors?"

I took a deep breath. I cannot say I was not tempted. This kingdom had gone through so many changes and upheavals in the past century that surely another one was possible. If the Pretender was successful in his bid for the throne, and I threw my lot in with him, would I not gain, and gain greatly, by my efforts? But that could not be incentive enough.

"Mr. Johnson, I do not style myself a political thinker. I can only say that my race has received an uncommon warm welcome in this country, and it would be ingratitude of the highest order to rebel against its government, even if some of its members seek to do me harm. I understand your cause, sir, and I sympathize with the depth of your beliefs, but I cannot do as you so kindly request."

The Pretender shook his head. "I say this not to be critical, Mr. Weaver, for it is the condition of all men. But you would rather live in servitude to a master you know than risk freedom with a new master. It is a sad thing that a person of your stripe cannot quit the clogs of subjugation. You may depend on no ill will on my part. When I am returned to my rightful place, I will beg you call upon me. There will be a place for you yet."

I bowed in return, and the Pretender left the room.

Johnson shook his head. "His Majesty is ever more generous and understanding than I am, for I will call your decision foolish to your face. I did imagine that you would say as much, but His Majesty wished to make the offer, and so it was made. The time may yet come when you change your mind. Clearly, you know where to find some of my brethren, so you needn't keep it a secret if you decide you wish to join us. In the meantime, I can only beg that you not repeat any of what you have seen and heard here tonight. If you do not wish to stand with us, I must depend on your gratitude for our preserving your freedom."

He now fell silent, and the room was full of our breathing and the clicking of a great clock.

"That is all?" I asked incredulously. "You intend to let me leave this place?"

"I have no way of preventing you from doing so but by means I should find distasteful. And as it happens, His Majesty is within a few hours of quitting these shores, so you can do little harm by reporting what you have seen—though I would request that you do not. I can only wish you luck in your quest for justice, sir, as I know that any bold endeavor on your behalf will serve the true king's interests."

Improbable though it seemed, Mr. Johnson intended to let me leave, though I now had information fit to destroy Mr. Ufford— though no evidence with which to support my claims. I have rarely felt as guarded as I did while leaving that house, but no bravos appeared from the shadows to cut my throat, and the greatest difficulty I faced in getting home was finding a hackney to carry me there.

I fell asleep marveling that Ufford would permit me to walk the same soil as he did with the information I possessed, but I soon found out he had no intention of doing so. I soon learned that the day after my meeting with Johnson, Ufford departed these shores—claiming health difficulties—and took up residence in Italy. In fact, he took himself to Rome, the very city in which the Pretender resided.

CHAPTER 18

Wᴵᴛʜ ᴛʜᴇ ᴄᴏᴍᴍᴇɴᴄᴇᴍᴇɴᴛ of the six weeks of election upon us, I thought to travel to Covent Garden and witness the procession of opening day. These events often have the festive atmosphere of a parade or a Lord Mayor's show, and if nothing else I knew it would offer me something of a diversion.

I had written Elias and asked him to join me, and as we were in so public a place, I chose to appear as neither Weaver nor Evans and instead resurrected the footman's livery for the afternoon. Enough time had passed since I'd used that disguise that I believed I might comfortably rely on it for a short period.

We first met in a tavern, that I might discuss with my friend the information I had so recently acquired. Elias, however, appeared most irritated when I first met him.

"I am sorry I ever devised this Matthew Evans character," he told me. "I cannot visit one of my patients without hearing of how he is the most interesting man in London. I was administering an enema to this pretty little creature, the daughter of a duke, you know, and Matthew Evans was all she could talk of. She had seen him at the theater. She had seen him at the assembly. I could hardly get her to notice her poor surgeon at all."

"If you have a young lady with her arse exposed to you and you cannot get her attention, I won't have you blaming it on me."

He coughed into his fist to disguise a laugh. "Well, let us discuss your situation. Have there been any new developments?"

"A few," I said, and proceeded to tell him of all that had happened.

He stared with disbelief. "The Pretender has been in London! We must inform the government at once."

"I said I would not."

"Of course you said you would not. What should you say, *I will betray you, so please let me go that I might do it at once?* Your word hardly matters in this case."

"It does to me. And he's gone now, so what does it matter?"

"It matters because if he is willing to risk a visit here, it can only be to bolster support of an imminent uprising. The ministry must be made aware of it."

"The ministry prepares every day for an imminent uprising. It will do just fine without our information. I'll not risk my life to tell a government that means to murder me that it must prepare for a crisis that it is already preparing for."

"You may have a point," Elias said thoughtfully. "Rabbit it! I wish I could tell my friends this intelligence. I should be quite the fellow in the coffeehouses, knowing this."

"You'll have to live without being the coffeehouse fellow, won't you?"

"Of course," he said sheepishly. "But what you tell me changes everything, as far as you are concerned. Despite what you were told at Ufford's house, you must consider yourself to be in terrible, terrible danger. These Jacobites have tolerated you because you've been useful to them, but poking around in their studies and discovering secret funding sources for an invasion and clandestine visits of the Pretender to these shores—well, it is the sort of thing that makes them nervous. You've got to be careful, or you'll end up like Yate or the witnesses at your trial."

"What are you suggesting I do?"

He took a deep breath. "Look, Weaver. You can depend upon none of these people to tell you the truth. If this Irishman Johnson is kind to you, it does not mean he is honest with you."

"No, but he might well have harmed me and he did not."

"Only because he thinks you may be of use to him free. He'll harm you plenty if things begin to appear otherwise."

"I know that."

"Then you had better accept that all of this Jacobitical intrigue is, for you, no more than a distraction. You are exerting all your efforts in an attempt to learn the truth behind who killed Yate and why."

"Should I not be doing that?"

"I suppose you should, yes, but as a means to an end, not an end."

"The end, I suppose, is politics."

He smiled. "I see you have learned something after all."

By the time we reached the Covent Garden piazza, it was already crowded with thousands of electors and observers, many of whom flew the colors of their candidate, and many more who were only there for the diversion. The crowd was packed in tight, cheerful and surly simultaneously, in the way of London mobs. These people delighted in entertainment but always felt an inexplicably sharp resentment that the entertainment was not so entertaining as they would like, that it did not transport them from their poverty or their hunger or the pain in their teeth.

As we arrived, the Tory candidates were entering the plaza, the Whigs having already made their entry. I saw hundreds of banners rise up in the air as Melbury made his way toward the platform, and not a few eggs and pieces of fruit flew as well. During his short speech the Tories seemed to have the advantage, and more than once I saw a Whiggish heckler dragged down into the mob to face I dared not think what torments.

Elias laughed softly at my surprise. "Have you never before observed an election procession?"

"I suppose I have," I said, "but I always thought of it as some sort of spectacle. Not having the vote myself, I never bothered to consider its political import. Now that I do, this madness seems absurd."

"Of course it is absurd."

"Do you not think it wrong that the nation elects its leaders in this fashion? Why, there is more danger here than at Bartholomew Fair or at a Lord Mayor's show."

"There's not much difference, is there, between this and a puppet show, but that here it is people and not puppets that are banged upon the head. But at least here there are thousands who have a say in the election. Would you prefer a town like Bath, where their Parliamentarians are selected by a small group of men who sit with their roast chicken and their port and determine who will keep their bellies the fattest?"

"I don't know what I prefer."

"I prefer this," he told me. "At least there's a bit of distraction to it."

And so, with the requisite amount of violence, the election commenced. How odd, I thought, that my hopes should depend upon a man I had once hated without knowing. But it was true enough that it was in my best interests for Griffin Melbury to carry the day. I was therefore not a little gratified when, in a coffeehouse the next morning, I heard the results of the previous day's tallies: Mr. Melbury, 208 votes; Mr. Hertcomb, 188. The man I despised, running on the platform of a party I mistrusted, had won the first day, and though I should have wished this man nothing but ill, fate had ordained that I must rejoice in his victory.

Not two days later—and two days in which Melbury bested the Whigs in the polls—Matthew Evans received a note that I found utterly delightful. Mr. Hertcomb himself wrote to inform me that I was invited to join a group of friends—including Miss Dogmill—for an evening at the theater the following night. I suspected that Miss Dogmill was not the sort of woman who would be so bold as to initiate a correspondence with a man, although I would have been pleased had she proved herself unfettered by such restrictions. I wrote to Mr. Hertcomb at once, telling him I would join him with all my heart.

The Whig candidate arrived at my rooms wearing a suit of a remarkable shade of blue, lit up with enormous gold buttons. He grinned sheepishly at me, and I invited him in for some wine before we proceeded. If he felt any worry that the first three days of the election had gone Melbury's way, he did not show it.

"I trust you have no geese about you, sir," he said impishly, still amused at events now two weeks past.

"None but are at their liberty, I assure you," I returned. I sensed at once that Hertcomb, who bristled under the harsh yoke of Mr. Dogmill, had taken a particular delight in my defiance of his master. Perhaps he had never before witnessed any man resist him so boldly, and his kindness to me might be all the rebellion he could muster. Or, I thought, he might be some sort of spy in Dogmill's service. In either case, I knew my business well enough to welcome this man into the bosom of my friendship—and to be careful all the while I did so.

"I do not believe that Mr. Dogmill would be partial to my spending my spare time with a man of Toryish inclinations, sir, but we need not say anything to him."

"I am not in the habit of informing Mr. Dogmill of my doings," I said.

"Well, then. It is for the best. In any event, Miss Dogmill seems to enjoy your company, and as I enjoy Miss Dogmill's company, I see nothing wrong with accommodating her inclinations, if you take my meaning."

I was not entirely certain I did. It was clear to me that Mr. Hertcomb had a liking for Grace Dogmill and that she had made it clear she had no intention of elevating their relations to a more legal status. Why then did he consent to my accompanying them? I could only imagine that he did not see me as a rival—or he had something else in mind that superseded his amorous inclinations.

"If I may venture to be bold," I said, "I have observed that, though he is your agent and you work quite closely with him, you are perhaps none too fond of Mr. Dogmill."

He laughed and waved his hand dismissively. "Oh, we have no need to be friends, you know. Our families have long been linked, and as an election agent he does a marvelous good job. I can't say I would stand a chance in this race without him.

"I am in far beyond my understanding," he went on, "and Dogmill is quite skillful at managing treacherous waters. Those Tories have a strong presence in Westminster, and if Dogmill is right,

there is more at issue here than just a seat in Parliament. If we lose
here, the country could find itself overrun with Jacobites."

"Do you believe that to be true?"

"I don't know if it is true," he said, "but it is what I believe." He
took a moment to look meaningfully into his goblet.

"What are your beliefs, then, sir?" I asked warmly.

He laughed again. "Oh, you know, the usual Whig sort of
things. Less Church and all that. Protecting the fellow with new
ideas from old money. Serving the king, I suppose. There are one
or two others, though I don't recall them just now. It's just that a
man can't always do what he likes in the House."

"You mean because of Dogmill?" I asked.

"If I may be honest with you, Mr. Evans, I must say that I
should very much like to part ways with Dogmill—after this election, of course. I tell you this in confidence. I am surprised to even
hear myself utter the words, but for whatever reason I find myself
taking a liking to you. And I have never before seen any man stand
up to Dogmill so boldly."

I laughed. "There is something in him that makes me long to
antagonize the fellow. It is the very devil that comes out of me."

"You should not do so lightly. He has a most horrendous temper. Last year, as I began to prepare myself for this election, I approached Dogmill to tell him that I wished not to use him for my
election agent. I had hardly even begun to speak when he turned
red and stammered and paced back and forth. He held a glass of
wine in his hand, and I tell you he shattered it with his brute
strength. He bled tremendously but hardly even noticed."

"What did you do?"

"I could do nothing," he said. "Dogmill stared at me. His eyes
were wild. Blood and wine dripped from his hand. He said, 'What
do you say to me, sir?' again and again, and did so in a voice that
would make the Devil himself tremble. And I merely shook my
head. He threw open the door, leaving a bloody handprint on the
paint, and we never discussed the matter again. I never spoke of it
to anyone."

"I am honored by your confidence."

"And I am impressed by your courage. I can only hope you will not suffer for it." He drained his goblet with an air of finality. "Now, let us forget these unpleasant matters and get on with our evening's entertainment."

Once we reached Drury Lane, I was met with a half dozen or so others, young people of both sexes. I exchanged names with each, but if I am to be honest I must say that I remember not a one of them, even the ladies, who were all quite handsome. I had eyes only for Miss Dogmill.

She wore a wonderfully flattering gown of pale blue with an immaculate and enticingly cut bodice. Her dark hair had been piled flatteringly under a matching wide-brimmed hat. She looked for all the world like the finest young lady in the kingdom, and I was delighted that she took my arm at once and allowed me to lead her into the theater.

"It is a pleasure to see you once more, Miss Dogmill," I said.

"I am delighted to be the source of such pleasure," she told me.

I observed that Mr. Hertcomb, who chatted amiably with one of the other young men, cast in our direction some significant glances. Again, I could not easily divine what it was he wanted of me, but despite his kind words, I was determined to remain on my guard around him. And if he wished to court Miss Dogmill, he would have a hard road to run competing with Mr. Evans.

I settled warmly into my smugness, though in truth here was something of a dilemma. As I strolled into the theater dressed in my fine suit and fashionable wig, arm in arm with a striking young lady, I could not have been more charmed with the role I had chosen to play. I was Matthew Evans, prosperous bachelor, presumably in search of a wife. I had become the subject of gossip among the single ladies of the beau monde. As we climbed the stairs to our box, I heard other theatergoers whisper my name. *That's Mr. Evans, the Jamaica man I told you of,* I heard one creature whisper. *It appears Grace Dogmill has snatched him up.*

And yet, for all of these delights, I could not stop reminding myself that I lived an ugly falsehood. If Miss Dogmill knew who I was she would recoil in horror. I was a Jew who lived by his fists, a fugitive wanted for murder, and I sought to destroy her brother. It would be cruel, monstrous cruel, to allow her to develop any affection for the persona I'd assumed by necessity. I understood that. And yet I was so enchanted by my habitation in this world that had always been denied me, I was ill prepared to heed the niggling voice of morality.

Could it be, I thought, that this was the sensation that had so seduced Miriam? Perhaps it had not been Melbury and all his charms but London, *Christian* London, that had done it. If I could have become Matthew Evans, with his money and his station and his license to move in society, would I have done so? I could not, even to myself, answer the question.

We all took our seats in the box, and I glanced over to the stage where the play, Addison's *Cato,* was already well under way. A fine choice, certainly, for this election season, for the play celebrated a great statesman who embraced civic virtue over fashionable corruption. No doubt the theater manager had thought to draw a large crowd with this choice, and he had successfully done so, but so volatile a play could easily ignite public passion—and it did.

We had been sitting not ten minutes when Mr. Barton Booth, in the role of Cato, began to deliver a rousing speech on corruption in the senate. A fellow in the pit shouted, "Corruption in the senate? We wouldn't know nothing about that one."

This drew a great laugh from the audience, and while the intrepid thespian plowed ahead with his lines, another man shouted, "Melbury's our Cato! He's the only one with virtue here!"

Now I looked up. Mr. Melbury was in a box across the theater from ours, and he rose and took a bow to the cheers of the audience.

Onstage, the players ceased their playing, waiting for the audience to return some small fraction of their attention. I could see that they would have a long wait. "Melbury be damned," someone else called. "The damned Romish Jacobite Tories be damned!"

At all of this, Hertcomb began to turn the color of an old farmer's cheese, and he slumped his head into his chest. The very last thing in the world he desired was that an incensed crowd of Tory theatergoers should recognize him. I can hardly say I blamed him. By the time I saw a few pieces of fruit take flight, I took hold of Miss Dogmill's arm. "I believe it is time I took you someplace less combustible."

She laughed good-naturedly in my ear. "Oh, Mr. Hertcomb is perhaps right to wish to avoid notice, but we've nothing to worry about. Perhaps they don't have such riotous audiences in the West Indies, Mr. Evans, but here they are no uncommon thing."

Now there were warring factions in the theater. Half cried out that Mr. Melbury should be damned, the other half encouraged the damnation of Mr. Hertcomb. The famous comedian of Drury Lane, Mr. Colley Cibber, now stepped foot onto the stage in the hopes of quelling these violent sentiments but was answered only with apples to his head for his troubles. I could tell now that the Hertcomb party was losing out, their voices being drowned by the Melbury camp.

And then I heard something that astonished me to my core. "God bless Griffin Melbury," one man shouted, "and God bless Benjamin Weaver."

It would seem that Johnson's praise of me in the Tory papers had taken root. Soon the cry, all but destroying all trace of the Hertcomb faction, was "Melbury and Weaver!" over and over again, as though we ran for the House together. And Melbury stood waving at the crowd, glowing in the premature glory of victory, while Hertcomb attempted to bury his face in his hands. Now the chanting was accompanied by the stomping of feet, and the whole building shook with the rhythm of the crowd's mayhem.

"Are you sure there is no cause for alarm?" I asked Miss Dogmill. I have been among boisterous theater audiences many times, and I felt I knew when a crowd had begun to turn dangerous. Melbury no longer waved and was attempting to quiet the crowd, but he was no longer of interest to them. Pieces of fruit, paper, shoes, and hats were now soaring through the air like sparks at a fireworks show. We were on the cusp of riot.

"No," Miss Dogmill said, her voice now shaking with concern, "I am no longer sure. Indeed, I begin to fear for Mr. Hertcomb's safety, perhaps even my own."

"Then let us go," I said.

The rest of our companions were in agreement, and we vacated the premises in a rushed if orderly manner, along with the majority of the patrons in the boxes. If the ruffians in the pit were to destroy the place, let them destroy only themselves. There was much murmuring about the unruliness of the lower orders, a sentiment Hertcomb heartily agreed with by nodding vigorously, though he hid his face behind a handkerchief.

Our evening entertainment having been prematurely ended, there was some discussion as to where to go next. As the evening was unusually warm for the season, the general agreement was for dining al fresco at a garden in St. James's, so we repaired there and enjoyed a hearty fare of beef and warm punch while the heating torches blazed nearby.

Hertcomb played his distress with a skill that would have impressed the thespians of Drury Lane. Though he glanced over at Miss Dogmill no more than two or three times each minute, he found comfort in one of her companions, a pert little creature with mouse-colored hair and a long thin nose. Not the prettiest young lady in town but certainly amiable, and I believed I could see Hertcomb find more to like about her with each glass of punch he swallowed. By the time he had put his arm around her waist and shouted out that dear Henrietta (though her name was Harriet) was his own true darling and the finest girl in the kingdom, I ceased to concern myself about his feelings.

As Hertcomb fell more securely into a delightful stupor, I allowed myself to relax and enjoy myself entire. Pressed into close conversation, I found Miss Dogmill's companions all sufficiently agreeable, if unremarkable. None of them had any particular interest in my story but the most minimal details, and I took some pleasure in having to tell so few lies over the course of the evening. Instead, warmed by drink and food, the roaring fires of the garden, and the nearness of Miss Dogmill's body, I could almost convince myself that this was my life, that I was Matthew Evans, and that there was no unmasking in my future. I now know I was overly optimistic, for an unmasking was to come, and very quickly too.

Perhaps if I had been enjoying less drink, I would not have permitted such a thing to happen, but after the evening's events I found myself traveling alone with Miss Dogmill in her equipage. She had agreed to take me home, and I had assumed that others would be joining us, but I soon found myself alone with her in the darkness of the coach.

"Your rooms are so close to my house," she said. "Perhaps you would like to come in first for some refreshment before going home."

"I should love to, but I fear that your brother might not wish me to pay a call."

"It is my home too," she said sweetly.

Here things began to grow delicate. I had long since come to suspect that Miss Dogmill might not be, let us say, the most scrupulous guardian of her virtue, and though I was never a man to resist the allure of Venus, I had taken far too great a liking to her to allow her to compromise herself with me while I remained in disguise. I certainly had no intentions of revealing to her my true name, but I feared that if I rejected her proposal I might seem to her something overly principled or, perhaps worse, uninterested in her charms. What could I do but acquiesce to her offer?

We retired at once to the parlor, and after her maid brought us a decanter of wine we were soon left alone entirely. A rich blaze roared in the fireplace, and two of the sconces of the room had been lit, but we were still largely veiled in shadow. I had cautiously taken a seat across from Miss Dogmill, who sat on a sofa, and I lamented that I could not very well see her lovely eyes as we spoke.

"I have recently learned that you paid a visit to my brother at his goose pull," she said to me.

"It was perhaps not the least provocative thing I've ever done," I admitted.

"You are a mystery, sir. You are a Tory, yet you seek the help of a great Whig when you arrive in our city. Then, rebuffed by him, perhaps unkindly, you attend him when he is certain to find your attendance infuriating."

"Does my having done so anger you?" I asked.

She laughed. "No, it amuses me. I love my brother, and he has always been kind to me, but I know he is not always kind to other people: poor Mr. Hertcomb, for instance, whom he treats like a drunken butler. I cannot but smile at seeing a man who does not hesitate to stand up to him. But it puzzles me as well."

"I cannot fully account for my whims," I said by way of explanation. "Taking upon myself the defense of that goose seemed to me, at that moment, the right thing to do. My doing so does not mean that I would not sit down for supper and eat the better part of a goose with great relish."

"Do you know, Mr. Evans," she said to me, "that you speak of yourself less than any man I have met?"

"How can you say so? Have I not, just this moment, expounded my opinions on goose and man?"

"You surely have, but I am far more interested in the man than I am the goose."

"I do not wish to chatter on about myself. Not when there is someone as interesting as yourself in the room. I should very much like to know more about you than hear myself speak of what I know so well."

"I have told you of my life. But you have been very withholding. I know nothing of your family, your friends, your life in Jamaica. Most men who make their living from the land love to talk of their estates and their holdings, but you have said nothing. Why, if I were to ask you the size of your plantation, I doubt you should even be able to tell me."

I forced a laugh. "You are surely unique of all the ladies I have known, madam, in wanting to be taxed with tedious knowledge."

Miss Dogmill said nothing for a moment. She then took a drink of her wine and slowly set down the goblet. I could hear the soft tap of the silver base against the wood. "Tell me the truth. Why did you call on my brother?" she asked at last, her voice heavy and somber. Something, I knew, had changed.

I tried hard to show that I saw nothing alarming in her tone. "I have thought to make myself a purchasing agent for Jamaica tobacco," I said, repeating the oft-told lie, "and I had hoped your brother would provide some guidance."

"I very much doubt he would do that."

"As it turns out, your doubts would have served me well had I known of them prior to my visit."

"But the results of your calling upon Mr. Dogmill cannot have surprised you. My brother's reputation as a ruthless businessman must extend to the West Indies. There is not a farmer in Virginia who does not fear his grasp. Do you mean to say you had never heard him to be ungenerous in these regards? Surely there was some other purchasing agent, some smaller fellow, who would have made a superior mentor."

"I wished to go to the most powerful," I said hastily, "for your brother's success testifies to his skill."

I thought she would press me now with another hard question, but I found I was mistaken. "I can hardly see you over there," she said. "Not even when I lean forward."

As it is so dark, I should have said, *I ought to make my way home.* But I did not say that. Instead, I said, "Then I must join you on your sofa."

And that is what I did. I moved next to Miss Dogmill, feeling the delicious warmth of her body as we sat only inches apart. I had hardly settled before I made bold to take her hand in mine. It was as though my higher self had become frozen inside me, and my baser instincts ruled my actions. The urge to feel her skin against mine silenced all other voices inside me. "I have longed to hold your hand in mine all evening," I said. "Since the moment I first saw you."

She said nothing, but she did not take her hand away either. Even in the dark, I observed an amused smile.

I had hoped for more encouragement, but I was willing to make do with none. "Miss Dogmill, I must tell you that you are the most beautiful young lady I have met in these many ages. You are charming and vivacious and lovely in all regards."

Here she allowed herself a laugh. "I must take that as a sound compliment," she said, "for you have a reputation as a man well acquainted with the ladies."

I felt my heart pound in my chest. "I? A reputation? I have hardly been on these shores long enough for such a thing."

She opened her mouth to say something, but she said nothing. Instead she leaned forward—yes, *she* leaned forward, and kissed me. Soon I had my arms around her sweet form, as we gave ourselves over to the delicious lure of passion. All of my determination to keep my distance from her was forgotten, and I cannot say to what degree we would have lost ourselves had not two things happened that cut short our delights.

The second, and less troubling of the two, was that the door burst open and Mr. Dogmill, along with a half dozen or so of his friends, entered the room with their blades drawn.

The first was that, in the very instant before our privacy was so utterly shattered by Dogmill and his bravos, Miss Dogmill broke off her kiss and whispered something in my ear. She said, "I know who you are, Mr. Weaver."

It was unfortunate timing, in more ways than one, that led Dennis Dogmill and his friends to break open the room at that instant, for I could not but conclude that all of this had been an elaborate trap. Having been lost in the pleasing fog of passion, I lamented that I was now in a position of having to strike dead this lady's brother if I did not wish to be returned to Newgate.

I leaped to my feet and searched the room for a weapon sufficient to fend off so many men, but found nothing.

"Get away from my sister, Evans," Dogmill spat at me.

Evans. He called me *Evans.* He was not here to drag Benjamin Weaver to prison. He was here only to protect his sister's honor. I breathed a sigh of relief, for it looked far less likely that I would have to seriously harm anyone.

"Dear God, Denny!" Miss Dogmill shouted. "What are you doing here?"

"Be quiet. I'll have plenty to say to you anon. And don't swear.

It is unladylike." He turned to me. "How dare you, sir, think to dishonor my sister in my own home?"

"How did you know he was here?" Grace asked.

"I did not much like the looks he gave you at the assembly, so I instructed Molly to contact me if he showed his face here. Now," he said to me, "we'll have no more rudeness from you. We are all gentlemen who know how to attend a man who would attempt a rape."

"A rape!" Grace cried out. "Don't be absurd. Mr. Evans has behaved in all ways like a gentleman, here by my invitation and guilty of nothing improper."

"I have not inquired into your opinion of what is proper and what is not," Dogmill told my victim. "A young lady of your age cannot always know when a man is using her ill. You need not worry, Grace. We will deal with him."

"It is very brave of you to face me with only six men at your side," I said. "A less stalwart man would have a full dozen."

"You may quip as you like, but it is I who have the power here, and you have nothing. You ought to thank me for intending to only give you one quarter of the beating you deserve."

"Are you mad?" I asked him, for he had pushed me too far. I knew that the person I pretended to be, Mr. Evans, could respond in only one way. "You may take issue with me if you like, but do so like a gentleman. I will not be treated like a serving boy only because you took the precaution of bringing a small army with you. If you wish to say something to me, say it like a man of honor, and if you wish to take up arms with me, let us do so in Hyde Park, where I will gladly duel with you on the day of your choosing, if you be but man enough to meet me."

"What is this, Dogmill?" one of his friends asked him. "You told me some blackguard was troubling your sister. It looks to me like this gentleman is here at her invitation and should be treated with more respect."

"Be silent," Dogmill hissed at his companion, but such arguments failed to hold sway. There were murmurs of agreement from the others.

"I resent this, Dogmill," the friend said again. "I was running a swimming hand at ombre when you dragged me from the card table. It's a scurvy thing to lie to a man and say things about sisters in trouble when there are no sisters in trouble at all."

Dogmill spat in the man's face. This was no trickle of moisture either, but a massive and agglutinated catch of sputum. It landed with an almost comical slap. The friend wiped it away with the sleeve of his coat, turned a rich shade of plum, but said nothing more.

Miss Dogmill held herself straight and folded her arms across her chest. "Stop spitting on your friends like a schoolboy and apologize to Mr. Evans," she said sternly, "and perhaps he will forgive this outrage."

I looked over at Mr. Dogmill and showed him my most winsome smile. I did it, of course, to mock him. I knew he found himself in a bind. Any man of grit would challenge me to a duel now, but I already knew he would not risk anything so scandalous until after the election.

Dogmill looked like a cat cornered by a salivating hound. He turned this way and that. He tried to think his way out of his trouble, but nothing came to mind.

"Get out. I'll settle our account once the election is resolved."

I grinned once more. "Well, I should be a rascal to be unsatisfied with an apology so kindly rendered," I told the room, "so I shall accept Mr. Dogmill's words in the good spirit he intended them. Now, perhaps you gentlemen would leave so that Miss Dogmill and I can be alone once more."

Only she, I should observe, laughed at my quip. All of Dogmill's friends appeared mortified, and Mr. Dogmill's muscles tightened so that he nearly collapsed on the floor with a seizure.

"Or," I proposed, "it might be best if I were to come back some other time, for the hour is rather late." I bowed to the lady and told her I hoped I should see her again soon. With that, I walked to the door and the crowd of men parted before me.

I had to make my own way from the parlor to the front door, and in doing so I passed a pretty little serving girl with sprightly green eyes. "Are you Molly?" I asked her.

She nodded dumbly.

I pressed a pair of shillings into her hand. "The same will be yours the next time you are supposed to inform Mr. Dogmill of my presence but neglect to do so."

I looked this way and that but saw no hackneys, and I could hardly expect Dogmill to volunteer his man to run one down for me, but I turned to reenter the house and request just that service. As I turned, however, I found myself facing Dogmill, who had followed me outside.

"Don't make the mistake of thinking me a coward," he said. "I should have fought with you on any terms to let you defend what you have the impudence to call your honor, but I cannot risk any action that might reflect badly on Mr. Hertcomb, with whom I am so nearly associated. When this election is complete, you may depend upon my calling for you. In the meantime, I suggest you keep your distance from my sister."

"And if I choose not to, how will you punish me? With another threat of a duel six weeks hence?" I cannot easily express the pleasure I took in making his outrage even more exquisite.

He took a step closer to me, no doubt with the intent of intimidating me with his great size. "Do you think to test me, sir? I may be shy of a public duel, but I will not be shy of putting my foot to your arse right here."

"I like your sister, sir, and I shall call upon her for as long as she wishes me to. I will not hear your objections, and I will tolerate no more rudeness from you."

I think perhaps I overplayed my part, because I next found myself at the foot of the stairs, in the wet street muck, looking up at Dogmill, who nearly smiled at my embarrassing position. An aching jaw and the coppery taste of blood in my mouth told me where I had been struck, and I ran my tongue along my teeth to satisfy myself that nothing had been knocked loose.

Here, at least, was some good news, for all remained properly affixed. Nevertheless, I was startled by the speed rather than the force of Dogmill's blow. I knew him to be a strong man, and I could not but believe he had chosen to reserve some of the power he unleashed against me. I had taken many such blows during my days as a pugilist, and I knew a man who could deliver a punch so quickly—so quickly I had not even seen it coming—could have deployed far more force than Dogmill had put into his attack. He toyed with me. Or he dared not risk killing me, perhaps. He thought me a wealthy trader, and he could not so easily escape the law should he murder me the way he did beggars and paupers.

It was Dogmill's strength that presented the greatest challenge to me. Were he a weaker man, a man whom I believed I could best easily, I would have had no difficulty in walking away from a fight. I would tell myself it was the right decision and think no more of it. It was the knowledge that he could, most likely, defeat me that made my decision more difficult, for more than anything I wished to return the blow, to challenge him like a man of grit. I knew I would hate myself for turning coward. I would lie awake at night and think of how I should have or might have or wished I could have answered his challenge. But I could not do it. I told myself I could not do it. I dared not risk revealing myself to Dogmill.

I sat up and stared at him for a moment. "You have taken liberties," I said at last, through a stiff jaw.

"Chastise me if you will," he answered

I damned him in silence, for he knew I would not stand up to him like a man. "My time will come," I said, attempting to drown my shame in thoughts of vengeance.

"Your time has come and gone," he told me. He turned his back and returned to his house.

CHAPTER 19

GRACE KNEW who I was. I cannot say if this revelation was more a distress or a relief, for I had at least the comfort of no longer having to lie to her. But how had she known me, and what did she intend to do now that she had discovered my true name? Fortunately, it was she who saved me from the torment of wonder, for I received from her the next morning a note inquiring if I would like to join her on the canvass. I knew nothing of how these things were ordered, and my innate curiosity would have compelled even if other circumstances had not. I wrote back at once, indicating my eager agreement.

My jaw was tender from Dogmill's blow, but miraculously it was not swollen or discolored, so I saw no reason to decline the invitation. At nearly eleven, a coach arrived covered in the blue-and-orange streamers of Mr. Hertcomb's campaign. If I thought, however, that I should find myself alone in that coach with Miss Dogmill, I was sadly mistaken, for it was that worthy, Mr. Hertcomb himself, who arose from the coach and met me with something less than good cheer. According to the letter of the law, he ought to be on the hustings each day for the duration of the polling, but in Westminster, where the election lasted for so long, no one insisted that the candidates endure such a hardship, and many men were known to make only brief appearances daily.

Inside the coach I found Miss Dogmill, adorned in a lovely gown of orange and blue colors. I sat across from her and offered her a thin smile. The grin she returned me was hearty and amused. She was possessed of my secrets, and I would have done anything to hear what she had to say, but I would have to wait—and she loved making me do so.

The equipage had only just begun to rumble along when Hertcomb, straining under the weight of his confusion, turned to me. "I must say, sir, I am startled to see you wish to join us."

"And why should that surprise you?" I asked, somewhat startled by his tone.

"You do remain a Tory, do you not?"

"I have had no conversion," I said.

"And a supporter of Mr. Melbury?"

"So long as he stands for the Tories."

"Then why should you wish to join us? You don't mean to do any mischief, I hope."

"None," I promised him. "I join you because I wish you well, Mr. Hertcomb, and because Miss Dogmill asked me to join your outing. You, yourself, have said that party is not all to a man. Besides which, when a lady as amiable as Miss Dogmill makes a request, it takes a foolish man to decline."

Hertcomb was in no way satisfied with this answer, but as none other was forthcoming, he made do with it as best he could. I did not like his new spirit of confrontation, and I could only imagine that he was caught between conflicting emotions. On the one hand, he wished more than anything for me to continue defying Dogmill. On the other, he wished I would leave Dogmill's sister to his own ineffectual attempts. Our coach, meanwhile, had turned onto Cockspur Street, and I observed that we were headed in the direction of Covent Garden.

"How do you determine the location of the canvass?" I asked.

"That is a good question," Hertcomb said, his tone lighter now that his curiosity had been aroused. "How *do* they do that?"

Miss Dogmill smiled like a lady's painting instructor. "My brother, as you know, is managing Mr. Hertcomb's election, so he coordinates with his underlings the names and addresses of the voters in Westminster."

"But there must be near ten thousand of them. Surely, each voter does not receive a visit."

"Surely, each voter does," she said. "Ten thousand visits are not so many when the election campaign lasts six weeks and there are dozens of canvassers willing to encourage each to do his bit for his country. Westminster is not a country borough where these things can simply be directed by the landowners. We require action here."

I had long heard of such things, of the great men and squires of the counties telling their tenants how to vote. Renters who defied orders were often forced off their land and pauperized. Once or twice the suggestion of secret voting had been raised in Parliament, but this notion had always been shot down immediately. What did it say of British liberty, the men of the Commons demanded, if a man were afraid to say publicly whom he supports?

"It is hard to believe that so many are willing to give up their time to the cause," I said.

"And why should that be so hard to be believe?" Hertcomb asked me, perhaps a little insulted.

"I only mean that politics is a very particular thing—in which people seem interested largely in their own gain."

"You are a cynic, sir. Can it not be that they are interested in the Whig cause?"

"And what is the Whig cause, if I may ask?"

"I see no point in arguing this matter with you," he said irritably.

"I do not seek a quarrel. I am most interested in hearing what constitutes the Whig cause. From my perspective, it appears to be little more than protecting the privileges of new men with new money and standing in the way of anything that would suggest there is more to seek than to enrich oneself at the cost of the world. If there is a more fundamental ideology that the party rests upon, I should very much like to know it."

"Do you suggest," Hertcomb asked, "that the Tory party is above seeking gain and advantage where it can?"

"I would never suggest anything of the sort about anyone involved in politics. I do not propose that there is no corruption among Tories. I am, however, asking about the philosophical foundation of your party, not the immoral practice of all parties, and I ask in earnestness."

Hertcomb quite clearly had nothing to say. He neither knew

nor cared what it meant, in principle, to be a Whig, only in practice. At last he muttered something about the Whig party being the king's party.

"If association is of such importance," I said, "I should rather you had observed that the Whig party is Miss Dogmill's party, for that is reason enough for any sane man to follow its banners."

"Mr. Evans attempts to flatter me, but I believe he has, in a way, answered his own question. I choose to support the Whigs because my family has always done so for as long as parties have mattered. The Whigs serve my family and my family serves the Whigs. I cannot say it is the most upstanding of the parties, but I know that none are above reproach; there is a certain pragmatic approach that must be followed. Nevertheless, if I could wish all of these politics and politicians away, I would do so in an instant."

"So you mislike the very system you serve?" I asked.

"Oh, immensely. But these parties are like great savage lions, Mr. Evans. They stand over you and salivate and lick their lips, and if you don't offer them a morsel of food now and again, they will eat you. You may stand upon principle and refuse to placate the beasts, but if you do so, all that will happen is that the lion will remain and you will be quite gone."

When we stepped out of the carriage at Covent Garden, I immediately pulled Hertcomb aside. "You and I are used to being on friendly terms," I said. "Have I done something to change that, sir?"

He stared at me, his face slightly less blank than usual. "I am not obliged to be every man's friend."

"I should not think you are. But as you have been mine in the past, I should like to know why you are not now."

"Is it not obvious?" he said. "I have a preference for Miss Dogmill, and you think nothing of trying to steal her affections away."

"I cannot argue when it comes to affairs of the heart, but I believe my fondness for Miss Dogmill was evident last night, and while you may not have liked it, you continued to be civil to me."

"I thought of it more, and I concluded I don't much like it—nor you either, Evans."

"If I believed you, I would respect your words. But I think you're hiding something, sir. You may confide in me, you know."

He bit his lip and looked away. "It is Dogmill," he said at last. "He has instructed me that I must no longer be friendly with you, sir. I am sorry, but the matter is quite out of my hands. I have been told that you and I are not to be on good terms, but that we are to be on bad terms as often as possible, so if you will cooperate in this, you will make my task much easier."

"Cooperate!" I nearly shouted. "You wish my assistance in cultivating you as my enemy? You will not have it, sir. I think it is time you learned that because Mr. Dogmill demands something of you, there is no need for you to provide it."

Here a redness began to spread across his eyes, like the plague of blood in ancient Egypt. "He struck me," Hertcomb whispered.

"What?"

"He struck me in the face. He slapped me as though I were a badly behaved child and told me he would serve me more of the same sauce if I did not recall that we meant to win a seat of the House of Commons, and that end is not generally achieved by being overly friendly with the enemy."

"You mustn't let him use you thus," I said, in a harsh whisper.

"What choice have I? I cannot defy him. I cannot strike him back. I can do nothing but endure his abuse until I win this election, and then I shall make every effort to free myself of his grasp."

I nodded. "I quite understand. You must let him have his way in this, but you and I need not allow his opinions to rule us. You may tell him you said the harshest things in the world to me, and I to you, and he will know no better. And, if we find ourselves in Mr. Dogmill's company, you may be as unkind to me as you like, and I promise I shan't hold it against you."

For a moment I thought Hertcomb would hug me. Instead he smiled as broadly and as innocently as a baby and then grabbed my hand, which he shook heartily. "You are a true friend, Mr. Evans, a true friend. After this election, when I sever my connections with Dogmill, I shall show you what it means to be well liked by Albert Hertcomb."

I could not but be touched by his affection, even though I was not his true friend. I would not have hesitated to ruin him if it would advance my cause, and, though I did not view the world as Dogmill did, under the proper circumstances I might strike Hertcomb in the face as well.

The canvass proved a strange and curious ritual. Miss Dogmill had a piece of foolscap on which the names of her voters had been written. There were indications if their political leanings were known to Mr. Dogmill, but most were not. I wondered why it was that so pretty a lady should be sent to so rough a part of the city to spread her message, but I found my answer soon enough. We visited the shop of one Mr. Blacksmith, an apothecary. He was in his fifties, perhaps, and had weathered his years not so well as he might have liked. When we walked into his shop, I thought perhaps he had never seen a creature so exquisite as Miss Dogmill in all his life.

"Sir," said Mr. Hertcomb at once, "have you yet voted in the general election?"

"I haven't," he said. "No one's been by yet."

"We have come by now," the Whig said. "I am Albert Hertcomb."

The apothecary sucked on his gums so that his face, in an instant, went from plum to prune. "Hertcomb is one I ain't heard of. Which one are you now?"

Miss Dogmill smiled sweetly at him and curtsied to show off the colors of her gown. "Mr. Hertford is the blue-and-orange candidate," she said.

The apothecary returned her smile sheepishly. "Blue and orange, is he? Well, those are fine colors, I reckon. What do ye have to offer me for the vote?"

"Why, justice and liberty," Mr. Hertcomb said. "Freedom from tyranny."

"I got as much of them as I'm like to have right now, and that ain't much, so try again."

"Half a shilling," proposed Miss Dogmill.

The apothecary scratched at the wispy bits of hair on his pate as he pondered the offer. "How do I know the other fellows won't offer me a better price?"

"You don't, but they may not offer you anything at all," Miss Dogmill said sweetly. "Come then, sir. If you will vote for Mr. Hertcomb, I will stroll over to the polling place with you right this moment. I will wait with you, and I will place the money in your hand myself." She took a step closer to him and placed her arm in his. "Do you not wish to accompany me?"

A great scarlet tide rose from the apothecary's neck and spread to his face and skull. "Gilbert!" he cried mightily. A boy of ten or eleven years appeared from the back of the shop. "I go to exercise my English liberties," the old man explained. "Watch the shop until my return. And know that I am familiar with every item in here. If there is one thing missing I'll beat you bloody on my return." He then looked up at Miss Dogmill. "I am ready for you to take me now, my dear."

It was clear enough that there was little to be gained from continuing the canvass without Miss Dogmill, so Mr. Hertcomb and I accompanied the happy couple to the great plaza where the polls had been set up, and together we waited in line with the voters. Miss Dogmill brought the old fellow to the tally master, who controlled the approach to the polling booths and decided in what order men would vote. Although these men were meant to be incorruptible, in less than two minutes she had convinced him to add this voter to an upcoming tally. Meanwhile, she chatted amiably with the apothecary as though there were nothing more natural in the world than for her to converse freely with so odd a man. Hertcomb stood awkwardly, wanting to avoid my gaze all the while yet seeming to desire conversation as well. My efforts to speak of something neutral, however, fell flat.

At last the apothecary stepped up to the booth. Miss Dogmill joined him and waited just outside, and we joined her as well, so we could hear all that transpired within. There was no better way of ensuring that the half shilling would not go to waste.

The man inside the polling place asked for the apothecary's name and place of residence, and then, when he had checked this information against the voter rolls, he asked for which candidate he chose to vote.

The old fellow cast a glance outside the tent to Miss Dogmill's gown. "I vote for orange and blue," he said.

The election official nodded impassively. "You cast your vote for Mr. Hertcomb?"

"I cast my vote for Mr. Coxcomb if he's orange and blue. That pretty lady with those colors there will pay me good coin to do it."

"Hertcomb, then," said the official, and waved the apothecary away so that the wheels of English liberty might continue to turn.

The apothecary stepped outside and, as promised, Miss Dogmill placed the coin in his hand.

"Thank you, my dear. Now, would you care to abandon these political-type sparks and join me for a dish of chocolate?"

Miss Dogmill explained that she should delight in doing so, but that her duties compelled her to continue the canvass, and so she left the old man both wealthier and happier than he had been that morning.

Not all of the names on the list proved to be so obliging. The next man we visited, a chandler, informed us that he was Melbury's man and Hertcomb be damned. He punctuated his thoughts by slamming his door behind us. Another fellow made us buy his meal in a chophouse and, upon our paying the reckoning, he wiped his face with a napkin, smiled, and informed us that he had already voted—for whom was none of our concern—and he was grateful for the bit of mutton. Finally, we visited a strapping young butcher, his forearms covered with blood as though he had just moments before been sticking them inside the cavity of a freshly slaughtered beast. He looked to Miss Dogmill and grinned so lecherously that had I not been in disguise I should have struck the fellow down for that offense alone.

"My vote is it that you want?" he asked. "I've heard there are things to be got for a vote."

"Mr. Hertcomb would be delighted to extend to you his gratitude," she said.

"Indeed I would," Hertcomb said.

"I don't give a fig for the gratitude of that scrawny bird," he said. "I want a kiss."

Hertcomb opened his mouth to speak, but nothing came out. Meanwhile, Grace had locked her eyes on the butcher. "Very well," she said. "If you vote for Mr. Hertcomb, I shall most certainly kiss you."

"Then, let's get to voting," he said, wiping down his arms with his apron. And so we were off once more to the plaza, where Miss Dogmill once more convinced the tally master to let her man vote without too much waiting. She remained by the butcher until he cast his vote, remaining remarkably cheerful in the presence of so low a man. After he had done his business, the butcher then turned to Miss Dogmill and put his arm around her waist. "Where's my kiss, then, lass?" he asked. "And don't skimp on the tongue."

Right there, before the world, she kissed him upon the lips. He pulled her closer and tried to force her mouth open, and he put one hand upon her breasts. This gesture brought the crowd, particularly those who carried Mr. Melbury's banners, to a cheer.

Grace attempted to pull away from him, but he would not release his grip. He began to tug at her gown in the most savage fashion, as though he intended to strip her naked in the middle of Covent Garden. A savage cry for *Melbury* arose at once from that candidate's supporters, who perhaps imagined that this ruffian was a Tory who chose to abuse a Hertcomb supporter, rather than a rascal who had sold his vote and now believed himself entitled to a rape in exchange.

Though I had no desire to call attention to myself, I saw I had but little choice, so I rushed forward and pulled Grace away from the brute's clutches. She gasped for breath and staggered backward, righting her gown as she did so. The butcher now took a step toward me and sized me up. He surely had the advantage of size and youth, and I could see that he had every intention of pressing those advantages.

"Nothing like a Whig slut. Now, you step aside, grandfather," he said to me, "unless you like the taste of your own blood in your mouth."

Perhaps I ought to have sought a more peaceable resolution, but after my encounter with Dogmill the previous night, I was in no mood to cower before this rough. Instead, I grabbed the fellow by his hair and yanked hard, pulling him to the ground. I pressed one foot hard on his chest until I could feel his ribs straining under the pressure, and then relented, only to stomp at him until he was quite unable to rise again. He grunted and made some valiant efforts to roll from my wrath, so I gave him one more kick for the mere pleasure of it. Then I raised him to his feet and pushed him away. Being a good fellow, he regained his balance and continued to run without looking back.

My performance received a warm cheer, so I bowed to show my appreciation, knowing full well that a refusal to acknowledge goodwill can lead swiftly to ill will. Somehow the fact that Matthew Evans favored the Tory candidate circulated quickly, for the cry for Melbury went out once more. I looked over to Grace, who appeared flushed and confused but not horrified. Mr. Hertcomb, however, was clearly out of sorts, and I knew that our canvassing for the day had come to a conclusion.

I cannot easily describe the frustrations of that day. I only wanted Miss Dogmill to myself that I might hold her or, perhaps, inquire of her what she knew of me and what she intended to do with this knowledge. Instead, hours had passed in close quarters with a rival while brutes of all descriptions had pawed at her mercilessly. I therefore breathed a sigh of relief when she informed the driver that as Mr. Hertcomb lived close by, he should be delivered to his home first. This news was hardly welcomed by Hertcomb, but he bore his displeasure silently if not well. After he was disposed of, Miss Dogmill suggested that we visit a chocolate house nearby, and so I held my tongue until we were seated together at a table.

"How did you like the canvass?" she asked me, with her eyes cast downward.

"I did not like it much. How can your brother allow you to expose yourself to such brutishness?"

"He is quite good at exposing the world to his own brutishness, though had he been there he should not have treated that butcher with the mercy you demonstrated. I attempt to keep from him some of the more unsavory elements of what a woman faces on the canvass, lest he forbid me participating. I have, in fact, used a wide variety of deceptions to keep him from learning the truth of how brutal the canvass can be for a woman. You see, it is the only involvement in politics I am permitted, and I should hate to surrender my role."

"And what would happen if Dogmill should learn the truth?"

Miss Dogmill closed her eyes for a moment. "Two years ago a carpenter to whom my brother owed some money grew rather desperate. He was none the most engaging man in the world, but Denny owed him more than ten pounds, which the fellow needed to feed his family. There are times when Denny will not pay what he owes tradesmen simply for the pleasure of watching them suffer and worry, and here was such a time. This carpenter seemed to understand that my brother teased him the way a child will tease a captured frog. So he sent Denny a note telling him that if he did not pay his bill, he would get his money by hook or by crook and that he would pluck me off the street and hold me hostage until justice was served."

"I presume your brother did not take this kindly."

"No. He went over to the carpenter's house, beat his wife unconscious, and then beat the man unconscious. He then took a note for ten pounds, spat upon it, and stuffed it in the fellow's mouth. He even tried to put it into his throat so he would choke on his money. I witnessed all this because the carpenter, in an effort to convince my brother I had been abducted, had invited me to his home, knowing I was sympathetic, pretending that he wished me to serve as an intermediary." She took a deep breath. "I should very much have liked to have stopped his violence, but there is no stopping him once he begins. I should hate to see him let loose with his passions in the midst of Covent Garden while the electors stand by."

"I can understand how you might feel thus."

"You seem to have your passions much more at your disposal, and I thank you for your efforts today. I cannot say that this was the first time I have ever been threatened, and it is a much finer thing to have a capable man by your side."

"It was my pleasure to serve you."

She astonished me by reaching out and gently, just for an instant, laying her fingertips against my jaw where Dogmill had punched me. "He told me he struck you," she said quietly. "It must have been very hard for you not to strike him back."

I laughed softly. "I am not used to running from men like your brother."

"You are not used to men like my brother at all. No one is. But I am sorry for what he did to you."

"Don't be sorry," I said testily. "I chose to let him use me so."

She smiled. "I have no doubt of your resolve, sir. No one who knows your name would make the mistake of doing so. I daresay my brother, if he knew who you were, would have hesitated himself."

"As you have broached the topic, I would fain discuss it with you."

She sipped from her dish of chocolate. "How did I know? I did the most extraordinary thing to make my discovery: I looked at your face. I have seen you before around town, sir, and I always remarked on your proceedings. Unlike some others, perhaps, I am not so easily fooled by the application of new clothing and a new name, though I think your disguise masterfully handled. The moment you came to see my brother, I thought I knew your face, and I could not rest until I hit upon it. At last it occurred to me that you looked uncommonly like Benjamin Weaver, but I was not certain until I danced with you. You move like a pugilist, sir, and the world knows of your leg injury, which I fear gave you away."

I nodded. "But you have said nothing to your brother."

"You have not been taken by the constables, so you may assume I have said nothing to my brother."

"And you do not think he will guess?"

"How could he? I don't know that he has ever laid eyes upon you—dressed as yourself, I mean—and there is no reason why he would suspect you come to him in disguise. He learned from Hertcomb about the chanting for Melbury and Weaver at the theater, and though he cursed at great length and with great vigor against Tories and Jacobites and Jews and the large franchise in general, he never once mentioned your name—Mr. Evans's name, that is. And, allow me to assure you, he was in no frame of mind to censor himself."

"Well, that is a relief, at least. But you know who I am. What do you plan to do?"

She shook her head. "I cannot yet say." She reached out and placed one gloved hand on my arm just above my wrist. "Will you tell me why you sought to connect yourself to him in the first place?"

I let out a breath. "I don't know if I should."

"May I speculate?"

Something in her tone caught my attention. "Certainly."

She looked away for a moment, and then turned to catch my gaze, her eyes as amber as her dress. I could tell that what she had to say could not be said with ease. "You think he had this man, Walter Yate, killed, and that he has put the blame on you."

I stared I don't know how long before I dared to speak. "Yes," I said in a rasping voice, just above a whisper. "How could you know that?"

"I could not reach any other conclusion. You see, if you had truly killed that fellow, as you have been convicted of doing, you would have no business with my brother. You would have no need to play at masquerade. The only reason you might take such risks is to prove yourself guiltless, and I can only presume that you now search for the man who did murder Yate."

"You are a very clever woman," I said. "You would do well as a thieftaker."

She laughed. "You are the first man to tell me so."

"So now you know all my secrets."

"Not all, surely."

"No, not all."

"But I know you think my brother is involved in Yate's death."

I nodded. "And does that place a wedge between us?"

"I cannot enjoy seeing my brother accused of so horrible a crime, but that does not mean I am blind to the possibility he may be guilty. He is, in his own way, very good to me, and I love him, but if he did this thing, he should be punished rather than let an innocent man hang in his stead. I could feel no resentment toward you for being the instrument of your own vindication. You could do no less. Indeed"—she lifted her dish and set it back down again—"Indeed," she said once more, "indeed, I think he may be guilty as you suspect."

I felt a tingle across my skin, the sensation one feels just before something of import happens in a stage play. I leaned toward Miss Dogmill. "Why do you say so?"

"Because," she told me. She paused, looked away, and then looked toward me again. "Because Walter Yate came to visit my brother not a week before you were said to have killed him."

I had been, for some time now, proceeding on the near certain assumption that Dogmill had orchestrated Yate's death, so I cannot say why this revelation so surprised and delighted me. Perhaps it was because this was the closest I had yet come to being able to prove my assumption, and though it was true, as Elias had certainly pointed out, that proof alone would not save me, it was satisfying for all that.

"Tell me everything," I said to Miss Dogmill.

And she did. She explained that, as I had already observed, she had a habit of peering in at who visited her brother, so she had been surprised to find a rugged, roughly dressed laborer in his parlor one day. He had refused to say much of himself, other than his name and that he had business with Mr. Dogmill. He had been polite but uncomfortable, clearly feeling out of place, which he well should have—seeing that he was but a dockworker sitting in the parlor of the wealthiest tobacco man in the kingdom.

"I thought it odd at the time that they should meet on such terms," Miss Dogmill said, "but I knew there were disputes on the matter of wages among the labor gangs, and that Yate was one of the leaders. It seemed to me likely that my brother had invited him to the house to make Yate uneasy by taking him out of his own world."

"And did you suppose more when you learned that Yate had been killed?"

"Not at first," she said. "I read that you had been arrested for the crime and thought no more of it than that you lived your life in a rugged fashion and there were bound to be incidents of violence. It was only when I discovered you to be hounding my brother that I began to wonder what role he might have played in all of this. It then occurred to me that what I took to be discomfort in the presence of money may have been another kind of anxiety. I cannot say what Yate wished to discuss with my brother, but I suspect that if you were to learn, it would help your cause greatly."

"Why do you tell me all this?" I demanded. "Why do you side with me over your own flesh and blood?"

Miss Dogmill blushed. "He is my brother, it is true, but I will not protect him in a matter of murder, not when another man must pay the price for it."

"Then you will help me to discover what I must do to exonerate myself?"

"Yes," she whispered.

For the first time since my arrest, I felt something like the swell of joy.

CHAPTER 20

I HAD NOT THOUGHT to return myself so soon to Vine Street, but I went there that night, unwilling to waste any more time. I was close to something, and I knew it, and I felt that Yate's widow might have the answer. I found her with her baby asleep in her arms, hovering over the fire of the stove. Littleton was there too, looking not a little provoked to see me once more. He answered the door with a pewter dish of peas and mutton fat in one hand, a hunk of bread gripped in his mouth.

"For a man with a hundred and fifty pounds on his head," he observed, while clenching the bread with his teeth, "you find your way to this part of the city with an alarming frequency."

"I am afraid I must speak to Mrs. Yate," I said. I pushed my way in without waiting to be asked.

Mrs. Yate looked at her baby and cooed and rocked and kissed. She hardly looked up to glance at my face.

"That baby don't even know you're there." Littleton spat his bread onto his plate. "Set it aside and talk to Weaver that he might be out of here the sooner." He turned to me. "I don't want them cony-fumbles from the magistrate's office coming in here and saying we gave you shelter. It ain't personal, you understand, but you're not a safe man to be near these days. I know you got your business, so go about it and be gone."

I pulled a chair closer to the widow and sat. "I have but one thing I must know. Mr. Yate paid a visit to Dennis Dogmill just one week before he was killed. Have you any knowledge of why they met or what they discussed?"

She continued to coo and kiss and rock. Littleton kicked her chair, but she ignored him.

"Please," I said. "It is important."

"It don't matter to me, important," she said. "It don't matter as I can't tell you what I don't know, and they can't do nothing to me if I don't know."

"Who can't?" I asked.

"No one. No one can say I said nothing. I didn't say nothing because I didn't know nothing."

"What is it you did not say?" I asked, urgently but gently.

"Nothing. Ain't you heard me?"

"Aye, he heard you," Littleton said. "He heard the worst bit of lying that ever escaped from human lips since Eve lied to Adam. Tell him what you know, woman, or there will be more trouble for all of us."

She shook her head.

Littleton walked over to her and knelt beside her. He put his hands on the baby. "Listen to me, love. They can't do nothing to you for just knowing what Yate knew, but if you don't tell Weaver what he wants to know, they might come and take the baby away and put it in the workhouse, where it ain't going to live but another day or two before it dies, longing for its mother."

"No!" she shrieked. She pulled the infant to her chest and rose from her chair, quickly walking to the corner, as though she could defend the creature from any evil in the world so long as it was hidden.

"Aye, it's true. If you don't help him, he won't be able to help you, and Jesus knows what will happen to the baby there." Here Littleton turned to me and winked.

I opened my mouth to object, for as much as I wished to know her secrets, I could not countenance such cruel extortion. But before I could speak, Mrs. Yate had already surrendered.

"I'll tell you, then," she said, "but you must promise to protect me."

"I swear to you, madam, that if you should face any harm because of what you tell me here tonight, my life and my strength will be at your disposal, and I will not rest until you and your child are safe."

This declaration, romantical as it was, seemed to soothe her considerably. She returned to her chair. Silence once more descended upon us, and I saw Littleton begin to utter something, no doubt harsh, but I held up a hand. Her words would come, and I saw no need to terrorize her more.

My supposition proved sound, for a moment later she began to speak. "I told him," she said, "I told him it would come to no good, but he wouldn't listen to me. He thought what he had learned was like gold, and if he could but reckon how to manage it, we would be rich for his efforts. I knew he was wrong. I swear to you, I said he would be dead before he was rich, and I was right."

"What did he know?" I asked.

She shook her head. "He wanted to meet with the Parliament man. The blue-and-orange man."

"Hertcomb," I said.

She nodded. "Aye. Walter thought he was the one who should hear about it, but the fellow wouldn't meet with him. Dogmill would, though. Walter didn't trust Dogmill, not for a moment. He knew what Dogmill was, but it was clear that it was talk to Dogmill or talk to no one, and he couldn't let his dream of getting rich slide. So he went to talk to Dogmill."

"What did they speak of? What did he believe would make him rich?"

"Walter said he knew of someone who was not what he was supposed to be. That there was one of the orange-and-blue fellows who was really with the green-and-white side. He knew the name, and he figured Dogmill would want to know the name too."

I rose to my feet. If I had understood correctly what I had just heard, I could not remain still for long. "Do you mean to tell me that Mr. Yate knew there was a Tory spy among the Whigs?"

She nodded. "Aye, that's right."

"And Mr. Yate knew the name of this spy?"

"He told me he did. He said it was an important man, and the orange-and-blue fellow would shit himself to death if he knew there was a Jacobite among them."

Littleton put down his pipe and stared. "A Jacobite?" he asked.

She nodded. "That's what he said. That there was a Jacobite that was one of them, and he knew the name. I can't claim to know much about things of the government, but I know being a Jacobite will get you hanged, and I knew that if a man pretends to be one thing and is a Jacobite instead, he'll do a lot worse than kill a porter on the quays to keep his secret."

Littleton and I stared at each other. "Not merely a Tory but a Jacobite spy," I said aloud, "among the Whigs."

"An important Whig," Littleton said. He turned to Mrs. Yate. "I wish I'd listened to you, love, for some things are better not to know."

"Aye," she said. "And after Mr. Dogmill come here himself, I thought I should never say a word of this to anyone."

"What is this?" Littleton spat. "Dogmill come here? When?"

"Just after I laid Walter to his rest. He come and pound on my door and tells me that he can't say if I knew what Walter known or not, but if I do and speak of it to anyone, he'll see me in the ground next to my husband." She stared at Littleton. "He grabbed me then in a place that's none of his business and told me that a poor widow belonged to any man that wanted to take her, and I should remember that if I wanted to stay alive."

I expected to see something more of a rage in Littleton, but he only looked away. "The laws belong to those which have the money," he said softly. "They can do what they please and they can take what they want—or at least they think so." He rose and walked over to Mrs. Yate and planted a kiss on her cheek. "You've been hardly used, my love. I won't see it happen again."

If I found Littleton's calm impressive, I could not say I shared it. With each passing day, the idea of fleeing the country appealed to me more.

No amount of questioning revealed more information. Mrs. Yate knew neither the name nor the station of the spy, only that he was an important Whig. After I had fully interrogated her, she retired to bed and Littleton uncorked a bottle of surprisingly drinkable claret. The need to drink wine exorcised all earlier needs to rid himself of my company.

"How could Yate have learned of this?" I asked.

Littleton shook his head. "I don't know. There's plenty of boys on the quays that raise a glass to the king across the water, but that's all talk that comes from the bottle. I can't think that Yate had any great connections with the Jacobites that he could learn a secret like this."

"But it seems he did."

"Aye," he agreed. "And now what? What will you do with this knowledge that you wrung from me woman?"

I shook my head. "I don't know, but I will do something. I knew that I would have to find something to frighten Dogmill, and I believe I have discovered it at last—at least I have discovered what it would be. I am close, Littleton. I am very close."

"You're close to death is what you are," he said. "I just hope you don't take the rest of us with you."

CHAPTER 21

O N RETURNING HOME, I drank the better part of a bottle to port to calm myself and went through the letters that had collected that day. I had begun to receive invitations to outings and parties and gatherings. People who read the name *Matthew Evans* in the paper wished to make my acquaintance, and while in some odd way I could not help but be flattered, I declined them all. I had achieved what I wished with Mr. Evans's reputation, and I had no desire to make him more conspicuous than I had to.

Of far more interest was a note from Griffin Melbury, saying that he would be by at ten to pay me a visit. Here was good timing, I thought. Or perhaps bad; I could hardly say which. My mind was already muddled with drink, and I did not know whether I was equal to formulating the questions I wished to ask.

Melbury's equipage pulled up precisely as the clock struck ten. The man came inside and greeted me warmly but refused to take any refreshment. "Have you heard today's tally?" he asked. "One hundred ninety-nine for Hertcomb and two hundred twenty to our side. We lead by nearly a hundred votes, and the election is but five days old. I taste victory, sir. I taste it. I tell you, the people of Westminster have had enough of corruption, of these Whigs who sell the soul of the nation to the highest bidder. But there is no time to rest. There's work to be done, Mr. Evans, and as you are eager to aid the Tory cause, I thought you would care to join me in it."

"I should be honored," I told him, attempting to hide my confusion. It was not the suddenness of the offer that put me off my balance, but the familiarity Melbury showed me. I had wanted him to like me, and now he appeared to do just that. I had wanted to make him my ally, and he was becoming so. But my feelings were uncertain. I disliked him, but not nearly as much as I wanted to. Melbury was stiff in the way of old-money men, but not hard or cruel or insufferable, and though his politics were not mine, he appeared to believe them with great passion.

I could only tell myself that the fates had shown Melbury their kind faces, and he did seem poised to win Westminster. I flattered myself that when I revealed my true name, and when I told him all I knew of the Whiggish corruption, he would do all in his power to aid me. That I found him too superior (or too married to Miriam) for my tastes hardly signified. And so the two of us entered his equipage, which began to roll noisily toward Lambeth.

Melbury hummed a few times and then coughed and snorted. "Look here, Evans. I like you tremendous or I would not have asked you to come with me tonight, but there is something I must say to you."

"Of course," I replied, not a little uneasy.

"I know things are oft different in the colonies, so I understand fully well you meant no harm. You must understand that I am not for a moment insulted or angry. It's just a bit of friendly advice, you see."

"I should be honored," I assured him.

"It's just not the thing to dance with another man's wife, you understand."

I felt my guts turn sour. "Mr. Melbury, you must not think that I mean—"

"Please," he said, with forced cheer. "I will not have any explanations or apologies. I only tell you this to keep you from perhaps finding yourself in an unpleasant situation with a less liberal gentleman. Or perhaps, if I may be so bold, a less uxorious one. I surprise you? Well, I think it no crime for a man to dote upon his wife."

"I should not think it was," I said stiffly.

"I presume one of the reasons you have come to London is to search for an appropriate wife?"

"Perhaps," I said.

"I tell you, marriage is a fit and proper state for a man. I have no regrets of it, but rather rejoice each day. But you'll get nowhere dancing with Whig harlots like Grace Dogmill or other men's wives. Perhaps it is the wrong thing to have spoken to you, I don't know. I only mean to aid you—though I admit to being of a slightly jealous temperament when it comes to my beautiful Mary," he said with a laugh.

"I do beg your pardon—" I began.

"No, no, I need no apology. Now, we shall say no more of it. It is forgotten. Are we in agreement?"

Here this villain wished to chastise me for dancing with Miriam when he had all but stolen her from my arms. I would have loved nothing more than to run my blade through him—if I were not depending on him to save my life. "We are in agreement," I assured him, grateful he could not see my face in the dark of the coach.

He said nothing for some minutes, and while I was glad not to have to make chatter with him, I began to find the silence oppressive. "May I inquire as to why I have been thus honored with an invitation?" I asked at last.

"You did express a desire to involve yourself in this race," he reminded me.

"I did, and earnestly too, but I doubt that every man who expresses such a desire receives the honor of an outing with Mr. Melbury."

"Well, there can be no doubt of that, but most men who wish to involve themselves in politics have not saved me from a Whiggish brute, so I am not as inclined to like them as I am you, Evans. Have you an engagement for two nights hence?"

"I believe not," I said.

"Then I shall provide you with one. I host a small dinner gathering where you will, I hope, meet some men of mutual interests. I beg you to join me."

I knew that my presence would be a hardship for Miriam, but if

I wished to solidify my bond with Melbury, I could hardly be seen to stammer excuses when generous offers were made. I must appear to be the most likable person in the world to him, so that when I happened to mention that I was not quite honest about one or two things—my name, my religion, my political inclinations, my money—he would not react with much displeasure. So I told him I was honored and would arrive most punctually.

"Very good. I think you'll like the company. Some very good Tories, you know. Men of the Church and their supporters. Old-money men, who feel the pinch of the stockjobbers and corrupt politicians. I promise you, they will have much to say about the latest developments."

"Some of which I find most perplexing," I ventured. I had told myself a hundred times I would not broach this subject, that it was foolish, even mad, to do so, but here in the darkness of the coach, where he could not even see my face, I took a false comfort in my sense of anonymity. With the easiest, most casual voice I could muster (and because of all this mustering, it must have sounded as false as gold-painted lead), I said, "What do you feel about the mob's association of you with this Weaver fellow?"

Melbury let out a barking laugh. Not a moment of hesitation. Nothing to suggest that he knew who I was and only waited for the right time to make his revelation. I could, for the moment, believe that Miriam had not betrayed my confidence.

"Weaver," he repeated. "It is a strange thing to what the mob will attach itself. The Whigs are to blame, of course, for embarrassing themselves at his trial, and the Tory papers cannot help but press the advantage when it dangles so temptingly in front of them."

"So you do not feel any kinship or affinity with this fellow."

"Let us be blunt, Evans. If I can take some advantage from the mob linking me with a renegade Jew, if I can strengthen the Church and push back the corrupt stockjobbers and foreigners, then I shall do so, but I should never break bread with the fellow. If he were to cross my path, I'd call the constable and take my hundred and fifty like any other man."

"Even if he is innocent, as the mob believes?"

"Innocent or guilty, I'd feel no disquiet to see him hang. You are new enough to London that you do not always know how things work. I can tell you that these thieftakers are all scoundrels, sir. They will happily send an innocent to hang that they might get a small bounty for the conviction. Jonathan Wild is only the most respectable of them, and Weaver would have the world believe that he is honorable, but that business with the murder reveals the truth."

This conversation should serve as a fine reminder, I told myself, when I forgot who I was and believed myself Matthew Evans. I could not become him, and Melbury was not my friend. He was merely someone from whom I wanted something.

"It is all a game, you know," he continued. "You make the mob believe that you think as they think. You get their votes and then you forget about them for seven years, that you may do some good. We did not make these rules that promote corruption. The Whigs did that. But we must live with them or die by them, and if I can use Whig trickery to run off the Whigs themselves, I shall not hesitate to do so."

"That's rather a sour view, is it not?"

"You saw the election procession, I presume."

I told him I had.

"That is our system, Mr. Evans. We haven't the Jamaican luxury of dropping our votes in a coconut brought from hut to hut by some naked African beauty. In London, it is King Mob who rules, and we must give his majesty a good show or he will have all our heads off."

"You told me once you thought the election but a spectacle of corruption. I believed you only said it because you were disordered."

He laughed. "No, I said it because it cheers to me to think of it as such. Spectacle can be orchestrated, chaos cannot. Take this Jew, Weaver, as an example. He believes he runs wild and dodges the law and the government, but we all use him—Whigs, Tories, all. He is but our puppet, and which party pulls the strings the hardest shall have its way with him."

I looked out the fist-sized window of the carriage for a moment. "For the nonce," I said, in an effort to change the subject, "I wonder about our current business?"

"Our current business is a delicate one. I should have sent my agent to order it, but he is not the most lionhearted man upon the earth, and we are now dealing with a group that requires some resolve. It is a voting club, sir, and they are not to be shown a sign of weakness. I aim to have this club, and I shall. Visiting them myself might keep the wheels effectively greased, and I thought having you by my side might keep my spirits up. I trust this is all amenable to you."

I assured him it was, and so we traveled in silence once more until we reached a coffeehouse on Gravel Lane. Here we decamped, entered the structure, and found ourselves in a disorderly place of business. The term *coffeehouse* is often used somewhat loosely, but here was one in which I doubted the eponymous beverage had ever been seen. It was full of rugged fellows of the lower middling orders, whores, and a band of fiddlers. The room smelled strongly of old beer and freshly boiled beef, heaps of which, covered with turnips and parsley, were upon every plate at every table.

We had hardly been inside an instant when a fellow rose to approach us with a most serious look on his face. He was dressed plainly, but for an abundance of lace and bright silver buttons. He had a long nose that pointed downward, a long chin that pointed upward, and eyes that were like two raisins.

"Ah, Mr. Melbury. I recognized you the instant you walked through the door, sir, the very instant, for I have seen you speak more than once. I am Job Highwall, sir, as you may have guessed, and I am most eager to talk business with you."

Melbury introduced me to Highwall, mentioning me as the man who had saved him from Whiggish ruffians and beaten the Whig butcher at the hustings. There could be no doubt that he had asked me along to lend an air of menace, but if Highwall felt himself endangered, he showed no sign of it.

We took a seat in a quiet corner of the coffeehouse. Highwall called for strong beer—the very thing for business, he said—and urged us to waste no time, for time was a most precious thing.

"Allow me to repeat what you already know, sir, and I shall thank you for your kindness. I represent the Red Fox Voting Club, Mr. Melbury, a most respectable voting club. You may look to elections past and you will always hear one thing again and again: The Red Fox delivers what it promises. I have heard that other clubs will promise the same to all parties in an election and deliver nothing to any. Not the Red Fox, sir. We have offered our services in every election since the days of the second Charles, and never once have we given a Westminster candidate cause to regret trusting us."

"Your reputation is unimpeachable," Melbury said.

"I should hope it is, Mr. Melbury, for the Red Fox does what it promises. I make you a pledge, sir, on behalf of the Red Fox, you may depend upon it. We are more regular and more dependable than the mail coach, sir."

"I have not come to question your reputation," Melbury said.

"There is no reason you should, sir. No reason at all."

"You and I are in agreement on that head. It is merely the numbers that we must discuss."

"Ah," said Mr. Highwall. "The numbers are the thing, sir. You may talk of this and talk of that, but it shall always be that the numbers are the very thing. Can you deny it?"

"I cannot," Melbury said. "I should like to hear these numbers."

"For that I cannot blame you. And so I shall tell you the numbers. Here are things as they stand, sir. We have three hundred and fifty men in this club, and they are three hundred and fifty men you may depend upon to do as I promise. They will deliver, sir, to a man. We are not a club that promises three hundred and fifty and delivers two hundred and fifty. No, we offer three hundred and fifty, and you will have it, sir, providing the numbers are agreeable."

"And what are the numbers, Mr. Highwall?"

"You must understand that to a man, sir, to a man, these three hundred and fifty I promise are Tories. They are Tories in their hearts and in the privacy of their innermost minds. I cannot tell you how many have said to me that if they could choose, they would choose to provide their service to Mr. Griffin Melbury, but you know as well as any man that business is the thing, and they will take their business to Mr. Hertcomb—who has made us an offer, you know— with a heavy heart if need be."

"I understand," said Melbury, not a little frustrated now. "I should like to know the cost of these three hundred and fifty Tories."

"You may depend upon the loyalty of these men, sir, these three hundred and fifty men, for the compensation of a mere one hundred pounds."

Melbury set down his strong beer. "That is rather a lot, don't you think?"

"I don't think so at all, Mr. Melbury, indeed I don't. Only consider what you are getting. Should you like to pay twenty or thirty pounds for the same number but, when the dust clears, as they say, receive only fifty votes for your money?"

"You ask more than five shillings a man. It is rather a lot."

"It is a lot, but you pay for reputation, you know. Reputation. I cannot say what Mr. Hertcomb's man offered, but I promise you I cannot go back to these men with less than one hundred pounds and look them in the eye. They will say, How could you take this offer when Mr. Hertcomb's man has offered so much more? What answer might I give them?"

"You might tell them that they are Tories to a man and should like to see me elected."

"Well, if this were preference, you would have a point, sir. But this is business, you know."

"I will offer you sixty pounds."

"Sixty pounds!" Highwall screamed as though Melbury had drawn a blade. "Sixty pounds! You shock me, Mr. Melbury. Indeed you do. I believe I must postpone this conversation, for you have so disordered me with your offer that I must be bled and purged before I can continue. Sixty pounds is the insultingest offer in the world. I cannot go to the boys with sixty pounds. Nor a penny less than ninety, for that matter."

"I propose seventy," Melbury said.

"The Red Fox Voting Club is worth far more than seventy pounds, but I honor you, sir, so I will accept eighty pounds in the interests of supporting your run for the House." And the two men shook hands. In this way, in the course of a few minutes, Mr. Melbury secured nearly a tenth of the votes he needed to win his seat.

Having concluded his business with Mr. Highwall, Melbury had enjoyed as much time in the company of the Red Fox Voting Club leader as he cared to, and he suggested that we retire to a far more fitting location. He chose Rosethorn's Coffeehouse on Lowman's Pond Row, a place known for its congregation of Tories of the better sort. Indeed, when we walked through the door, Melbury was fairly thronged by a company of well-wishers, but unlike men of the lower orders, these knew well enough to leave off after a time and let the fellow be. Once he had made his rounds and introduced me to far more men than I could possibly have recalled, we took our seats.

He promised me that their claret was of the highest quality, so I drank as he suggested, and we ordered a cold fowl to wrest our appetites down.

"Does the business with the voting club shock you?" he asked.

"Should it?"

"Well, you are from the West Indies, after all, and I suppose life is much simpler there. You are probably unaccustomed to ordering things in quite so circuitous a manner there."

"I assure you," I said, without malice, "that bribery has found its way to the West Indies."

"Oh, such an ugly word, bribery. I hate to call it so. I think of it as a mere transaction, and there is nothing wrong with a transaction, surely. I only sting over the cost. You know, in the last election, I believe I could have secured the same votes for ten pounds, but these clubs know what they're about. Even at so dear a price, it is far cheaper than canvassing three hundred and fifty men all the way to the hustings."

296 | DAVID LISS

"Are there other, equally delicate, methods of securing votes?"
I asked.

Melbury only winked. "The election is young yet," he said.
"We shall see what develops. But think only of what is in the balance: honor, integrity, the future of the kingdom."

"May I impose on you to ask a question?" I ventured. All night
I had struggled with myself as to how I would raise the issue. I
could find no natural or organic way to bring it into our conversation, and at last I settled for being abrupt. I was, after all, new to
the nation, and if Mr. Melbury believed I was an ignorant West Indian, I might comfortably avail myself of his beliefs.

He seemed only too eager to play professor at the university of
modern politics. "I shall endeavor to answer any questions you
might have," he assured me.

"To what extent do you depend upon those who are Jacobitically inclined for your votes?"

The eager smile was gone in an instant. Melbury stared as
though I had dropped a turd on his dinner plate. Though the light
was poor in the coffeehouse, I believe he paled. "Please," he said.
"If you must speak that word in public and in my company, do so
in the most quiet of whispers. You will make no friends here by
even mentioning that such people as you alluded to exist in the
world."

"Is it as dangerous as that to even mention them?"

"It is. You know, Hertcomb and Dogmill need but the slightest
excuse to paint us all as a gang of traitors in service to the false
king. We must do all in our power to keep that weapon from their
hands." He took a sip from his goblet. "Why do you ask, sir?"

"I am merely curious."

He leaned forward and spoke in the most hushed of voices.
"Allow me to be blunt, Mr. Evans. I like you, sir. You have my
gratitude for your service the other day, and you will always have
my esteem. But if you are, yourself, a man who supports the political camp you have mentioned, I must beg you to never speak to
me again, appear by my side, or attend any event at which I am
present. I do not mean to be severe, but I will not have the taint of

those reckless mutineers trouble my reputation or my political aims."

"I thank you for your honesty," I said, "but I can promise you most earnestly that I am not myself of that persuasion. I ask because these people are spoken of so frequently as being in league with the Tories. I wished to know if they were a group to be courted or not."

"Not openly, of course. If they wish to cast their votes for me, I shall be silently grateful, but I shall never speak a word to encourage them or to make them believe that I should ever support their monarch against my own. Do not mistake me—I believe His Majesty has made some grievous errors, particularly in regard to his ministry and his support of the Whiggish party—but I should rather a Protestant fool than a canny Papist."

I saw I could ask no more on this matter, and I should have changed the subject at once had Melbury not taken that task upon himself. "We have had a trying experience with Mr. Highwall," he said, with some levity. "Let us unburden ourselves with some recreation."

Perhaps because of my own proclivities, I thought that Melbury was suggesting that we should find for ourselves a pair of willing women, and I admit I rejoiced at the notion—not because I was thus inclined myself but because I wished to see proof that this man was a poor husband to Miriam. I saw proof of this soon enough, but not how I imagined, for the vice of Melbury's choice was not whoring but gaming. He led us to the back of the tavern, where several tables were set up and gentlemen played at whist, a game I confess I have never been able to fathom. Elias once swore to me that he could teach me the game in less than a week's time, but as cards are meant to serve as amusement, this seemed to me a most foreboding promise.

Nevertheless, there was more to be mastered here than my enjoyment, and if I wished to keep Melbury as warm to me as he had become, I had no choice but to be a good sport in his diversion. I therefore sat by his side as he took up an empty chair at a table. He introduced me to his companions, all of whom seemed to have mastered the acrobatic task of managing simultaneously a pot of drink, a box of snuff, and a handful of cards.

Melbury began at once to involve himself in his game, seeming to forget I was in the room with him. Indeed, the experience was rather mortifying, for in the space of a few minutes I went from being his particular confidant to nothing more than an attendant. He made quips with his fellow cardplayers, he threw bits of money around, he drank with great enthusiasm. Once or twice he would turn to me and make some sort of quip but then, in an instant, forget about me again. I could hardly blame him. Though he had haggled with Highwall over a matter of twenty pounds, now, in less than an hour, he lost more than three hundred. During one hand, he thought he should win a mighty pile of money, but one of his opponents won unexpectedly. I could see the loss hit Melbury hard, but he turned over the money with what looked for all the world like indifference and thought nothing of throwing more coins into the fire for the next hand.

After nearly an hour of this treatment, watching Melbury surrender far more in losses than I should dream of having earned in two years combined, I thought it most prudent I take myself elsewhere, before Melbury began to see me not as a valued companion but nothing more than another toadeater.

As I attempted to devise the most effective way to make known my decision, a man I had never seen before came and leaned in between Melbury and myself. He was of middle years, and even in the light of the coffeehouse I observed that the stubble of his beard grew in gray. He was a thin man with sunken eyes and sharp cheeks and as many teeth missing as present. He wore an old suit, clean but threadbare, and he carried himself with a strangely artificial dignity.

"Ah, Mr. Melbury," he said, as he thrust his way between us. "How good to see you, sir. I had hoped to find you here, and here you are."

Melbury's face darkened. "Excuse me, gentlemen," he said to the cardplayers. He then grabbed this man by the coat sleeve and pulled him across the room.

I knew not the best way to respond, but I certainly did not want to sit like a mute blockhead with the whist players, so I rose to follow Melbury. He now sat at a table with his new companion, and as I approached, I heard him speak in hushed tones.

"How dare you come to me here?" he said. "You may be certain that I shall instruct Mr. Rosethorn to deny you entrance in future." He turned to me. "Ah, Evans. I may ask you to do for me now what you did in Covent Garden the other day."

Certainly my presumption had not done me harm.

"That is not very good-natured of you, sir," the fellow said to Melbury. "You have already denied me entrance to your home, and a man must do his business where he can; indeed he must. And you and I have business, Mr. Melbury. You cannot deny it."

"What business we might have is not for a public place such as this," he said. "Nor can it interfere with me when I am meeting with gentlemen."

"I should like to do our business privately, indeed I would, but you have not made it possible to do so. And as to your meeting, it appeared to me to involve your casting to the wind that which might be better applied elsewhere."

"How I spend my time is not your concern," he hissed.

"No, indeed. Your time is nothing to me, and you may use it as you like. It is your money: That is my concern. It is very unkind of you, sir, to spend it so recklessly when there are those who await an already tardy repayment."

"I must ask you to leave," Melbury said.

The fellow shook his head. "That is not so good-natured of you, sir. Indeed, it is not. You know I might be far more insistent than I have been, but I have been both kind and patient in light of your status. But I may not be kind and patient in a permanent way, if you catch my meaning." Here he paused and looked over at me. "Titus Miller at your service, sir. May I inquire your name?"

"Have you no manners?" Melbury nearly shouted.

"I believe I have quite good manners, Mr. Melbury, for I was taught them by my grandmother. I am polite and deferential, and I pay what I owe. I see no harm in wishing to know a gentleman's name, and unless there be some reason why I cannot know, I shall think you very ill-natured for not telling me."

I could see that Melbury would not yield his ground and speak my name, and I did not wish that it should become so contested an issue, so I resolved to end the matter myself. "I am Matthew Evans," I said bluntly.

"Well, Mr. Evans, do you count yourself a friend to Mr. Melbury?"

"I have not known him long, but I believe I may aspire to that station."

"If you are a friend to him, you might wish to assist him with his embarrassments. Indeed you might."

I could see why Melbury had such little patience with this fellow. "I believe Mr. Melbury's affairs are his to speak of, and if he wishes my assistance in any matter, he may speak to me without your permission."

"I fail to see why a man should not be good-natured if he can be," Miller said, "and you are choosing to be ill-natured, which is a thing I do not love. I shall not speak to you of the precise nature of Mr. Melbury's embarrassments, as you do not seem to want to hear them. I only say that if you are his friend, you will offer him some assistance. As I best recollect, his other friends have done so in the past, but they are perhaps not available to do so now."

"Miller, I shall have you removed if you do not leave of your own accord."

He rose. "I am displeased it has come to that, but I suppose there is no helping it. I shall go then, sir, but I think you may find that our business together has taken a turn in an altogether new direction. I do not love to be ill-natured, but a man must do his business as best he can."

The next night I had one of my appointed meetings with Elias. Before I could even begin to speak, he met me with a broad grin. "I see that you may wear all the disguises you like, but you cannot contain your nature."

"What do you mean?" I asked, as I took a seat.

He slid a Tory newspaper toward me. In it was the story of the great hero Matthew Evans, who had recently saved Mr. Melbury from an attacking Whig ruffian. Now he had stepped forward to save the life of an unnamed Whig whore who had set about selling her virtue for votes. When one customer determined that his vote was worth more than the lady would acknowledge, Mr. Evans presented himself and, without regard for party affiliation, sent the villain running.

I returned the paper to Elias. "I had no idea these events had become so widely known."

"You must be careful of this sort of thing," he told me. "You don't want to draw attention to yourself, not as being a man of strength. It is a fine way to be recognized."

"It was no frivolous whim," I assured him. "I could hardly stand by and let this ruffian grab Miss Dogmill's bubbies with impunity."

Elias gave a bored half shrug. "As to that, I cannot say. You know her bubbies better than I. Nevertheless, you ought to be more careful."

"I wonder, if Dogmill had learned of this, whether he would be more happy that his sister had been saved or angered that I was the one to save her. He is very protective of her, you know." I then repeated the tale that Miss Dogmill had told to me: that of her brother attacking the tradesman who had "abducted" her.

"What a marvelous tale," he said. "And very instructive too, I think. I might use a dramatic version of it in my *History of Alexander Claren*. Perhaps I could have a rogue who merely pretends to have abducted a girl—with her consent, of course—in order to make her father—"

"Elias." I interrupted his reverie. "Are you suggesting that I abduct Miss Dogmill and wait for her brother to come smashing through my walls like a baited bull?"

"Oh, no. Nothing of the sort. I want to use it. If word of your doing such a thing were to get around, the passage in my narrative would seem derivative. And right now, I think it quite the best idea I've had. No, you'll have to come up with your own story, I think."

"It *was* my own story," I said.

"Then you'll just have to come up with a story I haven't stolen from you."

I then brought him up-to-date with all that had happened in those very eventful days.

"I know that Titus Miller," he said. "He is a dealer in bills. He has bought up one or two of mine in the past, and he is merciless—merciless, I say—in hounding his debtors. I heard once that he pushed his way into a bagnio where a shopkeeper was enjoying an assignation with a pretty little chestnut-haired harlot, and he refused to leave until this fellow had paid what he owed. I suspect that Melbury might have some rather painful encumbrances if Miller is troubling him."

"Well, as you say, a Parliamentary race is a costly business."

"These would be older debts. No one would trouble him for expenses of the race *during* the race. But I was made to understand that his wife, if you will excuse me for mentioning her, came with a handsome fortune."

"Mrs. Melbury was surely clever enough to settle her property separately at their marriage. Perhaps Melbury is ashamed to speak to her of these debts. I have seen him at play, and these may be debts of honor, which he fears to mention to his wife. But Melbury's encumbrances are the least of my worries. I should rather hear what you have to say of this Jacobite business."

"Well, it's the very thing, isn't it? If you can demonstrate that there is a highly placed Jacobite among the Whigs, you will have exactly what you need. You need only wait to see how the election ends. The Tories will do anything to keep the information quiet, for they will look like traitors. You know how excitable the public is; they'll blame the Tories for what the Jacobites have done. And the Whigs will do anything to keep the information quiet, for they will look like rubes. All you need do is identify the man, and you will be well on your way to freedom."

"All I need do is identify him? I imagine this man's name is a closely guarded secret."

"I imagine as much too, but if someone like Yate could uncover it, it will be a mere fribble for a man of your talents. By the way, have you heard the result of today's polling?"

I told him that I had not.

"For Hertcomb, one hundred eighty-eight. For Melbury, one hundred ninety-seven. His lead increases each day."

"That is bad news for Hertcomb."

"I am afraid it is bad news for Melbury as well. Dennis Dogmill will not let go of Hertcomb's seat easily."

"Which means what?"

"Unless I miss my guess," he said, as he took a bite of boiled turnip, "it means election violence. And a great deal of it."

Elias's pronouncement proved to be disturbingly prescient. The next day a group of four or five dozen men descended upon the hustings, declaring there could be no liberty without Hertcomb. Several of their number were posted just outside the polling booth, and when a man who had voted Tory emerged, the ruffians would taunt and jeer and even strike the fellow. Each man who stood up for Melbury merited an increasingly severe response, until anyone who dared cast his vote the wrong way was beaten mercilessly.

Melbury, along with every Tory of note in the city, cried out that the army must be called in to disband the rioters, but it was a sad truth that the mayor and the aldermen and a vast majority of the magistrates in the city made a habit of breaking bread with Dennis Dogmill and Albert Hertcomb, so they pronounced that a bit of election-season violence was inevitable and that it was better not to react too strongly lest the tempers of the troublemakers be even further inflamed.

I made a point of visiting the hustings myself that I might see to what extent this violence manifested itself. I saw it was cruel and certain, and that it surely cost Melbury his votes. That day ended with one hundred seventy votes for Mr. Hertcomb but only thirty-one for his opponent. Only a few such days of unrest could undo

Melbury's lead, and if Melbury did not win, my chances of clear-ing my name diminished to near nothing.

It was for that reason, and some others, that I observed some-thing else with great interest. I saw that, unless my eyes deceived me, the men who rioted against Melbury were Greenbill Billy's porters.

CHAPTER 22

I DID NOT LIKE that my fate should be bound as closely as it was to a man like John Littleton, but I saw no way to avoid calling upon his services once more. I wrote him and asked that he meet me in a tavern on Broad Street in Wapping. I went undisguised, for Littleton knew nothing of my Matthew Evans persona and I thought it safer that way. He had thus far proved himself willing to aid me after his own fashion, but I could never know when I might have asked too much or provided too great a temptation.

As it happened, Littleton was eager to meet with me. The entry of his rivals into the political fray seemed to have utterly disordered him. His men knew not how to respond, but many believed that if Greenbill's boys were rioting, surely there was profit to be had in riot and Littleton ought to be able to secure their share of the spoils.

"It's all in chaos," he said to me, swallowing down his beer as though he had been deprived of drink all day. There was a bruise on his face, just under his left ear, and I wondered if he had been brawling—with his men, perhaps?

"What do you know of it? What does it mean?"

"What does it mean?" he repeated. "What do you think it means? Dogmill's got them paid off to riot against Melbury. What could be more plain?"

"But why would Greenbill accept Dogmill's money for such a thing? Does he not wish to see Hertcomb out of office and Dogmill taken down a notch?"

"You're thinking like a politician. That's your problem. You ought to be thinking like a porter. They've been offered money, which is enough, but they've been offered money to make mischief, which is even more. As to matters of right and wrong, they hardly signify, but that's all took care of just the same. Greenbill went out there and told his men that if Melbury gets elected it will ruin Dogmill, and if Dogmill is ruined, they can forget any work this spring. It's as simple as that. They must wish well to their master, for the only thing worse than being under his boot is to have no master at all."

"Can Greenbill believe this? Can he believe that if Dogmill no longer brings in tobacco, no one will bring in tobacco?"

"I only know he believes in the silver that Dogmill surely gave him to tell this tale. And, when you think about it, it is but one more talk. It is like unloading a ship—work for which Dogmill pays Greenbill and Greenbill pays his boys. Nothing's changed but that there's a little more winter work."

"How long will they riot?"

"I think only a few more days. Hertcomb and Dogmill can't hold off the soldiers much more than that. In the meantime, I have contacted Mr. Melbury and let him know that he don't have to take this lying down."

"You would send your boys out to fight Greenbill's?"

"It's been a long time coming this way. I don't see no harm in letting it play out as it might."

I was in beyond my capacity. I knew it to be so. Did I wish for more rioting or less rioting? Did I wish to see Melbury, a man I once despised as a rival, triumphant? Surely he would put things right. Surely I could count on him to restore my name if he was elected. But there was a twinge of pleasure in seeing his electors cower in their homes, afraid to step up to the polls. He had been too ambitious. He had taken on what did not belong to him, and now he would know the taste of failure.

My vengeful thoughts were shattered, however, by the arrival of my landlady, Mrs. Sears, who informed me in a most disapproving tone that a young lady wished to call upon me. I could not have been more delighted to see Miss Dogmill walk into my chambers.

I rose in greeting. "As ever, I am delighted to see you, Miss Dogmill."

She closed the door behind her, nearly upon Mrs. Sears's face. "I believe myself worthy of this enthusiasm, for you have no better friend, sir." She sat without waiting for my invitation—an act that, when performed by me, seems invariably hostile and defiant but only made this lady appear breezy and at ease. "I've brought you something you may wish to see." She then set a series of letters down upon the table.

I picked up one and examined it. It was unsealed and addressed to a gentleman in York. "What is this to me?"

"These are letters, Mr. Weaver, four letters that my brother has sent to gentlemen of whom he is aware—though he knows none of them personally—who have lived for some years in Jamaica. He has written to all of them to inquire if they are familiar with Matthew Evans, grower of tobacco and charmer of sisters."

"And you have rescued them for me," I said.

"I thought they would be better off in your hands."

"I think you are right, but when they go unanswered, will not your brother grow frustrated and try again?"

"I suppose that depends upon how long they go unanswered. Surely you have no intention of remaining Matthew Evans forever."

"I find that there are advantages," I said.

"Hmm. I believe I do as well. In any event, if you do plan to continue your pretense longer, you might consider answering these letters yourself. I do not think Denny knows any of these men well enough to recognize their handwriting; I don't believe he's even met any of them in person. You could very easily provide him with precisely the information he does not wish to hear—that Matthew Evans is a well-respected gentleman planter who has lately left for England."

I thought her solution a good one, though another approach I liked better occurred to me. But more of that anon. For now I rose and put the letters upon my writing table. "I thank you for these," I said. "They may well have saved my life."

"Then I believe you owe me something in return," she said, rising to greet me. "You must kiss me."

"This penalty I shall pay gladly," I told her.

I walked to embrace her, but she held me back for a moment. "We are alone here and have all the privacy we could desire. There is nothing to inhibit us but our own inclinations."

"I have thought the same thing."

"Then there is something I must say to you. I know you to be a man of honor, so I wish that we might not misunderstand each other. You and I may share a fondness. We may, for all I know, share what is commonly called love. But you are not to ask me to marry you. Not out of affection or out of what you might imagine to be an obligation. I do not wish to marry—not you or anyone else."

"What?" I asked. "Never?"

"I will not be so foolish as to talk of never, but I will talk of now. I only wished that you not misunderstand me or act out of what you might think an obligation that should make both of us uneasy."

"It would hardly be proper for a woman of your family to marry a man of mine," I said, with a bitterness I did not feel.

"That is surely true," she said good-naturedly, "though you must know that such rules would not lead me to act against my own heart. If I were to marry, I can think of nothing more delicious than the scandal of marrying a Jew thieftaker. But I think I will, for the foreseeable future, avoid matrimony entirely."

"Then I shall not force you to act against your inclination," I said.

She smiled at me. "Besides, I do not believe I should like to marry a man in love with Griffin Melbury's wife. Do not look at me thus, sir. I know who she is, and I saw what you looked like when you danced with her."

I pulled away from her. "My feelings for her are not pertinent, as her heart is not free."

"No, it is not, and that is a very distressing thing. But my heart is free, and you are welcome to make what use of it you will."

And here I shall draw a curtain against the rites of Cupid, which are too delicate to write of and must be left to the reader's imagination.

The hours I passed with Miss Dogmill were delightful and too quickly used. After she departed from my rooms and faced the gantlet of Mrs. Sears's scowls, I found myself alone and the time passed most miserably. I ought, I suppose, to have been full of good cheer. I had found that this beautiful woman was more than happy to be an agreeable friend of the most amiable sort. I no longer had to pretend to be something I was not with her, and she wanted nothing more of me than my time and companionship. Certainly she was not the first young lady whose company I had enjoyed since losing Miriam to Melbury, but she was surely the most agreeable, and I did not like that emotions should be divided. Perhaps I felt false to my hopeless love by feeling such fondness for Miss Dogmill, or perhaps I only regretted the waning of the pain itself. It had been for so long all that I had left of Miriam. I hated to see it dissipate.

These reflections were shattered when Mrs. Sears informed me that there was a lad at the door with a message for me, and he would not depart until I had read it. I impatiently tore it open.

Evans,

I am in a bad way and need your help at once. Follow this boy, and lose no time in meeting me or all will be in ruins. The election—nay, the kingdom—may stand or fall on your actions. I am, &c,

G. Melbury

I felt some remorse in having delighted in Melbury's difficulties when this same man so clearly thought of me as his friend. Nevertheless, I had to remind myself that the friend he thought of was not *me* but a fiction called Matthew Evans. He had no idea who *I* was, and if he had he would almost certainly not have come to

310 | DAVID LISS

me with his problems. It might yet develop, I thought, that Melbury could resent the freedoms I'd taken with him, and he might never help me when he learned of the falsehoods I had perpetuated.

I followed the boy to an old house near Moor Fields Street in Shoreditch, and in this place I was greeted at the door by none other than the bill collector, Titus Miller. "Ah, Mr. Evans," he said. "Mr. Melbury mentioned that you were a man upon whom he might depend, and it would seem you have shown yourself to be dependable. I have no doubt that Mr. Melbury will relish your company."

"What is this?" I demanded.

"What it seems to be," he said. "Most things are, you know. Most things are not deceptions but just what they seem. Mr. Melbury has been ill-natured enough to overlook some of his debts that I have bought up, so I have insisted he tarry here awhile and consider what consequences his reluctance might have on his bid for a seat in the House. Tomorrow, if he does not become more good-natured, I may have no choice but to forward his care to that of the King's Bench—a prison where many men who have refused to meet their obligations are wont to congregate."

So that was the nature of Melbury's distress. He had been taken to this sponging house, and here he would remain for twenty-four hours unless he could convince someone to meet his debts. Clearly, he imagined that someone to be a wealthy Jamaican planter.

I have never loved sponging houses, and I say that while fully admitting that I have, on one or two unfortunate occasions, had the opportunity to examine their interior operations very closely. It is something of a shame to our British method of justice that a man may be taken off the street and held against his will for a full day before being turned over to the courts. During that day he must eat and drink and sleep, and for all of these accommodations he must pay the proprietor of the house far more than the market would bear if the customer had the freedom to try his luck with a competitor. A dinner that might cost him a few pence at the chop-house across the street would cost him a shilling or two in a sponging house. And thus have many men gone into debt and, finally being caught, found themselves in more debt than ever before.

I insisted that Miller take me to Melbury at once, so he led me through a house cluttered with old furniture, rugs rolled up and stacked in corners, crates and trunks unopened. Here were the goods men had bartered for their freedom.

Miller led me up a flight of stairs, down a hall, and up another flight of stairs. He then removed from a hook upon his coat a rather large key ring and, after a brief search, identified the necessary object.

The door creaked like a dungeon gate, but the accommodations were tolerably respectable. The room was of a manageable size and contained several chairs, a writing desk (there is no more important occupation for the man in a sponging house than that of writing letters to friends with money), and a rather comfortable-looking bed.

It was on that item that I found Melbury, stretched out and looking mightily relaxed. "Ah, Evans. Good of you to come." He leaped up with the grace of a rope dancer and took my hand warmly. "Miller here would have had me writing letters all the day, but I sent only one, for if a man does not know whom to turn to in a crisis, he is a poor man indeed."

I should have thought to say that a man who cannot keep out of a sponging house is a more fitting definition of a poor man, but I held my tongue. I likewise restrained myself on commenting on the honor of being the only man summoned to meet his needs. "I came as soon as I received your note," I said.

"I do admire a man who is punctual," Miller volunteered.

"Oh, leave us alone, would you?" Melbury snapped at him.

"There is no cause to be uncivil," Miller said, seemingly injured. "We are all of us gentlemen here."

"I have no interest in hearing your notion of who is a gentleman and who is not. Now get out."

"You have been ill-natured, sir," Miller told him. "Very ill-natured indeed." He then backed out, closing the door behind him.

"I should like to have that fellow horsewhipped," Melbury told me. "Now, come sit, Evans, and have a glass of this wretched port he sent up. For what he charges, he should blush to ask me to drink this filth, but it is better than nothing, I suppose."

I ought to have hesitated to drink a wine that came with so weak a recommendation, but I joined him all the same. We sat near the fireplace and Melbury smiled, as though we were visiting in a club or in his own home.

"Well," he began, after a painfully long pause, "you can see that I've gotten myself into a bit of a fix here, and I need someone to get me out. As you have mentioned to me on more than one occasion a desire to be useful to the Tories in this election, I naturally set upon you as the very man for me. I have no doubt the Whig papers will make much of this incident. I have every reason to believe that it is Dogmill who has encouraged Miller to act so ungenerously. Not that a wretch like Miller needs any encouraging, but I smell a collaboration here—one that shall be answered with strength, I assure you. But our more immediate concern is that we can ill afford to feed the Whig papers something so scandalous as debtor's prison. I trust you are in agreement."

"In the most general sense, certainly," I said, with a weak smile. "But I wonder precisely how much this erasure of scandal will cost."

"Oh"—he waved a hand in the air—"it is nothing. Nothing. The amount is so small, I hesitate even to mention it to you. I am sure a gentleman like you must spend twice as much in a year on nothing so important as hunting. I trust you like to shoot, by the way. This year, after the season, you must join me at my house in Devonshire. There is excellent shooting there, and I flatter myself that many a man of consequence in our party will be there to enjoy the sport."

"I thank you for your offer," I said, "but I must beg to know the amount you require of me."

"Look how grave you have become. One might think I was to ask you to mortgage your estate. I promise you, it is nothing so severe as that. It is a trifle, a mere trifle."

"Mr. Melbury, be so kind as to name the amount."

"Of course, of course. The bill is for two hundred and fifty pounds, no more than that—excepting, of course, a few odd pounds for my stay here. There have been a few bottles of port, you know, and some meals. The paper and pen are a bit expensive too, which I find outrageous. But I should think two hundred and sixty pounds will more than answer our needs."

I could hardly believe that he would speak of these sums so freely. Two hundred and sixty pounds surely signified, even to a man such as Matthew Evans. Why, it would be more than a quarter of his fictitious income. For Benjamin Weaver, however, it would mean the loss of the bulk of the money I had taken from the house of Judge Rowley. I did not know how I could afford to pay out such an amount, though I knew excusing myself should prove a mighty setback.

"If I may be so bold, Mr. Melbury, I have been made to understand that your wife is possessed of a large fortune."

"Do you mean that she is a Jewess, sir?" he asked me pointedly. "Is that your meaning? That I have married a Jewess, so I must not want for money?"

"I do not mean that at all. I say only that I have been told she came to your union possessed of a large fortune."

"All the world thinks that because she is a Jewess she must have money. My life, I should have you know, is not a production of *The Jew of Venice* upon the stage; all my wife must do is rob her father of his moneybags, and all will be well. I am sorry to tell you, sir, that there is a great rift between the truth and the stage."

"I have said nothing of rich fathers or moneybags."

"Very good," he said, taking my hand. "I am sorry I grew warm with you. I know you meant nothing. You are a good man, Evans, a monstrous good man. And I have no doubt that you understand that a man cannot run to his wife's petticoats every time he faces a danger. What sort of life is that?"

Was I to conclude then that I must surrender nearly every penny I had in the world so this man might not trouble himself to ask for money from his own wife? The very idea enraged me. Of course,

I could also find no pleasure in the idea that he would squander Miriam's small fortune on his debts while he gambled without remorse.

"I should think the bonds of matrimony would reduce a man's squeamishness."

"Spoken like a bachelor." He laughed. "Someday you will take the vows yourself, and you will see that it is a bit more complicated than you now flatter yourself. But as for now, what say you, Evans? Are you able to help defeat the Whigs here or no?"

What could I say? "Certainly."

"Splendid. Now let's find Miller and kick him through this world."

As we had been locked inside the chamber, we found Miller by pounding upon the door. Melbury then gleefully told him that I would sign for the money, and that once the election was over he would return to make Miller answer for his rudeness.

"As to what you call rudeness, I can say nothing," Miller told him. "It is not a rudeness to demand what is yours. I think it ill-natured to refuse to give what you owe, but I will say no more of that. As to the signing of notes, I fear that it is a ticklish matter. You see that the note that led Mr. Melbury here today was signed freely, and yet there was to be no money behind it. I should like something more than airy notes for my trouble, Mr. Evans. As this kingdom has learned from the South Sea Company, it is one thing to put your promises to paper but quite another to honor those promises."

"The South Sea men are a pack of Whigs who know nothing about honoring promises," Melbury mumbled, clearly out of sorts at having been likened to the Company directors.

"Whigs and Tories are all one to me," Miller said. "If a man is not good-natured enough to keep his word, I care nothing for his party. And for the moment, I care only for knowing how I shall receive my money from Mr. Evans."

I confess I could not blame the fellow for his concern, for I had no desire to hand over a note to this rascal. As I was not, in any honest manner of speaking, such a person as Matthew Evans, my signing a note in his name would constitute a forgery—a crime with which I might be asked to pay with my life. I had every hope of being able to vindicate myself in the matter of Yate's death; as to the injury done to Mr. Rowley, surely the world would forgive it as the hasty action of a man more sinned against than sinning. But if I were to begin generating money with false notes, that was another problem altogether, and it was a risk I was unwilling to take in the service of the man who had married the woman I love.

I cleared my throat and addressed Miller. "You can hardly expect me to have so large a sum on my person."

"I might hope that you would. I might ardently wish for it. But as to expectations, you are surely right. It is the unusual man who carries with him so much ready cash for no particular reason. I hope, therefore, that you will allow me to call upon you at your home—let us say in five days' time—and there I will ask you for the sum we have here mentioned."

"Splendid idea," said Melbury.

I nodded my agreement. I had grown to depend so much on Melbury's success in this election that I would risk almost anything on his behalf.

"I hope it is a splendid idea," said Miller. "I hope so most fervently, for if Mr. Evans fails to be able to make his payment as promised, I shall be forced to begin with you anew, Mr. Melbury. Under the circumstances, you may not hide in your home or leave town. You must be in the metropolis, visible and, so, vulnerable. I hope you will not play any ill-natured games with my patience."

"I should like to play a game with your head, Miller. I should like to play a game with your head and a large stick, but as to your patience, you may be certain I shall leave it be."

"That is all I ask of you. That and to refrain from being quite so ill-natured."

Conducting himself in the fashion of a man leaping with vigor from a favorite bagnio, rather than one released from a sponging house by someone little more than an acquaintance, Melbury called for a hackney and ushered me inside.

"I trust you have no pressing plans. You have some time just now?"

"I suppose I do," I said, thinking only of the impending visit by Titus Miller and what that might mean for my finances.

"Very good," he said, "for there is a place I've a mind to visit."

The place, it turned out, was a tavern called the Fig Tree far to the west in Marylebone. I had now had my ear to the political ground for some weeks, but even if I had not, I still would have recognized the place as a notorious gathering spot for Whigs of the most ardent nature.

"What should lead us to such a place?"

"Dennis Dogmill," he said.

"Do you think it wise to confront the man in the heart of his own stronghold?"

"I am beginning to care less and less for *wise* and with greater fervor for *bold*. Is it mere coincidence that a pack of thugs descend on the polling place, meant to terrify every liberty-loving elector away—at the precise moment that blockhead Miller descends on me with a new vengeance? I tell you, Dogmill and Hertcomb have smelled the scent of their own defeat, and it is not pleasing to their nostrils. Now they wish to throw our fat upon the fire to appease their Whiggish gods, but I shall not tolerate it, and I mean to tell them myself—in public and before as many of their supporters as choose to listen."

"That is all very good," I said, "but I must ask again if you think it wise."

"How can it not be wise when I have my most stalwart friend by my side? The Whigs have learned once, and in the most painful fashion, that it does not pay to apply violence to Matthew Evans. I think they may learn the same lesson tonight."

It would seem, then, that in Melbury's mind I had become both his banker and his henchman, and like a hired Swiss I was to put myself in the way of whatever danger he chose for no other reason but that he chose it. I hardly relished my new role, but neither did I bid him to stop the coach or attempt to persuade him to alter his course of action.

We drew up outside the tavern in question, where a large crowd was now congregated. The men were not of the rough sort who had begun to plague the polls—these were respectable men of the middling order: shopkeepers and clerks and lawyers of unremarkable success—and they were hardly the kind to erupt into violence, so I let out a sigh of relief. I let out another when I saw that this throng awaited entry into the tavern. Melbury, I presumed, would be too impatient in his wrath to wait for a period of time—which might stretch to hours—in order to speak a few cross words to men who would pay him no mind. I soon discovered, however, that I had underestimated his resolve. He approached the crowd and announced in a booming voice that we would pass through, and the authority in his tone did the business. The men—bemused and irritated—stepped aside. They grumbled as we passed, but we passed all the same.

Inside, the scene was nothing short of riotous. A great sheep roasted on a spit over an open fire, and with each turn a new piece was cut off and placed on a plate, a prize for which a hundred hands rose up in greedy anticipation. The air smelled of charred meat and strong tobacco and of the spilled wine that formed sticky puddles on the floor. In the center of the tavern, tables had been cleared away to make a great space, and those men who did not clamor for mutton like starving prisoners had gathered in a circle here, some cheering, some moaning and clutching at their heads in horror.

Melbury nudged me. "That's where we'll find him," he said, pointing to the circle. He led us around to a spot he reckoned would be the most propitious for our point of entry and began to make a path through the crowd, easily five or six men deep. We had burrowed about halfway into the depth when I saw the spectacle that so entranced the onlookers. A pair of mighty cocks—one black with white streaks, the other white with bits of red and brown—circled each other with unmistakable menace. The black one moved slowly, and I could see that its feathers were heavy and wet, but because of his color and the poorness of the light, it took a moment for me to recognize that it was his own blood that dampened him.

The black bird reared up and leaped at the white, but it was obvious that its strength had been tapped. The stronger bird, unencumbered with injury, easily dodged the attack and, with the wounded aggressor off balance, spun around and leaped in turn upon the poor creature. It was only then that I saw that their claws had been affixed with small blades, which augmented the damage of their natural weapons most terribly. The white bird gave his opponent what was surely a finishing blow, and the black cock turned upon his side and fought no more.

A mighty noise rose up from the crowd, and money at once began to change hands. After half a moment, enough quiet had descended that someone began to speak. Because it was hard to hear, it took a moment for me to recognize that it was Dennis Dogmill's voice I now heard.

"We shall present another match for your entertainment in an hour's time," he announced. "For now, those of you who find yourselves having chosen the wrong bird in this contest may take some comfort in knowing that the losing beast was a member of the Tory party, and it is said in the vicinity of the henhouse that he was of a Jacobitical bent. And there are other reasons to rejoice. We dominate our opposition at the polls, and we may soon rejoice in the victory of Whig liberties over Tory absolutism."

The crowd answered this proclamation with far more laughter than it deserved, but then the men began to dissipate, some toward the mutton, which continued to rotate agreeably and yield meat, others to the barrels of wine that sprung cheap drink lavishly and freely. There could be no mystery, however, as to where Griffin Melbury received his sustenance. He strode boldly up to Dennis Dogmill and Albert Hertcomb.

"Has your blood sport sufficiently satisfied your portion of the electorate, or will you continue to depend upon roughs to make a mockery of British liberties?"

"It can hardly be a mockery to permit the unenfranchised to

express their opinions as best they can," Hertcomb proposed. "I suppose some men are inclined to the French way of doing things—using soldiers to beat down any man who might say something not to his liking."

"I'll not listen to these lies," Melbury said. "You must know that if your roughs do not disappear, the election must be contested by the House."

"Perhaps so," Dogmill agreed, "but as all signs indicate that the Whig majority will be as strong, if not stronger, than ever, I need hardly doubt what conclusion that august body will reach."

The calmness of the words, the ease with which they were spoken, the confidence of victory to which they testified—despite the Tory candidate's still possessing the lead—only served to inflame Melbury further. "Damn you for a rascal, Dogmill! Do you think Westminster is a pocket borough to be assigned to whomever you please because you spread your money around? I think you will soon learn that British liberty is a beast not easily managed, once uncaged."

"I beg your pardon," Dogmill said, "but I will not have you or *any* man address me in such terms."

"I am available for redress if you think yourself wronged."

"Mr. Dogmill does not believe in defending his honor during the election season," I volunteered. "Something to do, I think, with the Whig electorate not respecting a man who values his name or reputation. I have found that if you press Mr. Dogmill hard enough, he will loose his temper and lash out, but he will never behave as befits a man of honor."

"Don't think I have forgotten about you, Evans," he said to me. "You may be sure that when the polls close you will learn the difference between a man you can abuse and a man of resolve."

"You misunderstand me," I said, "if you think I doubt your resolve. Any man who can convince the very fellows he beats into poverty to rise up against the man who would make their lot easier is a fellow of great resolve, I should say."

"What, those porters?" He laughed. "I thank you for your compliment, but you must not think I had anything to do with their behavior. Rather, you misunderstand the nature of life on our is-land, Evans, being so new to it. Those low fellows will love the man they serve, so long as he continues to pay them, and the less he pays them, the more he will be loved. We may speak of British liberty, but the truth is these roughs love to feel the lash upon their backs and the boot to their arses. I gave them no encouragement to stand up for me. They did as they, in their limited way, under-stood to be what was right."

"Those fellows are good Whigs," Hertcomb said, "and no amount of agitation will turn them Tory."

"They are neither Whig nor content to be trod upon," I said. "You play a dangerous game with their liberty."

Dogmill took a step toward me. "You are a fine man to speak of liberty," he said. "Tell us, if you will, about the liberty of the Af-ricans enslaved on your lands in Jamaica. What freedoms do they have to speak their minds? Tell us, Mr. Evans, how much you raised up the downtrodden laborer on your own plantation."

I fear I had no words at my disposal, for I had never taken the time to think of that aspect of my disguise before, and though I knew that arguments for the justness of slavery were to be found in print, I was familiar with none that I could utter without feel-ing foolish. I suppose, if I had rehearsed them, I might have been able to offer some clever rejoinder in defense of a practice that, truth be told, no honorable man can endorse. Yet I should rather have defended all the wrongs in the world than stand there, as I did, looking bashful and confused, leading Dogmill to believe that he had scored a mighty blow against me.

To my shame, Melbury came to my rescue. "A man invested in the trade of human flesh can hardly criticize another for being a customer in that trade. Your sense of the truth is as crooked as your sense of honorable electioneering. I come here, in the midst of your revels, to give you both notice that I will not stand by and see this election corrupted. I do not fear you and I do not credit your reputations. You may call me out or not, according to your own sense of honor. But what you will not do is defeat me, not by trickery. You may run this race fairly or you may simply run. What you will not do is buy a seat in the House of Commons. Not here. Not in Westminster. I have placed myself as guard on the bridge of liberty, sirs, and corruption may not pass."

With that he turned on his heel and led us from the heart of the beast, not affording either man the opportunity to respond.

Once in the hackney, Melbury congratulated himself on the prettiness of his speech. "I told him a thing or two. Not that he will much care, of course. My words will mean nothing to him."

"Then why trouble yourself to speak them?"

"Why, because I made certain that a few men of the Tory papers were in that crowd, and they will be certain to print my words for the world to see—just as the world will see that I was man enough to speak them in the very den of the enemy. Dogmill and Hertcomb are now probably laughing to themselves about what a fool I am to come trouble them with my sanctimonious speeches, but I believe they will make quite a stir. Any man who is undecided in this election will rejoice in my determination to fight the corruption of hired ruffians disturbing Tories at the polls."

"And how do you propose to fight them? Do you plan to hire your own ruffians?"

He cast me a look I might have anticipated had I asked if he intended to kiss Hertcomb on the lips. I sensed I greatly disappointed him. "I leave those sorts of tactics to Dogmill and the Whigs. No, I shall defeat their violence with virtue. Their men cannot riot forever. The king will have to send in soldiers sooner or later, and when the polls are once more quiet, the electors of Westminster will be more eager than ever to cast their votes for me."

I begrudgingly admired his resolution, but the next day, when I visited Covent Garden, I saw that men had taken to arms in the Tory cause. I might have excused Melbury and believed that these rioters acted on their own volition, but it seemed to me all too obvious they had been hired to do their work. The men who fought back in the cause of Griffin Melbury were Littleton's porters.

CHAPTER 23

THE SCENE at Covent Garden was scarcely to be believed. I might easily have imagined myself in Lisbon during the time of the Inquisition, or perhaps some medieval capital when the plague ravaged the lands. I wanted to see the events for myself, and I spent no small amount of time in the debate of whether I ought to attend as Evans or Weaver. Though I feared Weaver might be seen, I had come to realize that every passing man did not take the time to examine the face of his neighbor to see whether or no he might be a fugitive. Evans, on the other hand, as a gentleman, might draw unwanted attention from the election roughs, so Weaver won the day.

I marveled that a few men and light purses could so easily topple the monument of our cherished British liberties. A few stalwart voters braved the dangers, but they were mad to do so. If a rough heard him speak his party at the polling booth, the elector would at once be pulled out and pummeled. Then the opposing men would make themselves known and raise their fists to the offenders. Spectators gathered around to observe the festivities. The crowd was thick with oyster women and pickpockets and beggars, and I held myself a safe distance from the mayhem, not wishing to become a victim to anyone's tricks.

In doing so I spied several men I recognized from Littleton's gang and could conclude that Melbury had decided to take the fight to Dogmill's doorstep. I took a bit of pleasure in this realization. For all his noble talk, Melbury was no better than the rest of them.

Nevertheless, the scene of confusion was not one I enjoyed, and after a small dead dog went flying through the air, nearly striking me in the head, I determined that it was time for me to depart the plaza. As I turned, however, I saw a man very far away that I recognized. I realized that I knew him, and his companion too, before I could think of who he was. And then it came on me all at once: These were the Riding Officers who had twice attempted to take me.

For a moment I froze in terror, certain that they had tracked me to this place and that they knew where I had taken up residence. Then I saw they were laughing and walking with the easy sway of drunkards. They were not there to follow me but to amuse themselves with the spectacle of violence. I nearly ducked away, relieved that I had seen them before they saw me. But then I had a better idea. I would follow them.

M y work here was not difficult. They took themselves to a tavern off Covent Garden on Great Earl Street and seated themselves in the back, calling at once for drink. I was able to find a dark corner for myself that gave me a fine vantage point but offered little risk of being seen. I called the barman over and inquired what these two worthies were drinking.

"They ordered wine," he said, "but wouldn't pay for nothing but what was cheapest. Finally settled for some very poor claret that's a week or more vinegar."

"Send them two bottles of your best," I said. "Say only they were paid for by a gentleman who overheard their order and then departed."

He looked at me quizzically. "There's something that don't sound right in that. Oughtn't they to know who it is that gets them drunk? Mayhap I should tell them your proposal and let them make up their own minds."

"If you tell anything of me, I'll break your leg," I said to him. Then I grinned. "On the other hand, if you don't I'll give you an extra shilling."

He nodded. "Well, then. Looks like I'll be doing some lying, don't it?"

"There are worse fates than being bought wine by a stranger," I said, to further soften his misgivings, but my efforts were wasted. The promise of the extra shilling had already done all that could be done.

I sat in my dark corner for the better part of two hours, slowly drinking small beer and eating some hot rolls I had the barman fetch for me from the baker around the corner. Finally, the two men rose, and rose most unsteadily. They called their thanks to the barman, and one of them approached the fellow and shook his hand. He was easily the more drunk of the two, so I set my cap at him.

I rose and followed quickly so as not to lose them, but I needn't have rushed. They remained just outside the tavern, dropping coins and then picking them up, only to drop them once more and then laugh. I remained in the dark of the doorway and waited an infuriating five minutes while they performed this ritual and then said their toddling goodbyes. One went off, presumably to safety. The other had a much harder fate awaiting him.

I did not wait long. As soon as he departed a more trafficked street, I quickened my pace. In doing so, I made my approach louder, but I was prepared to take that risk, given the depth of his inebriation. Nevertheless, he turned, startled at the sound of my approach. He stopped and opened his mouth to speak, but I silenced whatever words he had planned with my fist.

Down he went into the muck, his fall softened only by the large dead rat that served as a pillow under his head. While he lay in confusion, I reached over and pulled his pistols from his pocket and his blade from his scabbard. I little doubted he was unprepared to use these weapons, but I saw no point in letting him try the experiment. Now he stared at me. A thin stream of blood ran from his lip, and in the darkness it looked as black as tar.

"Do you recollect me?" I asked.

I could see the drunkenness spilling out of him. "Weaver," he said.

"That's right."

"I wasn't bothering you."

"Not tonight you weren't, but you might recall that you've tried to arrest me once or twice in the past."

"That is only business," he said.

"And so is this. Tell me why, precisely, Riding Officers are seeking to bring me in." I knew the answer full well, but I wished to hear it from his own lips. He hesitated a moment, so I grabbed him by the hair and yanked him up to a sitting position. "Tell me," I said again.

"It's Dennis Dogmill that wants it," he said.

"Why?"

"I don't ask such things. I just do what he tells me."

I thought about this: how to find out information that would be of use to me. "How do you know what he wants of you? How does he contact you?"

"It's his man," the Riding Officer said. "All the customs men meet at a tavern near the Tower called the Broken Lamp, on Thursday nights. We get paid what we're owed, and if he's got special instructions, he tells us then. Sometimes if it's urgent, such as when you broke loose, we get a note, but otherwise it's always a Thursday."

I sensed I was getting close to something. "And who is his man?"

He shook his head. "I don't know. He don't say his name. He just pays us. If you want to find out, you can come Thursday."

Good advice, but how could I dare to go if he knew I would be attending? "Where do you live?" I asked. He hesitated a moment, so I kicked him in the ribs. "Where do you live?" I asked again.

He groaned. "In Mrs. Trenchard's house off Drury Lane."

"You know I do not work alone," I told him. "You have been thwarted by my aides in the past and you will be again, if you don't leave the metropolis without mentioning a word of this to anyone. You may come back in a few months, but if I see you sooner, or if any of my allies see you sooner, we shall not hesitate to burn Mrs. Trenchard's house down about your ears and with you still in it too." I gave him another kick to cement my point, though I don't know that my efforts were required. "Now get away," I said, and watched him attempt to push himself to his feet.

I then walked off slowly in an effort to show my contempt. I would not know if my warning had meant anything until I visited the tavern come Thursday.

As for Littleton, I wanted to hear from his own lips that Melbury had hired him. I could not say what this information would give me other than the satisfaction of knowing the woman I loved was married to a liar, but that seemed reason enough. I awaited him as he came out of Mrs. Yate's house that morning, and when he turned a corner I grabbed his arm.

"Off to do some rioting?" I asked.

He flashed me his easy grin. "It's good weather for it, I think. I guess you've seen me and the boys down there, giving as good as Dogmill's boys, and then some. We might not be able to make them go away, but we can keep the odds even. Sooner or later, Dogmill will agree to a truce."

"That's Melbury's thinking, is it?"

He made a face as though he'd tasted something sour. "Melbury be damned. That tightpurse wouldn't pay for a good riot if the election depended on it, which it does."

"What?" I demanded. "If Melbury isn't paying you, why are you rioting? Surely it is not for the pleasure of facing off against Greenbill and Dogmill."

"I won't deny there is a pleasure, but it's more than that. We're getting paid, I can tell you, only not by Melbury. It's a risk, you know. If Dogmill wishes, he might send us to the devil for rioting against Greenbill, but I don't think he will. If we go, he won't have nothing but Greenbill's boys on the quays, and then they'll be able to set their wages as they like. No, this way we get a few shillings in our pockets to get us through the winter, and we have a fine time as well."

"Who pays you?"

He shrugged. "The devil, for all I know. A dapper Irishman called Johnson offered me the coin if I would take Melbury's part. It seemed to me too fine an offer to turn away; the boys had grown restless at any rate." He stopped to stare at me. "Now that I think on it, did you not inquire of me regarding a man named Johnson? Is this the same?"

I shook my head. "No, I don't think so."

That evening I sat in my room, staring at a book without reading. Mrs. Sears knocked on my door and told me I had a visitor, so I dusted myself off and walked into my sitting room, where I found myself face-to-face with Johnson once more. He bowed to me and then politely dismissed the landlady.

"These are fine rooms you've taken, Mr. Evans."

Until he spoke my name, I don't think I recalled that in our previous encounter, Mr. Johnson had known me only as Weaver. It was now evident that he had discovered my false persona. I had made every effort to be careful when leaving and returning to these rooms, but I had not been careful enough.

"Please have a seat," I said, unwilling to show my concern. I offered him some port, and he took it gladly. I then poured a glass for myself and sat across from him.

"Let us be honest with each other," I said, having in that instant decided to take the more direct approach available to me. After all, Johnson, and therefore all the Jacobites, now knew my secret. Dissimulation and caution would get me little. "You have discovered my disguise, and you wish me to know it. What do you want of me?"

Johnson laughed agreeably, as though I had just recalled something witty from a mutual past. "You're a suspicious man, sir, though I cannot say I much blame you. Yours is a difficult situation. I shall therefore be direct with you, as you have honored me with your forthrightness. I understand you went to visit Mr. Littleton today."

"That's right," I said uneasily, for I began to see his meaning.

"And you inquired of my business."

I smiled. "I did not know it was your business until I inquired."

"Ah," he said. He swirled his wine about his goblet. "Well, now you know."

"Yes, I do."

"I'll thank you not to concern yourself with it." He set down his glass of wine. "I understand your affairs are important to you, and I shall not interfere if I don't have to, but you must understand that I cannot permit you to trouble yourself with what I do or to whom I speak."

"I am not certain what you tell me. Am I to refrain from speaking to anyone lest it be an acquaintance of yours?"

"You needn't be so dramatic," he said. "I shall be plain with you. Leave these riots alone, sir. Leave Littleton alone. He is no concern of yours."

"It may be no concern of mine to interfere with the riots, but I should very much like to know more of them."

"Of course. As I have said, we've no desire to see you harmed or captured. While you are free and an enemy of Dogmill, you do our cause as much good as we could hope. I only wish you might clear your name by implicating Dogmill immediately. That would provide us with just the thing."

"It would provide me with just the thing too, I assure you."

He laughed softly. "Of course. I speak of strategy, but you speak of your life."

"You are quite right. And you cannot blame me for wishing to understand the mechanisms behind these riots. My difficulties are directly related to this election, and I must do all I can to understand the mechanisms that work against me."

"Of course. But we shan't privilege you over our cause."

"I would not expect you to. But I do not see why my inquiries disturb you. I shall keep what I learn to myself."

"For now, you will. Let me say this, Mr. Weaver. You would not want to learn anything that might make you our enemy in the future."

I nodded. Johnson liked that I roamed around the city making things uncomfortable for the Whigs, but he did not like the idea that I might prove my innocence and then be at liberty to speak of what I knew of the Jacobites. I had already indicated an unwillingness to side with his cause, and Johnson feared that, should I vindicate myself, I would reveal what I had learned of him and his allies to the Whigs.

"I owe you a debt of loyalty," I said. "You assisted me in the matter of the Riding Officers, and I shan't forget it."

"And you will say nothing about us to the ministry once you are safe?"

I shook my head. "I don't yet know. Should a man hold his own honor above concerns of treason?"

He appeared nothing if not amused. "You can see that I am right. You must not learn what you do not wish to know." He stood abruptly. "I trust I have made myself clear."

I stood as well. "Thus far you have. I cannot say I entirely understand what it is you are asking of me."

"Then I shall be plain. I am asking nothing of you, but you must understand that we are not some gang of thieves you cross and then outwit. We have left you alone thus far, sir, because you have achieved a certain popularity, and to move against you might cause us some difficulties. But please know that if you threaten us in any way, we will not hesitate to destroy you."

Mr. Johnson's speeches turned out to be nothing but pretty sentiment, for the next day Mr. Dogmill's friends in the city could no longer stomach turning a blind eye to the violence and posted soldiers in Covent Garden. Had they marched upon the rioters, no doubt great violence would have resulted, for those who would destroy and murder and rob never love to see their English liberties curtailed by that most venomous of beasts, the standing army. Fortunately, these dragoons were deployed with uncommon strategy, stationed in the piazza long before dawn, so when the porters arrived they saw they would be met with a disappointing welcome and slinked off, satisfied that they had performed their duty for more than half a week.

During that time Melbury's lead had suffered serious attrition, but there could be no doubt it would now recover, for the sentiment in Westminster was one of dissatisfaction with Dogmill's influence. The rioters had been a gamble, and a bold one, and the Whigs had hoped to ruin the Tories' lead. But it had only strengthened their cause, and for that I was grateful. I now had little doubt that once Melbury sat in the House, he would do all he could to serve my cause and send his old enemy to ruin.

As the day was Thursday, I spent my time preparing to take myself that night to the tavern mentioned by the Riding Officer. Here was a risk, for I had no choice but to depend that he had followed my advice and fled the metropolis rather than face my wrath. I would, nevertheless, take precautions, the most significant of which was that I thought it best to attend to my business as Matthew Evans, not as Benjamin Weaver. If the Riding Officer had not held his tongue, the men there would be keeping watch for an escaped felon, not a finely dressed gentleman. Of course, because they looked for me in particular, they might well see through my disguise more easily than men not seeking me out. Nevertheless, I was determined to take the chance.

For all my determination, however, I did not entirely believe I would learn very much by going to this tavern. I already knew that Dogmill bribed the Customs men. The world knew it, and the world did not care. What, then, would I discover? The one thing I hoped to learn was the identity of the agent who paid the Customs men. This person might well be Dogmill's primary tough, the fellow who executed the violent orders. I held out the faint hope that I might that very night learn the identity of the man who had actually beaten Walter Yate to death.

I took a seat in a dark corner, ordered a pot, and hoped to make myself as unnoticed as I might. Here was no difficult task, for the Customs men busied themselves with their own concerns.

They began to arrive at eight in the evening, as they had been advised to do. I understood well how they were being used, for this was an all too common bit of treachery perpetrated upon the laboring man. On rare occasion their wages would arrive at eight as they had been promised, but most times they would not arrive until eleven, so there was nothing for them to do in the time of waiting but eat and drink. For this consideration, the tardy pay-master would receive from the tavern keeper a little something for his troubles.

After nearly two hours I grew impatient and even considered abandoning my position, but I found that my patience was well re-warded. Some few minutes after ten, a man arrived and was greeted by the cheers of the customs men. They drank a bumper to him, and after he distributed wages all around, they drank another. They even bought this fellow a drink and treated him as though he were a king in his own right rather than an underling merely per-forming his master's service.

It was Greenbill Billy. The leader of the labor combination worked in the service of the very man he claimed to resist.

My meeting with Greenbill now began to make far more sense to me. He had asked me what I knew of Dogmill's involvement, not to discover for himself but to measure my own understanding. He had urged me to take my revenge against Dogmill, not in the hopes that I would act but rather so he could report back to his master on my willingness to do so.

I now observed him among the Customs men. He was good enough to let the men buy him a few drinks, but he appeared eager to move on afterward. Though they begged him to stay longer, he tipped his cap and bid them good night. I wasted no time and was out the door after him in an instant. To my relief, he took no hackney but appeared content to walk to wherever it was he was intending to go. I might have followed him to learn where he went. I could then pursue him on my own terms at my own leisure. But I had already enjoyed my fill of waiting and deferral. I would wait no longer.

When Greenbill walked past an alley, I broke into a run and knocked him hard in the back of the neck with both my hands clasped together. I had hoped for a bit of good luck here, that he would fall face forward and not catch sight of me, and this time the dice rolled my way. He fell into the alley's filth—the kennel of emptied chamber pots, bits of dead dogs gnawed on by hungry rats, apple cores, and oyster shells—and I pushed him down hard, knocking his head into the soft earth. Desperate for some way to maintain my anonymity, I then ripped the cravat from around his neck and hastily wrapped it around his eyes. Using one knee to keep his arms pinned, I tied the blindfold tight and only then rolled him over so that his face was out of the muck.

"You seemed mightily keen on yourself at that tavern with the Customs men," I observed, affecting an Irish accent. I did so both to protect my identity and to create a likely fiction as to the identity of his assailant—that is to say, a Jacobite agent. "You are not so keen on yourself now, are you, my spark?"

"Mayhap not," he said, "but at the tavern I was not blindfolded and wallowing in shit. It's hard to be keen on yourself when you've got that working against you."

"You wallow in far worse than shit, friend. I have been watching, and now I know your little secret."

"Which one is that? I'm burgeoned with so many, you know, I doubt you can have learned them all."

"That you are in the service of Dennis Dogmill. I believe that revelation might ruin your reputation among the porters."

"And so it would, boglander," he admitted, "but at least it would make it inevitable that Dogmill would find a more dignified post for me. You think to frighten me by revealing that little tidbit. Why, you'd be doing me a favor. So go ahead and do your Irish worst, Dear Joy. We'll see who benefits and who ends up with nothing for his trouble but a dish of boiled oats."

In a move I had learned during some of my less honorable performances as a fighter, I rolled him over and grabbed his arm, which I bent hard behind his back until he yowled quite unhappily.

"It's the Scots that are famous for their oats," I told him, "not the Irish. And as for my worst, well, bending your arm isn't nearly so bad as what else I have in mind. So now that you see I'm in no mood for nonsense, perhaps you'd like to answer a few of my questions. Or do I have to give another demonstration of my earnestness?" And I pushed hard against the arm.

"What?" he shouted. "Ask me and be damned."

"Who killed Walter Yate?"

"Who do you think, you blockhead?" he growled. "I did. I knocked the fellow over with a metal bar and killed him as he deserved."

I remained stunned in silence. I had been seeking the answer to that question for so long now, I could hardly believe what I had just heard. A confession. An admission of guilt. We both knew I could do nothing about it. Without two witnesses, the confession had no value in a court of law, even assuming I could find an honest judge. But it meant something to me to know that I had finally learned the answer to so pressing a question.

"Did you do it under Dogmill's orders?" I asked.

"Not in the way you mean, Teague. Things ain't always so clear."

"I don't understand."

He sucked in some air. "Dogmill said to take care of Yate, so I took care of Yate. I don't know if he meant for me to kill him or not. I don't know if he noticed Yate was dead or not. He only knew that a man he wanted out of the way was gone, and that was enough for him. Dogmill's a great merchant, and to him it don't matter if the likes of us live or die. We're not real men to him, only vermin to be brushed away or squashed—it don't matter which. It only matters to him that we trouble his quiet or we don't."

"But you killed Yate without remorse."

"You say it was without remorse, but you don't mitigate it for certain. I done what I had to in order to keep my place. That's all. I can't say it was good or bad, only that it had to be remunerated."

"And why Benjamin Weaver?" I asked. "Why did Dogmill choose to blame him?"

If my question made him suspect he was in Weaver's hands, he did not show it. "That I can't tell you. I thought it an odd choice meself, and not a man I would have trifled with for no cause. But I never thought to ask Dogmill his motives. They're his own, and I suggest you inquire yourself."

"And what of Arthur Groston, the evidence broker, and the men who testified at Weaver's trial? Did you kill them as well?"

"Dogmill said make it look like the Jew is out to protect himself, and that's just what I done. It ain't nothing more than that. It ain't as though I had something against those sods."

I said nothing. There was no sound but that of both our breathing, thick and heavy in the night air. There was no easy course for me now. I could not bring the man to a justice of the peace or a constable, for the route of honest procedure was foreclosed to me. It could be that an honest judge might inquire honestly into these affairs, but that seemed a fond hope. Therefore, either I could kill Greenbill for what he had done and exact my own petty justice, or I could let him go, perhaps to walk free of the crime of murder, perhaps to lead me better to a chance of clearing my name. The former seemed more satisfying, the latter more practical.

If I let him go, however, he might take himself forever beyond my grasp, and should I be recaptured and hang for his crime, the memory of this moment would be the bitterness of my last days on earth.

I relaxed my grip on him. "Go," I said in a low voice, just above a whisper. "Go and tell your master what you have done in his name. And tell him I am coming for him."

"And who are you?" Greenbill rasped. "An agent of Melbury or the Pretender—or both? If I am to tell him, I must know what to say."

"You may say he will face justice soon enough. He can't hide from me—from us," I added, lest my indulgent speech be understood too well.

I released him and stepped back, allowing Greenbill to struggle to his feet. The arm upon which I had worked my mayhem hung limply by his side, but the other pushed into the filth so he could right himself. Once to his feet, he used his good hand to untie his blindfold, and then he scurried off. I watched him go and felt a remarkable sadness. Before I knew all the facts, I had had the hope of a wondrous discovery that would clarify everything and make my course seem certain and inevitable. I had found just the opposite, the murkiness of ambiguous orders and cowardly deeds. And I hardly knew what to do next.

CHAPTER 24

THE FOLLOWING NIGHT, a Friday, I made ready to answer Mr. Melbury's invitation to dinner. I thought with some irony that if I were not a wanted criminal, I should very likely be attending my uncle and aunt's house this evening in celebration of the Hebrew Sabbath. Instead, I would be dining with a woman who was once their daughter-in-law and now a member of the Church of England.

I dressed myself in the best of the suits Mr. Swan had labored over, and I took myself to Mr. Melbury's home, where I arrived at precisely the time called for in the invitation. Nevertheless, I found Melbury occupied, and I was asked to cool my heels, as the saying goes, in his parlor. I was there only a few minutes before Melbury uncloseted himself, emerging with an older gentleman dressed in clerical colors. This man walked with a cane, and then only with a great deal of difficulty, and appeared to be in the most fragile of health.

Mr. Melbury smiled at me and introduced me at once to his guest, none other than so famous a personage as Francis Atterbury, Bishop of Rochester. Even I, who followed events of the English Church no more closely than I did events of the Italian buggery, had heard of this luminary, well known to be one of the most eloquent proponents of restoring ancient Church privilege and power. But having heard of him, I felt myself ill at ease, knowing little of the forms belonging to such a lofty personage. I merely bowed and murmured something of what an honor it was to meet his grace. The bishop forced a smile and returned my kind words with some skepticism before hobbling from the room.

"I'm glad to see you once more," Melbury said. He handed me a glass of claret without asking if I should like one. "Forgive his Grace's taciturnity. He is in great pain from the gout, and you know his wife has died of late."

"I did not know, and I am sorry to hear it. He is a great man," I added, knowing that Tories, in general, thought so.

"Yes, I hope he will be in a better mood for dinner, for he makes most entertaining conversation when he is feeling lively. Now, you and I have some things to discuss before we greet our other guests. I read with interest some time ago of your adventure. That incident at the polling place has won us no small share of votes, sir. You are now famed as the Tory Tobacco Man, and you serve as a living idol to the differences between our two parties. Your rescue of Dogmill's sister has become very well known and celebrated, and though you stood up for a Whig canvasser, you have much gratified your own party." He paused for a breath. "Nevertheless, I have given the matter some thought, and it is unclear what you were doing canvassing for Hertcomb in the first place."

"I did not engage in any actual canvassing," I explained, feeling like a schoolboy who had been caught at some silly infraction. "I merely attended the canvass. I am, after all, friends with Miss Dogmill."

"There can be no friends in politics," Melbury said to me. "Not outside of one's party, and certainly not during an election year."

I ought not to have shown my teeth, but I'd begun to grow weary of Melbury and his belief that I lived to serve him. His forcing my hand with that bill collector, Miller, had soured me not a little. And, I assured myself, no man but a toadeater would fail to let forth his indignation at this usage. "Perhaps there can be no friends in politics," I said softly. "But I remind you that I am myself not running for the House and might be friends with whom I please."

"Just so," Melbury agreed affably, perhaps now fearing he had been too critical. "I just do not like to see you succumbing to the enemies' wiles, even if the enemy uses a handsome sister to do his bidding."

"What?" I exclaimed. "Do you say that Miss Dogmill's interest in my company is only to serve her brother?"

Melbury laughed again. "Why, of course. What did you think? Is there some other reason why she should suddenly attach herself to a Tory enemy of her brother's at the very moment of the election? Come, sir. You must know that Miss Dogmill is a fine-looking woman with a handsome fortune. There are countless men in the metropolis who should like to have achieved what you have achieved so easily. Do you think there is no reason for your success?"

"I think there is a reason," I said, somewhat heatedly, though I could not fully account for the rise in my passions. I only knew that, absurd though it might be, I took some umbrage that Matthew Evans had been insulted. "The reason is that the lady likes me."

I think Melbury felt that he had pushed the matter too far, for he put a hand on my shoulder and laughed warmly. "And why should she not? I only say you must be careful, sir, that Mr. Dogmill does not try to use your fondness for his sister to his advantage."

This was *not* what he had been saying, but I saw no point in pressing the matter and let him retreat comfortably. "I understand what Dogmill is," I said. "I shall most certainly be careful of him."

"Very good." He refilled his goblet and drank down half of it at once. "I asked you here tonight, Mr. Evans, because, in speaking with some of the more important party men, it has come to my understanding that no one has much familiarity with you. I know that you are new to London, so I wondered if you might not relish the chance to make some valuable acquaintance in the party."

"You are very kind," I assured him.

"No one would deny it. However, there is something I would ask in return. When we first met, you made certain allegations to me regarding the men down on the docks and their connection to Mr. Dogmill. I may not have been wise to dismiss what you had to say, for these porters I understand have become instrumental in the riots against our cause. But you will find that I am willing to listen to you now."

It was generous that he should choose to listen, but I had not any idea what I would say. One of the liabilities of this false persona was that I was often asked to fabricate information at a moment's notice, and I found it difficult to keep all my lies clear in my head. "I don't know what more I can tell you," I began, as I tried to recall what I had told him in the first place—something to do with Dogmill paying out the customs men, I believe. "You told me that what I had to say is known to all."

"I don't doubt, I don't doubt. However, I should point out to you that this election season is nearly a third gone. With the riots dispersed, I should be able to salvage my lead, but I should like to have some more ammunition at my disposal if I can. So if you have something to say, I beg you say it now."

I was about to make another denial or repeat what I had already told him of Dogmill, but then another idea came into my head. I had, up until now, been nothing but the most ardent of Melbury's supporters, and I could not but see that he recognized my loyalty. But in the same way that a man begins to despise a woman who offers him no resistance, I wondered if Melbury began to think the less of me for the ease with which he had used me. I therefore decided to apply to the situation some feminine wiles.

I shook my head. "I wish I could tell you more," I said, "but it would be premature to speak. I can only promise you this, sir. I am at this moment in possession of information that would destroy Mr. Hertcomb, but I fear it might harm your side as well. I must seek out more details in order to reveal that Hertcomb is the villain here and no one else."

Melbury drained his glass and refilled it without looking to see if I required more (which, I recall with some pain, I did). "What do you mean by this? It could destroy Hertcomb and harm me? I have no idea of what you speak."

"I have hardly any more idea myself. That is why you must be content for me to wait until I have the information I require."

He squinted at me. "You speak like a Gypsy fortune-teller, Mr. Evans, with your cryptic promises."

"I shall speak more when I can."

He darkened. "Damn it, Evans, speak now or you'll know what it means to defy me."

I faced him and would not avert my eye. "Then I suppose I shall know what it means to defy you. For you see, Mr. Melbury, I honor you and the Tory party too much to deliver unto you something that might do you more harm than good. And I would rather you hate me than see me as the source of difficulty."

He waved a hand in the air. "Oh, bother it! I suppose I ought to let you do as you see best. You have already served my campaign marvelous good, and all that by only being yourself. But I hope you will not hesitate to let me know if I may assist you in your labors."

"I am most grateful," I said.

All seemed, once more, easy between us, but I did not entirely believe the performance. Melbury was uncommonly agitated. Though the riots at the polling place appeared to have quieted, and had done so with the Tory lead still intact, there was still adequate reason for concern.

He placed his hand on the doorknob but then halted and turned to me. "One more thing," he said. "I know it is a delicate matter, so I will have my say and it will be finished. You do not like that I suggest alternative motives for Miss Dogmill, and there is no reason why you should like it if you are fond of the lady. I will only say that even if her heart is pure and her morals are beyond reproach, you must recall that she is subject to her brother's poison and perhaps even her brother's subtle directions. She might harm you in a thousand ways without even knowing she does so. I ask you to be cautious."

I had already swallowed enough of his suggestions about Miss Dogmill, and wished to hear no more. I attempted to hide my resentment, but I could feel my face reddening. "I will keep your caution in mind."

"And if you will not keep that in mind, keep this: I knew her when she was but a child, and I will swear upon any Bible you might choose that she used to be enormous fat."

I could only presume that Miriam had been advised of the guest list, for she showed not the slightest hint of surprise when she saw me from across the dinner table. She did, however, flash me a look of anger. It was fleeting, and no one would have thought anything more than that she might have had a burst of toothache or some similar pain. I understood her meaning well enough, however: I should never have accepted her husband's invitation.

And I should not have. Would I have respected her comfort and her unstated wishes had not my very life been in the balance? Most likely, for increasingly Miss Dogmill had come to fill the void in my heart that Miriam had left. It still pained me to look at Miriam, I still winced with longing at the way she laughed or held a knife or dusted a piece of lint off her sleeve. All of these little things retained their baffling magic, but they were no longer devastating. I could watch Miriam and not want to seek out the nearest bottle and drink myself senseless. I could endure her charms. I could even think fondly of them, and of her, and of the promise of love between us that had seemed so real that some days I could have been no less surprised at the absence of her love than I would have been by the absence of my arms and legs.

But that promise was gone. I had long understood this, but I now came to *believe* it. And though I knew I might proceed with other matters—those of the heart and otherwise—there was a sadness in my acceptance, a sadness that was perhaps even more profound than the sadness of loss I had felt every day when I lived in inconsolable longing. I understood now, finally, as I sat at the table, that all hope for me and Miriam was gone. Her husband would not simply disappear, as I had somehow, in my core, believed he might. Instead I saw things as they were: She was married and a Christian, and I sat in her formal dining room pretending to be a man I was not, putting her marriage at risk. She was right to glower at me. She would have been right to knock me in the head with a pot of boiled chicken. I wished I could tell her so, but I knew this desire too came because I sought my own comfort, not hers.

There were perhaps a dozen guests at the table that night, Tories of no small importance and their wives. Dinner was interesting and lively. Much discussion of the election took place, including the role of the mysterious Mr. Weaver, for here was a lively topic, and the wine had been poured with uncommon generosity, so perhaps the less attentive diners neither noticed nor cared of their hosts' displeasure. No one showed any sign of recalling that Miriam had once belonged to the nation of Hebrews.

"I find the whole thing utterly amazing," said Mr. Peacock, Melbury's effusive election agent. "That this rogue Jew—just the sort of person we might have all argued ought to be hanged, even prior to his being found guilty of murder—should emerge as so amiable a spokesman for our cause."

"He is hardly a spokesman," said Mr. Gray, a writer for the Tory papers. "He does not do much speaking. It is the rabble who speak for him, which is mightily good since these Jews are famous for being inarticulate, and their accents are most comical."

"You may be confusing the true accent of the Jews with that portrayed on the stage by comedians," said the bishop, who appeared to be in better spirits than when we had met earlier. "I have met with my share of Jews over the years, and many of them speak with the accents of Spaniards."

"Am I to understand that a Spaniard's accent is not comical?" asked Mr. Gray. "I must tell you this is news indeed."

"Many Jews have no accent at all," said Melbury somewhat dourly, for he was in the awkward position of having to defend his wife while ardently hoping no one recollected her origins and became aware that he was now cast in the role of defender.

"It is hardly their accents that need concern us. But this Weaver fellow, Melbury. You cannot love having your name yoked to his."

"I love that he gets me votes. In truth," he said pointedly, "he gets me far more votes gratis than those men I pay to get them."

Mr. Peacock blushed not a little. "It is a fine thing to get votes, but must we get them any way we can? Mr. Dogmill gets votes for his man by sending rioters to the polls."

"Surely," said the bishop, "you do not think it harmful that Mr. Melbury merely raises no objection when the rabble idolize him in the same breath with which they idolize Weaver? What would you have him say, *Continue your praise of me, but no longer praise that other man you like*? We shall see how the mob likes their support being served with *that* sauce."

"But if Mr. Melbury is asked to answer for his endorsement later," Gray pressed on, "it could prove something of an embarrassment. I say, if in the final days of the election you have a clear and decisive victory, it will be time to disavow the Jew. You do not want your enemies in the House using it against you."

"Mr. Gray may have a point," the bishop conceded. "When you stand up to speak out against privileges being handed out to Jews and dissenters and atheists while the Church is starved, you do not want to give your enemies ammunition. You do not want to hear it said that you speak pretty words for a man voted in on the coattails of a murdering Jew."

I cannot claim to have concealed my discomfort perfectly during this exchange, but uneasy though I was, I would not have traded my place for that of Melbury or Miriam. At least I was in disguise. The crowd at this table insulted their true lives freely and cruelly, and almost certainly ignorantly. I could see that his wife's dubious past was a heavy burden for Mr. Melbury to bear. Each mention of *Weaver* and *Jews* made him wince and redden and drink from his glass to hide his discomfort. Miriam, for her part, turned paler with each comment, though I could not say if her ill ease was born of shame, her concern for me, or her observations of her husband's displeasure.

Soon enough, a new topic of conversation was on the table. Miriam slumped in her chair with visible relief, but not her husband. He remained stiff, holding himself with unnatural erectness. He gripped his knife until his hand turned crimson. He bit his lip and gritted his teeth. I could not think he could stay in this state long, but he did for more than half an hour, until the other guests could not but discern that their host had become angry and sullen, and an uncomfortable silence crept across the table like a plague. We endured this awkward state for ten excruciating minutes, and our discomfort only broke when, during the somber dessert, a servant jostled a bowl full of pears, sending a half dozen or so onto the floor.

Melbury slammed his hand down at the table and turned to his wife. "What the devil is this, Mary?" he shouted. "Did I not order that fellow to be gone two weeks ago? Why is he now scattering pears on my floor? Why is he here? Why? Why?" And with each *why?* he would slap his palm down, sending our plates and goblets and silver rattling as though there were an earthquake.

Miriam stared at him. She flushed and reddened, but she did not look down or turn away. Her lips quivered, and I knew she longed to give him an answer, but perhaps she had nothing to say that he wanted to hear, and so she remained quiet. She said nothing while he slammed the tabled and shouted out his question. Glasses rattled and silver chinked, and far more than a few pears nearly bounced onto the floor. But still he slammed and shouted until I thought I would go mad with rage.

And then I heard a voice say, "Enough, Melbury."

I could hardly have been more surprised to see that I was the one who had said the words. I was on my feet with my arms limp by my side. I had spoken clearly and loudly, but not forcefully. It had done its business, however, for Melbury stopped shouting and slamming and looked up at me.

"Enough," I said again.

The frail bishop reached up with one hand and touched Melbury's arm. "Sit down, Griffin," he said gently.

Melbury ignored the bishop. He stared at me, shockingly without a hint of anger. "Yes. Yes, I'll sit."

And so we both returned to our seats.

He looked to his guests and made some quip about wives being too easy on servants, and all did their part to make the incident pass as easily as possible. By the time dinner had finished and the men and women had moved to their separate rooms, I would have sworn from my observations that the incident was utterly forgotten.

I, however, would not so easily forget.

The next morning, I could not have been more astonished to receive the following note:

Mr. Evans:

I cannot easily imagine the difficulties you face in your unique and perilous position, though I find it hard to believe that any dangers you face would have necessitated that you accept my husband's unfortunate invitation. Nevertheless, you did so, and I fear you have seen him not at his best. I know you are a man compelled by a keen sense of justice, and I have been awake all night with anxiety over the possibility that you will choose some impetuous course as a result of Mr. Melbury's conduct. In an effort to forestall any such actions, I believe it is necessary that I meet with you to discuss these events. I will be this afternoon at the Monument for the fire at four. If you wish to see me at peace, you will be there to meet with your friend,

Miriam Melbury

At least, I thought, she did not sign her letter *Mary*. Of course I would be there. I could not but attend. I did not know what it was that she feared I would do: knock her husband down, challenge him to a duel? Or was there something else? Did she fear that in my anger I would learn something of him she did not wish me to know?

I had little to do with my time until the meeting, and I found myself to be in no mood for going out-of-doors, so I was in my rooms when my landlady knocked upon my door to say that there was a man below to see me.

"What sort of man?" I asked.

"Not the best sort," she assured me. Her analysis proved to be correct, for she showed Mr. Titus Miller into my rooms.

He stepped in and looked around, as though he were inspecting the space for his own use. "You live comfortable," he said to me, as soon as Mrs. Sears had closed the door. "You live mighty comfortable, I see."

"Begging your pardon, but is there some reason I ought not to live in comfort?"

"There might be a reason or two that I know about," he said. He picked up a volume that I had taken from Mrs. Sears's collection and examined it as though it were a precious stone. "Time for books and all matter of fancy words, I see. Well, your time is your own, I suppose, or it has been so, at any rate. But that is business, and we have not yet got to business, have we? Perhaps a glass of wine might put us all at our ease." Miller put down the book.

"I am quite at my ease," I told him, "and I hardly think that because I have agreed to pay a friend's debts that you are entitled to speak to me in such a voice or to behave with such insolence."

"You may think as you like, of course. I shan't be so ill-natured as to prevent you. But I should very much care for a glass of wine, Mr.—well, I won't call you Evans, since that's not your name, and I won't call you by your real name, since it might distress you to hear it spoken aloud."

And there it was. I suppose I knew it would happen eventually. I could not remain disguised forever without someone discovering the truth. Of course, Miss Dogmill had done so, and so had Johnson, but neither wished to do me immediate harm. I had no confidence that Miller would behave with equal benevolence.

I turned to him. "I am afraid I know nothing of your meaning," I said helplessly, clinging desperately to some hope that I might deceive my way from this desperate situation.

Miller shook his head at the sadness of my efforts. "Of course you do, sir, and if you pretend otherwise, I might just as well go explain it to a constable instead of you. He'll understand my meaning plain enough, I expect."

I poured myself a glass of wine but offered Miller nothing. "If you wished to visit a constable, you would have done so already. But I perceive that you would prefer to deal with me." I took a seat, leaving him to the awkwardness of standing. I had been reduced to such petty victories. "Perhaps you had better tell me what it is you want, Miller, and I will tell you if it is feasible."

If he bristled at being made to stand while I sat, he showed none of it. "As to being feasible or no, I should think there would be no question. I mean to ask nothing that you cannot give, and I need not tell you the consequences of refusing to provide it."

"Let us forget the consequences for the moment and think instead of the request."

"Oh, you are now all business, I see. No longer putting on airs and wigs. Did you think no one would recognize you, all dandified as you are? I recognized you at once, I did. Maybe you can deceive the common sort of fellow with those trappings, but I am far too perceptive. I've seen you about town far too often, always with a sneer for a fellow such as me, only doing his business."

I leaned forward in my chair. "You make some very pretty speeches, but no one wishes to hear them. You may go home and praise yourself upon your own time, Miller. Do not think to waste my time with glorifying yourself. Now tell me what it is you would request."

If I had insulted him, he showed no sign of it. "The request, then, is for the two hundred and sixty pounds for Mr. Melbury's debt, as has already been promised, and another—shall we say—two hundred and forty for my good wishes, which will bring the entire amount to five hundred pounds."

Only by summoning all of my resolve could I keep from reacting to this sum as it deserved. "Five hundred pounds is a great deal of money, sir. What makes you believe I have it at my disposal?"

"I can only guess what you have, but as you have been willing to provide two hundred and sixty for Mr. Melbury, I am forced to speculate that this sum, large though it may be, must represent only a portion of it. In any case, I see from the papers that Mr. Evans has made a marvelous name for himself in town. I don't doubt that a gentleman of your stature should have little difficulty raising funds against the earnings of his plantation."

"You wish for me to borrow money from trusting gentlemen and let them suffer the consequences?"

"I cannot tell you how to raise the money, sir. Only that raise it you must."

"And if I refuse?"

He shrugged. "I can always return to Mr. Melbury for his debt, sir. He will pay one way or the other, as he cannot afford to sit out the remainder of the election in a debtor's prison. And as for you, if I cannot get two hundred and forty pounds from you, I know I may at the very least get one hundred and fifty from the king. If you take my meaning."

I took a drink of wine. "I take your meaning to be very ill-natured," I said.

"You may take it as you like, sir, but a gentleman must always pursue his business, and that is no more than I have done here. No one can say it's more that I've done, and no one can criticize me either."

"I will not speak to that point," I said, "only the other. As to the sum, you may perceive that it is a very large amount, not easily at my disposal. I must have a week."

"That cannot be. It is not so good-natured of you to ask for it."

"Then how much time do you think fitting for the raising of this sum?"

"I will come back in three days, sir. Three days, I say. If you do not have the money for me, I fear I must take actions we would both prefer to see avoided."

Mrs. Sears had seen this villain enter my rooms. Would she notice, I wondered, if she never saw him emerge? But tempting though it might have been, I was not willing to commit that most egregious of crimes to protect an identity that was already doomed. Miller had recognized me. Sooner or later, another would recognize me as well. Perhaps that person would not be so kind as to come to me with this intelligence but would go to the constables instead. I had no choice but to let Miller go and to use the three remaining days as best I could.

I remained uncommonly silent as I considered my options, and Miller must have known what sorts of possibilities occurred to me, for he grew very pale and uneasy. "I must go at once," he said, hurrying toward the door. "But you will hear from me in three days. Upon that you may depend."

And so he left, and I knew then that my hand was forced. I had not as much time as I would have liked, but I hoped it would be enough.

I arrived at the Monument a quarter of an hour in advance of our appointed time, but Miriam was already there, enveloped in a hooded greatcoat. The hood was pulled down low, to keep her identity a secret, or perhaps to keep mine. Even in that bulky mass, however, I had no problem recognizing her in an instant.

She did not see me approach, so I stood for a moment to watch her as flurries of snow landed about her, melting as they touched the wool of her coat. She might have been my wife, I thought, if . . . but there was no *if.* I had begun to see that with painful clarity. The only *if* I could summon was *if she had wished to be,* but she had not, and this was the most painful *if* imaginable.

She turned as she heard my muted footsteps in the newly fallen snow. I took her gloved hand. "I hope you are well, madam."

She let me hold on to her for as long as she could without risking a rudeness, and then withdrew the prize. Here was our entire relationship in miniature. "Thank you for meeting me," she said.

"How could I not have?"

"I cannot say what you might think best. I only know that I felt the need to speak with you, and you have been so good as to oblige me."

"And I shall always be thus," I assured her. "Come, shall we get a dish of chocolate, or a glass of wine?"

"Mr. Weaver, I am not the sort of woman who may freely visit taverns or chocolate houses with a man not my husband," she said sternly.

I attempted to show no sting. "Then let us stroll and talk," I said. "With your hood, all the world may think you my illicit lover, but I suppose there is no helping that."

The hood spared me from the distaste she no doubt registered. "I am sorry you saw Mr. Melbury lose his temper last night."

"I am sorry it happened," I said, "but if it must happen, I am not sorry to have been witness to it. Does he lose his temper with you often?"

"Not often," she said quietly.

"But it has happened before?"

She nodded under her hood, and I knew from the way she moved her head that she was crying.

Oh, how I hated Melbury at that moment! I could have torn the arms from his body. Had not this lady suffered all her life, shuttled from family to family, from one keeper to another, until the most fortuitous of events had left her financially independent? I could not have been more astonished when she had sacrificed that independence to a man like Melbury, but she had taken a risk, such as we must all take in life. It was a terrible tragedy that she was to suffer for her venture.

"Is he violent with you?" I asked.

She shook her head. "No, not with me."

There was something she would not yet say, yet I knew I could draw it out. "Tell me," I said.

"He breaks things," she said. "He smashes them. Mirrors, vases, plates, and goblets. Sometimes he throws them in my direction. Not quite *at* me, you understand, but in my direction. It is unpleasant enough."

I drew both hands into fists. "I cannot endure this," I said.

"But you must. You see, this is why I wanted to meet with you. I knew you would not rest until you found the truth, so I came to tell you the truth, but you must bother us no more. Griffin is not a perfect man, but he is a good one. He means to do important things for this country and to unmake this knot of corruption that binds our government."

"I don't give a fig for the knot of corruption," I said, "only for you, Miriam."

"Please don't address me so familiarly, Mr. Weaver. It is not right."

"Is it right that you should be under the torments of a tyrant?"

"He is no tyrant. He is but a man with weaknesses, such as you all have. It is only that some of his are more pronounced."

"Such as gaming," I said. "And debts."

She nodded. "He does have those weaknesses, yes."

"It is well, then, that you settled separate property upon yourself, lest his debts destroy your fortune."

She said nothing, so I knew then what I had already suspected. "He has destroyed your fortune, hasn't he?"

"He needed money to obtain the seat in the House," she said. "He lost so much at play that he could not afford to stand for Parliament as he had long meant to do, as others in the party had expected him to do. But there were debts. He assured me that once he was elected there would be opportunities to make the money back. So you see it is vital that he get his seat, for if not we shall be quite ruined."

"This is the good and virtuous man who will unmake the knot of corruption?"

"He is not the only man in this city to succumb to the evils of gaming."

"True enough, but if he picked pockets he would hardly be the only man in this city to be guilty of that crime, either. That would not mean he was the more virtuous for it."

"You are a fine man to talk about virtue," she said.

I turned to her, but she looked away.

"Forgive me, Benjamin. Mr. Weaver. That was both cruel and false. Whatever else may be said of you, I know you are a man who loves what is right above all else. But though you strive to do what is best, you sometimes do what you know may be wrong. I don't believe that makes you a bad man any more than it makes Mr. Melbury one."

"The difference is that these things I do that you frown upon are in the service of what I think my duty. I can hardly believe that Mr. Melbury thought it his duty to destroy his wealth and that of his wife at playing whist."

"You are unkind."

"Am I? You talk of being ruined. What do you mean by that?"

"Just what I say. We shall have no money, no credit. Should he not win the seat in the House and receive the protection members enjoy, and if creditors press their case, we shall have nowhere to live. Mr. Melbury's parents are long since dead. He has no siblings, and he has pressed those of his extended family as far as they will go. He must be in Parliament. He will do such good there. And—" She paused. "And only Parliament can save us now. I don't know what you need or expect from him, or what you hope to gain by making Mr. Evans his fabulous friend, but you must know that you are playing with my life as well as his. He must win that seat. He must have it."

"And do you think I wish to keep it from him? You must know, Miriam, that I have invested everything in your husband's election. I am Dogmill's enemy, not his. I cannot say I am delighted to be in such a position, but the truth is that I also wish for him to obtain the seat in the House."

"Why should you want that?"

"Because when he is elected, it is my hope that he will use his influence to help me."

Miriam turned away from me. "He will not," she said quietly.

"What? How do you know? He has no idea who I am. He cannot know that I am not Matthew Evans, can he?"

She shook her head. "No, you can be sure he does not. But he will not help you, all the more when he discovers you have deceived him with your masquerade."

"But surely he will understand the necessity—"

"He will understand nothing," she hissed. "Can you not see that he hates you? Not Matthew Evans, but Benjamin Weaver. He hates Benjamin Weaver."

I could not understand it. "Why should he hate me?"

"Because he knows—he knows we once meant something to each other, and he is jealous. It is because we are of the same race. He fears I will revert. Every time your name is raised, he seethes with anger. He cannot forgive that you have brought him votes, that you, no matter how unwillingly, have aided his campaign, for in doing so you have worked your way into our lives and our home."

"There is no need to be so ungenerous with your lives and your home."

"There is for Mr. Melbury. He has an idea that I will sneak off in the night to run away with you."

"I have the same idea," I said.

"Can you please pretend to gravity?"

"I'm sorry. But why should you have told him about us?"

"He wanted to know if I had entertained any lovers between my first husband's death and my marriage to him. I did not want to tell him, but I did not want to lie either, and so he learned who you were to me. I never had any intention of telling him such things, but he has a way of making people say what they do not wish to."

"Yes, that way most likely involves throwing things at you. Can you not see he is a cruel master, Miriam? Can you not see he has a black heart? He may not be inclined to villainy, but there can be no greater encouragement to baseness than debt. You speak of the good he will do in the House, but if you think that a man who faces ruin will vote his conscience rather than his purse, you are sadly deceived."

"How can you say so?" she cried.

"How can I not? Melbury speaks of Parliament as saving him from debt, but you know full well a member makes nothing for his service. The only money to be made in the House is through the sale of favors and by making great friends among the powerful and cruel."

"You may speak of destroying Mr. Melbury on principle, but would you sacrifice me for your principles as well?"

"Never," I said. "I would give you the bread from my mouth. But you must know that, because of what I have seen, I would not hesitate to see Melbury destroyed. I will not go out of my way to harm him—I will swallow my anger and do what you wish—but I will not protect him either, and I will not serve him."

"Then we have nothing more to say to each other," she told me.

"How can you tell me so?"

"Are you mad?" she asked me. "He is my *husband*. I owe him all the loyalty in the world. You speak to me as though he were but a rival to you. But you must understand that you can be nothing to me now but a friend, and you decline that role. You would do what you wish in order to satisfy your own sense of right and wrong, but it is not only Mr. Melbury who will be trampled, it is me as well."

"What do you ask of me, then?"

"You must promise me to do nothing that will harm him."

"I cannot. I have told you that I will not seek to harm him, but I will not protect him, and if I have the opportunity to sacrifice him to serve my aims—knowing what I know of him now—I must take it."

"Then you are no friend to me at all. I will thank you to stay away from me and my husband. I understand that you must encounter him now and again in your guise, but if you come into my house again, I will tell him who you are."

"You would do that to me?"

"I do not want to have to make a choice between you, but if you force my hand I will choose my husband."

CHAPTER 25

$\mathbf{M}$Y DECEPTION was coming undone rapidly, so I had no choice but to act. Miriam had made it clear I could hope for little from her husband. The debt collector Miller knew who I was, and I could not count on his remaining quiet for even as long as he had agreed.

None of this came as a surprise, of course. I had known I might be discovered before I had secured my liberty, and I had been contemplating a plan for some time now. I therefore risked contacting Elias and met with him in a coffeehouse. He was none too thrilled with what I asked of him, but he agreed in the end, as I knew he would.

That resolved, I contacted those who needed to know of my plans. I then took the notes that Grace had given me, those written to Dogmill's contacts in the country who had spent time in Jamaica, and fashioned an answer that best suited my purposes.

Grace was, in a very passive way, central to my plans, and I met with her in a chocolate shop that I might explain everything to her. She had shown herself to be nothing but an ardent supporter, but I was nevertheless preparing to move against her brother, and I could not take her cooperation for granted.

She arrived before I did at the shop on Charles Street, looking radiant in a wine-red dress with an ivory corset. The other men—and indeed the women—stared at her openly as she sipped her dish of chocolate.

"I am sorry if I'm late," I said.

"You're not. I only wished for the chocolate."

"Many ladies would hesitate before drinking at a chocolate shop alone."

She shrugged. "I'm Dennis Dogmill's sister, and I do what I like."

"Even to Dennis Dogmill?" I asked, as I took my seat.

She stared at me for a long moment and then nodded. "Even so. How hard will you be with him?"

"No harder than I have to be. For your sake," I added.

She put both hands on her dish but did not raise it. "Will he live?"

I laughed aloud, which might have been unkind, given the gravity of her question, but I had no plans to act the assassin. "I am not so foolish as to pursue perfect justice, or some flawed idea of what that would be. I want my name and my freedom. If the guilty can be punished, so much the better, but I have no illusions."

She smiled at me. "No, you don't. You see everything clearly."

"Not everything."

She laughed now. I saw her lovely teeth dark with chocolate. "You mean me, I suppose. You want to know what happens with Grace Dogmill when all of this has resolved."

"It is a luxurious question, for it depends upon my having escaped the hangman's noose and regained my reputation. But yet, I have wondered."

"It would be improper for a woman of my station to have a friendship with a man of yours."

"I understand," I said. I had heard this position before, after all.

She smiled once more. "But if I find I have had something stolen, I may need to pay you a visit. And, sadly, I am none the most cautious of my belongings."

With Miss Dogmill fully willing to lend me aid, I had nothing to do but wait to take the appropriate steps on the heels of the notes I'd sent. It seemed to me unwise to wait too long. Twenty-four hours were enough to induce the anxiety and anger I wished for.

More than that might produce action. Less would result in insufficient emotion. These were, however, a very anxious twenty-four hours, and I knew I should be happier if I found some occupation for myself. Fortunately, there was one more task left to me, and if it was not wise, it was at the very least justifiable. I therefore found myself in need of calling one more time upon Abraham Mendes.

He answered a note I sent him and met me that evening in a tavern off Stanhope Street near Covent Garden. There was something amusing upon his face as he saw me. Perhaps he thought that if I should manage to extricate myself from my dangers, I should never bear the same contempt for him or his master. How little he knew me if he believed it. Nevertheless, Mendes served me as I hoped he would, and I left my meeting with him hopeful that all should go as I wished.

As I anticipated, I received a note the next day, and it was very much to my liking.

> Evans,
>
> I know who and what you are, and I promise you that you cannot succeed in any plans you may be pursuing. If you end this charade now and vacate the metropolis, you may yet live.
>
> Dogmill

I wrote back at once, suggesting that Dogmill meet me that very evening at a tavern close by Whitehall. I chose the location because I knew it to be popular with Whigs, and I believed it would make him more comfortable and confident. Such was what I required of him. When I received a note in return confirming our rendezvous, I made my final preparations and fortified myself with a glass of port.

I arrived nearly half an hour late, for I wished Dogmill to be there in advance of me. I had no doubt he had arrived early, but I had no wish to surprise him and catch him unprepared. I arrived and asked the innkeeper for Mr. Dogmill and, much as I had anticipated, he told me I might find him in one of the back rooms.

I walked into the room to find Mr. Dogmill sitting at his table with Hertcomb at his side. Standing behind them, with his arms crossed, was none other than Mr. Greenbill. I was surprised that Dogmill should want another man to threaten violence, but perhaps he was, in this case, not willing to take risks. I was further surprised that he would risk Greenbill's presence in the room, for he had obviously gone to great lengths to hide his association with this porter. I could only presume that Dogmill had little intention of leaving me in a state fit to report what I knew.

All appeared agitated, as well they might be. I grinned at Dogmill and Hertcomb. "Good evening, gentlemen," I said, as I closed the door behind me.

Dogmill glared at me. "You will have to be very careful if you do not wish to die this night."

"I cannot say how careful I shall be," I told him. I took a seat at the table and poured myself a glass of his wine. I sipped it. "This is quite good. You know, from the look of this place, I should hardly think they would have claret of this quality."

Dogmill snatched the glass from my hand and threw it against the wall. It did not break, no doubt to his disappointment, but it did splatter rather ferociously, staining Mr. Greenbill, who attempted to appear as though his dignity had not been assaulted.

"Where is my sister?" Dogmill demanded.

I stared at him. "Your sister. How should I know?"

"Allow me to put him to the question, Mr. Dogmill," Greenbill said, taking a step forward.

Dogmill paid him no mind.

"I know who you are," he told me, through his teeth. "I took the liberty of writing to some gentlemen from Jamaica." He now held up the letters I had forged. "I have been informed that you have used the name Matthew Evans before, though it is not your true name. Instead, you are a scoundrel known as Jeremiah Baker, a confidence trickster, who has made his wretched living by abducting young ladies and then demanding money for their safe return. One of these gentlemen, upon receiving my note, rode all the way to London to warn me of you. Shortly after receiving this intelligence, I thought it wise to make certain of my sister's whereabouts, but she had not then been seen for more than a day."

I took a glass that I presumed to have been Dogmill's and emptied the contents upon the hard dirt floor. I then poured a fresh helping from the bottle and sipped from it. "You have thus saved me the trouble of informing you of the current situation. We may now agreeably come to terms."

Dogmill slammed his hand upon the table so hard I thought it should break. "There are no terms but that I shall get my sister and then I shall rip your head from your neck."

Hertcomb reached forward and put a hand on Dogmill's shoulder. "I don't know that you are giving the fellow a reason to negotiate in good faith."

"Nicely said, Hertcomb."

"Don't think to play my friend," he said petulantly. "I restrain Mr. Dogmill out of concern for his sister, not you. You betrayed my trust."

"Your trust is hardly so precious a thing that one need treat it with care," I answered.

Hertcomb opened his mouth but said nothing. I thought he might weep, and I confess I felt some remorse at having spoken to him so, but I played a part, and I would play it to the end.

Dogmill took a deep breath and turned to me. "You had better understand, Baker, that you have chosen to cross the wrong man."

"This," I asked, "is your idea of negotiating in good faith?"

"It is," he said, "for I tell you the truth. You shan't get a penny from me. Not a farthing. I will not endure that a fellow of the lowest sort like you should force me to pay to see my own sister returned. Instead, I shall offer you something else. If you send my sister back unscathed, I will give you a single day before beginning my pursuit of you. In that time, if you are wise, you can get yourself gone and from my grasp, for if I do catch hold of you, I will rend you to pieces. That is the best offer I can propose."

I shook my head. "I must tell you, it is not what I had in mind when I took your pretty sister, tied her hands behind her back, and shoved a rag in her mouth."

Greenbill, standing behind his master, suppressed a grin. Regardless of his loyalties, he liked a good bit of violence against a young woman when he could have it.

I thought that Hertcomb would be called on once more to restrain his friend, but Dogmill did not move. "You may have thought to gain something else, but you shan't. You must now decide if you wish to sacrifice your life along with your hopes of wealth."

"Most men," I said, "are willing to part with a few pounds if it will save the life of a person they love. And it is you who are threatened here, not me. It is time you recognized that."

"You think I have nothing more to show for myself than bluster?" he asked. "You've tasted a small portion of my wrath, you may recall. But I have more than that." He turned to Hertcomb. "Have Mr. Gregor walk in."

Hertcomb rose and disappeared for a moment, only to return with a tall thin gentleman in tow. He smiled at me and took a seat.

"You know this gentleman, I believe?" Dogmill said.

"I do," I answered, for the gentleman in question was Elias Gordon.

"Mr. Gregor here is willing to swear out an arrest warrant for the theft of some notes you took from his home in Jamaica. So you see, you are very much in my power."

"Would you do what he threatens, Mr. Gregor?"

Elias was nervous, but he appeared to be enjoying himself. There was something of the dramatic in this performance, and he could not help but indulge. "I think you know quite well what I am willing to do," he said.

I did know, for he had already done it. He had convinced Dogmill of the urgency of the danger against Grace. I had wanted the matter resolved at once, and Elias had strolled into Dogmill's house to make certain this would happen.

"You see, you have no options," Dogmill said. "You must do what I tell you, or you will be destroyed."

"Well," I said, "as that is the case, we may yet work for ourselves a compromise. I am willing to forgo any demands of wealth, given the dire nature of my situation. What say you to exchanging your sister for some mere information. Does that trouble you so much?"

He blinked a few times as he attempted to make sense of my proposal. "What information?" he demanded.

"Information regarding Walter Yate," I said.

Here Greenbill turned flush and something I could not quite identify flashed across Dogmill's face. "What should I know of it?"

I shrugged. "Something, I hope, if you wish to see your sister again."

"Why is this important to you?" he demanded.

"Idle curiosity," I said, taking a sip of wine. "If you tell me why you had him killed, and a few other details, I shall free your sister. It is as simple as that."

"I had him killed?" Dogmill repeated. "You must be mad."

"Perhaps I must." I finished my wine and set down the goblet. "I shall be off, then. You may leave a note here in the next forty-eight hours if you should happen to change your mind. If not, you can depend upon never seeing Miss Dogmill again." With that I rose to my feet and began toward the door.

Greenbill now walked over to block my way.

"I shall not let you leave," Dogmill said to me. "I cannot endure that my sister is in your hands, and you shan't leave here without telling me where she is. You may speak of all the forty-eight hours you like, but one way or another, sir, this will end tonight."

I smiled at him, a pitying sort of smile. "Do not make the mistake of thinking that I work alone. Mr. Gregor can attest to my cleverness, I believe."

"He is remarkable clever," Elias said. "You had better hear him out."

Dogmill glared at him but turned back to me. He bit his lip while he attempted to think of what he could say to make me remain in this room on his terms rather than mine, but in the end he came up with nothing. Thus far, my plan continued to work.

"Speak your wretched proposal," he said at last, "and hope it saves your life."

"Very generous. Now, you must know that if I do not return to my set meeting place at a given time, my associates have instructions to move Miss Dogmill to a location they have not told me of. If they do not hear from me in one day, they are to remove Miss Dogmill from the miseries of this world. You may, therefore, threaten to torment me until I reveal what you want to know, but

I believe myself strong enough to last until the first time of crisis that I mentioned, and once that time has passed, you will never be able to find your sister again unless I am at liberty and wish for you to find her. So I tell you, sir, get your dog from my path. Either treat me like a man now or be resolved to do so another day, but I shan't endure this bullying."

Greenbill stared at me, and Dogmill at Hertcomb. Hertcomb stared at his shoes.

Finally, Dogmill let out a sigh. "Damn you, you rogue. I shall tell you what you want, but you must know that it can do you no good. If you wish to use this information against me, it will be worth nothing, for the testimony of a single witness has no weight in court, and the testimony of a man such as you is worth less than nothing."

"Perhaps," I said, resuming my seat, "but that is my concern and none of yours. I only wish to hear what you have to say for your-self in the matter regarding Walter Yate. You have my word that if you speak to me openly and honestly, you will see your sister's safe return this night."

At long last, Dogmill took a seat at the table, and Hertcomb sheepishly joined him. Greenbill, for his part, remained at the door, looking very much like a goose awaiting the season of the Christian nativity.

"You had Walter Yate murdered by your friend Billy, here," I began. "Is that not so?"

Dogmill smiled thinly. "Wherever did you get such an idea?"

I returned the smile. "From Billy. A few nights past, I knocked him down, affected an Irish accent, and asked him a question or two. He was most accommodating."

"I don't care what this blackguard says," Hertcomb interjected. "You may depend that gentlemen do not engage in murder and deception. That is the province of the likes of you."

"If you are so troubled, Hertcomb, I will tell you that I am sorry I wounded your tender heart," I said, "but your heart has nothing to do with this. Gentlemen are much more brutish creatures than you would allow."

Dogmill, for his part, was glaring at Greenbill. I could see what happened inside his churning Whig mind. Why had Greenbill not confessed this mysterious nocturnal interrogation? That he had not done so had put Dogmill at risk, and I could not but doubt that he would, in exchange, provide Billy with very little shelter.

"I don't know what this rough told you, but you may depend that he had very little to do with Yate's demise. It is true that he had been causing difficulties for me, but I only asked that Billy silence him. I never specified how that might happen."

"Surely you must have known that murder might be one method used."

"I never thought about it. I neither knew nor cared, and frankly I still don't. I cannot say why you do."

"I have my reasons, I promise you. Do you mean to tell me that Billy never once spoke of his dealings to you?"

"We spoke of it. What is it to you? Do you think to confuse the world with these tales that no one will believe? Do you think that if you cannot extort me into paying for my sister's safety you can do so in order to protect me from scandal? You know me not at all if you think that."

"I know you as well as I care to," I said. "I only want now to know your motivations. Why did you have Yate killed?"

"I asked Greenbill to remove Yate from my sight," he corrected, "because the fellow was a nuisance and a troublemaker. He and his labor combination with its communist notions was too great a danger to my business."

"Come, now. Was there not some matter of Yate's knowing of the existence of a Jacobite spy among the Whigs?"

For once, I believe I had truly unbalanced Dogmill. "Where did you hear that?"

"Your problem, Dogmill, is that you have no regard for laboring men. You think them no more than beasts to be driven and tormented and consumed. But unlike beasts, these men have the gift of speech, and they talk freely. By listening to them one can learn a great deal."

"Perhaps it is so, but I shan't listen to leveling cant from an abductor of women."

"I prefer to think of myself as a redistributor of wealth," I said, thoroughly enjoying this role I had adopted. "But you have evaded the question. Did you believe that Yate knew of a Jacobite spy?"

"He came to me and told me that he knew of one, and he wanted money from me in exchange for revealing the name. In other words, he was but a vile extorter, much like yourself."

"And did you come to terms with Mr. Yate?"

"Of course not. I do not deal with men who resort to extortion."

"No? Not even when they are your own men? Did you not have Mr. Greenbill here send threatening notes to a priest named Ufford?"

Dogmill and Greenbill exchanged looks.

"You are mightily well informed," Dogmill told me, "though I cannot imagine what this information will do for you. I had him send a note or two to the meddling Jacobite priest. What of it?"

"As to that, you need not concern yourself. But let us return to the matter of the Whig conspirator. You were content that you should never learn his identity?"

"I did not believe that Yate knew anything. He only wished to squeeze some money from me."

"But you had him killed regardless."

"This is but a matter of semantics. If I send a man out to fetch me a new snuffbox, would you call me to account if the man knocked down an innocent to steal what I had sent him to buy? Now, you've asked me your questions, so let me ask mine. When shall I see my sister?"

I said nothing.

He stepped forward. "Listen to me. I have indulged you; now you will tell me what *I* want to know. When shall I see my sister?"

I must have waited too long to answer, because he slammed his palm down on the table. "I have had enough of this," he said. "If you think I shall simply let you walk out of here in the hopes that you return my sister unharmed, you are sadly mistaken. I thought to beat the information out of you, but I cannot risk anything so bold, so we shall instead take a ride to the magistrate's office. You'll soon find you have little to gain by remaining quiet."

"Perhaps," I said merrily. "But on what charges shall you bring me to the magistrate? You cannot prove that I have done anything with your sister."

"I have these letters," Dogmill said, slamming them down on the table.

I felt that the moment to reveal all was now at hand. "Those letters reveal both less and more than you have realized." I picked them up and held them out to Dogmill. "Examine them once more, if you please. I hope that if you look at all four at once, you will notice something you have not before observed."

Dogmill looked at them and then Hertcomb. Both shook their heads. They saw nothing.

"Perhaps I did a better job than I realized," I said. "Look at the hand."

And then Dogmill's eyes went large. He moved from one sheet to the next, until he had examined all four letters. "They are written in the same hand. It is disguised in each, but it is the same hand."

"In truth," I said, "I wrote those letters. They are a fabrication. The gentlemen you contacted never received your messages."

"You speak nonsense," Dogmill stammered. "Mr. Gregor here can testify to that."

Elias rose and walked over to where I stood—no doubt so that he would stand less of a chance of being pummeled by Dogmill.

"Mr. Gregor," he explained, "is also not what he seems, and is here to bear witness to something far different. So, you see, we have two men now to testify to what has been said. Your case is much harder than you've suspected."

I grinned at Dogmill. "Your lovely sister was kind enough to provide me with the notes you wrote to your Jamaica acquaintances, and my friend Mr. Gordon was good enough to impersonate a Jamaican you have never met in the flesh. Of course, Miss Dogmill is unharmed and was never in any danger. She is not my victim but my confederate. I asked her to remain hidden for a few days, that I might be able better to perpetrate this fraud. You will find her with her cousin on Southampton Row. You may rest assured that she removed herself there voluntarily and without duress. Her sole aim was to assist me in my plans."

"And why should she do so?"

"Because she is fond of me," I said.

"She is fond of an impostor, though I have no idea who you be in truth. A Jacobite spy? The one they call Johnson?"

I laughed. "Nothing so remarkable, I assure you."

"Then say who you are and speak what you want. I grow tired of this masquerade."

I then leaned forward slightly, removed my hat, and plucked off my wig, allowing my natural hair to fall back behind me. "You used your influence to see me wrongly convicted. I will now ask that you use your influence to have that conviction overturned."

It was Greenbill who recognized me. "I thought I knowed you from somewhere," he said. "It's Weaver."

Dogmill's jaw dropped. "Weaver," he repeated. "Under our nose all this time." He now looked at Greenbill and back at me. And he smiled. "Well, you've got yourself a bit of a problem, Weaver. You see, if it's evidence exonerating you that you sought, you are a man short, for you cannot stand witness in charges leveled against you. Your friend's testimony in this matter won't serve you much good if he cannot corroborate it. Your voice will count for nothing, as you are implicated in these matters, so you might as well have remained hidden and far from me. I think I shall resolve this evening by bringing you to a magistrate, collecting a nice bounty, and forgetting about you. My sister might have been beguiled by you, but her sympathy won't save you from the hangman."

It was then that the door opened, and, as per our arrangement, Abraham Mendes walked in. He had no weapons drawn, but there were pistols visible in his pockets. He meant to make an impressive entrance, and with his bulky form and ugly scowl he did just that.

"No," said Mendes, "but my oath will. I heard all that was said, and I'm afraid you've got some difficulties now, Dogmill, for you've two men who will substantiate Weaver's claims, and all the Whiggish courts in the world can't deny justice now."

I could not restrain a simper. "Your position is not so strong as you once thought."

"Mendes." Dogmill spat. "This is some ruse by Jonathan Wild, then?"

"Mr. Wild ain't complaining, but Weaver asked me to stop by, and I did it as a favor to him mostly."

"You see, the matter is quite turned now," I said. "I think you should look rather shabby before the courts when you have Mr. Wild, the thieftaker general, sending his lieutenant to testify against you."

"It is a sad thing," Mendes observed, "much like the tragedies of the stage. Once all of this is revealed, Mr. Melbury will have the advantage."

Greenbill's lips trembled, for he understood at once that he was to stand sacrifice for his master's whims. "You bleeding curs," he said. "I'll negotiate your throats in my hands."

"I for one," I announced, "am getting quite tired of your misuse of words."

He grinned. "Well, I do it on purpose, don't I? It puts the likes of you quite off the mark in estimating me."

"I don't feel as though I've missed the mark," Mendes said. "As you'll find out when you come to your uncomfortable end at the bottom of a rope."

"The only uncomfortable end is your arse, you buggering Jews," he said, and raised his pistol at Mendes, fully prepared to eliminate my corroborating witnesses. Hertcomb and Dogmill shouted out, and with good reason—it is never wise to fire a pistol at such close quarters unless one be utterly indifferent to whom it might strike—and Elias opened his mouth in a pantomime of horror. Greenbill for all I knew was full of such indifference, but the rest of us were not, and we all dropped to the floor—all of us but Mendes, who appeared utterly indifferent to the prospect of a ball in his chest. The lead, however, hastily fired by an unsteady hand, missed its target entirely, lodging itself instead in the wall, where it propelled outward a nimbus of dust and smoke and chips of wood.

We all of us breathed our relief, but the duel was but half over. Seeing that Greenbill had spent his shot, Mendes retrieved a pistol from his pocket and returned fire, far more successfully than his opponent. Greenbill attempted to dodge the ball, but Mendes had either a better hand or better luck, and his adversary went down upon the floor. Within seconds a pool had begun to form around his neck.

He pressed his hand to the wound. "Help me," he gasped. "Damn you all, get me a surgeon."

We remained motionless for a moment, for there was not a superfluity of sympathy for Greenbill in that room. Mendes could hardly have cared if a man who had just tried to shoot him should be gathered to his fathers, Dogmill must surely have realized that the blackguard was of more use to him dead than alive, and I, for my part, felt that this man had received no more than he deserved.

"Is no one going to fetch a surgeon?" Hertcomb asked at last.

"What's the use?" Dogmill said. "He'll be dead before one gets here."

Elias had only now recovered his senses. "I'm a surgeon," he recalled, and began to rush toward the fallen man.

"No." Dogmill stood between Elias and Greenbill. "You've done enough harm for one night. Stand back."

"He's a surgeon," Mendes said, with apparent boredom. "He's not lying. Let him through."

"I presume he's not lying," Dogmill said, "but he will have to pass me to administer to that man."

Elias turned to me, but I was disinclined to interfere. Here, after all, was more evidence against Dogmill if we needed it, and as to the porter—well, I could not but think that he deserved no better than he got.

Greenbill, groaning in pain as he was, seemed to understand that Dogmill stood between him and his only chance at life. He attempted to say something but could not, and his breath began to come out rasping and wet. We stood in silence for three or four minutes, listening to Greenbill's gurgling breath, and then there was silence.

It is an odd way to pass the time, waiting for a man to die. I thought to lend him comfort. I thought, in his final moments, to torment him and tell him I knew his wife to be unfaithful. But I did nothing, and when he died I felt, all at once, that perhaps he had not been so bad as I thought. Perhaps I was the bad one, for doing nothing to save this life, wretched though it was.

"I'm glad that's done with," said Dogmill, who clearly had no such thoughts of remorse.

"It's a deuced thing, all this shooting and dying," Hertcomb said. "Dogmill, you told me there would be no mayhem. Surely this must qualify as mayhem."

"Only just," Dogmill said impatiently. He looked around the room for a moment. "Let us be frank," he said to me. "You have threatened me, I have threatened you, and a very low sort of fellow is now dead at my feet. I propose we retire to another room, one with fewer dead men in it, open a bottle of wine, and discuss precisely how to resolve this difficulty."

What else was there to say? "I agree."

As these matters touched him very nearly, I sent a note to Littleton—to whom I had related some small portion of my intentions for the evening, and who had been on notice to come if called. Though he was certainly an important player, Dogmill would not countenance that Littleton join us in our negotiations. He would not sit on equal terms with a porter, he said. It was disquieting enough that he would have to sit on equal terms with a thieftaker and convicted murderer. For my part, I thought it very hard that my status as a convicted murderer should be thrown in my teeth by the man responsible for the killing for which I had been convicted, but I saw that his position was weakening and there was little to be gained by pressing the point. In the end, Dogmill agreed that the porter might remain in the room if he stood. Littleton took no offense, gratified as he was to witness Dogmill's being pressed to the ropes, and would have agreed to stay on had he been asked to hang upside down.

The rest of us sat, and the innkeeper, whom Dogmill had given two shillings to stay his hand in calling the constables, provided us a bottle of canary. We therefore sat together as old friends.

"As I see it," Dogmill began, "Mr. Weaver has been hardly used by Mr. Greenbill, and though I am sorry that this came to a period in violence, I am delighted that the truth has been discovered while I looked on. The press has embraced Mr. Weaver as its darling, and it is only right that we all step forward together to announce how Greenbill tricked me into trusting him and the world into blaming Weaver for his crime. He surely would have killed us all had not Mendes behaved so bravely."

"Here, here," said Hertcomb. "I think that is a mighty fine solution to our troubles. Mighty fine."

"And all goes back to how it was," spat Littleton from across the room. "I don't very much like that."

Mendes said nothing, but he met my eye and shook his head, as though I needed further instruction—which I certainly did not.

"Wages can be raised," Dogmill grumbled to Littleton. "These things can be ordered. And I should like you to recall that if there is no Dennis Dogmill, his ships will no longer need unloading, so don't get too ambitious in your ideas of comeuppance."

"You may go to the devil, sir," Littleton said, "and London will still need its weed. On that you can depend, so don't think to frighten me into worrying after your well-being."

"I'll thank you not to swear at me," Dogmill said.

"Mr. Littleton," I said, before the porter could reply with more sweet words, "you may be sure there will be justice for you and your boys before we are done here tonight. One way or the other."

"I thank you, Mr. Weaver."

"Allow me to make a proposal," I said to Dogmill. "I will agree that the blame should be laid upon Mr. Greenbill, who did, after all, kill four men more or less upon his own initiative. I should like to see you hang for your role in it, but I am not so naïve as to believe I could easily bring such a thing about, and I don't know that I am willing to risk trying the experiment. I will therefore not threaten you with the rope that so lately hung around my own neck. I will, however, threaten you with this election. Once my name is cleared, I may speak freely, and as the Tory press has already shown a willingness to be kind to me, you may be sure they will lap up any information I might choose to provide them."

"And you will refrain from doing this under certain circumstances?"

I did not like that Mr. Hertcomb should be returned to office, but I also did not like that a villain like Melbury should find a place in the House—not now that I knew of his treatment of Miriam. And if Dogmill could not have Hertcomb in his pocket, he would have another man instead. I could only do so much against this circuit of corruption, but I would do what I could.

"I will remain quiet until the end of the election. I may choose to speak at a later date if I believe it is in the public interest, but not until this race is long past decided."

"Unacceptable," he said.

I shrugged. "You haven't a choice, sir. You may allow me to remain quiet now, or you may encourage me to speak now. Later is to come later."

He stared at me, but I saw that he could not argue with my logic. He could do nothing to keep me quiet but have me killed, and I think that he might well have had enough of attempting harm to Benjamin Weaver.

"And in return?" Dogmill asked.

"In return, I want some questions answered. If the answers do not lead to the discovery of new wrongs, I will do as I say, and we may all leave here free of any threat of the law over our heads."

"Very well. Ask your questions."

"The first, and the most pressing, is why you selected me to take the blame in the death of Yate. Surely there was some other unfortunate who would have proved a more willing victim. I hope I do not flatter myself if I say that the world knows—or ought to know—that I am not a man to step with resignation into the noose. Why choose me for your victim?"

Dogmill laughed and raised his glass in salute. "I have asked myself that question. But you see, it was an accident. That's all. You were at the quays that afternoon dressed as a lascar, and Greenbill thought you *were* a lascar. He saw you and said to himself, Why, there's the perfect fellow on whom to put the blame. By the time I realized who you were, it was too late to undo the accusations. We had no choice but to prosecute and hope for the best."

"But you did more than hope for the best. You exerted your influence to make certain that I would be convicted."

He shook his head. "You are wrong. To my knowledge, no one ever asked that judge, Rowley, to act so harshly against you. If you must know the truth, I wished he had not, for his prejudice was so blatant it could only have caused us harm. I, myself, preferred that you be acquitted and a new man found on whom to put the blame. Or, more likely, the victim would be forgot and the matter would close itself."

"So why did Rowley do it?"

"I don't know. Shortly after you sliced off his ear, he retired to his estate in Oxfordshire, from where he has refused to answer my letters. Were it not an election season, I should travel there myself and get the answers from his lips."

I could not believe what I heard. "And what of the woman," I said, "the one who provided me with the lockpick?"

"I know nothing of any lockpicks."

I ground my teeth. What could all this mean? I had begun my persecution with two cardinal assumptions: that I had been singled out for this murder to suit some purpose and that the person who had singled me out had controlled the actions of Judge Rowley. Now I learned that both assumptions were false, and while I was happily close to ending my legal troubles, I was no closer than I had been to the truth.

"If what you tell me is right, I must press you on some other details. I have operated on the assumption that you turned against Yate because he knew of an important Whig with Jacobitical ties."

"It ain't no assumption," Littleton pronounced. "It is the Lord's truth."

Dogmill sighed. "He did claim to have such knowledge, yes, and I asked Greenbill to quiet him because of that claim. But as to the truth of it, I have ever been in doubt. He offered me no evidence, and it could well be he was only looking to make a bit of silver from my anxiety. Where, after all, would a man of that stamp have the opportunity to meet an important Whig that he might discover him to be a Jacobite?"

And there I sat up straight, for I knew the answer. The very ob-
viousness of it struck me in the face. I had taken too much without question and ignored facts that stared at me boldly.

"You may be certain that Yate knew the Whig," I said, "and I
believe I now know who he is too. I see that as soon as we are finished here, I must leave London for several days. Upon my return,
I trust that your machinery will have resolved the legal troubles
hanging over my head. If not, I promise you, you will have every
cause to regret it."

Mendes agreed to contact the constables for us, for as Jonathan
Wild's man he would be able to wield the most influence and keep
us all out of the compter for the night. He strutted around in his
glory while we waited for the magistrate's men to answer his sum-
mons. He sipped at wine, and picked at cold fowl he had ordered,
and stared most oddly at Dogmill. It was almost as though Dogmill
was some newly got printing Mendes hung on his wall.

At last, the tobacco man could no longer endure the rudeness.
"Why do you gape at me so?"

"I must say, Mr. Dogmill," he answered, "I was only thinking
that Mr. Wild will be most delighted with this turn of events. You
and he have long been enemies, but now you will be friends, and
he will relish having so amiable a friend as Mr. Hertcomb in the
House."

"What?" I shouted. "Mendes, I did not call upon your aid so
you could deliver Wild a Parliamentarian to order about as he
pleases."

"It may not be why you done it, but you done it all the same.
We now know something about Mr. Dogmill that is very damning, and Hertcomb is Mr. Dogmill's man. That makes Mr. Hertcomb Wild's man now as well." He turned to me. "And don't say
nothing about it. I've pulled your neck from the noose, Weaver.
You'll not gripe about my taking a thing or two for my troubles."

None of us said a word. I had grown so used to calling upon
Mendes for his aid that I confess I had forgot who and what he

was. In that instant I almost wished I had remained forever in exile rather than put into Mr. Wild's hands the member for Westminster. I had allowed the most dangerous man in London to become even more dangerous.

Mendes, sensing the horror of the room, glowed like a maiden in love. "There is one more thing," he said to Dogmill. "Some years ago I had a dog by the name of Blackie." And with that, he removed his pistol and struck Dogmill in the head.

The tobacco man collapsed in an instant. Mendes turned to Hertcomb.

"This filthy cunny crossed me. Three years ago it was, but I ain't forgot it. You see him there, lying on the floor, blood coming out of his head? You see it, all right. Don't you forget, Mr. Hertcomb. Don't you forget what happens to someone who crosses me."

We awaited the arrival of the constables in silence.

CHAPTER 26

I TOOK THE mail coach to Oxford-shire—a journey of some length under the best of circumstances, and fortune was not to provide me with the best of circumstances. It rained hard nearly all the way, and the roads were in horrific shape. I remained in disguise as Matthew Evans, for I could not depend that news of my innocence would reach the provinces as quickly as I could, and I did not care to find myself arrested. However, I faced other trials of a nonjudicial sort. Only halfway to my destination, the coach became caught in the mud and turned over. No one was hurt, but we were forced to make our way on foot to the nearest inn and make new arrangements for ourselves.

A trip that ought to have taken less than a day took me nearly three, but at last I arrived at the estate of Judge Piers Rowley and knocked upon the heavy doors of his house. I presented my card—that is to say, Benjamin Weaver's card—to the footman, for I would have no pretense with this man of the law. I hardly need tell my reader that I was invited inside at once.

I waited no more than five minutes before Mr. Rowley joined me. He wore a large flowing wig that effectively covered his ears, so I could not see the damage I had done him. I did perceive that he appeared tired, however, and much older than when I had last set my eyes on him. Though a heavy man, his cheeks looked sunken.

To my surprise he offered me a bow and invited me to sit.

I was not comfortable, and remained standing longer than suits a gentleman asked to be at his leisure.

"I see," said the judge, "either that you are here to kill me out of revenge or that you have discovered something."

"I have discovered something."

He laughed softly. "I hardly know if that is the answer I most wished for."

"I do not believe my arrival here is good news for you," I said at last.

"It could not have been, but I knew it would come. I knew no good would come from prosecuting you, and no good would come of your escape. But a man's choices are not always his own, and even when they are, they must often be painful."

"You sent the woman with the lockpick," I said.

He nodded. "She is my sister's serving woman. A pleasant sort of girl. I can arrange for you to meet her, if you like, but I think you will find her much less devoted to you than she once pretended."

"No doubt. Why did you do it? You both ordered me destroyed and set me at my liberty. Why?"

"Because I could not bear that you should be hanged for a crime you did not commit, and I had no choice but to see you convicted and to sentence you to death. I was made to do it, and I would have been ruined if I had not. You must understand that I was ready to face that ruin rather than commit murder, for I perceived what I had been asked to do as murder. But then I alighted upon this idea. If you could break free of prison, I thought, you would flee, and I would have done my part safely. I could hardly have imagined that you would be so determined to vindicate yourself."

"Knowing what I now know, I am sorry I was so hard with you."

He put a hand to the side of his head. "It is no less than I deserve."

"I cannot say what you deserve, but I think you deserved less, for you did try to tell me the truth. You were ordered to see me hanged by Griffin Melbury. You told me the truth that night. I accepted it as a matter of faith that you had lied. I presumed you were attempting to prey upon my ignorance and set me at your enemy, for you are a Whig and he is a Tory. But you told me the truth all along."

He nodded.

"And he could so command you because he is a Jacobite, and so are you."

He nodded again. "After your arrest, he convinced some high-ranking men in our circles that you were a danger to our cause. I cannot tell you their names, but I can only tell you they believed him, for Melbury is a convincing man. The order came to me, and I dared not disobey, so I tried to defy it as best I could."

"Why did Melbury wish me hanged?" I asked.

He smiled. "Is it not obvious? Because he was jealous of you—and afraid of you too. He knew you had courted his wife, and he believed that you suspected him of acting against the Hanoverians. He thought you would, out of love for his wife, inquire into his doings, discover his political connections, and expose him. When Ufford hired you, Melbury was beside himself with anger and fear. He was certain that you would discover his link to the priest and then expose him before the world. But then you were arrested, and he could not resist the chance to remove you forever."

"If the Jacobites wished me harm, why have I been spared and even held up as their darling?"

"After your trial, when the mob began to rally around your cause, and when Melbury could not show justification for his anger toward you, his wishes were disregarded. He longed to see you destroyed, but he had no support within the party. He was quite angry, you know. He was convinced you would do all you could to destroy him for his loyalties to the true king."

"But that is madness. I would never have been aware of his true loyalties had he not pursued me."

Rowley shrugged. "It is ironic, I suppose, but hardly madness. We all do what we must to protect ourselves."

"As you did with Yate. I suppose now I understand how it was that he was not convicted when he sat before your court."

"He knew my secret. I cannot say precisely through what channels, but sometimes we men of breeding are not nearly so cautious as we ought to be around those beneath us, and I fear there are those in our circle who are truly foolish. Some pair of loose lips has cost me dearly."

"And they will soon cost Melbury," I said.

"It will be hard to prove him one of the exiled king's party. He has hidden his connections well."

"That's true enough. I've never heard that anyone truly suspects Melbury of supporting the old king."

Rowley laughed. "They ought not to. I don't believe he does. But Melbury has had some financial difficulties over the years, and a year ago he struck a bargain: He would link himself to the cause of King James in exchange for funds to run his campaign. I must tell you that there are those in our organization who have grown weary of paying his gambling debts, and Mr. Melbury has become something of a liability."

"But he has power," I noted.

"Of course. If he is elected to the House, as it seems he very well might be, he would be in a position of some influence. I could not have directly defied him when he ordered me to find you guilty, so I did what I could."

"And now what will you do?"

He looked at me. "I think that is up to you, sir."

"I suppose it is," I agreed. I had not had the time to consider the consequences of my visit. I had not anticipated that Rowley would prove the cooperative informant that I now saw before me, and his cooperation made me inclined to find some solution that would not end in his execution for treason.

"I propose," I said at last, "that you flee the country. My name, sir, will by now have been cleared owing to other activities, and I do not require a confession on your part. I cannot allow you, in good conscience, to maintain your post and exert the will of your corrupt masters, but neither would I see you die for what you have done either, for you did choose to spare my life. I believe you found yourself in a difficult position and you managed it as you thought best."

Rowley nodded. He must have known, long before I had arrived that day, that he was defeated, for he made little complaint of what I had proposed. "And what of Mr. Melbury?"

Indeed. What of Mr. Melbury? I could not allow a man who had used me so hard to go unpunished, but neither could I countenance that Miriam should share in the ignominy of a general discovery of his treachery against the Crown. Were he arrested and tried as a traitor, the shame should destroy her.

"I shall manage Melbury," I said.

Rowley blinked but once to show his understanding. He then asked me if I would be his guest for the night, and I thought it rude to decline. He thus indulged me in a splendid dinner and the choicest samples of his wine cellars. I departed in the morning not a little regretful that I had, in effect, exiled this man from his country. I had long thought him an unprincipled villain, but I now understood that villainy in most men is but a matter of degree.

CHAPTER 27

BY THE TIME I returned to London, the papers were full of the news that I had been exonerated of any wrongdoing in the death of Walter Yate. The Tory papers blamed the Whig courts. The Whig papers blamed the Tory agitation of laborers. No one blamed me, and that was easily enough to keep me satisfied.

At Covent Garden, the violence had diminished considerably. The Whigs, understanding that they looked foolish in the revelations surrounding my name, were less willing to use such extreme methods of dissuading voters, so Dogmill ran his campaign as best he could, only to lose in the end to Melbury by fewer than two hundred votes. Wild, at least, was denied his Parliamentarian. Dogmill retired to tend his tobacco business. Hertcomb simply retired to a life of leisure.

I saw little of Miss Dogmill after my return. It was one thing for her to be seen about town with a gentleman only she knew to be Benjamin Weaver. It was another for her to be seen with Benjamin Weaver. I understood that our worlds did not touch, and I did not seek her out, though she came to me once a few months later, having lost a watch. I spent several weeks in her employ before she discovered it had fallen behind a sofa.

As for Mr. Melbury, he never took his seat in the House. The summer after his election, a great scandal was discovered in which the Bishop of Rochester, whom I had met in Melbury's house, was revealed to be the leader of a great Jacobite conspiracy. Mr. Johnson himself, whose true named was George Kelly, was tracked down by the King's Messengers. They burst into his rooms unannounced, where he managed to hold off half a dozen of them with a sword in one hand while, with the other, he gathered his papers and tossed them into the fire—thus concealing the identities of many of his conspirators. Nevertheless, no small number of men were arrested and disgraced, and I have little doubt that Melbury would have been among them had he lived so long.

Less than a month after the close of the polls, however, Melbury met with a terrible accident coming home late one night from a gaming house. He was found in the mud the next morning, a great wound to his head. The magistrate determined that there was no motive of robbery, as his goods had not been touched. Many men testified that he had been drinking to excess that night, so the coroner determined he might as easily have fallen to his destruction as been struck. Though his injuries had all the signs of a violence done to him, his death was ruled to be no more than an unfortunate misadventure.

I attempted to call on Mrs. Melbury to offer her my condolences, but she would not receive me. I could only presume that she held me responsible for the death of her husband, as she returned one of my notes with a quick scrawl indicating that she would never speak to me again.

ACKNOWLEDGMENTS

Many thanks to Frank O'Groman for helping to demystify the world of eighteenth-century elections. I would also like to thank Jim Jopling and John Pipkin for their insights and suggestions on early drafts of the manuscript.

As always, I am in debt to the people at Random House, particularly Dennis Ambrose, and, once again, my editor, Jonathan Karp, whose humor, wisdom, and insights make my job so much easier. I cannot sufficiently thank my agent, Liz Darhansoff, for her guidance and friendship.

I must also put on paper my gratitude to my family, my wife, Claudia Stokes, for her help, support, and patient listening; and our daughter Eleanor, for reasons that are too obvious and silly to articulate. And as no book would be complete without thanking at least one animal, I must mention my appreciation for Tiki, who always made sure I was up for breakfast—his, not mine.

ABOUT THE AUTHOR

DAVID LISS is the author of *The Coffee Trader* and *A Conspiracy of Paper*, winner of the 2000 Edgar Award for Best First Novel. He lives in San Antonio with his wife and daughter and can be reached via his website, www.davidliss.com.

ABOUT THE TYPE

This book was set in Bembo, a typeface based on an old-style Roman face that was used for Cardinal Bembo's tract *De Aetna* in 1495. Bembo was cut by Francisco Griffo in the early sixteenth century. The Lanston Monotype Company of Philadelphia brought the well-proportioned letterforms of Bembo to the United States in the 1930s.